The
Abstract

ALSO BY Goodloe Byron
i
Revisions of
As Reverence to a Rose

The Abstract

Goodloe Byron

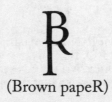

(Brown papeR)

A BROWN PAPER BOOK

Copyright© 2005 by Goodloe Byron

First printing.

ISBN 13– 978-0-615-15046-8

Random House: Excerpt from 'Inferno' by Dante Alighieri. Translation Copyright ©2002 by Anthony Esolen. Reprinted by permission of Modern Library, a division of Random House Publishing Group, Inc.
Cover Illustration © by Jack Davis (?) for *Witches Tales* October, 1971. Copyright © 1971 Eerie publications, attempts have been made to contact, for further information please write to the address below.

Drawings by le Goodloe

BROWN PAPER PUBLISHING
P.O. BOX 3954
FREDERICK, MD 21705–3954
WWW.BROWNPAPERPUBLISHING.COM

"How fine an ape of Nature's works I was."

–Dante Alighieri

The
Abstract

Part 1

(oh, this horrid way of life)

There was a time when he was young, as well as a later time when he would be old, but now there were only times when he was asleep, as well as begrudging times when he was awake. At that moment, he was moving from one to the other.

That is not to say that he was growing old, but that he was not quite awake.

He had been waking up for four hours now. In the third hour, he had decided against eating a chocolate bar, opting instead for a yolky egg thing over top of a pork and potato mixture. Supposedly, this entrée was offered at an awful restaurant nearby during vague hours.

Not that he knew what time it was. He could not be bothered with such details.

Giving up on all of that, he decided to change direction, and walked down the hill towards a water fountain in the park.

He walked down the hill.

He jogged over.

Turned the knob.

No water, turned off for winter.

A kid studied him as he growled dry matter loose in his throat. He stopped this behavior as the mother came up to reprimand her son for staring at the deadly man. He smiled to her, attempted to flirt a bit, spat once she ushered her child away.

He got it into his mind that they, the woman in particular, wanted him to leave the park. He felt resentful of this, and stayed, leaned his neck into one of the trees. He decided that those two would have to leave before him, as a matter of principal.

He has a right to be here.

That incontrovertible bit was not true, altogether, as he was not a citizen, a membership which accorded one with the public, and thus to the facilities of a public park. But here, in the sense that here is a place in the world, he has a right to be here, in that sense at least.

Somewhat true to his word, he did not move for a while. When he did, it was not to leave so much as to circle a tree for purposes of exercise. He looked at the kid, not at the mother.

The territorial dispute was between them.

The mother's presence seemed a physical representative of the social standing that the boy had over him. The boy was not paying him any mind, enjoying the park, ignoring. He was left to wait like a scavenger with no stomach.

He would not fit on the swings, he could not see what fun could be had on the wooden bridge.

After a few minutes he was eager to leave, and counted his steps.

At what would have amounted to 'many' steps, if he had not gotten distracted, the other two left. He stared at the car for some time, kicked several scraps of wood out into the grass.

Before leaving, he took two pills from an envelope in his jacket, and slid them onto his mouth, attempted to gather saliva with his tongue. The powder began dissolving, causing him to gag. He was able to swallow one, the other he spit out.

* * * * * * * *

On the way home he stepped over the curb, looking ahead to see a dog with matted dust in its hair. White hair, black, with a black eye. Its nose was stuck in a paper bag, grease spots. It was trying to lick the grease, but ended up pushing the bag around as it moved.

How stupid, haha.

In a cobweb of his mind, however, he did not believe this with his whole heart. He liked this dog. It reminded him of an old cartoon. He held out his hand as a cat claw, throwing out a playful hiss. The animal panicked, off away, pushing the bag along the ground, mad scramble, bag crackling as it slid. It stopped, removed its nose from the paper bag to look back at him.

He kissed to it, and found nothing in his pockets but the key card and key to his hotel.

Maybe good enough.

He waved the key card to the dog, as if it were a bit of food. He made a benevolent face.

The dog eyed him nervously.

It picked up the bag in its mouth, then took off. He made rat sounds with his cheeks. The poor thing did not turn back to him, disappeared up the road.

Perhaps the dog did not like rats.

His stomach lurched a little. He felt out of shape physically. To counter this, he threw two imaginary punches and gave himself the title of 'The Boxing Man'. Though, even with this title, he did not know how to fight properly.

He walked up the wheelchair access ramp between the two stores with yellow signs, one he knew to be a pharmacy where the good-looking girl worked.

From here he could see his hotel.

Sadness, he remembered that his hotel room was filthy. The problem was far enough along that he had actually put the 'do not disturb' sign on the doorknob, ashamed of the mess or whatnot, did not want the maid to see it.

Oh, if only he'd had the courage not put up that sign, his room would be clean.

He put his hand on a young sapling, in order to look a certain way. The bark was covered with something tacky. Sap. He withdrew his hand, rubbing his fingers. Was this sap? Or something more disturbing? He would have to go home and wash his hand. He really had nothing better to do anyhow.

He descended through the haggard ivy, mulch kicking into the space between his sock and shoe.

He jumped down the last two steps.

On the corner, a man vending things from a small cart was reclining against a wall, listening to music. His lip was stuck up into his mustache. His daughter was dirty, cross-legged on the pavement reading from a textbook and so on. The father said something to her in a private language. He imagined it was something intimate.

Something that had never been said to him.

Alas.

* * * * * * * *

One of the hotel clerks had, somehow, gained access to his name. They'd exchanged a few words before this, though none of it had given him the impression that the guy would bother investigating his past.

He entered the lobby, looked around.

He didn't see that clerk, which made him relieved yet lonely.

He then heard his name.

Actually, the clerk called him Bramdon, which was not right.

He turned to see the clerk pushing the ring finger of one hand into his other fist. The clerk asked him something using some words that he didn't understand. The clerk rephrased the question to ask him if he was going to give himself pleasure in his room.

He became terribly nervous. He might have been going to do just that. He was not sure he said, which the clerk did not understand.

Then his confidence returned as he thought for a moment. No, he said, because the maid, who was related to the clerk somehow, does not knock on doors, he said, before entering.

The clerk laughed about this, then asked what he had been doing outside, it being early afternoon, on a weekday none the less.

Shouldn't he be drinking?

What?

These insults were now angering him.

He spit onto the tile in front of the desk and, in a smooth gesture, pointed to a mop sitting against the wall. The clerk took this surprisingly well. He became much angrier when he gleaned that the clerk had no intention of cleaning it up. Not so long as he was there, at least.

What a filthy hotel.

He felt as though he were chewing his cheek between his molars. And. He was.

The clerk told him that one of the staff had the elevator stopped on the top floor, everyone had been using the stairs. He shook his head as he headed to the stairwell, passing the clerk's desk onto the carpeted area.

His senses told him that the clerk had followed him into the hallway. He made a point not to stop, indignant. He did not stop as the clerk misspoke his name.

After the third time, he stopped. When he turned he saw

that the clerk was carrying a coffeepot. He stopped walking. He waited for the clerk to explain himself. The clerk's little face made some eye contact.

Yes, he asked, his eyebrows down and such.

The clerk held out the coffeepot, reminding him that he had claimed to have broken his coffeepot the other day. He felt his cheeks heat, embarrassed that the clerk was apologizing to him. He accepted the pot. The clerk told him that he himself had stolen this, personally, out of one of the other rooms. He thanked the clerk, looking on the red vest for a name tag, finding none.

He offered his hand and they shook hands for a bit.

* * * * * * * *

For the time being, he had ordered up a television to the room. Thus far the investment had not paid off, as he could not really follow any of the shows really. The only real entertainment he'd gotten from it was when he wrote on the screen with some shaving cream. He had tried to think of something clever, ended up with a curse word. And now the shaving cream had disappeared, cleaned off by the maid. Though she still had not removed, or touched, his collection of empty wines. She did not approve, he assumed.

He noticed the hiss of the heater.

Yes, interesting.

He could do something with that.

After much meditation, he was struck with the impulse to pour water on the valve, in order to see how hot it was or such. He took one of the coffeepots on the desk to the bathroom, filled it with water, on his way back he used his toes to remove one of his shoes.

He poured the water onto the radiator pipe.

Some of this water transformed into steam, how delightful.

So, the experiment proved his hypothesis that the radiator was hot. But he could think of no logistical behavior that would be influenced by this conclusion. He placed the coffeepot on the floor, freed his hands, swept his palms across the comforter.

If only he were tired enough to go to sleep.

Went over to the television, turned it on, lay down.

He counted spikes in the plaster over the bed instead of watching the television. He also asked himself what he was doing, without reprimanding himself too harshly. He felt as though he were crying, but he wasn't upon inspection.

When he further examined himself, he actually found that he was quite happy, in a strange way. He considered writing that lady he knew to tell her all the reasons that he thought of that he was happy.

On the television a conversation carried on, the only words he recognized were probably incorrect. These people talk very fast, quite quickly. He stuck his canine tooth into the crevice underneath. He thought of how many languages he knew. This list included the sounds from the television, and ended at a word for the first palisades, spoken by the old natives.

For a while he tried to make this word have significance of some sort.

He gave up in order to check if there were any channels in his own language. Though there were none yesterday. Today there are. Still none.

His mother, back at home, had once been in a television commercial, which he had watched with her when it had come on the television.

He felt strange.

It was just as well to stay in bed. He actively defiled the memory by figuring that his parents might have had sex that night. He had heard a doctor type person once describe this as splintering the crib by re-conceiving it as a cramped space.

* * * * * * * *

He stretched out on the floor, used the towel for a pillow. The entire room was as quiet as he was quiet. He examined his cuticles, which had turned orange at some point. He could not recollect how this had happened.

Was he just unclean?

Had he eaten pistachios,

Or, dipped his fingers in a glass of orange finger dye?

He guessed that the stains were maybe the result of coffee. He looked over to the desk. The maid had left more coffee mix out for him. This begged the question, could he drink this coffee? His stomach felt fine, but had been out of sorts recently.

Standing up, he saw that she had left him two decaffeinated pouches, instead of one of each. He felt cheated. He called off the whole thing. He looked back at the floor, then at the lights coming from the hall.

He dreamed of receiving something, a sign or opportunity of some sort.

He saw that someone had slipped a pamphlet under the door, walked over to it. The thing was hand folded, with pencil marks covered in transparent tape.

He took the paper over to his desk lamp. His coffee mug was in the way. It was stuck to the table, he marveled at this, the adhesive properties of whatever. He needed to use all the muscles in his hand to remove it.

The brochure offered a laundry service, independent of the hotel. Pencil drawing of a man cradling dirty clothes, waiting in line to use the laundry machine in a laundry room that looked reasonably similar to his personal experience. He imagined that one of the staff had thought up this little scheme. The drawings looked like the work of a kid. Each sighted a different problem with doing one's own laundry. Lack of change for the washing machine, lack of time, tough stains. The last indicated that the machines often broke, which had not happened yet, though it evidently might, someday.

The brochure did not even offer prices, just a phone number. This might be for the legal whatnot of solicitation. The whole operation was probably illegal somehow. Maybe he could report this to the hotel management. He entertained the idea that they would provide him with a week's free lodging.

Not that he needed that, really.

He began worrying that the artist could draw better than himself. When he was younger, he had been proud of several recurring scribbles in his notes. Most notably of one named 'The Elastic Maniac!'

He hoped that he was being modest, looking for a pen so that he could compare the drawings side by side. There was a pen in the drawer, he walked to the drawer. He remembered that this pen had no longer worked since he'd begun using it to stir iodine into the tap water.

He dropped the paper on the floor, stepping on it halfheartedly.

He squeezed his lips into a kissing shape, closed his eyes. He did not sigh, but he was able to make his eyes water.

* * * * * * * *

The night was night, yet again. He left his room, with no

destination inside, without any want of fresh air. He'd hoped that one of his neighbors would have a woman in the hall, but no.

He saw that there was a flickering light coming from the room up ahead. Currently, this room was being rented by a man with a biblesque name that he could not remember.

On his way, he observed that someone had ordered food up from a restaurant, leaving the box outside as though it was room service.

He opened the lid, waved his fingers.

A piece of buttered toast, how enticing.

It was pretty cold, so it was not so enticing actually. He felt like a vagrant looking through garbage for something to eat, which was true, in a sense. He winced his tongue to his teeth, disgusted. Disgusted by the very idea that he himself had planned, nearly executed. He threw the toast back into the box.

He shuddered.

He resumed his interest in the flickering lights ahead of him, but walked slowly, knowing that it would be nothing too special, that he would have nothing to do once he was done with this. He hoped that he was about to eavesdrop on a couple watching pornography.

He tiptoed softly, there were still no sounds from the television, even outside the door. A piece of hotel stationary had been speared on the door handle.

knock

This was underlined emphatically.

He concluded from the evidence that he had been half-right. The volume of the television was muted. The ceiling lights turned off. A sign to ward off trespassers, meekly worded. So, that fellow was watching pornography by himself then? Good for him, how pathetic, he thought.

He decided that, if it were him, he would instead place a sign on the door that explained exactly what he was doing in scientific terms.

That is, if he ever had sufficient ambition to rent pornography, that was.

His laugh twisted from his nose in the form of air, a whimpering sound.

He decided to kick off his shoes, to feel the carpet on his

socks, to walk by sliding his feet ahead of him.

He was amazed to discover that the pattern of the carpet depicted a series of musical instruments. He had always thought that it was just gaudy.

He felt apprehensive about leaving his shoes behind, but figured no one would steal them.

When he came to the stairwell, he decided to sit with his calves over a stair. He yawned, breathed through his nose for several minutes. He sat in a small emotion for some time.

He began tonguing his thumbnail.

He should go back for his shoes.

He imagined several incidents, such as forgetting them, the pornographer finding them, a janitor throwing them away. In the end he decided not to retrieve them, in order to prove to himself that none of these things would happen.

The back of his right knee felt it was developing a rash.

* * * * * * * *

The window looked into the vending room. Through the smudged fingerprints, through the crosshatched wire, through the window, he saw that the night auditor had retreated here from his desk, and sat against the wall, reading.

Or, at least, seeming to read.

The auditor looked up at him. Rats.

He was not particularly hungry, but decided to explain the whole 'staring at you through the window' thing by buying a bag of corn chips. He pressed open the door, saying hello informal, as though addressing a friend or peer. He heard a book close, he looked through the glass.

Quickly following this he realized he had not brought any money with him.

He planned it out perfectly; he would tap the glass over the item he would appear to have selected, fish through his coat pocket dramatically, find no change, curse, nod, leave, not return. A whole little show, a social dance of sorts.

He tapped, fished, cursed, and that went well. But then, just as he reached the door, the auditor called to him.

Hand outstretched, loose change.

He closed his eyes, waved.

The auditor would hear nothing of it. He even went to the machine, using his left finger as a bookmark, inserting the coins, welcoming him to make his selection.

Awkward quiet followed.

He could not remember the item he had tapped at.

Why not, he went for the bag of curls, input his selection, watched the snack package unhook, hang there, drop to its death, and picked it out of the holding chassis.

Turn around.

There's that guy again.

He realized that he would probably have to offer some of the curls to the auditor, exchange a few words, thank him, offer some sort of repayment.

He might even have to invite him to his room so that he could pay back the loan.

he'd also have to eat these awful things.

He opened the bag, offering the first handful to the auditor.

The auditor accepted, then asked, in a crude version of his language, which city he was from. He chose the most recognizable city within some distance. The auditor mentioned a type of music particularly associated with that area, holding his hands up, started pantomiming a horn or something.

Yes, he said.

Yes, exactly.

He mentioned several street names, while drawing his jaw in to yawn. It came out that the auditor had not heard of any of these. Why would he have, considering that these streets were, secretly, unrelated to the music? The auditor was excited by this. He felt bold, somewhat excited. It seemed they were developing a genuine rapport.

He looked down at the auditor's wristwatch, but it was moving quickly.

He offered the auditor another handful of snack food, which he took. This made his next gesture, a handshake, somewhat impossible. He ended up patting his hand on the auditor's elbow. He held up the bag as he left.

It occurred to him that he did not want to bring the bag into his room. It was nearly empty. He figured he could place it in the ashtray upstairs.

* * * * * * * *

As the hotel's clock radio did not work, it was his travelling alarm that went off at five in the morning.

What was strange about this was that he did not remember

setting it. The alarm's volume grew louder as he did not respond. As he had no reason whatsoever to wake at this hour. True and false. True; he could not remember what purpose being awake now would serve. False; as he had no job, nor great social doings, he had no reason whatsoever to wake at any hour.

And yet he could not sleep for more than ten hours a day.

The alarm kept beeping.

He had already been somewhat awake anyway.

He had, in fact, been somewhat awake for some time already. He used his arm to snake a pair of pants and then somewhat catapulted them onto the alarm. This worked well enough. He could no longer hear it, so much.

His mind still remained in bit of a dreamy state. He was currently thinking of an amputated cube, without any arms to speak of.

He could still hear the alarm.

He thought of the airplane pictured on the back of the alarm. This reminded him that Garret's father was involved in the airline industry. He thought of a pilot's hat, thought of pilot, of pilots wearing a pin of sorts on their suits, which he could not picture and so on. Once he realized this, he came to understand that he was awake enough that his imagination would no longer generate itself automatically. He actively tried to keep it going, think of the cockpit of an airline. No. He tried to remember the professional terminology for the pins that pilots wear.

Desperate, he then tried to think of what he had been thinking of before thinking of that last thing he thought of. He remembered the amputated cube, but now it didn't do anything for him.

He wondered, in general, how various people were doing.

It would not be probably altogether too early to call them, considering the time difference. The first questions that someone would ask another person in another place.

What time is it there?

He would have to say. Oh, well, it's five o'clock, five thirteen or so.

Long night?

He could probably say yes. He would probably have to.

Considering that he was not going to call anyhow, he might as well say no.

Why so early?

Because so and such, a famous actress, has started snoring.

Because I have a series of investments, or financial dealings.

Because I set my alarm.

I'm not sure why I set the alarm, I can't remember that part of the night. Yes, it was that sort of night. Actually, he remembered that it was not that sort of night. He didn't drink, though he had taken two spoons of cough medicine. He even remembered setting the alarm, but the motive remained unclear. More of a sudden resolution to wake at this hour.

Change life, get organized, wake at five.

He needed to use the toilet, so, in the end, he did end up waking.

* * * * * * * *

It was early enough in the day that the people at the police station treated him with a first-customer type politeness. One of the officers even asked if he was thirsty. He had said yes. The officer brought back a glass of water, in a stein, no less. He said that his wallet had been stolen, which meant, they seemed to know, that he had lost it.

Since he was not a citizen, they would have to wait until their customs consultant began her shift, about forty minutes ago. Until that time, they invited him to sit on the couches in the waiting area. He asked if she was normally late. The officer shifted his allegiance at this point, informing him that she was, in fact, a single mother.

He wanted to ask, 'so what?'

He could not muster the courage.

Several complimentary newspapers were provided. One was typeset in a font that relayed that it was a newspaper for children. He realized then that the bit about the mother had begun working on him. You brave woman. He would even pander to her about traffic around schools.

He pushed the newspapers around on the table to see the pictures.

The theater section had run a picture of a burlesque woman. Her entire thigh uncovered.

He made a noble attempt to read the review. That word was probably something like sultry, it even shared syllables with the word for hot. The caption confirmed that the woman pictured was in the play.

The bear has made its grandiose.

That cannot be right.

The bear, has made, its grandiose.

Would this be an idiom of some kind? He came up with no sensible interpretation.

He then began thinking that some lucky someone must have gotten to stitch sequins into certain areas of the costume.

Ah, if only.

He noted several details of the waiting room. The cover to the ceiling lights had come unscrewed. The carpet had cookie crumbs ground into it. The cloth of the sofa had hardened there. It occurred to him that this might be dried blood, this being a police station and all that. He lifted his eyebrows. This would mean that they had made someone wait here while they were bleeding. If it were so, he felt like chastising the entire department for treating people in such a rude manner. The entire department was confused, poorly run, no sympathy for people in the waiting room, when they're bleeding no less. Ridiculous, he didn't care if they were widowed grandparents.

Hm, that's not dried blood, probably.

Nothing else to do, he resumed the theater section.

He saw that he could go see this show, in fact. He could go see it that very evening at seven. For. For that much? That much to see what, at best, amounted to a burlesque show. For that he could go see a real one for an entire week. He could even wear a dinner shirt, even bring a pair of tiny binoculars.

He laughed out loud.

* * * * * * * *

The shower would take a while to warm.

Maybe he should start using dental floss. His gums hurt just thinking of it. He instead decided to use his fingernails to scratch some plaquesque stuff off his teeth.

That.

That is disgusting.

He ran his fingers under the faucet for awhile, until they were sanitized. Perhaps the shower would heat up faster if he left the sink on. Perhaps he could flush the toilet too. That would do it. He had left a coffeepot on the toilet? Oh yes, he had used it to replenish the water more quickly, as he had needed to flush it twice following that impressive bowel movement. He should place it in a more proper place, some time in the near future, such as next to the coffee maker. He checked the temperature in the shower.

It was warm enough now.

He drew back the curtain, stepped into the tub. The water against his chest was much colder than it had been against his wrist. He shrieked and retreated to the wall, holding out his foot to monitor the rising temperature. The water flicked around, some went to the curtain, some sprinkled his knees. He put his foot down after feeling that the soap residue left in the bottom of the tub was quite slick. He noticed that the maid had left a fresh paper-wrapped bar of soap in the soap holding alcove. The water had already soaked the paper into pulp. He reached over to grab it, attempting to avoid the water, even though it was a difficult gesture, even though the water had heated.

He sat down in the tub cross legged, adjusting himself so that the stream hit his back. He unwrapped the soap, throwing the paper outside somewhere. The soap was dry enough that he could draw basic mathematics on the dry tile. He held out his hand, gathering water. He smeared the water on the shower drawing. It ran down the tub, into the hair of his ankle.

He decided to stay here for a while, get extra clean.

Some water struck his chest area, and he pictured that he was on a boat deck, swimming trunks, brine, barnacles and such. Assuming the sensation of warm sea mist would be roughly similar to this shower steam. He then thought about deep-sea fishermen, drawing in large fish. He had once heard that a tuna was the size of this entire tub. Actually, he had said the bench they were sitting on when he'd told her that, which was, maybe, even larger.

If only he could get a hold of one of these gigantic fish, and use it for his own purposes.

He could keep it in the bathtub.

He ran his hand over the back of his neck. He suspected that his hair was getting long.

He also examined several hairs growing from his chest. He performed a chest hair inventory. The water from the shower grew a little colder.

A wave of feelings occurred to him.

The water grew colder. He felt that he wanted this bathing ordeal to last longer. He felt that if he turned the water pressure lower the hot water might last a little longer.

He felt the knob on the shower head as he turned it down.

* * * * * * * *

That day, he called his bank to assure himself that his finances were holding up. They were holding much better than he had hoped. He had spoken to a woman at the bank, and tried to tell her that he was travelling, to give her the impression that he was a globally operating man of the world, but she did not seem that interested, giving him his balance, thanking him for some reason, hanging up first.

Now he was in the lobby.

He went up to the clerk, to ask how much he was paying for his room. The clerk asked him if he was renting a room.

The clerk had assumed that he was sleeping in the lobby toilet.

He rubbed his left eyeball as a response. He decided to ignore the statement altogether. This did not work properly. The clerk was waiting for some type of verbal response.

He thought of a good one, and it took some time to figure out the proper wording. The clerk waited with a toothy smile.

He could not go into the rest room because he was afraid of catching diseases from the clerk's family.

The clerk took this rather poorly.

He had crossed a line somehow.

He stared at the clerk, who looked down at an empty mug of pens and gave him a figure for the room. It was very reasonable. He waved, then did several calculations. He called the clerk back.

Did they also have another room available at that rate?

The clerk asked if he was going to start selling his sister in it. He felt that this was copying his earlier statement about diseases, felt proud, no need to respond to it, as he had no sister anyhow.

He rolled his eyeballs.

No, he was serious about this.

The clerk said that yes, there were other rooms in the hotel.

Well then, did they have one up higher than his?

Yes, they did. The clerk seemed genuine when he asked if he wanted a better view, to change rooms. He said that he was quite satisfied. He was interested in renting out an additional room, at the same rate. The clerk was confused about how to do this.

While waiting for the clerk to ask him why he was doing this, he became confused about the reasons himself.

Why?

He could put some stuff inside it.

bags, garbage.

He let the clerk decide how to rent the room, instead choosing to bite his lip, coming up with several reasons, one being that the second room would have a better view of things. The clerk asked for his identification.

He said that this had been lost. The clerk should have copies.

He said to arrange the billing directly to his bank account, which he had already arranged for his current room. The clerk wrote some things down. He scratched his beard, or, more accurately, the oddly patterned facial hair that grew when he did not shave. While the clerk looked through the keys under the counter, he came up with something.

For hosting parties, he said.

The clerk nearly glanced, but didn't.

* * * * * * * *

He could not find the envelope. But he did remember seeing it in several different locations. It was not on the bathroom counter, it was not in his dresser, it was not in the drawer, he made sure it was not on the bathroom counter, not in the pocket of his coat, perhaps under the sheets, not under clothes, not in the wallet pocket of his coat. He ran out of ideas. He imagined that he had placed it somewhere distinct then. But where? He had definitely had it that morning. He sucked air over his lips, then chewed chapped skin.

He checked the bathroom counter.

He placed the mouthwash into a more organized place. He folded up the washcloth, put it on the toilet lid. He thought that he had once seen the envelope under the curtains.

While he moved, he deduced that the maid had stolen them, and sold them on the black market. But he doubted that she would know what they were. He also entertained the idea that she was somehow related to someone of the criminal underworld. Then of course, she was keeping them from him because she thought he should not have them. How misguided. He ruffled the curtain up. Nothing. She did not understand though, that he had gone to great lengths to get those.

There was no place in the vicinity of the bathroom that they could be hiding.

He looked at the bathroom counter.

It occurred to him that brushing his teeth might somehow apply to his current predicament.

He then had a vague memory. He opened the closet door, as he had opened the closet door. He had placed something in the safe, which allowed one to set the combination when locking the door. He tried several combinations. He tried the day of his birthday, the month of his birthday. Instead of trying the year of his birthday, he switched to trying numbers with crude connotations.

Fifteen.

There we go.

The safe opened.

You win an envelope! And some loose change.

After taking two pills from inside the envelope, he decided to leave it in the safe. He left the combination alone. In the bottom of the closet, he saw a pair of pants that he had not worn that week. They were probably much cleaner than the ones he was currently wearing.

He picked them up, he placed them on the bed. He had some trouble removing his belt, the leather had frayed. It remained a very nice belt, his only one. He thought of buying a length of cord for casual use, and using this one solely for upscale social bits.

He took the pair of pants off the bed. He pulled the belt through the belt loops in a cautious way. He entertained the idea of changing shirts, as he tucked in his shirt.

There we go, you handsome devil.

He would like to go out into the hallway, to share himself with the world.

Carpe diem.

He went out into the hall.

* * * * * * * *

There was a woman standing at one of the doors, working with the key. Her face he could not see because she had let her hair fall to cover it. She was wearing a dark blouse, loose, he could not judge the shape of her breasts, but she had bent over nicely, wearing a knee length skirt.

He intended to slow down enough to appreciate this for a tic, before continuing on to wherever he was going.

She seems to be having some trouble with the door.

He was a little cautious, because he had not seen her face. This gave the woman a certain short-lived mystique. He even shuddered a little, somewhat on purpose. She had been quiet. She started cursing the doorknob, pushing aside a strand of her hair and so on.

She accused it of being born out of wedlock.

What would she say in a more private situation?

He thought some things. He tripped a bit on the carpet, but came out of it gracefully. He became somewhat nervous. He did not know how to pick the locks anyway. That was what he planned on doing. He stood behind her, but turned his standing into a very slow amble, while he phrased the correct wording, deciding if he even wanted to try.

She turned to face him.

This threw him off.

He was quickly torn between spitting out the half-finished sentence in his mind, examining her face, and assuming control of his body language.

Her face was alright, though she did have faint acne scars.

He figured that she had said something to him. But what?

He emphasized his accent. He said something that seemed charming enough. He said that he was sorry, that he hadn't heard her.

She had darker kind of eyes, but she was a little younger than him.

What?

She had repeated herself, he nearly missed it again. She pivoted her head, held up the key. The way she pivoted her head was intentionally girlish, which made him sniff. She wanted help with the lock, he figured. This was a delicate situation.

She was in luck, he knew how to pick the locks.

Not a forward thinking thing to say, really.

He rolled up his shirtsleeve for some reason, imagined that he would try this for a minute or two, seem stupid, wish her well, go back to his bathroom that evening. He guessed that someone who knew how to pick the lock would use a tool of some kind. In his pocket he found a subscription card for a magazine. He folded it, stuck it into the door, stuck out his tongue.

He guessed that he should just jiggle it around for a while.

He heard a sound.

The door went a little open!

He was caught for some time between being amazed with the luck of it, and pretending that he had expected this to happen. He stood, said a few things about the door.

He even gave her the subscription card, saying that she should just have this just in case.

He leaned against the door frame as they spoke.

* * * * * * * *

From the height of the garden area, he could see further down the street. Not many people were out at that hour, though it was not late. At first he did not see the panhandler huddled on the carton, but then the guy fell into a coughing fit. This went on. There was a genuine hack to the cough.

He has, perhaps, pneumonia?

Though he did feel cold in his shirt area, his armpits were sweating.

He had not applied enough deodorant.

The panhandler's hack was still going on. What was that guy's problem? The longer it continued the more fakeish it seemed. He thought of what he wanted to do. The trees planted along the brick were not doing so well. He thought of several things to do. Why was that man still coughing?

It had changed, at this point, from a cough into a growling-type behavior.

Then the panhandler noticed a younger couple nicely dressed coming that way but consciously looking at the other side of the street, though there was nothing there all that interesting. Some type of exchange was about to take place. He could feel it.

He was certain.

The panhandler removed a cap or something from his head, holding it out to the girl. The couple, however, was too interested in examining something over there, a mailbox or an empty space over the intersection. Nothing was going to come of this. It was too thought out, practiced, impenetrable.

The panhandler said something that stopped them.

What a brave man.

Actually, it was not so brave; the boy turned, replied, the girl did not try to stop him. That is the girl did not try to stop him until the panhandler's standing revealed that he was taller and more formidable than the boy.

Who would have thought it, with all that huddling over?

So he had been right, something had happened. He had even prophesied it. He lost interest in what was happening to think about himself. What an odd, almost supernatural, talent he had for this type of thing. He remembered a television program where an investigative organization would be on the look out for just this ability. He could have been a great asset to society.

He was startled by a word of great force.

The standing gesture had not ended the conflict. The two nearly chest to chest.

Fingers were flying in the space between them. The panhandler's technique was to be quiet while the difference in size occurred the boy.

He walked over to a bench to get a closer look. He judged that he still was not close enough to be obligated to do something.

How typical, the girl was trying to end it, the boy pushed, also trying to end it.

The ragged creep stumbled back, surprised. Instead of retaliating normally, he slurred, then kicked his carton in the young man's general direction.

It was a good kick, but it missed.

End of conflict.

* * * * * * * *

He spoke with Sabrina in the elevator. She had decided that he was a particular type of man. Was he a fan of Gatton? She had also decided that he would love this. What was it? She described it by listing several other things he did not know.

Oh, it was music that she liked.

He decided not to say that he did not know what she was talking about. Instead he noticed things about her; that she wore perfume, that she wore a coat with some fashionable style to it. He leaned back against the elevator wall. The elevator stopped on his floor.

He didn't move.

She was confused. She started pressing the button to close the doors. He lived on five right? Had he pressed two?

She had left her blouse unbuttoned at the top.

He pressed the other button, saying that often both had to be pressed to close the doors. The doors closed. The incident with the elevator doors had distracted her.

So, Gatton?

Oh he would love it. If he was in to this or that. Pure so and so.

He felt somewhat demeaned by the assumption that he knew these things. He was truly at a loss for words on the subject. He mentioned the town that he was from, a type of music. He approximated several names that he had heard from someone else.

Oh, that's grand.

That was not her type of music though. This was much more, oh she did not know. She closed her eyes, waved her hands. The motion looked half arousing, but another half of it looked pretty vain. He did suspect, however, that she was from a wealthier social bit than himself.

She petted his sleeve when she said that he'd love it.

Did he have a record player in his room?

He said that he had not brought his record player, which was somewhat true. She said that she had the record up in her room. She offered to lend him her record player for a few hours, but he could see that she did not really want to do this.

He can rent one from the lobby, nothing to worry about.

Oh did they have them there?

Oh yes, he rented a television.

And they also have record players.

She is so excited.

She would give him the record, with no rush to return it. She said that he must be going mad without any music. She had a couple of freckles on her chest. The skin on his neck felt bare, irritated. She had even bought a traveling record player.

She motioned for him to follow her. The conversation broke.

He wondered if she would have trouble with the door.

It seemed she would, but it didn't turn out that way. He stayed at the door, but saw that she had left out some of her clothes.

Some black things on the floor.

He looked away, then looked back.

There was the record player on the desk. A little like he had imagined.

She told him to come inside, asked him to close the door behind him.

* * * * * * * *

He thought about differences in temperature of the cement barriers in the parking lot. The wool of his pants was thin enough so that when he sat on it he could feel a temperature. He had not brought anything with him except his keys. He looked up to the window of his room.

Window closed, lights off, the curtains drawn half-way. He imagined the air in his room would be stagnant, and he felt dismayed. He could picture a smell that would be there. What a filthy animal, the human being. This made him aware of a gas build up in his lower back.

Cautiously he let this pass, no one was around, he was outside.

He saw a plume of smoke pass from the brick to the light.

He decided to investigate, but while he moved to see he considered letting it go. He could see an elbow. He became aware that he had moved further into the parking lot as he brought the smokers into sight, as a means of maintaining his radial distance.

It's the maid, speaking to some man.

Oh bones, this man was better looking than him to boot. He assumed that they were courting one another. The maid was wearing on oddly large jacket. The man was resting his foot on a brief case.

The maid looked up at him.

He was just taking a casual sideways stalk through the middle of an empty parking lot, nothing to it.

The man did not know him, but called him hello something, hello close friend, when the guy saw that he did not understand the first bit. He said hello back, in a dubious way.

He wanted someone to explain what was happening here, but that never happens.

He was trapped now anyhow.

He walked closer to them, deciding that asking for one of the cigarettes that they were sharing would be the easiest way to be on his way, leave them to themselves and so on. The man reached into the pocket of the maid's jacket, whipped out a cigarette, held it out, said his name.

The maid had somehow whispered his name then.

He had not caught this.

Perhaps he was not perceptive enough for this little encounter, at the moment.

He took the cigarette, the box of matches. He said thanks, and pardoned himself.

The man said they were just taking a break. Having a cigarette.

The smoke scraped his pallet. It was disgusting.

What were they taking a break from, oh you know, the man kicked a briefcase at his feet. He had been sent here to deal with a will.

You're a lawyer?

He was not a lawyer.

He was an actor!

But until things got going for him he was working for a lawyer.

It went on like that. The maid looked over at him every once in a while.

* * * * * * * *

He tried not to let the mesh bag touch his back. This was impossible given the way he was carrying it. There were no sounds from the laundry room.

Good.

He pressed open the door. All the lids were open, no one was using any of them. What unbelievable luck. He could use two machines simultaneously. He looked over at the vending machine that sold detergent. There was some blue thing over there. Someone had left a large bottle of laundry detergent.

What unbelievable luck.

It was probably empty. He decided to put the laundry into the machine before checking this. Because he was using two machines, he decided to separate the light clothing from the dark, as a fancy butler might. He began picking out the light clothing first. He could not take his mind off the bottle of detergent over there.

Someone might come back for it before he got to use it.

Someone might come back while he was in the process of using it.

He decided to check right away then. It was nearly full. He grabbed it, filling both of the machines, even the one he had yet to fill. He placed the bottle where he found it.

Approximated the correct angle. Thereabouts.

He began loading the other machine, happy with himself.

He did feel a little guilty. He actually felt pretty bad about this. He thought of the person coming back while he was there, remembering the exact weight of the bottle, accusing him of theft. He decided to be as quick as possible.

He selected light for light, dark for dark, he inserted several coins into the machines.

They clicked on.

It was then that he realized that the person would not be coming back for the detergent anytime soon. If the person had just used the detergent in the washing machine, then some clothing would be in the dryers, all of which were currently empty.

He was very proud of this rationale. He ran his hand over the dryers.

They were all cold.

If someone came back anyhow, he would just curse at them for accusing him of theft. He had lived in this hotel for so long, they come in here for a weekend convention or such, then accuse him of stealing their soap, treating him like that.

It was even incidental that he had stolen the soap.

He should even admit it. This was his laundry room, he lived here, all properties herein abandoned so on. He wondered if there were not, in fact, some law that backed him up. If they wanted, he was ready for it.

That would do it.

His agitation settled after a little while. Once the detergent had dissolved he felt much better. No evidence. He thought about going back to his room, but decided to guard the dryers.

He put the bag on the table, instead of leaving it on the floor. This was all he did that time.

* * * * * * * *

It was later in the evening that he had returned to his room. For no particular reason, he took one of the towels, ran it beneath the sink. He applied the cloth to his neck. That felt very nice. He wrapped the towel around, tucking it into his collared shirt, looking as though he had been in an automotive accident. The towel soaked his shirt, annoying, but he decided to stomach it.

He found that the movement capability of his neck was dampened by the towel, but that was to be expected.

He paced up the room to the curtains.

Nothing out the window. He paced over to the bed.

He had left several business cards on the desk, but why? He had no intention to call the numbers listed on them. He should have just left them at the bus stop where they had been taped to the metal.

This one here was for a woman. This one for a credit counselor. This one, thicker tack board. That one, stationary.

The activity did not hold his attention for long, he did take another glance at one of the cards.

The water on his neck was getting cold. He took off the towel. He tried to fling it into the bathroom. It landed on the doorknob, hanging there. This seemed like more of an accomplishment than if it had landed in the bathroom, so he left it. He sat down onto the bed.

Maybe it was time for a catnap.

Because several items of clothing currently occupied the area by the headboard, he decided to lie lengthwise on the bed.

Sweet comfort.

He attempted several dreamy thoughts. He ended up thinking about cracks accumulating in his bones. He pictured tiny buttons on a picture of the spinal cord. This, naturally, lead to him thinking of brains. He had never seen one in person, but had heard many great things.

A terrible sound tore out.

He flew into a state of alarm. He rolled over.

Noise.

He looked around the room.

The fire alarm? He couldn't think right.

He was going to burn up. The noise was not coming from that direction. It sounded like a siren from an old war bit. For some reason, his eyes started to tear up. He rubbed them with his thumbs as he stood up. That sound. He couldn't think like this. It was coming from outside. He looked over.

The alarm clock radio

has turned on?

Well that's new.

He could not figure out how to turn it off. He did know how to turn the volume down, but he jerked out the power cord and it fell from the bedside table and that worked fairly well.

The noise stopped.

His panic, though, remained. In order to release it, he cursed the clock, firebrand saboteur. He took the jacket from the headboard, and used it to whip at the device repeatedly.

He stopped, standing, sucking air through his nose. He closed his eyes.

It was no use. He was awake once again.

* * * * * * * *

He recognized that he had been here for much longer than was customary. He had had the good sense to dissuade the waiter from becoming irate by giving a large gratuity in advance when he had brought him a glass of orange juice. He hoped that the waiter would be held in check by the chance that there was more where that had come from.

There was not.

In fact, that had been the only money in his pocket.

The corner booth he sat in was rather comfortable. Last night he could not sleep very well, which he was proud of. It made him feel that he was a complicated sort. A mysterious personality. Why, just the other day he had been flirting with a woman and left while she went to the bathroom. Complicated types like himself often had problems sleeping because of emotional so and such.

His emotional problem had involved a runny nose.

As well as a nap from two to six.

He had, however, left the hotel once his sinuses were clear, because he wanted his room cleaned. He also did not want one of the housekeeping staff to wander into the room while he was sleeping. He also wanted to go somewhere, and needed some vitamin content in his diet.

He liked these telephones on the wall to the rest room here. He also liked the bar area being so reminiscent of an underground politics ordeal.

Yes, yes, a very nice place indeed.

He then remembered that he had promised to call Jacob a long time ago. They were speaking on the phone, he had said that he needed to use the rest room.

He had promised to call back in five minutes.

That was some months ago.

He began thinking that he would ask the waiter for change for the bill that he had given him, pretending like he had been waiting for it this entire time. He could use this money on the telephone, call Jacob up right now. He could even play up his inability with the language. That would definitely work. He could pretend to be a man of no language at all, a man with no mouth, with skin over his mouth where there was a mouth normally. His face drooped down. How would he breathe then, like with a runny mouth?

He jerked his head back and it cracked into the wall behind the booth. It was more startling than painful. Still he held his palm to his hair, blinked, spread his eyes wide.

Had anyone seen him?

The waiter was looking his way.

He pounded his fist on the table several times and resolved to not sleep right now, by willpower means.

They were probably working up the nerve to kick him out. He felt like a drunk. He felt ashamed that he was not drunk at all. He had no excuse whatsoever.

The door creaked open. Several middle aged madams walked into the restaurant exclaiming to one another about a story, then about how much they liked the ambience. They agreed to ask for a menu. The waiter went off to greet them.

He was saved. He decided to leave while he had the opportunity.

* * * * * * * *

He finally found the record where it had fallen behind the desk. He pulled one side of the desk away from the wall, then leaned over the top to grab the sleeve. The space was tight enough that he needed to turn two of his fingers into pliers to grab it.

There it was.

That morning Sabrina had been in the lobby. He had not thought about the record until she asked how he liked it, which meant that she wanted it back. He had planned to go grab it for her immediately. But he had not listened to it, and feared that she might quiz him about his favorite parts.

As they did not, in fact, rent record players in the lobby, he had been forced to call several pawn shops in the area until he found one. It was expensive and heavy, but he had some time to return it.

He could not figure how to make it work.

He recognized that the disc was placed on the center pin. But when he turned it on, nothing happened. There was no manual to explain the process. Oh that's too bad, at least he could now say that he had tried to listen to it.

He fooled around with the switches for awhile, just for good measure.

He was almost disappointed when the music began.

During the first minute or so, he stood next to the machine. He then studied the jacket sleeve. The sounds made it difficult to read. He saw that the entire recording would last about an hour.

A whole hour.

He decided to sit down.

He watched the record spin around for some time. He watched the name of the music rotate.

He closed his eyes to listen.

He took several objects out of his pockets that were digging into his thighs. Why did he have these paper towels?

One of the instruments sounded like a car breaking down in a meticulous fashion.

He pursed his hands. They started to sweat so he stuck them on their respective knees. His posture began to bother him, as it had lately. He thought that if he sat straight for a couple hours, this problem would be cured. Maybe it would be best to lie down on the floor. It was much harder than the bed, so he assumed it would take less time to straighten the bones.

Perhaps it would be done in one hour.

He began to click his teeth together at one-second intervals.

It had probably been about ten minutes now.

He tried to pick out the most impressive musician, but got nowhere in this.

He could probably just listen to the first half of the record. If he did this he was a third done already. He could say that the first half had been his favorite, which would be trueish. He laughed out loud.

In fact, he would tell her that his favorite part was the second half of the record.

Oh it was absolutely remarkable, a real improvement.

Part 2

(frightening developments)

One

He muttered several profanities, but, despite this, the rain swelled more. He was still some distance from the hotel, no socks, three grocery bags. The loaf of bread was what worried him most. The thin wax paper was quaint, but could not endure this rugged weather. Secondly, he worried about the grocery bags filling up with water. The soft drinks, iodine, and frozen etceteras, these things would be fine, he guessed, so long as he got home quickly. He had realized that the quickest way back to the hotel, the only way he knew for certain, lead him through the open field right there.

Of course, he had not really thought about it.

Those tall stick plants had matted down, obscuring a dangerous topography. The ground was muddy, he could feel through his sneakers. Altogether a deadly time and place.

Out of logic, as well as frustration, he decided that he could get rid of the bread.

He cloud sling it into the air that way.

He set down the remaining bags so that he could do this properly. He rotated his waist.

Waka!

The bag flew off into the field, making a hissing noise, but it did not get too far. The rain had pushed it down or something, which meant that it did not count as an accurate measure of strength. He imagined that it bounced a few times, but he could not verify this.

He picked up his bags, carried on.

Well, that was stupid.

He considered going after the bread, but did not feel up to the task. What upset him most about it was that the cold cuts were no longer a practical purchase.

There would be a gulch he would have to cross, filled with barren trees.

The rain running from his eyebrows felt warmer than his skin. It dripped into his lower lip, tasting of salt. He smacked his lips and realized that it also tasted a bit like his shampoo.

Which was not altogether unpleasant.

He held his lips closed. He had to get home, he had these groceries to worry about. His inner soles were damp, squeaking with his weight. His shirt stuck to his pectoral muscles. In his peripheral vision, an orange light.

He stopped to look at it.

It sat on dark shapes.

Someone else would think this was pretty.

That was his impression. He continued walking, finding that the act was made much easier if he kept his eyes on his feet. He only hoped that he would not walk into a branch, or spear or something.

The soap, or whatever it was, ran into his left eye, blinding him, so he closed that one and, as he couldn't very well put the bags in the mud to free his hand, began whipping his head around in order to fling the stuff off of him. But that did not work well.

Even blind, he was able to see the gulch up ahead of him. The security light had turned on, fooled into thinking that it was dusk.

He took very wide steps across the pathetic stream. His skin rubbed against the zipper of his pants. He stopped.

He decided to be a little more cautious while he maneuvered.

No need to rush. He tried to think of an expression. But he couldn't recall one that dealt explicitly with zippers tearing off the genitalia.

* * * * * * * *

An address occurred to him that might be it that morning. He hoped it was correct, at least. The letter he wrote was not too obvious.

He even wrote several paragraphs at the beginning to throw off anyone who happened to open the letter. Just in case it was the wrong address.

As he had no other, he decided to use the forbidden envelope. He had placed the remainder of the pills inside his pocket, figuring that he could find a case of some kind to use instead, some mints or so on.

Out of a mix of paranoia and a need to get outdoors more often, he had not sent the letter at the hotel, and, instead, walked to the local post office, which is where he was right now.

Waiting in line.

A mother with a glazed expression studied several criminal notices. Her kid was going mad, walking on the floor like a crab, shrieking every once in a while. He surveyed the area to find someone who was as annoyed with this as himself.

The shipping clerk?

In fact, this chap was so irritated that he stared at the mother. He determined that the mother's interest in the notices developed from this awkwardness. Her angel, her darling demon, walking like a crab at age so and such. His father would be so proud the next time they let him out for a few days.

He used his thumbs to straighten out the crease in the envelope, or, at least, attempted to do so. This was a terrible idea. The type of thing one reads about, wondering how in the world someone could be that stupid.

Wait a tic.

This operation would go much better if he scratched out his return address.

What he meant was that it would go better if he had not written it. Then no one could trace it back to him. Including, it occurred to him, the recipient of the letter.

He had also written the phone number for the hotel so that there would be some way to contact him. It warned beneath the number that it was a hotel. The check that he enclosed was for a larger amount than necessary.

The shipping clerk called him over to the desk.

He should say something about the little rat, establish camaraderie.

No, wait, he loved children. la la. No need to give himself away.

He held the envelope beneath the desk at first. He requested an international stamp, but only one. Just one, he instructed. The clerk picked up the letter.

The clerk can mail the item right here, for a cheaper

price.

oh can you?

This was how it ended then. He knew, in his mind, that there were several things he could say to avoid this, but he could think of none. He squirmed a little, then handed over the envelope.

He looked at his hands.

The shipping clerk said that the envelope was, something, folded. Yes, he said, it was folded, without any feeling. Several things were written down. The clerk turned over the envelope and looked at it. He sighed, looked down at his shoes.

oh bones, curses.

All done.

He looked up.

He walked from the room with lightness in his face.

* * * * * * * *

At some point, it had been decided that they had to go see a film being shown at the community center. The exact time that this occurred was still mysterious to him, but he looked forward to it that day with sporadic enthusiasm. She had finished a conference call somewhat late, but had come to get him immediately afterwards. At the time, he had presumed she no longer intended to do so.

The community center was located next to the public library.

Yes, well, who doesn't know that?

She had not been here long but knew the town much better than he did.

Several old people were setting up fold out chairs in front of the projector. Drinks were being poured into plastic cups. He saw the poster outside advertising that there would be a discussion of some sort following the feature.

This was not his prime environment.

She told the volunteer that she had already paid for the tickets. Her clothing was a little thin, folded up at some fat on her waist. Her adolescent demeanor dispersed when it seemed that there were problems with the reservation. Then she became venomous, speaking so quickly that he could not understand the conversation.

She demanded to speak to someone. Hair came loose.

He found this attractive.

The volunteer conceded.

And everyone stopped for a second or two.

She grabbed his arm, tugged him inside. Did he catch that? They almost did not get in.

He explained a slang term that he knew for old people. He explained that it referenced flaking skin, as though the person was losing pieces of himself. She was delighted, she laughed forcefully for some time.

Hahaha.

haha.

Where did he normally sit?

Before he answered she led them to the middle. She took the seat on the makeshift aisle. His only seating preference was that he did not have to sit next to someone. The woman next to him gave no acknowledgement. Sabrina looked around the community center, appreciating it in some way. She seemed to consider, for a moment, that she might not like it, but then nodded, finding that she did.

He smiled at her.

The lights dimmed

It was shouted at someone or other that they just had to flick the thing on the bottom. When the movie began, it was silent for the opening credits. He tried, at first, to understand the dialogue.

It was the anniversary of an event.

The old man was a retired soldier, he had a gun in his desk drawer. His son came into the office with important news. He did not catch the news. They must go immediately. The son helped his father with the steps, but then ran down the hill.

The drunk guy had run his car into the water, he was singing. He wanted to die. The son pulled the drunk out of the water, slapping him. The soldier was somehow able to resolve the situation without getting wet.

This whole place smells like dead skin.

They put the drunk on the table. The soldier asked for hot water like a doctor.

He looked over.

She did not answer.

* * * * * * * *

There was something extremely suspicious in the way the clerk misspoke his name. He acknowledged the name rather automatically, out of habit, which was unfortunate. He was certainly trapped into a joke at his expense. He walked through the lobby, as he passed the desk the clerk asked how he was that day.

He made a crude gesture while he walked off. Not looking.

He had won.

The clerk came out from behind the desk. He pressed the elevator button several times, and looked that way.

He was thinking of him and

The clerk was holding a paper. He began to suspect something was wrong. Maybe someone had died. The clerk motioned him over toward the couches, but did not ask him to sit down.

What?

He scratched his armpit. The clerk waited for a while to start speaking. The clerk was wondering how much he paid for his rooms. He said that he did not know the exact figure. He had thought he was getting a discount, but he was wrong. The clerk said that he was paying that much for a room that he was not even using. In his hands was a brochure of some kind.

Ah.

The clerk explained basically, he had gotten this in the mail. A warehouse was closing down, the bankruptcy had prevented technical things from happening. Normally these things did happen, but the forms declared otherwise. Considering special legal conditions, the merchandise things could not be moved around. The merchandise would be blown up or whatnot with the building.

This merchandise was available at absurd prices.

Below their original cost.

If he acted quickly.

Right now, in fact.

He tried to leave a little. The clerk grabbed his arm. Listen, he could buy many things with some money. The clerk could sell these things, as he was a good salesman. He could sell things to the guests.

He slapped the brochure out of his hand.

While the clerk picked it up, it was revealed that what he meant was that he could sell things like mouthwash, etcetera, razors at the desk.

It annoyed him that this was starting to seem very reasonable.

They would split the profits down the center. They could even use the profits to buy even larger quantities of this absurdly priced inventory. What was the trick? He could not see it. He said that the little venture would shut down the moment the warehouse was exploded.

Just until then.

Make some money.

He then realized that this would give him weight on the clerk. It would be nice to get a little respect for himself. Just a small amount of money. Who knows? Maybe the investment would really pay off. He agreed, in his mind, to write the clerk a check for the price of one week's lodging. Maybe this was his chance to become a legitimate man.

He cut him off. He said that he would get a check from his room.

He walked back. The clerk smiled.

This was too chummy.

He said that he was buying the look on his face when it all went to pieces.

* * * * * * * *

This area he had wandered into was much shorter. The buildings had an old-fashioned look to them. He passed beneath a blue awning. A gaunt man examined him from inside, but saw that he was not a customer, then resumed his seat on the counter top, back to the window. He saw that several movies were on a shelf in the back of the store. The thin man picked up a telephone, resumed speaking to someone as though there were no chance he would come inside.

He didn't want to anyway.

The hooded shirt that he wore clapped against his thigh. He had forgotten to throw out of a set of disposable utensils in the pocket.

Yet another thing to do.

He looked ahead for a trash can to throw them in.

There was one over there, but it was across the street.

Several prints were labeled with prices. One showed a touch of nudity, but it was too highbrow to arouse him really. The woman was sterile, he imagined that if he had sex with her she would probably ask him afterwards to contrast the experience to an economics graph. Or something like that.

Hello.

A liquor store.

He looked inside for some time. He walked off, then returned to buy a small flask of rum. The floor was smeared with a thick film of unknowable smut. It still reflected the ceiling lights though, which made him a little dazed. The man at the counter was very old.

He wondered if he drank every night.

He must, how pitiful.

He dug through his pockets for exact change. He began to suspect that he did not have it. He found the coins in the pocket of his shirt, pricked his finger on the fork. He went on his way with a politic 'thank you'.

He looked behind him, tossed the bag out onto the street, sticking the rum into his wallet pocket.

He still had to find a trash can though for these other things. There would probably be one on the way back home. He felt strange that his excursion had ended at a liquor store in such an organic way. Who'd have guessed?

He began to feel a little blue.

Trash can.

He dropped several receipts, some coins, and the utensils into the bag. He then checked that he still had the rum, then walked off. His feet felt a little sore, his hair a little windy. Though neither sensation was bothersome on its own he stopped on a stoop to compose himself.

He rattled his feet unstuck from his socks, then matted his hair.

Stepped up to the window so that he could look at himself.

He saw that the building offered language services. Classes? It did not say. He could use a few classes of some kind. So long as they were one on one. He decided to write down the number, but had no pen.

He was so set on the idea that he sneaked around looking for one.

He found a flyer advertising a few services.

He crushed it into his pocket, pointed a finger toward some unseen destination and went on his way.

Two

He had no business in the bookstore. The only thing he could think to do there was to purchase a coffee on the second floor. The girl there was an attractive teenager. She asked him how he would like his coffee prepared.

Black, he thought.

Normal, he said.

She looked at him cruelly.

With nothing then?

He took the coffee over to the window by the books about war. The paper cup spilled a little onto the carpet, but he did not tell anyone about this. The bench there was not very comfortable to sit on, but he found a way.

He wanted to draw the curtain closed.

He managed this, with a little effort.

He blew on the coffee, but it was too hot. He let it rest upon the windowsill. The wood was angled, but he found a position that the coffee would stand without falling over. He examined several book covers about spies or such.

He could not stop looking over at the coffee to see if it was still hot. It would take awhile to cool off. He went to go find a magazine that he could read. The only magazine close to the coffee was a journal of photographs, which he did not take. He picked up a compilation of satirical drawings from old newspapers. The reproductions looked appealing, he could see folds in the newspapers that were not there now.

He realized too late that this book was incredibly boring. A big waste of time really. The drawings were not funny at all. He closed it, leaving it on the bench beside him.

Maybe the coffee was colder now.

It had cooled sufficiently that he could drink it, if he took small sips. The flavor of it was much stronger than he liked. There was no taste of water. He had paid for it. In the future he should probably just bring the packets from his hotel room wherever he went. A glass of hot water was probably free of charge.

Too much in his mouth at once.

He spit it back into the cup.

He slapped his esophagus, and decided to take a break from this coffee drinking. He looked over the railing to the bottom floor. A woman was reading a book of some kind.

She wore glasses, which seemed routine. She would probably be interested in him if he cleaned himself off a little. Wear a mortarboard, talk about his article in that one section.

What caught his eye was a children's book at her feet.

Was she going to buy that?

What a vine of tarts this country. He felt very lucid, he even thought of some pretty accurate things to say about this. The next time he used the telephone he would toss out a few of these little pearls. A place where everyone wanted to extend pre-pubescence. To file reports, and grope each other, the way that they would have when they were young, see movies, so on, neotenic etcetera. For some reason. My field agent's reports are still muddy.

I'm fine, I just thought I'd tell you.

* * * * * * * *

After only a few harmless glasses, he'd become vilely intoxicated. Some fresh air would help. He staggered a little.

Was this something that someone else would notice?

To be safe, he had gone to the back of the parking lot. He had not worn a jacket, which had been a good decision at first, because the cold air penetrated his senses. He had not brought his key card, which was a bad decision from the get-go. The only solution was to wait until someone was going into the hotel. Or maybe wait outside dying until dawn.

He shivered, but perhaps the cold would stiffen his joints so that he could walk in an ordinary way. He hadn't been so meek about his habits before, but in his mind, the management might decide that this was an evictable offense.

The doors were closing in. He would be trapped.

Actually, the doors were closed already. That was the bigger problem. He made several smooth motions in a fighting stance. He then tried to raise one foot from the ground.

That wasn't happening.

All of his grace, the little that remained, had left him.

That cheap liquor he had bought had proven to be much more costly than advertised. He combined his slurs and shivers, bracing himself against the wall. When he concentrated on his stomach however, he would feel almost hot. He became overconfident in the verity of this, and considered removing his shirt, hooting like a lunatic.

Car doors shutting, unintelligible talk.

He sneaked over to one of the walls. His stealth was so meticulous that he arrived in time to see the doors shut on him once again. He could see light from the lobby window, spreading onto the dead grass. His thoughts then concentrated on the possibility of knocking on the window. He could apologize to the night auditor. He knew two of them, if it were these two, he wouldn't even have to apologize.

He danced a cold dance.

He decided that he should go over to the window to see if one of the auditors was at the desk.

No one there.

Probably sleeping.

He cursed them for leaving their post. This was the emergency situation that they had been trained for. One of the tenants in a deadly crisis, freezing outside the window. He banged on the glass, then retreated a few steps. That would wake them up.

What was that noise?

A pigeon crashed into the window right there, then flew off. Lucky too, he had seen the whole thing while he was locked outside.

The night auditor's head popped up from behind the desk, one he did not know. He summoned the courage to draw himself into a visible area. The man stretched then walked toward the door.

He looked upset.

The night auditor opened the door. He said thank you. He then asked why the hotel needed to pay someone to sleep in the lobby at night.

* * * * * * * *

In the morning he searched his room for entertainment of some kind. There was a matchbook on the toilet. He used a match to light a match until the whole book had burned up. The smell was pleasant on the nose.

Alright, so now he had gotten rid of those pesky matches. Now what?

He did not really have to use the toilet, but tried to for a while. He was able to urinate a little bit, but that was all. He washed his hands in the sink, using a new bar of soap.

He cleaned off the counter, placing everything into his toiletry kit. He decided against wiping it off with a damp cloth, in favor of picking up some things in the main room. He took several cups, stacking them one on top of the other. He collected his jackets in a pile on the chair. Under the desk, he found the record player.

He had forgotten to return that, hadn't he?

He sucked on his teeth, then knelt to it. He pulled it out onto the carpet, to the limit of the power cord. He did not remember how to make it spin around, but that was easy enough to figure out. He turned it on, but found that it would not spin unless he tricked it into thinking that there was a record on the pin by depressing a small button.

He looked around the room for a roll of tape that he didn't have.

He remembered that the soap he had just opened had tape on it, so he went back to the rest room. The glue on the tape was not very adhesive. He thought that it would not work, that he might just make a note to buy some the next time he was out. Tape was a very practical item to have around the room.

Very carefully, no room for mistakes.

The button was extremely weak, the used stuff was enough to hold it down. The record player began to spin. Marvelous. He considered what to do with his invention, but the only use he had for it was to rotate several slips of paper he found in the immediate vicinity.

The cups weighed too much, the machine stopped. So he stuck with the slips for the time being. He stood up, looked down.

It was awfully expensive for a paper-rotating device. At least he was using up the hotel's electricity. He felt like he was getting them back in some way for things.

He resumed cleaning by stacking the cups once again, placing them on the desk.

A conversation slipped beneath the door. It was barely audible, and the female's enunciation was poor. Still he could make out that they were speaking casually. He thought that they referenced a local sight, one that he himself had found.

He had several things to add to what they were saying, if they were tourists. They should know that the bandit's grave was actually only speculated to be the right one. The rest he hadn't really bothered to see yet.

* * * * * * * *

He thought many awful things about his life from his bed. He could see birds outside the window. He wrapped the sheets around himself, though he was fully dressed. He made soft noises on his lips, which helped somehow. It had been so long since he had been right with himself. He felt he could feel deeper into the texture of the linens, they went from smooth to being a prickly landscape. He thought that he was now experiencing their true nature somehow. He had seen beneath the sheets, so to speak, to a microscopic thing. He placed his hand through the buttons of his shirt to rub his stomach. His hands were much colder than his skin. He did not think a whole lot of things about this. He stopped breathing through his mouth to try to unclog his nostrils. The air filled him up, but, in the end, he had to exhale.

He knew that that pharmacy had once carried some sleeping aids, maybe they still had them. Maybe those would work.

But work to what purpose? He would probably wake up just the same, more pills, then and again until he could not sleep any more ever again for his entire life. He eased himself by forming his lips into a circle, as though he were doing something dangerous. He felt that he could beat these sensations, if he moved correctly.

If he made no mistakes, no slips, how could he fail to beat this strain?

His consciousness began to disinterest him, replaced instead by disgust that the windows could not be opened all the way. Probably because they were trying to keep him from falling out the window. They were so mistaken. He was going to suffocate in here. Maybe, if he could just reach his hand out the window and fan in little bits of air, he could fill the room by bit with things he hadn't already breathed. They would probably escape under the door into the hallway, and everyone else would get the fruit of his labor. All that hard work for nothing.

He stared over at the lines on the wallpaper.

He could not make them into anything though. They could not be made into a shape that would help him out of his current scrape.

He began to suspect that the phone was off the hook. It was not though. Perhaps he had turned off the ringer. He lifted his head, hopeful. There was no switch on this side though, he could not remember seeing one ever at all. But there was a chance that he had been asleep, missing the call. They might have left a message down in the lobby for him.

He could go check.

This could be done just as easily from the room. But for some reason, he decided that his chances were much better that it had happened if he walked down to the lobby in person.

If he waited a few minutes, the percents would go up even more, so he just needed to wait until the last possible moment, when he could take no more.

* * * * * * * *

Because he did not want the call to show up on his hotel record, he decided to make use of the phone booth across from the vending room. He checked the folding door, judging that it would probably muffle his voice enough. He checked the rates written on a card beneath the phone. He had brought enough change to use the phone for forty minutes, if the call was local, as he imagined.

He inserted several coins, then pulled the flyer from his pocket. He dialed.

He waited for it to connect.

No one was picking up. The paper did not say the business hours, but he had planned that early afternoon would be the perfect time to call.

Hello?

The voice was gruff, he suspected that he had dialed the wrong number. He asked about hiring an interpreter.

Wrong number.

He became a little frightened that he would not have sufficient change to call again. He hoped that the number on the flyer had not been printed incorrectly. It began to ring again.

He prepared himself to deal with that man once again.

A woman picked up the phone, saying the name of the business quickly. He said slowly that he was interested in hiring a language translator. The woman responded in his language, though she was poor at it.

For what dates would he like?

He said that he was not sure yet, but it might be for several occasions. She checked the two languages. He said yes. She asked what the occasion would be for. He did not understand this, could she clarify? She listed two options, one being for a public address, the other being an interview or meeting. He chose the second one. She began looking through something.

He said that he would prefer a woman.

He thought that she would be fine, if she was one of the interpreters. She sounded young at least. He hoped that she would not ask why he preferred a woman, figuring that she would already know the answer to that. He rubbed his fingers on a notch in the wood shelf that the telephone sat on. He put his head against the glass to look down the hall.

She said that she would need specific dates.

In response, he said that he could just talk with the interpreter. He could figure out the exact times. She was somewhat confused about what to do. He said that he would leave her his phone number, that she could pass it on to the interpreter when she found her.

How very sly to say 'her.'

He asked if she had a pen. He then gave his name, his contact information. He asked when she expected the interpreter would get to it. She said that she could not give an exact time. He avoided the questions she asked about the project. The only thing he said was it would be private. The rest he would prefer to keep secret.

Three

He kept to himself for a little while. He became disinterested in eating the contents of his refrigerator before it went rotten. He felt a compulsion for something warm to eat, recalling that there was a food cart that roamed in the vicinity of the hotel. He had checked on the rising street, but it was not there today. The temperature was warm enough that he could check several locations before he gave up.

However, the cart was not at the intersection by the salon thing. He had never seen it there, but the area seemed like such an obvious place that he was convinced it would be there at the time. The street lead up into the park area, which, he decided would be his last hope.

He knew a view from the hilltop where he would be able to see much of the land.

With this in mind, he left the sidewalk for the grass.

His calves hurt, but he suspected that this was not due to

regular exercise.

Excuse me.

The voice came from below him. He disregarded it at first. Though there was no repetition, he turned back.

A small man.

He waited for some time to have the business explained to him. The fellow began jogging up the hill towards him, dropping his glasses. As the intruded upon party, he did not need to move. But, feeling beneficent, he then took several steps closer. The man spoke when he was still some distance away. He concentrated on the fact that the man was bald, attempting to figure out what animal he reminded him of.

Had he seen something go by?

This was an unanswerable question. Had he seen a little girl go by here? He had not really been paying such close attention. He asked how old.

Eight?

No, he didn't think so.

The man then went into a lengthy description of what she was wearing. Then explained that he was her uncle, that had last seen her thirteen minutes ago with odd confidence in these details.

No, he hadn't.

The man seemed genuinely out of ideas, out of breath. He looked off.

Thank you.

The man started running down the hill.

Wait.

He wanted to give a piece of advice to this gentleman.

There was a police department up one of these streets.

The man thanked him again.

Following this, he did not feel appropriate immediately resuming his search for the food cart. On the other hand, he did not feel that he had to drop it entirely in order to go look around for the girl wearing such and such that he did not remember.

He ended up standing on the hill, looking around for a minute or two.

He wished he had been standing next to someone throughout the scene so that he could say something along the lines of that being a tragedy. He looked into the brush, to see if he could see the dim shape of a girl.

Not there.

There was really nothing to do but move up the hill, where he could see further.

* * * * * * * *

The first few bottles that he selected he had no intention of buying really. It was not that they were too expensive, or that he had a particular vineyard that he would prefer, or year, or country, or picture. He had, he figured, as much experience in these things as an aficionado, considering that a man can only drink so much, no matter how educated he was in the subject. Despite this, his throat felt more comfortable in the clearance aisle. He had been beaten down, he felt, into feeling this comfort. Despite this, it remained genuine.

One of the labels was coming unglued.

There we go.

He decided to get a few bottles, in order to prolong his next visit. The quaint motif of the store rattled him slightly. He suspected that the clerks exchanged several words about him, his purchases, every time he stopped by. Though perhaps the purchase of many bottles at once would amplify their derision, it was better to get it all done at once, than to have his feelings picked at, bit by bit.

He was ready to go.

But he noticed a group of young affluent types.

They were petting one another, pointing, selecting wines. One had, how adorable, indicated a certain laughable brand. He insisted that this was the one for them, that night. The boy then pantomimed hiding it in his coat.

He himself had three bottles of this kind beneath his arm.

He picked through several corkscrews.

Despite the cold, the girl wore a short dress. It would be legal, in principal, for him to sleep with her. He then decided that the men would not know how to do that.

One of the clerks had taken it upon himself to ask if that would be all, indicating the bottles he had brought to the register. He looked over at the group, then back to the clerk. He thought the clerk had probably done this to protect the young clientele.

He could save face if he made some vicious, undeniable,

slander. But there weren't any.

Oh no.

He remembered that all the money he had brought with him was crumpled up in his pockets.

He straightened the bills on the counter, and slid them over. He stared at a pattern in his line of vision, while the clerk counted out the change, dropped the change into the paper bag, with the receipt, instead of handing it to him like a human being.

He left unhappier than when he had come.

His emotions went about.

He looked over at a bakery across the street. Then he hoped that he would meet a friend by chance.

While he was walking home, he thought of throwing out the bottles entirely, but that would do nothing for no one. Instead he kept his eyes ahead of him. The historic graveyard remained between two streets. He hoped that it would distract him.

He thought what a rein they'd had on him just now; making him feel like this, when he did not care one way or the other.

* * * * * * * *

The first thing he would do when he got back was probably eat, or take a shower. He needed to do both, as he had done neither maybe for some time. He also felt a bit of tension in his digestive system. It was mostly coffee, so it would be unpleasant. This, and the fact that he wanted to take a shower, he decided it would be best to use one of the toilets in the lobby before going upstairs. He rattled through his pockets, then removed his jacket, which was longer in the back.

He found his key card.

He stopped at the door for a short period of time, then looked over.

In the lobby, a hired worker was replacing pieces of the ceiling that had received water damage. An idiot must have stopped up the toilet on the second floor.

Before laughing, he mentally confirmed that this area did not coincide with his own bathroom.

Someone made a mistake, haha.

If he intends to use the lobby rest room, his first trial will be—ask the befabled clerk for the rusty key. They had recently installed a lock on it. The guy behind the desk was not someone he had spoken to before. Still, it was fairly easy for him to go request the bathroom key.

The new employee was a little disturbed by the question, the lobby toilet was ordinarily used by the staff. He assured him that it was a common practice, he was a 'preferred' resident on the second floor. The fellow did not move until he indicated the key on the back counter. The key changed hands, he promised to be quick about it.

Success.

Now if only he could abuse this power. He wished that he had conscious control over his bowels. If so he would have taken a particularly nasty one, as a method of revenge for that guy being so suspicious. That would certainly do it. He imagined the clerk's face puckering up the next time he went to urinate.

But, as far as that was concerned, he would have to wait and see. He set off toward the bathroom, twirling the key by its wooden thing, holding his coat over his arm.

Bye.

For some reason, he realized that this venomous word had been addressed to him. He turned to see Sabrina passing by the hallway, towing her luggage behind her. She did not stop, kept her head down quite intently. She passed from his line of sight soon after he saw her. But still, he could hear her voice as she requested the bill for her room, it had lost most of the fury from a moment ago.

He was not sure what exactly he wanted to do then. Thoughts of the bathroom seemed minor. He quickly thought up a little speech in his mind to say to her. It made solid points, very effective. It would only get better as he revised it that evening.

* * * * * * * *

What brought him out of the room, at that time, was restlessness, as well as a desire to purchase a drink of some sort. He had brought no money with him. He instead headed up to the third floor for no apparent reason.

He considered using the stairs while he waited for the elevator. The doors took awhile to open, they were breaking down, probably.

Three.

One floor, that's right, busy man.

He didn't really care about that though. It was a short ride up. The doors did not seem as slow from the inside. He stuck his hand in his pants to scratch his waistline.

Nails of smoke grazed his eyes, agh, he convulsed.

Someone was in the elevator waiting area.

He removed his hand, to be polite. The guy was not watching him though. Instead he was reading some papers, sitting on the ground. He had brought the complimentary plate into the hall, using it as an ashtray.

He did not really feel like being here anymore now, but he couldn't just jump back into the elevator. He could walk over to the stairs. The guy had definitely seen him, but was paying no attention.

Until he walked past, that is. Then the guy held up one of the papers, keeping his head down at first.

Read that.

He took the paper, slavish. When he saw that it was not written in his language, he asked what it was. The lines were very short, handwritten.

A play, a new play that he was working on.

He read a line or two of it, but it was written in a dialect or something. He called it very nice though. He asked if the guy was a writer. Yes. The guy stood up, took the paper, then began reading it to him. It was starting in the middle somewhere. The guy tried to make his voice sound like a politician. Then he paused to explain that the two characters had just gotten fired from their job.

There were a couple curse words, which he understood.

The writer guy started to trail off, reading it to himself, smiling. He said that that was interesting, he had never met a play writer. The writer guy introduced himself as his whole first and last name.

Then the writer guy said he could call him Tristan.

He, on the other hand, just said his name like a normal person.

The guy picked up on his accent quickly, asked where he was from. Once all these questions were resolved, the writer guy asked him to say a few things.

He couldn't think of anything to say.

He felt demeaned a bit. He expanded on some things they

had already said to one another. He said that they should just talk, he would prefer that to this.

They began to just talk for a few minutes or so. They talked about the town at first, then about traffic, what the writer guy was doing. He talked about some specific places, he said a few things about what he liked to do.

* * * * * * * *

When the phone rang, he was not sure what to do. It was probably a friend. It was probably the clerk from downstairs. Though he was currently engrossed with sitting at the desk, he decided to answer it.

It took some time to find the receiver, but whoever it was did not hang up.

Underneath the towel, there it is.

Hello?

He had not meant to say this in a rude way, but he had. The caller was caught off guard, then asked if he was available. A woman. As she said his name, he went through women's voices in his head.

Who is this?

It was Hannah calling from the so and such, calling with regards to setting up an appointment. He fumbled with a curt response. His voice became much warmer.

She said they could speak in his language, if he would prefer. She had a western accent when she said this. She sounded quite natural, real sophisticated lady.

She repeated the bit about the translator. He remembered clearly that he had asked for a woman.

He asked for dates that she would be available.

She responded by asking him about the project; he'd been a little obscure about it in his message.

He got into the bed, gradually wrapping himself in the sheets. He explained that it would be a smaller thing, a series of interviews.

Yes he had said that.

The conversation had divided. He could not figure out what it was she wanted from him. A series of interviews, it seemed simple enough.

Who?

He felt inadequately prepared for this line of questioning. He said it was going to be with a few people. Some different people on different occasions. He had been waiting for her to get back to him to schedule it all.

That did not satisfy her.

He reached out with his imagination, looking for a way to explain himself. He said that one of the people was a local play writer. She corrected him, which was annoying and rude. He was going to interview the playwright about what he was working on, his work with dialects.

A series of interviews with artists.

Pretty much.

That was what she wanted to know.

He got a little bold, he explained that he was writing it for a magazine that she wouldn't know. They were going to have all the interviews locally. He, his magazine, would pay for the transportation. She should wear a dress.

He had to back up there, and say a professional looking bit, not a casual one.

He asked if she had microphone equipment. The question disarmed her. She said that normally the journalist provided the equipment. Interesting. He had meant, though, for her own purposes. He himself preferred to take notes by hand as he was a member of the old school.

Yes, well.

He has to go now.

He did manage to set up a meeting time to show her the interviewing room. The whenever following the whatnot.

He hung up. He calmed down over the next few minutes, went over what he'd said and wrote it down for memory.

Four

The sunlight had taken up the other side of the street from his. He cupped his hands to his mouth, warmed them, then placed them back into his unzipped coat. The plastic bag on his elbow slapped his thigh with every step. He had been walking. He had been walking so long that skin between his legs had become irritated. He looked like a cripple, he was sure of it.

He had procured the microphone equipment.

Success.

And he no longer had a record player sitting around, taking up space.

It was heavy enough that he should have taken a taxi. It was too late now. He did not know who to call, what the number was, where a phone was, where he was, exactly. He also felt that this experience would be good for him. It was something he would be able to brag about to someone. I once walked so and so far in winter, no taxis or complaints.

A pair of old men stood outside, on the stoop of what looked to be a medical building. The bearded one began eyeing him, for no reason, from some distance. Because he was conscious of it, he assumed at first that this was due to his limp of sorts.

The glance continued as he approached.

The other geezer noticed that his friend was no longer enchanted with their conversation, followed the glance back, over the banister, to him. This one however, did not see what the fuss was about, smiled, then turned back.

He was close enough now that he did not have to look at them. He began putting on a face that seemed as though he was in deep spiritual reflection. He said a few things to himself aloud, things of no real consequence.

He passed.

He heard a nasty name.

The old man spit to the side, then muttered.

He withdrew one of his hands from his pocket, returning the gesture by clasping his testicles through his pants. This was all he needed to say, it seemed. He turned his head back to the sidewalk.

He heard some arguing. A door open, a door slam. That sort of thing.

He had not resented the insult at first. He began to think that he should have walked up, then cracked the guy in the head with the bag. If he got his leverage right, he could bring it over the top of his head, and down. That would do it, no doubt about that.

It would have also broken the microphone.

He complained to himself about this place, full of spite, etcetera, stupidity. They did not understand a list of things. So backward in their thoughts that they do this, that, without wind, fire, blah, or rain. He began to think of home, which he did not always think of. Now he wanted to go straight back. He would leave that same afternoon.

He wanted to go home, but the irritation of his skin from walking was making it hard enough to get back to his room.

* * * * * * * *

Angelo was in a jovial mood, his oily lips were stretched into a tight smile. Not today, not today. He himself felt quite the opposite. He didn't feel up for a little hassle. He tried to communicate this somehow.

Angelo, however, called him over to the desk.

Not today. He walked by.

His mail.

Angelo held out a roll of envelopes, held by a rubber band. He had not picked up his mail for some time, largely because he assumed that it did not contain anything worthwhile. He looked at the roll.

A yellow envelope.

He drew up to the clerk, thanking him. He took off the rubber band, which shot away somewhere into the lobby. He leafed through the mail. He looked at the cover of a magazine for a moment too long.

It was a teenaged girl magazine.

'gorgeous actors' or something.

Angelo laughed, then laughed. It really wasn't that funny though, not even embarrassing. The magazine was not his, it wasn't addressed to him at all. Angelo tried to say something, but every word wheezed back into a hacked giggle. He threw the magazine over the counter. The complex aerodynamic of it caused it to miss Angelo, who had, by this time, regained enough composure to say that he had dropped his magazine.

The yellow envelope had something inside.

Some guy, what a something, sarcasm, if only you could take him to the dance.

It had no return address.

He could not open it here. He put the rest of the mail on the counter. Angelo had been waiting all day for that, it was sent here by mistake. He cut the conversation short by asking him to put the remaining mail back in his box.

Then he left.

Angelo called after him.

Where was his sense of humor?

His mind was clouded, unable to respond cleverly. His brains hurt, he had this envelope, he did not really need to be polite at this point in his life. He could not wait for the elevator doors to open. He decided to take the stairs.

The envelope was constructed well, it would not open. He found a small string hanging loose from one end. He wrapped it around his finger, pulling so tightly that it hurt.

There was another envelope inside, with a note paper-clipped to it.

So and such. A violation of the instruction. In an idiotic risk.

Never contact them again.

He felt the little envelope, full of little pills. He was happy, but a confused happiness. There were definitely twice as many in there as last time. Never again though seemed a bit harsh. He could probably just do it right next time, it would not matter so much. He was a valuable client; they had even short-changed him a little.

Haha he took two steps at a time.

He folded the envelope over his index finger, look how thick it is, twice as thick as before. How had he lived so long? He could definitely have one with a glass of water and ice right away.

* * * * * * * *

The racks and shelves were full of clothing to the tall ceiling. This was making it much harder to find what he wanted. He did not even want it really, but needed a suit coat, shirt, pants, a belt or something. He felt he did not really have a sense of style that he wanted them in. Just something a bit better than showing up in his underpants.

The suits were sized in a complex system of numbers and adjectives.

Why can't they just say normal size?

He found himself looking at a glass case of accessories, which would fit anyone.

Wallets, money clips, watches, knives, metallic boxes.

He needed a wallet, in case he ever wanted to pay for something.

The salesman made the approach seem casual, not looking, holding his hands behind his back. He must work on commission. He spoke before the salesman got a chance to seem to notice him.

He wanted to take a look at that wallet, he tapped the glass.

The salesman had brought the keys with him. He unlocked

the case.

The knife as well.

Which one?

With the plaque.

The salesman offered that they also offered a complimentary engraving of three letters, if he would like to get his initials done.

He wanted the wallet as well, he reminded.

He tried, once this was done, to walk away with the two items. The salesman, however, insisted on holding them. Would that be all? He said that he still needed to get a suit. Not something expensive or high fashioned. He rolled some saliva onto his sore throat. The salesman tried to guess his size, which he said was about right.

Onward.

They walked through some place.

He did not want anything feminine or anything.

What he wanted to get at was that he did not want to look like the salesman.

Unseen to the salesman, he picked up a gray necktie that he liked while walking past the display. The salesman stopped in front of a rack of brown suits, leafed through them, then noticed the tie.

Gray would not really work with this particular suit. He assured the salesman that this was the one he liked, to the response that it would be better to select a tie to go with the suit he liked than backward. The salesman wanted to snatch the tie out of his hand. He looked down.

This tie was really classy, he liked it.

He assured the salesman that this would work with anything, which was the end of the matter. The salesman gave up on him, which was okay. He deferred to the salesman on the suit, which looked fine. He would take it, on the condition that they had it in his approximate size.

The suit pants had a little pocket that the knife would fit into. He could put the wallet in the jacket too. Now he was almost done, how easy.

He wanted a black shirt.

To go with the tie, he explained.

* * * * * * * *

He was a little drunk, his running nose made it worse. In a fit of responsibility, he had brought the masking tape with him up to his room on the fifth floor, which he had thought to do yesterday. There was a bit of wallpaper coming loose. He hadn't considered asking the hotel staff to deal with this problem for his own reasons. The key was deep in his pants, he felt around for the edge of it, taking the opportunity to itch himself.

He knew that it would be cold, but he had not prepared for this. Last night he had left the window open on purpose, hoping that the circulation would clear the room of a dank smell. He walked around the room, thinking of what he would use to reach the top of the wall.

He could see his own breath, even though he was inside.

He remembered that the heat had been turned off in his apartment once, when he'd had that apartment with his roommate oh so long ago.

He shook the shelving unit, it was steady enough that he probably wouldn't die. He could climb to the top, then sit, then use the masking tape.

It was worth a shot.

He gradually moved the unit over to the corner of the room by walking it on its edges. He left enough space between the wall for his legs. He put the roll of tape in his mouth. He climbed up one of the shelves, it held pretty well.

After two shelves, he found that he would have to snake himself into the space on top of the thing, which would be impossible for an ordinary man.

The shelf began to rock.

He looked over, out the window to the parking lot.

Rats, death.

A stupid idea. Thought up by an idiot.

Due to his animalesque agility, He was able to shoot himself between the ceiling and the shelf. He pushed out his stomach to squeeze the shelf, keep it from falling.

Good, good.

Now all he had to do was apply said tape.

His mouth was full of saliva by this point, which, when he lowered his head, dribbled onto the tape, then onto the floor.

He could not imagine one of the hotel staff doing this for him.

He applied the masking tape successfully. Then again, and again, just to be sure. He saw in his vision that the paper had begun to peel in other places in the room.

He blasphemed, then decided that this would be enough, as it was the most noticeable spot.

Instead of dying, he decided it would be best to just slide off the back of the shelf and fall. He slithered himself back. It was working. Then he fell back.

My jaw!

Nose.

Whump.

He did not pick himself up immediately after that. He realized that his lip was swollen, but did not feel anything about this. It had been a conscious decision, of sorts.

He dipped his finger in his mouth.

He drew his hand back and looked at it a bit, proud to see that he was bleeding.

* * * * * * * *

That morning the bed and shelf remained in the room, though he had given Angelo some money to get rid of them for a while. He had thought it best to call her and say that they should meet in the lobby of his hotel. They could probably go on a walk. He could show her all the lovely things he knew, local plants or such.

He found the entire lobby area was deserted, which was fantastic. He didn't want them ruining his little scheme.

Telling people that he was not a journalist or so on, saying that he drank wine every night.

He was so happy that there was no one there to ask him why he was wearing this suit, why he had shaved, why he had a scheduling book with him when he was clearly not in high demand.

He made his best effort to remember her name, but it never lead to anything. He had done a couple of exercises that morning, felt fit enough for it all. It was rude for her to not show on time. She had better apologize to him, or he would definitely fire her. There was nothing to read in the lobby. What was he doing, what was he going to pretend to be doing? He decided to open his schedule. Wrote a few things, then drew a poor picture of the mustached stranger in the September part. It was okay though, he could picture what he had intended it to look like.

The car that pulled up into the parking lot was a real piece of junk.

The woman was younger than him, but that is not to say that he found her terribly attractive. She wasn't really dressed up or anything, he thought he had told her to do so.

He hoped that this was her, but also hoped that it was not.

It was definitely though. She was twenty minutes late.

He closed the book, watched her as she walked up to the door. She would need a card.

She cupped her hands, looking inside. He waited until she saw him to get up.

When he opened the door, she slid inside, shaking precipitation from her scarf.

He hadn't noticed it was raining.

She said that she was supposed to meet someone here. She did not think it was him.

The translator?

She took his hand, apologizing for being late. She'd gotten lost or something. Obviously she hadn't spent the time correcting her makeup, doing her hair.

Hannah.

He said that the room was not yet prepared, but that this would be the location of the interviews. He wanted to go over some of the finer points of the scheduling, so that he could set dates.

The only condition she made was that she would be leaving for a weekend to see her sister, two weeks from now. This gave him some leverage, he pretended that he had set that Saturday as one of the cursory dates. He could figure it out though.

Well then.

Does she want to see the room anyway?

(the interview process)

One

Brushing his teeth was extremely difficult due to the rotten feeling in his shoulders. Even getting the paste onto his toothbrush would have looked, if anyone were watching him, needlessly courageous.

This disease, whatever it was, had reduced the amount of saliva in his mouth at any given time. Due to this, he became extremely aware of the texture of the paste, of the brush, the color of his poor man's teeth, which he could not see at all beneath the white paste, but were definitely not that color.

He had never been exactly sure how long he was supposed to scrub. Left to his nature he would do it for just a little while, sometimes though he went on for a long time, in the impression that that was what other people do.

He spit it out. Then spit out some bile type stuff.

What a masterpiece of work he was.

He took out the allergy medication that he'd gotten for free in the lobby. He did not think he had allergies. But these would probably cure his runny nose, itching, sneezing, restlessness anyway.

They might even knock him out for a few hours, that wouldn't be too bad at all. Some toothpaste was still in his mouth, the taste of which was never intended for his stomach.

In the area immediately around his bed, his master bedroom bit, he flung off the towel to facilitate the drying process. He didn't want to sit on the comforter though, to do so seemed dirty.

He should go stand in front of the window.

With a little rental sign hung on it.

Hey up here, yes I, up here. That was the funniest thing he could think to say. He could imagine though that the men would not blame their women for leaving them on the sidewalk for a few minutes.

He would give them a thumbs-up afterwards.

She'll be down in a minute, thank you for shopping, a lovely day, don't hesitate in the future.

When was he going to trim his hair almost bald? He had decided to do that yesterday. The toenail scissors in his bag were not going to cut it. They were too short, and he had used them to trim his nostrils, without following a proper sterilization procedure. He was not going to ask one of the staff to do it, and he hadn't seen a barber poll in this

this stupidsburg.

Poetry, no one has ever quite put it that way.

When he finally moved, he felt that his testicles had dried to his legs. He freed them, then shook them around for awhile to make sure this would never happen again. What happened to him next was that he could hear the maid unlocking the door.

He cleared his throat to speak.

Wait.

What if he let them walk in on him like this?

I'm nudeish.

No big thing of it.

we're all people.

His heart shuddered. Then he waited for what seemed like a long time before he saw her head peak in through the doorway.

* * * * * * * *

The graveyard was such a pathetic scene, but he wanted to see if anyone famous was buried there. He didn't think so, because the other place had made such a to do about it.

He saw that one of the names was flaking off, this made sense because whoever it was had died many years ago.

Two kids were putting on faces by having a conversation sitting on the ground smoking cigarettes. Look at them, sitting on the ground, how continental. Kids are always like that. When he was a kid he had done a few nasty little things. He used to go around with his father's army coat on, hadn't he? Hadn't he probably done this just to shell out himself to the public? He did not even remember the reason. Evidently it was done in a different way here, sitting on graves and all.

Nowadays people could tell what he was a lunatic without

his trying at all.

He thought he knew the dead woman's name from somewhere, but he did not pursue the memory for very long. He figured that he was mistaken.

What occurred to him next was that the sandwich shop across the street was so close to a graveyard.

He should go buy something.

He decided to walk up the street to the pharmacy and buy some actual medicine so that he would not spew junk all over the translator girl, whenever that happened.

He took off, but first, he went over and told the kids that they should stand up. They did not respond immediately.

They said that they didn't want to. They had their freedom. Despite this bold verbal demeanor, the ratty looking one was definitely spooked, he could see it on his face.

Since he was older than them, they eventually relented. He told them to get out of there, which they put up a ceremonial protest to as they did. They walked away, huffing about him without any accuracy. Talking about stupid misimpressions of him.

He felt so good with himself about this. How easy it had been to fold them up like that. Even though he did not feel any passion for it. The tall one kicked the gate as they walked out onto the sidewalk.

Bravo, young man.

He followed them for a little while until they began to walk faster and ducked into one of the side-streets. He felt that they might have just learned a thing or two that would help them out once they had gone through puberty.

He figured that people must have done that to him all the time when he was young, with the same impenetrable nonchalance. He did not remember a single incident of it happening, but he never remembers anything.

He knew that he would go and grab the medication from the pharmacy, he would give a smile to the girl there. She could lock the door, and lay down behind the counter where no one could see.

She was the one he really wanted anyway.

* * * * * * * *

The weight of paper in his arm was quite satisfying. He knew that he would be able to arrange something with one of the two literary magazines, both of which had printed contact numbers on the inside of the front cover. He had written both numbers on the length of skin between his thumb and index finger, but had purchased the magazines anyway as reference things.

He set them both down on the bookshelf. Already there were three glasses that he had gotten from the closet, as well as a bar of deodorant, a small amount of loose change, a knife, a package of supposed aphrodisiacs, various slips of paper, and two nails; all of which had accumulated unintentionally, and he would have to remove before the interviews took place.

The couch from the lounge area was situated in the center of the room. He sat on it, then moved the phone into a position that he could make the calls while reclining.

He dialed the first four numbers, but then stopped for a meditative reason.

Alright.

He dialed the number again, waited for the connection to go through. He was calling in regards to an interview.

He hung up.

He had just thought of a good tactic. He could say that he had already set up the interview with two or three of the authors. He had lost their contact information at an airport or something. He just needed the contact information for professional reasons.

He dialed the number once again, finding that he remembered it off hand. This time he got all the way to the receptionist, then requested for the receptionist to connect him to an editor. He needed to speak to someone in charge. He shifted into a position that would allow him to look through the open window.

He could see the neighboring roof.

The access door to his roof was locked, but it'd be nice.

He put the phone down onto the couch, then jogged over to the bookshelf to grab the magazines. He checked to see which one he had just called, then looked over the contributing authors. He selected the second, third, and fourth authors from the list. He picked up the receiver once again.

Is someone there?

Sorry, I placed you on hold.

He explained the situation as best he could, omitting the bit about the airport. The man on the other end of the line did not understand immediately. He redrafted his statement twice using different terms. The man then understood, but remained confused as to why he had called the magazine.

He pinched a growth in his inner armpit with his free hand.

He wanted to call the authors.

Did he have the phone numbers?

The man explained that, though he did have the phone numbers, for legal reasons, he could not divulge them at that time. He then countered this by saying that he was in a lot of trouble. What could he do? The man thought about it, demonstrating this by sighing a few times, blowing some air into the phone.

* * * * * * * *

He had gone to Tristan's room that morning to roll off a list of subjects that he would probably talk about during the interview. He had written most of them down afterwards on some typing paper.

What are you working on? Who are you? You work in the theater? How much money do you get paid? Is it true, the rumors about the theater?

The list went on like that for a while. He had told Tristan that he should probably wear a tie, because the interpreter he had hired was a prim girl. Tristan had been very excited about the whole thing.

He had put on his suit and left at roughly four o'clock to meet Tristan and the interpreter in the lobby's waiting room. He went a little early to ask Angelo to leave for a while, or, barring that, not to bother the three of them. Angelo was offended by the suggestion, but he explained it once more as a matter of business professionalism.

Angelo had propped himself up on the counter afterwards while he waited, then got around to asking if he could be interviewed too.

He did not dignify the question with a response.

Tristan was the second person to arrive in the lobby area, ten minutes early. Angelo said hello, and they began talking for a little while.

He chewed his cheek and shook his head.

Tristan came over after a while then sat on the chair next to him. He welcomed him, then began staring out into the parking lot, giving short answers to Tristan's questions.

She was not even late yet, but the entire operation seemed about to fall apart.

He began feeling the wallet inside his suit jacket.

He mimed hanging himself with his necktie.

Tristan laughed politely.

Her car pulled up exactly on time, which meant that she was a minute late when she walked into the lobby. Tristan asked if this was the lady.

He said yes and tried to make eye contact with Hannah as she walked into the lobby, but she immediately focused in on Tristan. She offered her hand, making an introduction of herself without letting him do it. Tristan did the same thing too.

He did not feel like joining in.

He suggested that they go to the elevator, leading the way. Hannah caught up with him, apologizing in his own language for the traffic that she had no control over. He said it was no big deal.

In the elevator, he noted that she'd done herself up a bit.

He took the key out of his pocket. At first he felt it was much colder than his palm, then it became warmer, he could feel the ridges in the joints of his fingers. He looked over at Tristan who was looking at the door, then at Hannah who was petting her wrist, then down at himself where he could feel how thin the cloth of his suit was, that it hung on him, opaque but paper thin.

Two

He had been cutting off the long sleeves of a shirt when the spider had first appeared. He had not immediately reacted to it, letting it sit on his toilet seat. The chances of it being poisonous were not real. It crept onto the underside of the toilet seat.

He should kill it.

He considered using the scissors in his hand, but declined to.

The complimentary shampoo and conditioner would do the job. Anything would do it, really, even his hand.

He took the bottle over to the toilet seat, lifting it, then finding that the spider had eluded him.

He did not give up there.

The hunt begins.

The spider had moved much further than he expected.

Where had it gotten to? It had sensed that its tiny life was in danger then, fled. He bent down on his legs then made a spider call, a clicking sound.

Peripheral motion drew him to look over there.

The spider was crawling toward the shower without any particular urgency.

He needed to get very close to it to accurately crush it with the bottle. He walked while bent over.

He hesitated, then slowly brought the bottle down onto the spider. He felt that he could hear the sound of its bones breaking.

He ground the bottle a bit, to kill it quicker, for mercy reasons.

The body of the spider was stuck to the underside of the bottle, while a fluid had spread out against the floor. He wondered for a moment if the body was now completely dry.

He withdrew the stopper from the sink, letting the water from the faucet pull the spider down the drain. He found a little lyric in his mind that his father used to sing out loud to him.

Something the naïve fly on the garden hose.

He used the bar of soap to sanitize the underside of the bottle. When he put it back into its place he found that the slickness on the bottom allowed him to slide the bottle on the counter top.

He made it execute a few daring maneuvers from ice-skating.

The shirt had fallen off the counter, letting him see how far he had gotten in cutting it. He took the scissors up then got the shirt off the ground. He used one end of the scissors to slice open the remainder of the shirt, then tucked the extra cloth into his pocket as he walked back to the bedroom.

He wanted to wrap the sleeve in masking tape, but he could not really think of what this would produce. A taped up cloth of some kind, a disgrace.

Instead of the tape, he found that he had left some clothing under the bed. He pulled out a sock then took this over to his laundry bag, placing it inside then drawing the cord to close it.

He considered making the sleeve into a pouch, in which to put loose change and resources. If only he had some thread, he could do it. He would need some string to open and close it.

* * * * * * * *

Angelo's cousin was taking her lunch break in the vending room. Or maybe she was just avoiding work for a while.

He followed her in there.

He wanted to get her a drink or something.

She said hello to him while she picked through her rain jacket for some change. He stepped between her and the machine, took a bill from his pocket. He asked what she wanted to drink. She said that it was fine she had change somewhere. He insisted. She said a name that he did not recognize, then pointed to one of the buttons.

She wanted the green one.

The machine clicked, then dropped the drink down into the basin. He let her pick it up herself.

His work was done, but he stuck around for a moment in the event that she wanted to thank him.

She did so.

He paused for a moment. It was time to go, he guessed.

She opened the can while he was turning around. She called his name out.

He always had trouble understanding what she said though.

He gleaned that she was asking about his article. Angelo had told her about it. He said that it was going well. She hadn't known that he was a writer.

Yes, he was, he said.

He did not really want to have the conversation. She was very shy with him, and spoke so softly, quickly. He complimented Angelo a few times for being a good person. She intuitively picked up that he wanted to leave, which he did not altogether want to do, but, once she said it, decided that it would be best.

Thank you, she held up the drink.

It was nothing though.

He pinned a smile up on one corner of his mouth as he walked down the hall. He could see a pale light coming through the window up ahead bright enough by contrast to the ceiling lights that he could not see through to the outside.

He could imagine that the time it would take to go out today and walk somewhere to get something to eat and bring it back would be so much that she would probably be done with her break by then anyway. He was hungry enough to eat a nice little thing that would not fill him up too much and he could get something more for her and maybe Angelo as well.

In the stairwell, he cracked his neck sideways.

Muh

He took giant steps up the stairs, four at a time. The process inhibited his travel time, as he had to brace himself against the rail in order to lift himself up.

He stopped, and began ascending the stairs like a regular human being. The stretching of his thighs a moment before had made them very frail and on in days. It felt like there was a single muscle fiber on the underside of his right leg that bent when he pushed up.

Is he getting old, or is this just a one time thing?

* * * * * * * *

Though the date was the same, he had never thought anyone celebrated the holiday. So many families had spread out blankets on the side of the hill for picnics.

Kids swarmed over the play-set, while their parents conversed holding beer bottles.

He saw that a few tables had been set up in the parking lot, that one may buy things. There was the scent and smoke of meat being cooked.

A portable cooking unit to make sandwiches.

He followed the arrowed flyers down onto the asphalt. The sign was written large enough that he could see the prices from a good distance, when the people in line were not obscuring it. Another, much less professional looking, guy was selling wine and beer out of a cooler for way too much. He was cold, and focused on the big plate of meat.

It occurred to him that it was the dead of winter.

What a hardy people.

He watched the line from a small distance, preferring to wait until the line had cleared and there would be no one waiting behind him. This took a long time.

He looked over at a large woman who had ordered brown thinly sliced meat dispersed in oily noodles on a paper plate. It looked good enough that he would get the same thing.

He gave up, got in line.

A man with a beer got behind him, then another. The two

began conversing.

They were happily drunk.

A splash of something cold spilled onto his neck, then ran down the middle of his back.

He turned around. The man was not looking at him. He took the man's arm, and extended it away from him.

The guy became quite upset about it, immediately assuming that he intended to steal the bottle. He said that the guy had spilled beer on him.

He should watch himself.

The man became apologetic, then placed the bottle into his jacket. He said that it was fine, which surprised him considering that he felt prepared to fight if it came to that.

He was now the next customer.

He said that he wanted the thing with the noodle, which he did not know the name of. There was a language barrier, but the drunk stepped in to say that he meant the whatever it was called.

He thanked him while he waited for the old woman to scoop it onto the plate, keeping a curt voice. The drunk began talking again about the beer incident.

He waved it off, then took his plate. He looked out the park into the city, deciding that he would rather eat it while walking somewhere else than stay here.

He stuck the fork into the food, scooped it into his mouth, reached an area of the parking lot that was not crowded, tasted fine, didn't know what type of meat it was.

After another bite, he decided that he did not want it, but he would eat it until he found a trash can.

* * * * * * * *

He provided Hannah with the phone number from his schedule book. As there was only one phone, he explained that she could sit at the table and relay how Mrs. Alton responded to his questions, and he would write that down.

She looked at him for a while before she dialed the number.

What did she want? After all, he was paying her money. He adjusted his position on the couch, pointing the microphone towards her instead of him. He took a pen out of his pocket, pulled a page out of the stack of paper on the table.

Hannah began speaking, someone had answered

evidently.

He had called before to explain the process to the woman, the time that the call would take place and all that. He imagined her sitting by the phone in a study, waiting around. Hannah turned toward him in her seat, but he held up his finger, explained the situation to the microphone.

We're talking to some lady on the telephone.

He opened the magazine to the first page of the story, folding its cover under.

His first question was for Mrs. Alton to say the title of the story and what it was about. Hannah listened, then explained that the title was an idiom that meant things one fantasizes. What she had been trying to do was to convey the position of a woman's effort to assert her femininity by also recognizing certain biases that

He interrupted.

He apologized, because the lady sounded like an indignant sort.

What he had meant was; would she summarize the story?

Had he read it?

Currently, no.

Because he could not read it, he added.

The summary took a while. He could hear a faint stream coming from the receiver. He watched Hannah's skirt wave from the heating duct in front of her. He thought he could also see the shape of her underwear at the top of her leg, but didn't really think about this too long.

The story was about a married woman who accepts a wager to cheat on her husband from her friend. Though she loves him and her family (etc.), she does not feel that an arbitrary sexual encounter will affect her if she does not feel for the man involved. While her husband is away, she drives into another city and meets Fergus, a man from a different culture.

Fergus is a poor guy, another sort of person, disenfranchise.

He started nodding.

Hannah took a while to say that the affair continues, which is what he suspected would happen.

But though she feels genuine love for her husband, she feels obligation to her lover who has been isolated his whole life.

They're going to kill each other, he thought.

Or one would kill the other.

Someone needs to die, at least.

When Marcus finds out about etcetera, she tells him why she did it. Marcus calls up Fergus, lying that she had been paid to sleep with him, thus Fergus suicides.

The lie thing was what he thought had happened, so he was confused for a little bit, and he waited for a moment that he could interrupt the conversation.

Three

He took a constitutional walk one day.

It lead him into a nice neighborhood full of stores, restaurants, that was pretty much it.

He had left his hair, for purposes of his own style, in a polygonish shape that had occurred while his head tossed during sleep the previous night. Little did he know that he would end up here, probably smelling too, he couldn't tell. Maybe one of these people would remark on his intoxicating scent, where could they purchase a bottle of this musk. He could hold out his armpit, invite them to whiff what they could of the sweat soaked into the cloth of his shirt.

Haha.

He declined to visit a subterranean shopping court.

He also had no need of such a sharp looking sweater.

However, he realized that he did need to examine the table of reasonably priced sunglasses. Several girls between the ages of twelve and maybe, if he stretched, twenty. He traced his fingers over the tinted glass, deciding to try some on that were dark blue. He looked around for a mirror where he could see his reflection, tried mentally to correct the skewed image of his face in the lenses on the table.

Those look great.

The girl with the greenesque shirt had said this.

She came up a little past his waist.

Did she like them?

Not for herself, she explained, but they fit his personality. She said he looked like something, good, he imagined. He asked if he should buy them. She smiled saying that he definitely should.

He wondered if she was joking with him.

The girl called over her blonde haired friend that had far

too many freckles on her nose. They conferred for a moment, then the second girl looked over at him, then concurred. He should get those. They looked handsome, they made him look like someone they couldn't figure out. Then they began giggling for some reason or another, looking down at their own feet.

What on earth was taking place here?

Should he get them or not?

He told them that they were right. He was going to buy these glasses.

He fished through his pockets to find the correct moneys. Several loose bills were in his jacket, but, in and of themselves, they were not enough to make the purchase. He felt the set of keys inside his pants, then probed through to find any coins that would form the complete price.

He did not have enough money.

The vendor asked him how much money he had.

He held out the bills, the vendor taking them, unfolding them, counting them. The two girls cackled at him once again, which made him finally decide that the whole thing had been a joke.

Did he care?

The vendor nodded, then took the bills over to a leather purse, placing them inside. He turned then smiled at the girls. How did they like his new glasses? They restated how good they made him look.

He laughed making sure that his laugh was louder than the others.

* * * * * * * *

At around dark, he decided that it was late enough to go to sleep, once again. He took off his shirt, let it fall, then his pants. He slid onto the bed, then drew the sheets around himself. He set his head down into the pillow, sounds of the bed compressing under his weight, looked through the dark of the room to the dark outside, ready to sleep now, did not move, went into sleeping mode.

Go.

He closed his eyes.

He breathed in a dreamy way.

He became aware of a clicking sound coming from somewhere that he would never know. He was always more comfortable on his side, so he got himself all set up that way, stuck his hands underneath his pillow to prop his head up at the good angle.

Much better.

Now he just had to bore himself to sleep. Like in the cartoons.

He began to think about the voting process.

He pictured the various kitchen sponges he'd had throughout his life.

His pectoral muscles had gotten in such sorry shape. He used to be quite fit. He used to go lift a bunch of heavy weights, but now he did not know where there was a gymnasium. Who was he trying to impress anyway? His muscles clearly preferred to be flabby, so why hassle them?

Now he was agitated. The linens were defective, trapping his body heat all wrong. He pushed them off, keeping the comforter over himself.

He felt much better.

You know, that clicking sound is probably coming from the refrigerator.

Genius.

That is definitely correct.

Perhaps the doodad has come out of its brass workings.

Maybe he should unplug it?

He got out of the bed, then walked over to the refrigerator. He was correct about the sound, evidently, as it did stop when he removed the plug. The only thing inside was a coffee pot filled with tap water, so no big loss there.

He wondered if it was going to leak all over the carpet.

Not his problem, necessarily.

He walked back across the room then lifted the comforter. The hairs on his leg had accumulated enough static that they prickled as he moved them down the cloth. He laughed a little in his imagination.

Hey, that refrigerator is broken, it got water all over my room. You'll clean it up? That's not enough. I demand emotional compensation.

After a while, he felt that the light coming in through the window could be resolved by drawing the curtains. He did not feel like he should have to go do this, just to get some sleep. He thought of how animals could just lay down wherever they wanted. Yet he had evolved in such a way that it was such an ordeal just to meet his biological needs. What a mistake that had been, and here he was paying the price for it.

* * * * * * * *

He had spared no expense in the purchase of the glass-bottle gin that he had bought. He intended to place it in the interview room, so that he could invite Alan to have some gin and tonic water. The offer stood for Hannah too, though he himself needed to keep his wits sharp during the process.

No thank you, I'm one of those religious guys.

In reality, he feared that he would drink it much too quickly if he began, and it would be such a mess if the interview went on longer than he expected.

He took the paper bag to the door, holding the ring of keys on his left finger.

He opened the door again, how exciting.

He was really giving this his all. He was proud of himself.

Where could he put this?

He placed the gin and the bottle of tonic water in the center of the table at first. This did not seem correct. He did not want those two getting drunk and spilling all over his recording equipment. It also would reduce the effect that he wanted.

Hey you two, you may not know this, but I have some gin, you can have some if you like.

You mean this gin right here in front of me? I hadn't noticed it. I'm fine.

He looked around. He figured out that the best place for it would be on one of the mostly empty bookshelves. He could set it there with the glasses, very subtle. He took the bottle over to the bookshelf, situated it on the second highest shelf, then shifted it onto the left side, with the glasses set right in a row next to it. Someone, probably Tristan, had left this pack of cigarettes on the shelf below. He took them up, shaking them to see that there were still some inside, then placed them into his pocket. The tonic water was problematic, as the packaging was visibly less fancy.

He tried placing it on the right side.

Just keep that one in the bathroom, out of sight. He stepped back.

Not to brag, but that is a stone classy set up.

He opened the bottle, so that they would not think he had bought it just for them.

To facilitate this, he decided to pour out half of the bottle in the bathroom sink.

He grit his teeth as he thought about that.

A senseless waste, in a wasteful and senseless world.

No, it did not have to be that way, he would spearhead the conservation effort, go get one of his coffeepots and pour some into that for safekeeping. He left the bathroom, then the room, falling into a half jog in the hallway. He turned over to the elevator waiting area. A dirty looking family was waiting for the elevator already. He stopped.

Then he clapped his hands.

How were they doing today?

The father smiled then nodded over at him.

He looked them over while the elevator approached. His excitement thinned out, and settled into the emotion of waiting for the elevator.

* * * * * * * *

Hannah explained that Alan was currently the assistant editor of 'Lines magazine', which he already knew. The magazine was a small press literary magazine that published short stories, poems, reviews, articles, whatever they could scrape together. Alan had laughed at that point, but Hannah did not add that touch to her translation.

He smiled from his position in the chair. Hannah taking a look back over at Alan, who was focused on the glass in his hand.

His next question;

Ahem.

How long have you been doing this?

He pointed the microphone over at Alan, who was doing some mathematics in his head.

At this particular magazine?

He nodded, figuring that this was what he wanted to know. Actually, he told Hannah, how long has he been working in all the magazines. Alan thought about the question, taking another sip.

He placed his back more against the chair.

Four years, and then before that he was a photographer for hire at smaller newspapers, then he became chief editor of captions at the Press. He held out the microphone at Hannah to make sure that it was getting this because he did not feel like writing it down. He reached into his jacket pocket to find that paper where he had some preliminary stuff that he'd written down that morning.

There it is.

He unfolded the paper. He realized that the bottom contained numerous drafts of his signature. He held the paper sideways so that those two could not see this.

Are you married? Are you married? Yes, two daughters. Yes, and he has two daughters.

Well, that's very nice.

Alan held up the glass to toast the compliment. He smiled, then adjusted his pants. He read the next question, then said it to Hannah, who explained the question to Alan.

What did his job consist of?

And, by that, he meant specifics.

He hoped that Alan would not answer this question as curtly as the other ones. He did not have too many more on his little paper. He could always make them up, of course, but it would be tough. The interview would have to last at least an hour or so, he figured.

He began to notice that Alan's suit was probably not from the same store that he had gotten his at. It was tailored and all. Ah, there you go, he could ask about this in the interview. Alan spoke in small chunks so that Hannah could tell him in bits. He looked down at the microphone, the previous owner had snapped a few wires in framework of the metal grill. He tried to push them down with his finger. They cut straight into the flesh of his fingertips.

He began sucking on his finger.

Pretty much what Alan did was desk type stuff. He said that he spends a couple hours a day using the phone, that he has to work with the printers, pretty much middle-man type stuff.

He asked if Alan liked what he did for a living, got paid well and so forth.

Four

He invited Hannah to a complimentary meal that he would pay for as a kindof thanks for doing such a bang-up job so far.

He said that he knew a place a mile or two away.

She offered to drive the both of them.

He was horrified at first at how much garbage there was in the passenger seat of her car. She needed to remove several paper cups and some rope from the passenger seat. He had to stick his legs down into the miscellaneous waste underneath the chair. She stared down at it, apologizing, calling herself a monster. After this she pulled her hair back over her ear, placed the car into reverse, craned her neck back so that she could blah blah.

He was almost positive that she would smash into one of the cars behind them.

She did not.

She was able to successfully maneuver through the parking lot, coming to a stop at the road. She began studying the traffic on both sides. She asked him to lean back in his chair so that she could see. He normally just stepped up over the wall here. Hannah found a suitable break in the traffic to turn the steering wheel far to the right and go.

She ran over the curb. The car lifted, then, smack.

There we go, her first mistake. If they were going to survive, it would be from his acute management skills.

Not that he knew the traffic laws.

Once she was out on the main roads, she felt calm enough to begin a conversation with him about his work. He began thinking of something actual to talk about. Did she know that it usually took him twenty minutes to walk this far?

She expressed interest, but immediately returned to asking him how long he had been a journalist.

He was not that much of a journalist, he said.

He was about to tell her that this was his own thing, but decided instead to watch the movement of the sidewalk out the window. If she wanted to know, he would tell her that he was paying for the whole thing out of his own pocket. He did not see the point in offering this piece of information himself.

What she meant was that, she did not know how long he had been doing these interviews. Maybe he had started out when he was not very proficient at the language, but, when she talked to him, it seemed that, now, he had enough grasp of it that he didn't really need an interpreter.

That's a nice compliment, he said.

He thought while she was talking that she had been

thinking about him.

The restaurant would be over here on the right, they had parking in the back, right there. She relented, slowing the car down, asking him if this was the correct one. He reminded her that he would pay for the food.

* * * * * * * *

The ball that he had found imbedded into the dirt outside and taken all the way up to his room, after a few hours, no longer interested him, and did not seem like it would improve his quality of life.

Nevertheless, he had let it sit there for a while longer until he thought of a good way to get rid of it.

The only thing that had occurred to him was to throw it out the window.

But that was just so bland.

The rubber or material was too old for it to bounce impressively. There was no one he could throw it at that would forgive him.

Then he had gone and checked to see if a machine was available for him to do his laundry.

People were using the washing machines, but none had yet progressed to the dryers. What angered him most about this was that it was the exact same situation as the last time he had checked, hours before.

They were all being greedy. He deserved a chance to use the machines as well. They always left their clothes in the machine for several hours anyway.

He was in the hall, when suddenly, a moment of inspiration. He realized that he could place the ball into the dryer.

Thud, thud, thud; it would be entertaining, mildly.

He had never done it before, at least.

He moved things around on the desk until he found enough change to use the machine, pausing, with a frown, to examine a broken but dry now pen that had leaked through the shirt underneath it, threw it against the wall. It ricochetted and stuck into the carpet and him happy, once again. A little spear, of sorts! He saw several coins were scattered across the first layer of the desk, exhumed them, walked toward the door, then remembered that he would need the ball if this was going to go smoothly.

He tossed the ball between his hands. Tada.

And now, behind the back!

He had to turn and follow the ball as it rolled back down the hallway. Its collision with his right ankle had angled it in such a way that it went much further than he wanted it to go. It ended up tapping against one of the doors on the odd side of the hallway, came to a rest against the door frame.

To save energy, he threw it down the hall toward the laundry room. It hit a low spot on the wall, just short of the door. He realized that he had thrown the pen as well just a bit before, and fancied that this meant such things were in his nature.

He should have been an athlete.

If only he'd paid himself more attention.

He took the coins from his breast pocket, rubbing them against one another. He made his way over to the ball, then opened the door and kicked it inside.

Which one would it be?

He decided that the one further into the corner would be the best selection, he put the coins in to pay for the joke.

* * * * * * * *

He could not see well enough outside the lobby window to see the shadow of the man that he had seen pressing his hands into the glass. He felt no particular need to investigate, but thought that, perhaps, someone had gotten locked outside.

The person, whoever it was, had probably seen him.

He could let them inside.

He walked over to the door. He stretched his neck to the side until he felt the bones shift and crack. He pushed the door open just barely enough to feel the lock disengage, expecting to hear someone say something to thank him, take the weight of the door from his arm.

He looked.

No one there.

Hello?

No response.

He was going to let the door close back into place. It was not his problem, obviously. But isn't that what's blah with society? He shifted his leg, felt the stiff shape of his key card in his pocket push against his thigh. He thought it over.

He was going well out of his way for this person. They'd better appreciate it.

The cold stepped through his face, into the lobby as he pushed the door fully open. His skin felt vaguely familiar to it, for he had felt this many time throughout his life.

Stepping out at night. Cold. The moon and all that.

The security light on the corner of the building gave a green tint to the asphalt. He rubbed his knuckle against his chest, until the friction warmed it up, then rubbed his hands over the opposite arms as if applying soap to himself.

They had probably gone to the opposite door.

He walked around, saying things to the hypothetical person. Were they there? Was someone locked out? If someone was out here they should tell him because he was going back inside. He had a key card.

He had, by that phrase, explained the situation so well that he could think of nothing else to say.

His testicles are freezing off, he informed them.

He reached the corner of the wall, then looked down the other side of the parking lot to see if they had tried to go over to one of the maintenance doors. He could see only a short distance, due of course to the scientific bit that the light made things outside of it darker.

Nothing.

He gave up.

Whoever it was could not hear him. He took the key card out of his pocket, ran it through the reader. The door buzzed telling him that he could pull it open.

He obliged.

He walked slowly through the lobby, suspecting that whoever it was would knock on the glass.

He stopped entirely at the corner wall, leaning against it like he had been waiting for some time.

He'd given it a good try, a real humanity gesture.

He had placed so much time into it all that he felt stupid abandoning it all. Obviously there was no one there, or the person was a vagrant trying to sleep in the lobby, or a list of on and on that he thought.

A cat, a black bag.

* * * * * * * *

Richard explained that he had given it some thought, and, through the interview process, he would prefer to be referred to as his pseudonym, because he felt that this was the man that they should interview.

Alright.

Gordon. Demarco.

He wanted to share a particular facial expression with Hannah; for her to look back at him desperately and he to look as though he knew how ridiculous this was but that she should keep her professional composure. She kept her eyes focused on the man in front of them, crossing his legs like a little girl would. Wearing the sweater with the argyle style.

His suit, he realized, had not been cleaned since he bought it.

No one said anything.

So Richard.

I'm sorry, it just came out like that.

So,

Gordon.

Hannah left this out, because it seemed like a mistake. He smiled with his eyes so tight that he could not see the two people in front of him clearly through the gray of his eyelashes.

He should do the whole thing with his eyes closed.

Gordon I like to close my eyes while I interview.

It helps with

No actually I just do it because I'm made of delirious garbage.

Gordon, I don't like you.

Gordon began pulling at the neck of his sweater, adjusting it, nodding at Hannah, preparing to answer. They looked so intimate just then.

He looked over at the bottle of gin on the bookshelf, making a point that he had not offered any this time and he was not going to do so. He rolled the microphone in a little circle through the air.

He rubbed his nose.

What the one he is writing now is about is a hospital patient who comes out of a long coma to find that he has been registered as an anonymous patient. The newspapers have all gathered around to interview him, quite like here, because he has acquired a type of celebrity after the story came out that he had been there for five years and they were going to terminate his life.

The people all chipped in, as these decent people tend to do.

But it turns out that he is not a resident of this country, and does not even speak the language.

Hannah began listing of things that Gordon had wanted to do with this, patriotism, satire, decency.

He wanted to say that, he, himself, did not speak the language here, so that was a very interesting coincidence.

Hannah would probably interject; it wasn't the same thing.

Not really the same thing at all.

He has an important fuh fuh going with himself, don't drag him down to your level.

He stared at the two of them, unwilling to proceed with his next line of questioning until it became noticeable.

He let it go.

He wanted to know how many languages Richard spoke.

He said Richard there because he was interested in how many Richard spoke, not Gordon, who wrote.

i too dance the empty dance of petty reason.

They were dumbfounded by his observation for a bit.

Richard said a little reflex humble-but-not thing, oh none with any proficiency, hahaha, though he'd studied eight.

Which ones?

Five

He had noticed that the grimy store across the street both had a window and sold, exclusively, lurid goods. This, in itself, was nothing special. However, there was a woman inside with a big stack of magazines. Her breasts stuck against the black sweater and all that, she wasn't bad looking. He stood across the street, waiting for her to make her purchase.

She looked at a rack of photographs stuck on the counter.

They were probably of men, weren't they?

She added several photographs to the purchase.

He had to wait for the clerk to count out the bills that she laid on the counter. He waited because, he didn't know why, blah, but had in his mind that she would see him across the street, and seeing as where she had just come out of, take him home for sex for awhile.

It took time for the transaction to take place.

He found a pack of cigarettes in his pocket that he had never purchased.

He stuck one in his mouth but he didn't have any matches.

She was asking now for a bag or something. The tobacco began to sting against the wet part of his lip and he could feel it getting soggy from his spit.

She was all set though, she thanked the clerk.

She walked over to the door.

She opened the door, then walked outside.

She did not say anything to him, but saw him.

Did she have a light?

She cursed at him, then he watched her head down the sidewalk. Shake, her breasts probably did not have a bra on. Then he could no longer see them. He listened though to the sound of her shoes against the asphalt as she got further toward wherever she was going.

Click click click click.

He kept his eyes on her the entire time, but she never looked back at him. He didn't even know if she had looked at him at all, which was a hasty judgment.

He was better than a photograph, he felt.

He hoped, that is.

Well, he was certainly less expensive.

As he turned down the more populated street, he began asking random people if they had brought with them any matches, never saying that's okay if they had not, heading off to the next person down. He was approaching the blue modernish store when he saw two boys blowing big wisps of smoke out into the air and not inhaling, leaning against the glass.

The taller one who currently had the cigarette offered it to him so that he could light it with the hot end. It was difficult to do.

No.

There we go.

He handed the cigarette back, thanking them without really thanking them. He considered lifting up the hood of his sweatshirt to increase his mystique, but never got around to it. After a block or so, he had allowed the cigarette go out, unattended too long.

He considered walking back to the boys. But, no.

* * * * * * * *

They had let him come along, but when they went to get in the car, Richard had taken the passenger seat.

He was stuck in the back, with no legroom to speak of.

The space behind Hannah was larger, but he chose to sit in the middle so that they would be irreparably aware of him.

He needed to spread his legs apart to fit at all.

The crotch of his pants was pulled tight from the position.

Hannah started asking lots of questions.

How long was the flight?

Not long. Here Richard thanked him for paying for the ticket and arranging seating, which made Hannah lose interest in the topic.

What radio station was Richard fond of?

He did not know of a particular one, whatever she liked.

He piped up that he knew of a particular station that was his favorite. In reality, he knew it through an advertisement sticker plastered in the stairwell of his hotel.

Richard said that that sounded good.

That was unexpected. Two in a row.

Was this guy chumming up to him?

Hannah changed the frequency. He clapped a little, yelped. After a minute the station began to bother him, but he pretended to smile.

He watched the traffic through the back window for a moment.

Blue, white, white, red, ugly color, yellow, white, black, black. Not that it stopped there, but he lost interest, instead seeing if his head could rest comfortably over the edge of the seat. He could see things through a tinted area of the back windshield, but they were things not worth mentioning, the sky or such.

His neck began to hurt.

In the shadow of his eye, he caught Hannah examining him in her rear view mirror.

Richard was looking through the window watching the other cars.

Aren't they just gorgeous this time of year?

Hannah was now mostly focused on the traffic patterns.

Richard made some comment about the vegetation.

His pubic area required a good scratching, but that could wait, or not happen.

One of the signs posted on the side of the road informed him that it would take another thirty minutes to reach the airport, at best. He couldn't think of anything to pass such a long amount of time. He made a pretense of reading one of the empty bags sitting in the back seat of her car, but it never quite captivated his imagination. He started talking about his sleeping patterns, but neither of them found the topic to be mutually enriching. He ended up picking at some dirt caught in the fabric of the seat.

He watched the speed of the car without focusing on the road ahead of him, wishing that he had something that he could throw out of the window that would allow the full impact of the fact to be illustrated.

He thought about how, if he had not come along, now she would be all over this guy while driving, without really letting this effect what he thought of himself.

* * * * * * * *

He skipped through most of the preliminary conversation that Angelo wanted to have by telling him that he needed a favor done.

He wanted to cancel the extra room that he was renting.

Angelo, instead of doing this, began to ask him what was wrong.

He just did not have a use for it anymore, that's all.

Angelo then began to ask about the reporting stuff that he was doing. Was it all done, that sort of question.

He said that it was, for the most part, done.

Angelo said that he would probably have to write now, wouldn't he? He looked over at the clock behind the counter, though he did not have such a pressing schedule, then reminded Angelo that he had to cancel the room, that he could speak with him later.

While this was done, he noticed that Angelo had left a line of shaving cream on his throat that morning, and, once he had noticed this, noticed that Angelo had done a terrible job of shaving, that is, if he hadn't intended to look like a hobo.

Rubbing his jaw while he says thank you and such.

He rolled his arm up through the air, as a gesture that had no clear meaning.

Back to the races or so on.

He felt the difference of temperature in the stairwell, but, again, felt nothing about it. He decided, without knowing what time it was, that it had been long enough that he could take one of his pills when he got back to the room. He was able to get himself a little excited about this, but he got tired of running up the stairs after a few steps, so he sank in for the long walk up to his room.

He pressed his sharper teeth down into the bottom row.

His stomach felt like it was infected for a few steps or so, but the pinch of it went away.

He felt the weight of the doorknob in his hand, then pushed it open. The light in the hallway was much brighter than the, whatever, blue that was in the stairs. He looked down at the carpet, then over towards the turn he would have to make.

He began to congratulate himself for canceling that room, what a wise economic decision that had been. He had done it without really putting it off.

It had been so easy too.

He turned the corner.

Another congratulations, for being almost back to his room.

He searched through his pockets for the key, saving himself a bit of time when he got to the door. He also walked toward the odd side of the hall so that he could see the keyhole in the handle sooner. This movement was not as efficient as the key finding initiative, as he had to cross back to the regular side of the hall when he got to the door.

Ah, welcome home.

* * * * * * * *

He waited outside of the hotel with Hannah for the guy to show up, explaining that he would prefer to do the interview at a public park.

Not so much for his sake.

These writer types like the open air and nature, he said.

She pushed her hands down into her jacket, pulling it outward, removing the shape of her body from it. She hunched around, letting her breath out as if she were blowing smoke.

He, on the other hand, was not bothered by it at all.

Except his ears, which threatened to shatter every time the wind touched them. Despite this, he was handling the temperature professionally, wearing no additional layers over his suit, and holding the recording stuff in his hand even though it was heavy enough that a lesser man would sit it on the ground while they waited.

Hannah went to the door, stating that she would be on

one of the couches. While she left, he offered her a cigarette, not at all surprised when she declined.

Little did she know, he did not smoke. And the only cigarettes that he had were both stale and in his room. He looked over through the window as she took a seat on the couch in an exaggerated way.

Not giving in to the cold, not a single step. He would not even get closer to the door.

Yes, even the seasons call me Master.

That's for sure. Then he thought it a few more times with variations in timbre, wearing his cold and sick smile.

He saw the bus pull up a few blocks away from the hotel, three passengers getting off. He strained his eyes to see if one of them looked like they could be the person he was waiting for, finding that they probably were not. He hoped there was a cripple or something that needed help getting off the bus.

A crippled intellectual would definitely be a nice addition to his project.

Nope.

The bus lurched from the parking break disengaging, then began to move down the road.

One of the passengers was holding an attaché case.

The guy was also coming toward the hotel.

This could be it.

The guy looked to be in his twenties, which was not good, needed a hair cut, and a list of other things, but he would have to do. He tried to remember the name, deciding that it was probably Roberto or something like that. He kept a strong eye contact, even though they were out of speaking range.

By the time the guy got up to the parking lot, they had acknowledged one another several times. He looked back into the hotel, saw that Hannah was watching him.

The guy waved at him, but did not offer his hand. Zachary.

He said that he had wanted to do the interview outside, but that Hannah, his interpreter, was feeling a bit cold. He looked over to what he could see of the gulch down the other side of the hill. Hannah had come outside to introduce herself.

(the malice of faint laughter)

Part 4

One

It was stupidly hot, for some atmospheric reason, when he woke up that morning. This, when combined with the heater in his room, had convinced him that he had come down with a plague that made people think briefly that it was summer before they died.

He had evacuated the room at two o'clock, stopping only to turn down the thermostat.

It was now two thirty; he imagined that his actions would have no effect until five.

He had spent the previous half hour taking his time to get outside, making a stop in the lobby to ask a custodian about the temperature. The response given was that the politicians were doing something wrong, which was probably incorrect. He himself did not supply an answer, finding that it was easiest to agree with the thing about politics, and move on.

He saw a pair of young folk looking for a dolly to take their bags up to their room. The girl was dressed in a shirt explaining something or other with a happy sun printed on her left breast. They wore sunglasses, but, other than that, were not dressed in hot clothes.

He went over to the closet behind the desk, taking the dolly out, then wheeling it out by the bags.

The guy did not say anything, but started tapping his foot, waiting.

Put the bags on yourself, I don't work here.

That he was all he needed to say to receive a little apology. Sorry sorry and all that.

The guy mumbling, lazy staff.

The girl pulled her smile wide and thanked him, but he could tell that she was involved with the guy in that sense. She even introduced both their names together. The guy said some casual have a nice day sort of thing while he tried to arrange the bags on the cart.

You need to do it like this, he said, placing the larger bag on the bottom. He got it to fit, waited for a moment expecting the bags to fall again. He then tried to think of the right words to explain weight distribution. The guy shook his hand, and the girl leaned in to thank him making it seem that she really wanted him instead.

It was nothing, he explained, helping people was his hobby.

He walked out of the lobby, there were many others in inconvenient situations that needed his help, obviously. A coin dropped at a crosswalk, a lack of toilet paper in the ladies room.

When he got outside he debated between the three or four directions available to him, one of which lead right back into the lobby.

He manipulated himself through his pant pocket.

I am able to mold my penis into three separate characters of the alphabet.

I just thought you'd want to know.

He rubbed his forearm against the lamppost, debated nothing, then took a seat on the concrete base with a view of his window.

* * * * * * * *

He found a bench. There were several dogs, so it might be a dog-walking park. He sat down, placed the apple juice that he'd brought beside him. He rubbed his hands together, cracked his neck to the left until he felt the pressure in his bones give.

So, dogs?

There was a fat guy dragging his feet with a puffy looking dog on a leash. The fat guy had worn a tight shirt that did not fit over his gut. That's great man, keep up the good work.

He stopped.

A fantastic looking female.

She was dressed in a whorish way, that's what made him love her. She did not care that the strap of her bra was out, things like that. He would have to keep his eye on this one. He smiled and smiled, then watched her a little more, cursing in a happy whisper. She remained out of to his charm zone, which was roughly an arm's length in radius. If she did come this way, he had a seat for her, right next to him. She kept her position by a tree, dragging an annoying miniature something or other. She would have to leave the dog in the lobby, of course, if she were going to come up to the room. He did not want that thing getting its teeth into his business.

I love miniature whatever, but me myself, my dog, is not miniature.

It's a metaphor, candy-face, he has a whole dictionary upstairs.

Hahaha, that is what he would say, isn't it?

He took the juice up to his mouth, swallowing a bit of it, disturbed to find that a piece of park debris had gotten in. He was able to swallow it down, then shook his torso to make sure that it settled on the bottom of his stomach. He blew his cheeks full of air, which was the way that cartoons looked when they were about to vomit. After awhile he stopped, letting the breath fall back into his lungs or wherever.

A man with addict's eyes walked up the sidewalk with a gray complexion. Their eyes met, he nodded, then turned his head back to face forward. He coughed then spit onto the bench, then made a groaning sound that did little to clear his throat out. The drug guy said hello informally as he passed the bench, then muttered something that he did not get. He toasted with his apple juice, but did not take a sip.

He wanted to look at that girl. She had disappeared. He looked over to the path, seeing that she was walking out of the park into the crosswalk. He was able to make out some skin that showed over her pants. From this distance he could not do anything.

Please, come back.

Several of the dog people turned their heads, not knowing what he'd said and to whom he'd said it. He let his eyes off the girl, looking out, with his juice resting on his knee.

* * * * * * * *

He rubbed the shaving cream between his hands until it thickened. He spread it onto his cheeks, feeling the hairs that had grown. He had waited so long to do this. It was going to be particularly dangerous. He turned the faucet, covering it in cream in the process, then ran his hands underneath the water until he shook them and the stuff flew around, off his fingers.

He picked up the razor, not knowing where to begin.

He held it against the underside of his chin for the first stroke. He drew the razor up his skin quicker than a cautious man would, then got the foam off the razor, targeted the area of his left cheek.

He did not feel the cut at all, but saw how the blood soaked into the white whatever residue. It was the entire length of the blade.

He admired it for a little while, then placed the razor in the sink to go construct a bandage out of something.

He considered toilet paper, but saw his phone book on the toilet, which he had brought into the bathroom at some point.

For some reason.

He turned to the middle of it, tearing out a slip of paper long enough.

He checked to see what the listing was. Hampton, Albert, Susanne, Theosomething.

He held the paper against his cheek until the blood served as an adhesive. The first time he let go the paper did not stick, so he held it on longer then a little longer to be sure.

There was a quiet knocking, quiet enough that he assumed one of his neighbors had a visitor.

Lucky guy, he supposed.

When the knocking repeated, he turned off the water then walked over to the door. He used his left wrist to avoid contaminating the doorknob with cream. He felt the bristles of the towel shift over his chest as he leaned his head over to look out the crack.

Oh, Angelo's cousin.

She had brought the towel cart up. She asked if he needed any.

Yes, thank you. He walked over to the cart, the carpet under his toes and all that. He threw the towel into the bag, taking two for himself, and threw one over his shoulder as the other had been a moment before. He thanked her again, pushing the door open.

She spoke to him.

What?

She looked down, enunciating, asking him if he was going to the wedding. He did not know. That was the end of the conversation, at first. She walked back to the cart.

What wedding?

The two, she pointed over there, are getting married. There were not enough people to sit on the man's side, it was bad luck to have it uneven, so. He could see her teeth, and a single hair that had come undone.

Angelo was going.

Why did she think he cared so much about that?

They needed one more.

He said that he was very busy that day, he did not think so.

* * * * * * * *

The coffeepot was full enough at this point that, if he moved quickly, he could pour himself half a glass. He took the glass up from the table, then hesitated, waiting for the right moment.

A drip fell into the pot.

He took the coffeepot, pouring its contents into the glass. He placed it back into its place.

drip.

Hooray.

He could feel the warmth of the liquid through the glass. He took it over to the window, looking down over all the view he had. It looked cold, though there was no precipitation to indicate the temperature. He blew into the cup, disturbing the steam coming off the surface. He could see coffee stretched thin over top of air bubbles.

He decided that it was time. He did not care if his mouth got a little burnt, he was tired of waiting.

The heat obscured the taste at first, and it did burn at the roof of his mouth. Once it had cooled he drew it back into his throat, then swallowed. He rubbed his tongue against the worst of it, soothing. He could feel the taste in his mouth, he could feel the warmth in his stomach immediately.

Something was terribly wrong.

The taste.

Somehow the coffee had been poisoned with liquid soap.

Horrors, he had not thoroughly washed the glass.

He was able to stomach the brunt of it. He braced his arm against the desk, danced a bit, concentrating his vision on the painting of wheat or something in a field. He summoned all his standing saliva by drawing in his cheeks. He moved them around until he had scraped off the soap. He was about to swallow it.

He spit it onto the desk, just to be sure.

It had passed.

To be certain, he tried to focus on something else.

What person had thought it was necessary to put a painting in the room? Of a farm or whatever no less. He had been all up and down this town, and there was no farm, that's for sure.

What were they getting at?

No good.

He was able to get to the bathroom, aim his face blindly at the toilet bowl before the first lurch of his stomach forced a sickly wind through his mouth. Nothing. He got to his knees, placing his head into the bowl. He could feel his eyes tearing, and the air inside the toilet had been cooled by the water.

He clicked his teeth.

False alarm?

Maybe maybe.

No.

The majority of it came out all at once, but he could feel that this was going to be quite a process. He pushed the top of his head into the edge of the toilet seat, pulling his lips in close, closing his eyes, crying a bit.

What a sight. If a photographer was nearby, they could split the prize money.

Thick saliva, he had to shake his lips to get the strand to break from his mouth. He fumbled around for the handle of the toilet.

* * * * * * * *

The wrapping of the sandwich remained cold from its position in the refrigerator in the deli. When he'd complained, they had offered to heat it for him, giving him a rough estimate of five minutes. He had wanted to go, and so declined the offer. He stepped off a curb of the street, looking across to the stoop of someone's town house.

He placed the sandwich down on the stair, then moved the newspaper over to the side so that he would have a place to sit.

He did not look down at the wrapping while he took it off, preferring to look at that more aesthetic bit of red over there.

He bunched the wrapping up, leaving it on the stoop.

Before he could take a bite, a little gust came by, pushing

the garbage over a ways.

He stared at it.

It took time for his sense of etiquette to form the argument for why he should pick it up.

Unhappy, he shifted both halves of the sandwich into one hand so that he could retrieve the garbage. He pushed it down into the pocket of his shirt, reverted to a sitting position.

The meat was soaked with liquidesque guts.

He would not be a repeat customer, but it was not that awful once the flavor of the condiments in the center of the bread obscured the stuff. They had offered to heat it for him and everything, so maybe it was his own fault.

Anyhow, he finished one half of the sandwich.

He decided to take a break. He placed the other half on the stair, then realized he might get a disease of some sort. He could find nowhere else to place it, and ended up sitting it onto the thigh of his pants.

Which, he admits, have not been washed for some time.

He watched a woman stack several whatnots on the passenger seat of a car through the window. He did not really care what they were. She tried not to let him know that his watching her was a demeaning experience, but he gleaned that she thought that anyway.

He could feel, at that very moment, someone watching him.

It was definitely a kid.

He did not look back, but heard a child's voice, calling for someone, dampened by the brick and windows and all the stuff inside the building. He did not know what it said. He heard a woman's voice drawing closer to the window.

Another set of eyes.

They were going to hassle him, weren't they.

He heard the woman call out for someone else, her husband he suspected. How far was this going to go?

The simple act of eating had spiraled into vague illegality.

He drew one of his arms inside his sleeve while no one was watching. The fabric pulled tightly over his elbow, then held his arm to his side.

They now would think that he only had one arm.

You poor soul!

But would it be enough?

He heard the door open behind him, standing up to go before any words got off, his sandwich falling, splitting open on the sidewalk.

Two

He was drawing up a letter that he was going to send to all the theaters, explaining why they should hire him as an actor. Bravery, not afraid to perform naked. That was the whole list, so far. His handwriting was not looking all that respectable. He put down some things about driven, no experience, wanted to show how it was done. He craned his wrist, which was cramping up, then placed the pen against the paper.

He should get that girl to translate this puppy.

His gravity violently shifted to the left, causing him to lean, then fall out of the chair, smacking his forearm against the desk.

He raised himself from the floor by pushing his left elbow into the carpet. His head was spinning.

He began shaking with laughter. He could not figure out what had just happened.

Watch out, his gravity is in the mood to travel.

He picked himself up from the floor. His forearm felt that it might be hurt, maybe.

A jagged black line where the pen had scratched him.

He saw that the pen had also cut through the letter about being an actor.

All his dreams, destroyed. Just like that.

He was not going to write another version of it, choosing instead to take another sip from the bottle of rum. He took it into his left hand, feeling the alcohol draw down into his throat. He was able to get it down into his stomach, then shook his head back and forth to recover from the sensation.

Will this be the end of him?

The nausea passed.

He smeared the letter off the desk, tearing it apart with his shoes. After the destruction process was complete, he had nothing else to do.

He kicked a fragment of it up, into the air.

It floated back down.

Then he felt a great charity in his heart. He would offer someone a drink from his bottle.

But who?

He could figure that out later, he thought, going out to the door. Before he was in the hall he figured out that he needed to offer a toast to the newlyweds.

He had seen them over in that side of the hall, going into one of the rooms. Like a seventeen or so. He would figure it out when he saw the position of the particular door.

He began moving with a stealth not altogether suited to the situation. He slowed himself down into a trot, then leaned over into the wall. The fabric of his shirt created a scrapesque sound against the wall as he moved. The friction began to make his shoulder feel as though it were hot, so he stopped.

He found the door, thinking to knock.

He heard a faint moaning inside, a girl's voice.

All right.

He held his head against the door frame, hearing the sound continue.

He could not hear any particular sounds that would indicate how exactly they were positioned.

He took the pen out, writing onto the label of the bottle. 'Congratulations!'

Then set it at the base of the door, oh so gently.

* * * * * * * *

He turned the corner into the back alley that was paved with old stones that nearly blinded him with their mild gray reflections outside the shadows.

An insignia of some kind had been mounted to the building between the windows.

Vandals had managed to deface it, a little, by chipping off one of the horns of the animals that looked like dogs with antennae.

He began to lean into his steps, then began to lunge forward, then turned his walk into a detectivesque retracing of footprints that were not there.

Hmm, interesting, quite.

He felt the sunlight strike his hair as he came out of the shade, but it was not warmer at all until he got a few steps further. He could see that the trash cans were obscenely overfilled. He could see the steam drifting out from a steel mechanism attached to one of the windows, which indicated that this was the back of a restaurant kitchen. He could think that the steam would be hot enough that he could step into it for a few minutes to warm up. He reasoned that the sensation would not be pleasant, probably.

An inclined ramp sank into the basement of the building. He said something about a wheelchair, to the tune of a kid's song he knew, running his hand over the barrier that removed the ramp from view.

Up.

He was able to pull himself up onto the barrier. His skin could feel how cold the rock was underneath his pants. It had never been intended as seating. He had some trouble finding a balance of his weight that would allow him to remain in place without any effort.

He heard, coming from the alley, a woman warbling something repeatedly to somebody.

As she repeated it, he picked the words apart. 'There you go.' She kept repeating it, wavering her voice like an awful bird.

There you go.

maybe it is a bird?

She was saying it to her kid he imagined, just so upset that she was abusing his ears without any care that she was doing so. What is wrong with your kid, that it needs you to treat it so stupid?

Oh, fuh fuh, I'm a mother too.

Eventually the woman stopped.

Afterwards he looked over to the corner of the parking lot, at some of the plants that were sneaking in over the walls. Hanging against the brick. No one yet concerned enough to cut them up.

This made him happy for a little bit.

He began to ask himself what he was going to do next.

What was his next big move?

Would he find a bathroom?

Would he, let's say, eat?

He began to kick the back of his feet against the wall. The rubber soles of his sneakers rebounded a little each time, moving his legs back up, but not so much.

He wished he had a lot of money.

Tons, tons of money.

As it was, things were tight enough that he could not really do anything he wanted.

* * * * * * * *

Someone had closed off the street, to conjoin the two blocks into a large complex.

Little did they know that he could see that the road had passed through the wall, once.

You sneaky demons, give him back his road!

Though the walk was not formally organized, he wanted to get to the opposite side of this wall, especially now that they were gumming up his plans.

He would have to go around the block.

He definitely would check to see what this building was, why it was so important as to impede his travel time.

He traced his fingertips against the wall as he stepped up the sidewalk, worrying that they would be cut by the texture if he kept it up.

He also felt, not really developing the suspicion, that they were trying to prevent him from getting to the other side. He wanted to see what was so special.

His stomach dropped, it felt very hollow, though he had eaten. He breathed out some of the air in him, trying to make it as cold as possible so that he could not see it in the air.

No luck.

When he turned the corner of the walk, he saw a flag hanging halfway up the building. It seemed familiar enough at first that he did not think it odd.

Hello.

All evidence indicated that this was his embassy.

That changed things completely. He decided to go inside, maybe they would offer him a soda. A seat in a well heated room, that would be a nice change of pace from this whole walking business. He walked up to the door, touching the handle.

It was firm, locked.

The man behind the desk looked up at him, to see who had made the sound of trying to get in. The man pointed his finger in a not so specific way. He looked around the walls, finding a speaker and button that he could press to communicate his needs.

Yes?

Let him in.

What was this regarding?

He was a citizen.

Did he have his passport?

No. His things had been stolen.

Oh.

The voice sounded happy about that.

The door buzzed. He took advantage of the opportunity to open the gate. He then found that the second door, a glass one, was not locked at all.

The waiting area had all these couches.

What ambiance, these fancy dim lights.

The man slid over a clipboard, even though he was a ways from the desk, asked him to sign in.

What a nice place we have here, he said.

The man chuckled, then agreed. It is; they try their best. Anyway it was not that busy this morning, so he could go see Miss Carter in room fourteen. They should be able to get him in and out very fast.

He signed his name very clearly, so that someone could actually read it, if they wanted.

The man picked up the phone, pointing again.

He lingered at the edge of the desk.

Yes, that way.

* * * * * * * *

That sound.

He had better investigate.

He moved quickly over to the door, throwing it open. He leaned out to look into the hallway to look where he thought the giggling had come from. He turned his head to the other side to see that there were three girls of blah age, two blonde, one wearing a red athletic shirt. They were towing their luggage behind them.

One was turning to look back.

Should he find cover?

She made eye contact, nodded at him.

How's it going?

The other two turned over to look at him. He could see all of their faces now. He began to count off the years since girls his age had looked like this. Old enough to travel independently of an adult escort, yet young enough to travel in groups.

Hmm. Yes, a prosecutable offence, definitely.

How are you? She responded.

He said that he was doing alright.

The one was finally able to get the lock undone. It took a moment for the other two to recognize this. Then they drained into the room.

No goodbyes, nice night so and such.

The conversation had ended. He hadn't even gotten to say what he was doing, other than that it was alright.

He stepped into the hall, since no one was there. He left the door open, leaned against the frame, petted his neck against the corner of it.

Noise erupted from the girl's room.

Evidently they had brought their own music.

He used to have a record player, it was pretty nice.

The sound grew louder. He clapped his teeth shut, spread his lips out to reveal an eerie grimace to no one there. Obnoxious. He was going to bang on their door. He stalked down the hall. Just one good smack, that would do it. The music was turned down, revealing girlish cackles that it might have covered a moment ago.

He wondered what was so funny?

He turned back to his door, studied the chaos of his laundry strewn around the room. He left the door open. He clapped his hands together as though he were holding a gun. He assassinated several items of clothing, then shot the picture on the wall. He might have killed a neighbor too, he wasn't sure.

Take that, you reckless music.

He swept off the bed with his forearms, then made the comforter flat enough that it the ridges would not dig into his stomach. He lay down, with his arms and head dripping over the bedside, bringing him face to face with the clothing he had evicted from the bed so recently.

He flicked them toward the window.

He heard two of the girls coming back down the hall.

What was wrong with them?

He thought, for a moment, about closing the door so that they would not see him. He decided against it, then actually became excited that they would have to look into his room, see his filthy little kingdom, him majestically reclining on the bed, inviting them in out of spite.

* * * * * * * *

At an hour in the evening, he could hear, dampened by the

window, a howling industrial etcetera.

Metal of some sort, with wind scraping through it.

Or it might be a bat.

The noises stopped. Whatever metal thing had been moved into a more aerodynamic configuration. Or the animal had eaten something. Some damsel it was taking back to the cave.

Help me.

Haha.

He felt his arms slack at the side of his body. He had been resting on his right hand for so long that he could no longer feel it. He pulled it out.

The hand would not obey his commands, but he could feel many sensations from it. It had been shaped into a claw of some sort, with the fingers drawn into the palm. He let it rest on his thigh, where it continued to be all prickly.

He also felt that he could not move his body. The toxins or whatever from sleeping had not yet worn off or so on. He had a hard time moving his mouth. He fantasized that he would remain in this position until someone discovered him.

Oh no, are you all right?

Moo moo.

He's not responding in any known human dialect.

Let's get this one to the something or other, you get his legs.

Get a photograph too.

'Sleepy Man Discovered, With Claw'

'fluent in cow.'

He could feel some feeling coming back to his hand. He thought that this was just like something he had heard before. It was like the old so and such tale wasn't it? his dad had mentioned in the car when he was going to school, in the parking lot? He grit his teeth, then remembered that it was like the coma guy story that that prissy fellow talked about.

It was also like the carnival people, the ones that you could pay to look at.

He had enough energy at this point to raise his torso, roll his shoulders from side to side. He was able to spread his fingers out far enough that his hand looked like a normal hand. He could reach over from the bed to the table. He turned on the lamp.

He opened the drawer.

He took out the hotel stationary, as well as the hotel pen. He also took the travel guide for the area that he had never actually read, which he could use as a hard surface.

The first line he decided was going to be from a newspaper.

Something to the effect of 'coma guy wakes up.'

He placed the pillow under his stomach. Then placed the paper in the pillow zone. He tried to think of a newspaper article.

They always say the city name, then the day.

Today was Thursday, he believed.

He remembered that the people had paid money to keep the man alive. So he wrote a line about that, then about how the people would be happy to know that he had woken up.

His hand hurt.

He read it back.

Sensational.

He should take a shower before he goes any further.

Three

He made fists inside the pockets of his pants, then angled his wrists to make the fabric as tight as possible. He found that if he pushed his fists forward, the pants would be flat in the front. When he pulled his fists back, the fabric formed noticeably into the shape of his genitals.

He decided to hold this configuration until he ran into someone.

He could feel that something he had drank had mixed with the gross substances in his mouth, the combination tasting almost sweet. He tried his best to clear his throat out with his tongue. He gagged, his eyes watered up. What a great idea that had been. He blinked his eyes until the water ran out through the tear ducts.

He saw an old maid coming this way.

He realized that he had allowed his wrists to go slack.

Quick.

He resumed the pants gesture, with his eyes off of her. He then turned his head in an oh hello sort of way. An oh hello, have you met my pants? She wheeled the cart in front of her, which was obscuring her view. He swept out to the side, which might look as though he were making room for her to pass.

She did glance down.

That was great.

He wanted to give a little clap, good job, but he managed to restrain himself.

He walked over to the door to the next cluster of rooms, opening it with his shoulder so that he could maintain this new joke he'd invented. The hall was empty. He looked down at the dust crumbs all over the carpet. Almost footprints. A high traffic area.

Should he find another unassuming victim?

He then looked over at the stairwell, wondering.

Was it time to buy a bottle of wine?

He did feel like buying one, as well as a little something to eat. Maybe some playing cards, or a little plastic thing too. He would have to grab his wallet from his room, which he could easily do.

He went over to the stairs, flicking his fingers to brush off a spot for himself. He let his legs hang down the stairs, their corners digging into a few points from the back of his knee to his calves. He breathed through his nose, feeling more serious than he had just felt with each breath. His eyes falling to the next flight, and his bottom eyelids swelling up a little.

He sucked on his cheeks, which felt like he looked like he was making some progress in pondering something of deep emotional import.

The wine, what was he waiting for?

He drew his head over to the rails so that he could see the bottom floor. He could see the head of Angelo's cousin standing over a grey basin that was full of empty towels. She wore a white thing in her hair that was holding it up that day. She began digging through the towels for some reason. He began wondering if she was brushing her hands against any that he had used.

* * * * * * * *

He was just beginning to get tired when the phone rang. He looked over at it.

Am I going to answer?

Of course.

He sat up in the bed, letting the phone ring a few more times to communicate that whoever was probably waking him up. He took the receiver from the cradle, then rolled his neck, then held it to his ear.

Hello?

He did not recognize his brother's voice at first because it came through so softly. But it was there in the speaker, saying hello, then saying his name as though it may not be him answering. His voice perked up, and he drew his back against the headboard so that he was in a position to talk for some time.

How's it going, he asked.

His brother was fine, just getting into his new apartment. His brother had gone out that night with Jake and those guys.

They had said hello, of course.

He felt that he should tell his brother what he had done that night, which was not too much. He ended up telling him an abbreviated story about a lady he had met that turned out to be crazy.

His brother said that such things happen.

His brother asked if he was sleeping.

He said that, yes, he had been. He pulled the pillow up behind him so that it rested in the small of his back. He saw the glow of the security light flat against the wall, making shadows of the curtains.

His brother made fun of him for being asleep.

Even though he insisted that it was not a problem, his brother told him that he should get to sleep that night, and call tomorrow. It was late there. The international rates were ridiculously expensive.

After this they talked for a few more lines to the effect of;

How was his new apartment? Fine.

Had he gotten furniture? He had ordered it, but it hadn't come.

they said goodbye several times.

They tried to hang up simultaneously.

He was surprised at how tired he actually felt. Then congratulated his brother for recognizing that he should get to sleep. He rearranged the pillow so that it was flat on the mattress.

He stuck his arms under it.

A few deep breaths or such.

He felt some intestinal gas in the pit of his stomach. He did not hear, but felt it passing into the linens, leaving a spot of warmth that he rubbed his knee into. It felt warmer now than his other bony cold one. He gave his other knee a shot at the warm spot, but found that it had cooled off.

He pulled the other pillow over to his chest, holding it with his hands until his stomach settled a little.

He then sandwiched his head between the two pillows to drown out dogs or something.

It was hard to breathe like this, his face became hot and wet, the air became useless.

* * * * * * * *

He drew the laundry from the dryer into his laundry bag, not bothering to fold it at that exact moment.

Pink hearts on white cotton.

Those were probably not his.

He already had them in his hands though, and could not stop the scooping maneuvers without dropping his laundry all over the floor. The yellow bag was getting full. He punched it down with a pair of pants that were still fairly wet.

Stupid appliance.

He took the last of the laundry into his hands, pressing them into the bag. He pulled the drawstring until the opening was closed. He pulled the bag up to his shoulder by the cord, which dug into the crooks of his fingers. He made a more comfortable grip then set off, destination his room.

He pushed the door open, letting it swing back after he had left. He whistled a constant tone through his lips, which were too dry. He began to cross through a list of suspected owners of the underwear. He could not really return them though. There was really nothing he could do at this point, except place them back in the machine, which was not really doing anything.

The bag slapped against his back with each stride, unless he took smaller steps.

He found his key in his pocket with his free hand.

It took some work to unlock the door while he opened it.

He slung the bag across the room, overshooting the bed. Now that he had two hands, he could use one to hold the door while the other freed the key from the lock.

He pushed the door into the frame, placing the key into the pocket of his sweatshirt. He wanted to postpone placing the laundry into the drawers, but he had not folded them yet.

He set the bag upright, then pulled it open.

He folded the shirt.

He folded the pants that were still wet.

Boxer shorts, you don't even have to fold those.

There they were.

To whom do these belong, and what to do?

Once again another ordeal.

They looked as though they had just been washed.

That would not do.

He stretched them out with his fingers, then rumpled them into a ball twice. He pressed the ball into his hands then ruffled it around. He lowered his arm, then rolled them under the bed.

Problem solved.

He wanted to be there when that came to an effect, to kick his shoe into the carpet and smile sheepishly. He would just have to wait and see.

Oh, you know, I just can't help it, I'm Mr. Seduce.

His suit pants were evidently not supposed to be washed. The stitching along the legs had torn beneath the pocket.

How sad.

He folded them up, placing them onto the other pants. He now had three piles going; shirts, pants, and miscellaneous. Each pile would get an entire dresser drawer to itself.

Pure class. That's all there is to say about him. He stuck his hand into the bag, pulling up another shirt for the first pile.

* * * * * * * *

He placed the cap onto the drink then pushed it down into his pocket, continuing down the sidewalk.

The sunglasses rested on his nose, giving him a little space to see what a difference they made. He could feel how soft his skin felt in the area that they protected, how dry his cheeks were by contrast.

The wind went up his sleeves, saturating his armpits with cold, though they were sweating. When he closed his arms to his side he could feel how the sweat had cooled off.

Newspapers on the street advertising.

Gates pulled shut over storefronts.

All that followed.

He had noticed, through countless hours of research, that

the stores in this area did not keep regular hours. Instead they were open sometimes, closing at other times, without any sense of duty to his shopping desires.

Not that he needed to buy perfumes, flowers, stuffed animals, hygiene products.

But, who knows, maybe one day they might be handy.

Or not.

The soles of his shoes were becoming far too thin, he could feel the topography of the sidewalk. He tried to see if they were thin enough to bend them with his toes. But, not yet.

He would have to make the turn two blocks up, by the yellow sign.

He yawned.

He spread further from the wall so that he could see the turn he would have to make.

There was somebody standing there.

Dancing.

A crazy person.

oh no.

He arranged his face into a fierce position. The sunglasses would help, he figured.

No eye contact. You are not interested in dance.

He moved back to the wall so that he would remain covered. He had a chance of making the turn unnoticed.

He felt inconvenienced, that's for sure.

He whimpered, letting the hum soothe the tides of fearishness. He darted toward the corner, where the guy looked over, saw him, called something out to him.

He wanted no trouble.

He said something or other to that effect, slowing down. This guy smells.

He felt his hand being taken in a slimy mitten thing. The guy pulled his arm, asking for money.

He shoved his whole weight into the guy's clothes, desperate to get his hand back.

He padded his pockets, thinking that he might have brought his knife.

It was not in his pants.

Something in his hooded shirt.

A menacing beverage.

He found the knife in his pants, pulling it out. His hands

were shaking, he had trouble unfolding the blade. His one palm was wet. The guy's clothes had been damp with some kind of crazy juice. The blade came out, its lock clicking into place. He held the entire thing out in one hand.

The guy had fallen over the curb.

The blade seemed pathetically small.

The guy sat up, coming into view of the knife. Neither said anything.

Backwards, keep the knife drawn.

He coughed twice, forcing his eyes open with an emotion. He rubbed his wet palm over the fabric of his pants.

* * * * * * * *

He found the note pad hidden between the mattress and the headboard. He reached his hand down into the mattress grabbed it.

The headboard scratched up the back of his hand when he pulled. He took the note pad into his other hand, examining the trail of the scratch, seeing that some skin had been pulled into a pile at his knuckles.

He held his fist to his lip, rubbing his tongue along the injury.

Note pad.

He read back what he had written so far.

It did not take too long.

Alright, so we've established that it was Thursday.

That's settled, at least.

And the people had paid money to keep the guy alive. That was nice of them.

He pushed the clutter on the desk to one side. He laid the note pad in the empty space.

He took the pen, placing a dot next to the last word on the page.

This is the most spectacular incident that this humble reporter or whatever has ever seen.

Many people have come to the hospital to see the guy.

How long was a normal article?

He should make some coffee. Regroup, plan his next move. He took the coffeepot from the cradle over to the bathroom. He waited for the water coming from the faucet to heat up, which would make it boil faster.

That way he could get back to writing his thing.

He saw that some steam was coming out of the sink basin. He moved his finger over to the stream, running it through the water. That should do it. He held the lid of the coffeepot open, filling it completely so that he could enjoy several cups.

He located one of the prepackaged coffee things.

Caffeinated, that's the one.

He pulled the bag apart until the seal broke. He popped the filter holding device on the coffee maker, then poured the water into the water holding mechanism. He flicked the switch, sat down, and resumed the pen.

He did not want to start until the coffee was finished. It would be irritating to have to stop writing to go find the glass, pour some coffee into it.

He decided to check the spelling of what he had written so far.

Hosspital?

He had picked up an extra letter somewhere.

The easiest way to correct that was to cross out the letter.

He could find no other mistakes, but decided that he needed to trace over the headline until it was thicker than the remaining text.

For realism purposes.

Such is life.

The coffee began to drip into the pot. He figured that he still had some time to kill. He crossed out the word hosspital, spelling it correctly overhead.

He added a few lines about how the guy's first words should prove to be the story of the century.

This cleverly set up the part about him being foreign.

Wait.

How did the reporter know that the guy was about to wake up?

That sort of thing normally happens out of the blue, in the literature.

He had been thinking about this entirely wrong.

A coma, idiot.

Four

Evidently, there were enough guests in the hotel that morning to warrant the reinstatement of the complimentary breakfast policy.

Which they advertised as provided each morning.

Someone had set out silver trays of eggs.

Two kettles of coffee, how decadent.

Which breakfast cereal would he like?

They hoped he was not allergic to raspberry muffins. Oh you are, well then, the manager will throw out the entire basket.

He went over to the basin of eggs, taking the spatula that hung from the side. He lowered it onto the surface of the conglomerated yellow thing, trying to flatten it out with his wrist power. The eggs flattened down. He removed the pressure, wondering if they would bounce right back.

Flat.

They slowly began to inflate.

Having ruined their appeal, he moved over to the next basin.

He took three strips of bacon for himself. Holding them in the tongs while he searched for a plate to place them on.

A stack of paper plates.

They'd thought of everything.

He took a scoop of eggs as well, hoping that there would be toast.

So he could make little sandwiches!

For good measure, he took one of the sausage links. Now he had everything. He found that some toast had been placed onto a red napkin. They had buttered it and everything.

He wondered who exactly had been assigned this duty.

They had probably considered coming up to his room, making him help out.

He took two of the one-person sized cereal boxes, reasoning that he could eat them later. Dry, if he must.

He placed his plate of food down onto the table, shifting it so that he would have a nice view of the wall. This allowed him to place the complimentary cereals he was stealing on the opposite chair, hidden from prying eyes. He pulled the seat out that would be his, remembering at the last possible moment that he would also indulge in a cup of free coffee.

He placed the cup beneath the tap.

The coffee smelled much richer in person. This wasn't even the ordinary stuff.

Fork. Grab that.

Tiny jellies. How had he lived without them?

He settled into the chair, first stacking the jellies on top of the cereal boxes.

He looked down at his meal.

Sandwich.

Using the fork, he dismantled the egg into shreds. He then piled these shreds into the upper left corner of the plate. The bacon he could not do anything with yet. Toast.

Why, they've cut the toast in triangles.

He appreciated that, actually. He preferred the triangle. This was going to be a great sandwich. He placed the eggs onto the toast pieces. He found that, while one sandwich would receive two strips of bacon, the other would have the exotic 'one bacon, one sausage link' flavor. He decided to create this stranger one first, as, if it were nasty, he would be getting the problem out of the way.

He raised it to his mouth.

It wasn't bad at all.

Thus is how he came to be happy.

* * * * * * * *

He walked down into the gulch that one glorious day.

The birds were most likely singing.

The grass was blowing around the place.

He concentrated his vision onto the blank color of the vegetation. The soil was not quite mud, but he could feel that it was wet, not sturdy standing ground. He pitched his weight backward while he descended into the gulch.

He looked over to the road beside him.

That would have been much easier.

He decided to capitalize on his poor decision by taking one of the rocks from the creek bed, then smacking it against the guardrail on the side of the bridge. He found a piece of shale large enough that he could pick it up. He heaved it over at the wall.

Bang, smack, all that stuff. The rock has been defeated.

He should make his escape.

He stepped onto the rocks in the creek bed, not particularly fast, at first, then deliberately slow.

Then he stopped, holding out his wrists in front of him.

Ascending the opposite side of this dangerous geographic etcetera proved to be more perilous than walking down into it. His footing slipped backwards twice. He devised a plan of grabbing onto some of the branches of the smaller trees.

It worked for the most part, until he stepped into some loose soil. He started to fall.

He refused to let that happen, spunk, determination.

He pulled fiercely against the sapling, finding that the best thing to do was to lean into it sideways.

He was now level with the road. He walked over toward the sidewalk, turning onto it, continuing in the direction that he really did not have to go. He looked back at the hotel.

His shoes had gotten dirt all over their tops.

He turned back.

He stepped up to the sign for the hotel, which was imbedding into the retaining wall that propped up the would-be flower garden. He kicked his shoes against it.

Chips of dirt, shaped like fossils of the traction marks of his sneakers, fell out.

He pulled himself up onto the retaining wall. He steadied himself, cautiously stood.

He was now standing on top of a wall.

He surveyed some stuff that he could see.

He petitioned himself for reasons to remain standing on the wall, finding that there were none. Excepting a small contingent of his kneecaps that were afraid of jumping down.

He walked along the wall over to the garden bed, then stepped through it.

Lucky thing he had cleaned off his shoes.

He walked up to the entrance of the hotel. He saw that someone had left a napkin in the trash. It was about to blow out. He snapped it up.

How was he going to do this?

He took the napkin into one hand, using the other to brace himself against the trash can. He lifted his left foot up, giving himself some space so that the dirt would not get on his pants, feeling as though what he was doing was, somehow, morally wrong.

* * * * * * * *

He saw Angelo at the front desk, then began rummaging through his pockets. The bullets were located eventually deep in the right pant pocket. He did not say anything, but walked over to the desk with the bullets in his hand. He slapped them onto the counter top.

They rolled a little.

Angelo studied the bullets.

All he needed now, he said, was a gun.

Angelo picked one of the bullets up, blowing the dust off of it, then commenting that these had already been used.

It would be enough to kill Angelo, he explained, because Angelo was incredibly weak.

Angelo asked where he had found them.

He insisted that he had not found the bullets, but had bought them.

For the purpose of killing Angelo, he explained.

After this, he was pretty much done with the conversation. He wanted to scoop the bullets back into his pocket, go back up to his room. Then, who knows? Do something else. Angelo had not set down the other one yet, though. He could not snatch it out of his hand without causing a scene.

Angelo asked if he could have one.

He said no, at first, but immediately recognized that he could not think of anything to do with them. He could not even think of a way to throw them out.

He said that Angelo could have one. Then made fun of him for wanting an empty bullet shell.

He left both on the counter, walking over, at first, to the elevator.

He waved over at the desk, telling Angelo that he did not want it. He turned so that he could use the master stairwell at the end of the hall.

He examined the red and yellow carpet as he walked.

Are those supposed to be vines?

He dragged his wrist against the wall until he came to the dining area.

Empty tables, a few chairs. He stepped inside, looking at the doors. Propped open.

Let's be civic.

He bent over, pulling the bolts up on the right door. Free at last, the door bumped into his head without any real force to it. He pulled away, allowing the door to swing closed.

He repeated this process with the left door. Leading it out into the hallway, letting it rest against his palm so that it closed gently.

He could see how dark it became inside the dining area

once the doors were closed.

He looked over to the stairwell, checking his itinerary with his imagination.

What luck, he had an open space right now.

He pushed the door open, which allowed enough light for him to memorize the location of one of the chairs.

The door closed.

Darkness.

Where's that chair?

Everything is black!

His fingers bumped into a rough, probably grey, surface. He held the backrest of the chair, drawing it out from the table that was probably there.

It took several seconds for his eyes to adjust to the lighting, during which time he realized that he hated this chair.

felt shoddy, the backrest etcetera.

* * * * * * * *

Some wild stuff was happening here.

He rubbed his head against the pillow, creating a scraping noise that at once sounded like;

So, huh, you lie to me Ray?

That was a great one.

Then he felt some watery sounds that turned out to be green fish all set up in a row popping their heads out of the river. Fat white lips, sparing no expense on the cute little eyeballs. Each one had something to say!

He forgot their exact words immediately; the ones further down the bank were not intelligible to begin with.

He should be dreaming, he imagined, but his stomach was not cooperating, digesting the remaining coffee in it. Providing just enough energy to keep him conscious.

His face, however, was completely exhausted.

It just wanted to get some sleep, refusing to open his eyelids and all that.

A different part of him was entertained. He wanted to know where this whole fish thing was going.

But they had swum away or something. All he heard was the faint hum coming from the clock.

He thought that flipping over onto his stomach would do something. He rolled onto it, trying to find a comfortable posture.

Sleep?

No sleep.

He wondered if he was uncovering a hidden trauma in the dark recesses of so and such.

No, probably not.

If this was a memory, he could not really imagine gaining anything by recovering it. Did I tell you about the time I was twenty, sitting by the river? The fish jumped out and sang to me for some reason.

It was disturbing, evidently.

And that Ray guy lied to me.

He was having a really good time with this, but enough was enough. He opened his eyes, fixed them on the window, then on the corner of the lamp shade, then on some empty space between his nose and the night. He started breathing through his nose.

He turned over to give himself a few punches in the stomach.

It had the opposite effect of a good effect.

He was now extremely aware of his entire body. An itch on his abdomen. The stomach thing. His nose felt colder than his left ear.

He was wearing his jacket?

Yes, but to what end?

While his initial plans to use the toilet were being drawn up, he thought about seeing rust along the side of a pole that was located towards the center of town. Before resorting to the bathroom, he opened his mouth wide to see if a little oxygen would do the trick.

He belched out some something. It felt nice, but did not have any real helpful result.

He rolled out of the bed, dragging the comforter onto the floor. He walked over it, into the bathroom, groped for the lights, removed his jacket, took down his boxers, sat on the toilet.

His stomach rumbled. He put his elbows on his knees.

He breathed quite smoothly.

He looked down at some water sitting on the grout between the tiles.

* * * * * * * *

He pulled out the correct tape, confident that this would be the one, though he had not labeled them.

He took the pen from the desk, writing on the tape. He had to trace the pen over it a few times to get the ink to stick to it.

The lid of the equipment was already open. He put the tape in, sitting down into the chair at the same time, waiting until he was seated to close the lid. He drummed the pen against the note pad, considered pressing the play button. He tore off the top sheet, examined his handwriting, then folded the sheet so that it could stand on the table.

He played the tape back.

He heard Gordon's voice coming to a stop.

He heard someone clear his throat.

That was his contribution.

Hannah.

She explained. What she does when she is writing is she tries to picture herself with an old group of friends. A very intimate circle of. Then she feels that. He picked up the microphone, which was hanging from the surface of the desk by the cord. He scratched it against the back of his knee. Truly unconstrained to say what. He looked down at the speaker, through a space in the grill.

Interesting.

Hey, that's me again.

He rewound the tape to get back to the story part.

He doesn't feel it's any harder from what you do, writing for a

Further back.

He looked down at his paper while the tape was rewinding.

He wrote down something about close circle.

He started the tape again.

So Richard.

Oh yeah, Richard, isn't it? He felt irritated about forgetting that.

Was this the right place?

Yes.

He heard Richard's voice going on into the details of the story.

Rrr.

He stopped the tape. Breathing, his fist wrapped tightly

around the stem of the microphone. He moved his head, closing his eyes. He opened them. He looked down at the player. He pressed the button.

No sounds played. He turned the volume up, then down, then up. He lifted the player up, dropping it against the desk. That did not work either. He looked down, seeing that he had pressed the button to record from the microphone. Oh no. He was recording over top of the tape. He rubbed his nose, then pressed his palm into his face feeling how cold his hand was.

He had better put a stop to this.

Right now. Immediately.

He said his name into the microphone three times, then pressed the stop button.

He pressed play.

anguages do you speak, Richard?

What?

He rewound the tape. Finding that, yes, in fact, all he had now was an accurate record of rubbing the microphone into the fabric of his pants.

He heard himself say his name a few times.

Did his voice really sound like that?

This microphone is no good.

anguages did you speak, Richard? I said Richard

Anguages? Oh no.

He bit his lips. His life's work.

Part 5

(escape!)

One

He made eye contact with the girl on the cover of the magazine. Her eyebrows were down, her lips puffed out showing her teeth gritting. The message was clear.

She was desperate, for him.

The wrapping on the magazine blocked his view of her chest. He was angry. The editors were interfering with his ability to make a discerned judgment. This poor girl, you must understand, she's having an emergency.

Haha, for her sake.

He tried his best to read the pink lettering on the top. He saw that the ending of the second word denoted that whatever was small. The adjective, he guessed, maybe, lusty?

Lusty tiny somethings?

He checked the price. Not on the back, not on the front. Whatever, he had enough money for it. He sighed, going over his finances in his mind's eye. He could skip a meal, drink some free coffee. Maybe he could just find some way to sleep the rest of the day. He was on his dumb budget.

He understood that the register man had been staring at him for some time now. He did not return the glance, but held up the magazine, asking how much it would cost.

Which one is that?

He felt embarrassed. He played it off by bringing the magazine up to the register. Before he got all the way there, the guy discerned which magazine it was, adjusted his glasses, said that it would be so much.

That much?

He dropped the magazine on the counter. Too expensive.

The guy told him to put it back, then, on the shelf.

What shrewd negotiating tactic. He was in the presence

of a master.

He studied his opponent.

His initial offer. Half the price.

No.

He acted casual. He turned the little rack of nudie postcards. What was the lowest price he could get it for then?

Why, that's the cover price.

He explained that he did not have that much money. This was not a very sympathetic man, no respect for poverty. He felt spiritually exhausted. He did not have the energy to refuse, though he did not want to purchase it now. He took the bills out of his wallet, placing them on the counter.

He took his change, the guy made him put it in the bag himself, and he actually fumbled at that. He stepped over to the door, opening it, feeling etcetera. He looked down at the pavement, then moved his chest up so that he felt the shape of his wallet resting on it.

Not today. He did not have to take this. He could use his imagination. He took out the magazine, studied the cover, trying to set the girl's appearance to memory.

He went back inside, then explained that he wanted to return the magazine. Too much money. The guy shook his head, exhaled, checked around, leaned in, offered to purchase the magazine for him, at an employee discount.

What would that be? He frowned, smiling somewhere in his heart.

* * * * * * * *

His new neighbor had seen him going into his room with the cans of beer. His new neighbor had clapped, then cheered him on, and he realized when he got into his room that he really appreciated this. He set the beer on the desk.

Yeah. That's right.

I'm going to drink some beer.

He pulled back the fingers of his right hand until he felt a cracking noise generating from the top of the knuckle. He repeated this process with his left hand.

Alright.

The metal tab at the top of the can was stiff, he stuck his thumbnail underneath it, using the nail to lift it to the point that he could get a good grip with his fingers. Once he had done this he pulled the beer off the desk, using his right hand to push the tab down, until it peeled the metal lip from the top.

I have always enjoyed the sound of compressed gas escaping through a small but expanding opening, in wintertime. It reminds me of the foliage pushing against the ruins of the one place with the setting sun in evening. Alone at dusk, caught in the dropping heat, sharing in the moisture of my wife's palm clasped in my own. As we watch the children do annoying stuff with the toys handed down by us to them, and then we go have sex for a few hours and never tell anyone.

The taste of the beer; delicious.

The aftertaste of the beer; not so much.

He had bought, he realized, a most rotten stuff. He took another sip, thinking that the appropriate audience of the taste was a drunk person.

He discovered that, if he took three to four small sips quickly, instead of one large sip, the aftertaste thing was not a problem at all. He became a little bold. He took five sips, just right in a row, then six.

Six was going a little far, that did not work.

He stuck out his tongue.

He yawned hoping to relieve some of the pressure from an excess of this gas. Forced his eyes wide.

He was staring at the wallpaper. He got the vague impression that he had done this at another point in his life.

Oh, yes, that would be last night.

He took the beer up, then grabbed the remaining two.

He walked out into the hallway, seeing that his neighbor was still in his room.

He knocked on the door.

He felt ready to take another sip of beer. He was in the process of sipping when his neighbor came out to the door.

He enjoyed the way this must have made him look.

He asked the neighbor fellow for his name, offering him one of the beers in the ring.

They could have a beer.

Constantine was thrilled, invited him to sit down at the desk, while he sat on the bed.

This room was so clean and bright. A nice exchange.

* * * * * * * *

He held the envelope against his chest so that he could remove one of his famous pills. He took it into his fist. He counted the remaining pills until he got bored with that, assured that there were several.

He placed the envelope back into the safe. He went to the bathroom to get some water involved in the swallowing process. He left the lights off turning the faucet on. He realized that the pill was in his hand still, so he placed it into his mouth, felt it dissolve. He cupped his hands under the faucet, then brought the water up to his mouth, sucking out a good portion of the pool, scattering the rest across the general sink area.

It went down just fine.

He used the toilet as an ordinary seat.

He could kindof see himself in the mirror.

Yes, he still looked his splendid self.

Someone was unlocking the front door to the room. He reached his foot out to the bathroom door, stretched his body so that he could reach it.

He closed the door, softly, and not all the way.

He saw Angelo's cousin enter into the room. She looked over to somewhere, to some of his stuff probably. She then propped the door open.

Why hadn't she knocked?

Able to answer neither this, nor the question of why he was sitting on the toilet in the dark while the maid cleaned his room, he did some other stuff. Such as, but not limited to; cracking his toes, sitting on his hand, and thinking that, maybe, some day, he would probably find some change and get a drink from the vending machine.

Angelo's cousin cursed.

She was mad about something.

He imagined that she was distressed over his laundry filing methods.

He stood up from the toilet, opened the door softly. He walked over behind her, thinking about the best possible way to startle her without seeming like he had really planned this out. He could see some of the hair growing on the back of her neck, not long enough to put up in a barrette.

Let me do that.

He walked over to some of the laundry, and began tossing it into the far left corner of the room. He could hear her gasp, then caught, out of the corner of her eye that she was holding her hand against her collarbone.

It took her a good amount of time to explain that the reason for this behavior was a result of startle due to the fact that she had assumed, during her original entrance that she would be alone in the room for the duration of the cleaning procedure.

Which sounded about right.

He smiled his smile, saying that it was no big deal.

He realized after saying this that it was not, really, a response at all.

He took out his laundry bag, assuring her that she could relax while he picked up.

He was delighted that she chose to spend this time sitting on the corner of his bed with her hands folded together resting on her lap. She laid back and sighed, tried to converse with him while he worked.

* * * * * * * *

He placed his hands against the window so that they would block out enough of the light that he could examine the interior of the car.

This one was too dirty inside, it wasn't what he was looking for.

He decided to save himself some time, somehow.

He surveyed the remaining cars in the lot. He rubbed his hands together.

That reddish one.

He walked over to the car, looking inside. He saw a stack of magazines, some cables of some sort, baby seat.

Curse you, car owner.

What about the big one over there?

One of these was going to have an alarm on it, that he would trigger somehow, and he would be done for, put behind bars.

He cupped his hands against the window, breathing heavily enough that he could not see inside. This guy, whoever, definitely liked soda. He moved over to the other colored small one, seeing something on the dashboard. He examined the flyer, though he could not really make out the meaning of the company logo.

It was yellow and black, but what color should it be?

He figured that this was probably what he was looking for.

He took the pen out of his pocket, writing down the letters onto his back wrist.

A job well done.

He walked back to the hotel door. He picked through his pockets blahblah key card blahblah opened blahblah inside.

Success.

No one was at the register, so he felt completely at ease. He looked through the cubbyholes for a directory, finding several items of strange significance. A small vial of cologne, which meant that Angelo's odor was not, entirely, just a bad biology, a lighter, which meant that someone wanted to light things.

A toothbrush?

He found the directory inside the bottom cabinet. He took it up onto the desk, then wheeled the chair over so that he could relax.

He sat down, pulling the directory into his lap. He consulted his hand.

He found the listing in the businesses section. He took the phone up, dialing the correct number.

A few rings.

The guy answered.

The guy put him on hold before he could say anything.

He held the receiver against his ear with his shoulder. He took out the cologne, opened it.

Nasty, that's the one.

He dabbed some onto his index finger, rubbed it into his neck.

The guy took him off hold.

Could you wait a second?

He put the cologne back.

He looked over at the elevator area, then outside.

He closed his eyes, sighed.

He was sorry about that, he's a very busy man, the reason that he called was he just wanted to ask a question.

Did they rent cars?

The guy said, oddly, that this was the case.

That was all he wanted to know.

Did he want to rent a car?

Not at the present moment, but he was considering it. The guy said that he should give a call back when he made his decision.

Click.

He looked out at things and felt good with himself.

* * * * * * * *

He explained, pretty much, that he had bought the microphone and everything at twice that price at this same establishment, and not so long ago that the economy had completely collapsed and everything was now worthless.

He had dealt with this man before, he suspected.

This was not a decent man. The man had a dirty white beard and everything like that, and went into streams of talk in some stupid, I'm-a-dirty-man, language.

He did not move his eyes from the counter, half closing them to communicate something about his general being. He began pondering which items he would break that would amount to an equal or greater value than the money he deserved. A baby guitar, that thing, a stereo.

And the man's fingers, why not?

He should first explain his views about violence in these troubled times.

He waved his hand forward for a while. The man stopped.

He brought his fist down onto the table as hard as he wanted to.

He did not say anything after that, but the man smeared his lips up, and contemplated the fist.

Wait, what I meant was

He brought his fist down onto the table as hard as he wanted to, which was much harder now. He could feel that the bottom knuckle of his small finger was not having a good time. He really wanted to stick his fist into his pocket, and rub it against his thigh. But, no, not the time for that.

Sorry buddy.

He explained that, as a human being, he was returning this item, which was faulty. He expected to be compensated in the full amount that he had paid for it.

Was the machine faulty? He wondered.

He indicated the tears in the microphone grill, and explained that it erases his tapes.

The man said that he had broken it then.

He wanted to say; Haha– it's not really broken at all, so I didn't break it– but that seemed inopportune.

The man's eyes went up, and then the man explained that

he did not have a receipt for the purchase.

Oh?

He pressed the button to make the thing pop up, and then took the receipt out of the deck. He handed it over. The guy studied the paper, trying to find some error that he had made.

Yes, that's right, I've got paper.

You're done.

Now was the perfect opportunity to remove his fist from the table and put it into his pocket like he wanted to do. He rubbed it against his leg, surprised at something to do with himself. He could hear the whistle of air pumping in and out of his nostrils.

He realized that couldn't think of anything to do. He wished the guy would just stop looking at the receipt.

He explained that he would be waiting right here. He went over to one of the corners and looked at several items as though he were shopping intensely. After a while, the man yelled out something about the whole fist thing, the authorities etcetera. Bah.

* * * * * * * *

Angelo came out from the desk to see him.

Whose car is that?

It's mine.

He puffed up, then stepped over to the side so that Angelo could get a better view of it. Angelo waved, then turned to walk back to the desk, saying that the car was not well constructed.

He looked out the window.

Angelo added that those cars always stop working for some technical reason. Obviously a jealous lie.

He made a crude gesture, then walked over to the elevators. He began wishing that he had parked the car in a spot that he would be able to see from the window of his room. He stepped into the elevator, he took out the complimentary key chain that had come with the rental.

He liked that too.

He took out his room key so that he could place it on the key chain. Why was this thing not moving up?

Evidently it was not so well constructed. Not like his new car!

Or,

He pressed the button that would take the elevator up to

the second floor. He took the key, sliding it between the two strips of metal that would hold it there. He then circled the key around the ring until it was settled, during which time the door to the elevator opened. He stepped out into the elevator area, but did not move to his room until he had finished with the key chain.

He put his finger through the ring so that he could twirl the keys while he walked over to his room. He stopped walking.

He made a triumphant pose that emphasized his muscle definition.

He walked down the hall, holding his hands behind his back, which he had seen someone respectable do somewhere before. He used this new key chain that he had and unlocked the door, and went inside to relax for awhile after that nerve racking drive.

He set his passport, as well as a copy of the papers down onto the desk, considered filing them in his dresser for safe keeping, then placed that key chain that he'd gotten, as a complimentary gesture, on top of the both of them, satisfied that, no matter how strong a wind came through the hall, it would serve well as a paperweight.

He took off his jacket, then got onto the bed.

Well, that's it for today, I guess.

Hmm, it seems I overestimated how long that would take.

By several hours.

He knew that he could not trust the hotel clock, which he had unplugged several times in the past. He guessed that, it was, darkish, well it would be a, some time, until the day was over. He studied the atmosphere for some telltale signs of the sunset, which amounted to various colors and seeing the sun go down.

He felt some pressure in the upper part of his nose, but he could breathe correctly through it, for now, at least. He could not really tell what the feeling meant. So he could not think of something he could do that would relieve it.

Two

He tried his very best to find two reasonably clean socks that were matching colors. He had laid the two that he found first, one white, one black, on the pillow.

There was one underneath the bed.

He folded it, to test how firm the fabric was.

That, is a dirty sock.

He decided to go with mismatched socks. It wouldn't be that noticeable.

And, if someone noticed, why were they looking at his socks anyway? They should just mind their own business.

He was incredibly unhappy when he looked down at his feet. Someone would definitely see that these two were not the same color.

Pulling on his nicer shoes, he remembered watching a program when he was younger or something. He could not remember the specific show, or the time that he was watching it, or what scene it was, what was happening etcetera, he couldn't remember much actually. Anyway, he knew that there was probably some piece of art or drama that made a big point of having the strange character's socks mismatched.

With the shoes on, it was not really apparent that the socks didn't match. This, added with the length of his pants gave him some serious confidence.

He was just wearing some socks.

Mind your own business.

He shook his pant legs down, boldly taking the door handle into his hand. He took several steps into the hallway before lifting his head.

His mind did not register at first that he was seeing something interesting. It looked like two people were standing against a wall, which was something he had seen before.

He noticed the way that they were moving in smooth patterns. He slowed his walk down, coming to a stop without thinking about it, a matter of pure animal instinct.

The woman pinned against the wall had closed her eyes.

Neither of the two had noticed him, he did not have to hide.

They were an attractive couple. It was a classy performance. The girl was attempting to hold a cigarette in her hand, but the guy was gripping her forearm, holding it against the wall, above her head. The cigarette dropped. The guy's other hand was wrapped around back, probably down her skirt, but he couldn't really see. Her other hand was wrapped around the guy's head, messing up his hair.

Hey this is great.

He tried to remember if he had seen them check in, but could not recall.

His door slammed shut behind him.

The girl let go of the guy's hair, pulling her arm down. She looked over at him. She looked like she would be angry in a few seconds. The guy stopped, but could not find the disturbance.

Time to go.

He walked down the hall the opposite way of the elevator, which was not very convenient. He began clapping his hands loud enough that those two could definitely hear him. They couldn't really come after him about that, considering he was perfectly within his rights.

He turned his head back, bringing them into his periphery. They were standing straight; the guy was shaking his head, looking at the floor.

* * * * * * * *

Let's take this stroll to a new level of intensity. He crossed down the block to walk in the woods behind the stores.

Half because he did not like the look of a few pedestrians. Another half because he was a very inquisitive sort of person.

The fauna here, it is somewhat fascinating. I believe this is called a stick, and this is called garbage. Of the bottle strain, of course.

He tried to kick the bottle over toward the asphalt, but missed. He lacked the ambition to go back and do it correctly, as, really, it was not the most important of his goals in life. He grabbed onto one of the saplings, but found that there was some junk on it. He wiped his hand against his jacket until the goo lost its adhesive quality.

It was still there, of course.

He made some sounds with his mouth.

They were entertaining, for a while.

He stopped so as to crack his back to see if that would help. No. He continued walking. The thought crossed his mind that he would probably be confined to a chair at some time in his life. He gave himself a rough estimate of ten years from now.

Unless he started eating celery or something.

He could see that the path through the woods forked off leading to the back of, I guess that's a, grocery store. People do have to eat. He looked over at some of the housing areas that he could see through the trees on the other side. He figured that there was probably a liquor store as well. He stopped to see if he had brought enough money with him to buy a bottle of wine, knowing that he hadn't, but maybe he might have.

He only had some coins, but, maybe, no.

No, it is just not going to happen. He closed his palm, sticking it into his pocket, letting it loose so that the coins dropped into the cloth. He kept walking and so on.

Hey there are two guys out on the receiving dock!

They're just chatting, incredible.

He nodded at them, but did not know what he was agreeing with.

He staggered around for a time.

Would it be nice to be drunk out here in the wild?

Probably not such fun.

He watched a posting on one of the trees. From its coloration he insinuated that it told him not to trespass, or maybe not to dump. Someone had vandalized it in the corner, which was good.

He decided that this walk was over, but did not turn around. He looked for a path that would lead him back to the sidewalk. There was one beside him that lead into the residential area, but he did not feel like doing that.

He found what he was looking for at a dead end of road. He stepped up onto the guardrail so that he could cross onto the pavement, seeing a way he had gone before ahead of him.

* * * * * * * *

There's the hotel, he held his breath. Yes, there it is, that's the hotel he's staying at, yes. He placed his hands into his pockets, drawing in his breath, looking at the pavement beneath him, which seemed to be moving fast, but when he looked back at the hotel it did not seem that he was making any progress.

Hey hotel, I want to talk to you, wait right there.

He walked some more.

He felt pressure building in his wrist, which he rotated. This did not do anything. He resorted to pulling the individual fingers. He hiccupped, hoping that it was an isolated event. He was now crossing the street, which meant that he was getting closer, but he had never timed himself, as he did not have a wristwatch.

And he had never thought to do so.

For the time saving aspect of the route, he decided to walk

over the mulch. That definitely saved several seconds of his life, which he could later use doing some great stuff. He saw the retaining wall in front of him, which he could bypass, if he really wanted, by climbing.

He hiccupped again; it was a painful experience. He tried counting off some time increments before he took his next breath, but it did not work out that way. He ended up reciting something that he remembered from etcetera. It rhymed and everything.

He made some eye contact with the reception guy, pointing his index finger at him through the glass. This gesture indicated that he had some serious business that needed attending. He fished through his pockets, found the key card.

He swiped it through in a professional or expertesque way.

He hiccupped, but he was able to control it.

When he came into view he could see that the guy was already leaned over on the desk, looking at him in an interrogative way. He checked around, making sure that no one was there.

He said that he was leaving for a while. He wanted to cancel his room so and so on the second floor.

The guy asked where he was going.

He explained that he was leaving, but that he would like, when he came back, to have the same room. Or the one next to it, at the same rate he had been paying.

Preferably the one next to it, he choked.

He pressed his fist against his lips, winced.

The guy explained that this would not be a problem.

He told the guy to have the forms or whatever ready for him in the morning. He walked over to the elevator. While he waited he took the room key off his key chain so that it would be ready for tomorrow. The elevator opened, he stepped inside pressing the right number without looking.

He hiccupped again, he thought he had finished with those. He scheduled a water drinking therapy when he got to his room. He would probably just drink from the tap. He was thirsty too so it would get that done. He walked into the elevator waiting area, key in hand.

* * * * * * * *

He looked through the window, up into the windows of the

house. They were dark at this hour, which was not too late. He hoped that they were asleep. He tried to stretch his legs out, but it was no luck. The best position he could make was to let his legs drip into the leg resting space.

He could feel the zipper of the pants that he was using as a pillow digging into his neck. He could not get to them without lifting up his head.

Someone was going to bother him.

He was positive.

He looked down at the space between the seats of the car. There was not much room down there, but someone would be less likely to see him. In the center of the floor, there was a large bump, which would destroy his back, but not forever.

Would it be worthwhile?

He imagined that he could lie down in the space, unpack all of his clothes and cover himself up completely. There was a space beneath the front seat of his car that he could use for air. To any passersby it would look as though the owner of the car just had a lot of clothes stuck in the back seat.

He must be a real fashion sensitive person.

That is going too far. It was all clean laundry, and he had spent the better part of half an hour packing it in an organized way.

He had parked in an unrestricted, park overnight if you like, area.

This, it seemed, should comfort him.

He muttered a stream of profanities. Not only did he have to sleep in this uncomfortable position, he also had people that would hassle him. His testicles were probably going to get frostbite too. It felt as though he was getting a terrible deal.

He had done his share of work in the past.

He wished that he were incredibly drunk. That really would solve everything. He would fall asleep quicker, probably a higher quality sleep, and anyone who hassled him would think that he was just being a responsible citizen or whatever and that he had done this so he would not run over a teenager who had just come from that dance, kissed the pretty girl.

He wished that he lived with the savages, they would have just banished him and let him go. Then he could sleep, and the only catch was that eventually he would be eaten by a fox.

Those are some devious animals, they say.

He could see his breath.

It was so cold.

He rolled up the window, which he had let down a little so that he would not suffocate. He leaned into the front seat, taking out two more shirts that he would use to cover his neck. He got back down, flattening each item of clothing so that all three shirts covered him completely. He stuck his hands underneath the pillow thing, where it was warmer.

* * * * * * * *

Driving on the roads in this area was a good time. He could see agricultural stuff, and some of the buildings looked old or something. He poured the cup into his mouth, finding that there was nothing left but ice. He chewed on some of it, feeling the stuff give way to his powerful jaw. He could see ahead of him that he was going to get to go downhill.

He put the car into neutral.

It came to a stop.

Then it started going backwards.

He was curious to see where this whole backwards thing would go, but he needed to save gasoline. He changed the gear, going forward once more. It was not until he felt in his stomach that he had crested the hill that he placed the car back into neutral. He went down the hill, but was somewhat disappointed at how slow the car moved.

He saw that he was going to get to cross over a tiny bridge. He turned his head to the side. There was some ice along the bank of the stream but he was moving too quickly to make a thorough analysis. He changed the gear again so that he could drive up the hill.

He saw that the road was going to swerve. He needed to make sure that it was going to swerve in a desirable direction. He had been driving North for the past hour or so, so he wanted to drive East for an equal amount of time.

He used his imaginary compass, which he had copied from a map during his juvenile state. It told him that the direction he needed to turn, if he was going north, was to the right. This road was about to turn West, or, as some people call it, left.

He felt that he needed to urinate.

The best thing was that he could pull over onto the side of the road. He waited until he got to the top so that he could look ahead, check to see how long the road went that way. He took the key out of the ignition, felt the buzz of the engine die out. He opened the door, walked around the front of the car, pushing the keys down into his shirt pocket.

He tried to pee on a rock, his accuracy was uncanny.

The rock changed from a dusty gray to a sleek blue, the urine running down its back into the gravel, blessing everything with improved color.

Would it freeze? If so, how long would he have to wait around to see this?

He could not make out how long the road was going west, due to geography. It was not such a loss of progress, as he could probably find a road going Northeast if he put his mind to it.

Back to the car.

He could have bought that map.

He started the car back up, sank into the back of his seat, and went further on his way.

* * * * * * * *

The stool was not suited for someone to turn on it, having a couple grooves on it that tried to make him face the bar. This was an upsetting etcetera, as he was trying his best to talk to the girl comfortably. He twisted his back into a position that, for a moment, under the excuse of getting settled into a new position, allowed him to take a long look at the side of her left breast, exposed through her sleeve.

He was drunk enough at that time to think that he should have every right to lean in and give it a little kiss, in a perfect world.

To live in such a place.

Sigh.

So anyway, yes I am passing through. This plppp looked fashionable plppp. She nodded.

Yeah she comes here all the time. He could see that she had dyed a streak of her hair red, for some reason. She had done something or other to this strand that allowed it to swing around, always falling over her eye. She had a kindof oval thing going on with her face, she kept closing one eye.

He made a practice of repeating her name over in his mind so that he would remember it while she talked. Rebecca Rebecca rebbeca

oh yeah?

berecca rebecca

your friends, over there, rebecca hey let's wave at them.
rebecca
what a good time
He was positive that he would not forget it.

One of the famous things about women is that they prefer you remember their name. Even when it is not a natural gesture, it is better to just do it!

Do this to relieve:

Lonesomeness, lack of bed, stiff neck, excess libido, odd situations.

Haha, like medicine!

She gave him some good tips about what there was to see.

He swore that he would put these to good use, though he was just passing through.

He tried his best to steer the conversation over to the fact that he had nowhere to stay that evening, but wanted to dress this up a little.

He had not yet checked in to a hotel.

She started recommending some good hotels? He kept saying such things as that sounds a good one, and where is that located? He felt he understood that she was explaining that she did not feel blah yet with him. Which was her right.

He kept trying, halfheartedly. He came up with a few jokes that really made her laugh.

Her friends indicated that they needed to go. She apologized. A final leap, telling her, as a matter of fact, that he would love to stay with her tonight.

She did think it over for some time. She wrote down her phone number on a napkin for him, left.

He put this into his pocket while she was looking back at him.

He eyed the something. He pulled out the number, wrote rebecca over top. The bartender complimented him on the nice number, which trampled his dream of walking out on the bill.

* * * * * * * *

The proprietor went somewhere into the office or whatever to check. He resumed eating the soup that had been recommended as something he needed to try. It had some eggs in it, some noodles, meat, and various vegetables. It was alright, but he had already picked out all the chunks of meat.

The guy came back with a big smile on his face, holding

the road map out to him.

Sweet benevolence.

He asked for a pen and piece of paper so that he could make the necessary notes.

He drank the last of his water.

There was a highway that he could get to if he traveled strictly north for some time. Until now, he had been blind.

His route until now had not been as accurate as hoped. He was off track, and his destination was actually further north than presumed.

There is the pen, use this paper place mat for paper, oh thank you thank you, sweet man.

He wanted to trace the route that he would need to follow straight off. The paper was opaque, and he could not see the map underneath it. He committed himself to drawing up a reasonable version of the information provided by the map. He labeled intersections and such, which he stopped doing as he progressed, figuring that the highway would have signs.

He looked up, finding no one in front of him. Water. He looked back down at his drawing. It was not a very accurate reproduction.

The guy set down a second glass of ice water in front of him. Free of charge.

Thanks.

How many times had he thanked this guy already?

He pushed his hand down into his pocket, drawing his finger across the seal of the envelope, then underneath it. He pulled one of the pills into his fist. Done and done and done, he swallowed the water.

He put spoonfuls of broth into his mouth. While he was doing this he tried his best to get a good memory of the map.

He was absolutely positive that he knew it by heart.

Where are you from? Oh yes, that's where the suspension bridge crosses the river before the highway splits in two.

He took out his wallet, and counted out enough to pay for the soup. He left a decent gratuity, as the guy had gotten him a map and everything.

He turned his head over to the window. He could not quite see his car. He debated whether he wanted to get back on the road so quickly. It was too cold to walk around.

He decided that he would look the map over for another

twenty minutes or so. That would give him some extra time to sit at the counter.

He would just say that he was a meticulous organizer.

Which is true.

If he ordered coffee that would probably give him some extra time too. He had seen people take forever to drink their coffee. It was acceptable to take forty minutes to an hour even.

Three

He returned to the coffee sitting on the hood of the car, clapped his wrists together. He hopped in place for a little while, trying to rouse his heart or whatever. He could see the steam rising out of the lid of the coffee. He sniffed, wiped his nose. He looked over to the highway above him. He could hear the traffic, and decided to take his time. He looked over to the curb.

Hello.

Anon, the good-looking hero man bends his back low.

In the year etcetera, darkest day of, the emperor.

Stirring the plastic of the cigarette package.

With a matchbook. He rattles it or something.

Hears news of echo, parting its lip to find.

Two free cigarettes. Hooray.

He decided to save one of the cigarettes for right now, to go along with his coffee. The matchbook had some interesting shapes on it, and yes, four matches.

That means two matches per cigarette, in the mathematic sense.

He cupped his hands together to protect the tiny flame from the horrible world. He puffed. The tobacco cracked or whatever, telling him that he was succeeding. The first bit of smoke came down his lungs. He inhaled again.

He dropped the match taking the cigarette into his hand. He coughed several times. His lungs were pulling inside out. He coughed out smoke into his hand. He opened his eyes, watching it lift up until it disappeared into the daylight.

Or was that just warm breath?

Having decided to take some time before he took another puff, he made flatulent sounds by squeezing air through his upper lip. He held his hand against the coffee, judging that it would still be too hot for maximum pleasure. He found himself unable to make the sounds with his lip anymore, and began to wonder exactly how he had done it a moment ago.

He sipped the coffee. It was not that bad if he blew on it and sucked his cheeks. He took the cigarette out. Hopefully, the two chemicals combined would give him some intense energy. He will be able to run the rest of the way, carrying the car on his back.

The cigarette had gone out.

He needed to take a class or something on how to do this.

He used one of the remaining matches, sad that he would not have three to use on the other cigarette. The first one went out before he could transfer the flame. He now would have only one match left. He would have to be cautious. He rubbed the match head against the flint on the back of the book. He was quick about it. The match went out. He puffed.

He did it!

He kept it going by continuously sucking in air. His throat hurt, but this was the way it would have to be done. He had only one match left, after all. He took a sip of the coffee, and tried his best to sit on the bumper of the car.

* * * * * * * *

He clicked his teeth. The car in front of him pulled up a little.

Here we go.

Then stopped.

He looked through his side window. He could see three girls gabbing about something in the red car a few over from him. They were probably going to a concert or something.

The tough looking guy was probably not so tough. Did he want to fight? Shall we see who, in the end, is the champion of the world? Will it be you or I?

He was extremely irritated by this whole traffic thing. The world was so crowded. If only he could afford to rent an airplane. He looked into the side mirror.

He saw a woman pulling out onto the shoulder of the road so that she could sneak past everybody. He made extreme eye contact against her, but she did not look. She drove slowly ahead of him, not fast at all, but he himself was completely stopped.

He held down the horn of his car, then began cursing at her. She looked away. How stupid and heartless you are. She probably needed to get home so fast because she needed to have sex with some plutocrat that she liked. She could at least look over at him and respond to his curses.

Up ahead she tried to pull back into the lane. She got in! Here he was, a multi-cultural ambassador of sorts, having his hard earned progress stolen by some etcetera.

He pulled his car onto the shoulder so that he would block anyone who tried to get past him.

Haha.

I am justice, back from the dead.

He ended up at an angle. He could see the forest off that way. The people on the other side of the road, going south, he confirmed, were moving much faster. If only he could go south. If only the world were round in a more practical way.

He felt, without actually seeing it, that a car was trying to squeeze by on the shoulder of the road. Lala, he did not care. The guy blared his horn, he looked over.

It was another woman! What was going on?

He gestured something that probably looked obscene, but had no actual meaning. She was just going to have to wait. Unless she had been shot, or was having a baby, and then, possibly, he would let her by.

He turned his rear view mirror so that he could study her expression without craning his neck.

She was wearing sunglasses, her mouth was stretched out. She had hair and all that, both hands squeezing the steering wheel.

With hatred.

For him.

Ha ha ha, slowly.

He pulled ahead a little, being extra careful to occupy both his lane and the shoulder of the road. There was no way she would be able to get by now. She even pulled her car into the lane behind him. He exhaled, picked at some crust on his nose, considered taking the shoulder like everyone else would.

No, he would not abuse his power.

* * * * * * * *

Yeah, it really was not that comfortable.

He titled his head back so that he could not see, really, the extent to which he had cracked open the window above his head. He lifted the empty can up, against the glass, then moved it upward to discover if the space were large enough to accommodate his littering impulses.

The can would not fit through the window.

So he rolled the window down.

The can dropped out of the car, falling onto the asphalt beneath it.

Someone is going to hear that.

And I don't care, really, that much.

He opened the next beer, wondering if this would be enough to knock him out for a few hours of sleep, or if he would have to drink the remaining three.

The fact that he was still enjoying the taste was enough to tell him that it probably would be some time before he vomited all over himself or whatever, then urinated in his pants, unconscious.

Not that it had to go that far, he was a sleepy sort of guy.

And these were some high quality pants.

The whole thing seemed such a process. He will be the most famous and wealthy man ever. He will invent a sleeping pill that gives you a hangover, and often gets you in trouble. He felt that he should be crying, or doing something that involved being a human. To this point, he began to mumble several phrases such as, the girl did not quite get it, all right, kitten, and death to something, but none of these lead anywhere.

Yes, yes, exactly it, but, what breed of kitten?

He needed to prop himself against the door, if he was going to retain his sipping power. The handle was digging into his neck, and he considered several different postures that could relieve this, possibly.

He thought again about just how intoxicated he would have to be to fall asleep to wake at an appropriate hour to carry on. The odd thing about it was that, if he succeeded, his sober self would not recognize completely what a hard job it had been to do this favor.

I had a few last night, I don't remember.

He heard a couple talking as they walked down the street.

He tried to lift himself up in his seat, spilling beer onto his shirt. What a tragedy. He began sucking on the shirt so that the beer would not freeze to his chest. He became engrossed in this act, and hardly noticed the couple passing by his window, probably trying their best not to look at him. The taste of beer, when combined with unwashed cotton and sweat was pronouncedly salty.

The saliva in the shirt settled on his chest.

Not pleasant.

He looked through the front windshield to the couple.

Ah, they're holding hands.

You darlings, I love you, here, have some shirt.

He picked the beer up from the divider between the two front seats, snickered.

* * * * * * * *

He sat down on the curb by one of the pumps, knowing that if he brought the bag of chips into his car, the packaging was going to be there for some time. It was better to just eat them here, and throw them out before he got back to things.

He pulled the bag apart.

No one would ever understand just how slightly disappointed he was at the scarcity of contents inside the bag. The food company had purposefully filled it with compressed air just to bamboozle him, take his money.

Ah, but they tasted so delicious that he forgave them.

In the future just tell him the truth, we've gotten to that point in our relationship. It just disturbs me that your chefs are so meek, they feel that I will not purchase their creations without being manipulated into doing so.

One of the teenagers going into the gas station decided to make fun him, try to get a few points at his expense.

The kid asked him something about his chips?

He responded, a little late, but entirely naturally, that they had more nutritional value than the kid's sister.

The others laughed at that, the kid looked embarrassed.

I win.

They walked inside.

For the next minute, he was completely infatuated with what he had just said. He marveled at how clever it was, how quickly it had come from the recesses of etcetera. He is a real talent at that type of thing. He wondered if he could find a job supplying clever responses to say when people are trying to get you.

Following this, he felt that he was old enough that he should never have to dignify anything said by anyone under the age of thirty with a response.

The chip thing was getting a little old.

He threw the rest into the garbage, then stood up. He stretched his back, then moved his hands through the air, very smoothly, almost spiritually so.

He watched the sign for the gas station, which was green and had a jungle cat or something on it.

It didn't do anything that interesting.

He continued his exercises, moving his hands to his chest and closing his eyes. He then removed the weight from one of his feet.

He then looked at his car, which still had the pump stuck in the fuel tank.

He walked ten steps, roughly, toward the car, then got nervous for some odd reason. He walked back to where he had just been standing, though it really made no difference which exact location he procrastinated from.

He went over and got into the car, mostly because he did not want to be in public when the teenagers walked out of the store, in the event that the kid had thought up a stupid retort.

He did not take the pump out of the tank, which he would have to do.

Someday.

He knew that he would have to get on the road, get into the good lane, avoid peril.

He was not up for that just yet.

* * * * * * * *

He had not made the appropriate notes on the exact location he had parked in, figuring that he would certainly recognize it. It had definitely been in a brick type of area, and he recalled that there was a laundry service nearby.

And, well, that was it.

He imagined that this place was diagonally down-left of his car, but he did not know to what exact coordinates he would need to something.

However.

He took the key out of his pocket, remembering that there was a device attached to it that would trigger his car alarm, for such emergency situations as these. He clicked the button.

He turned his ear out.

His ear reported that many things were audible, but made no mention of a car alarming sensation.

He made an extended smile at the girls passing by the shoe store. He thought that he might ask them if they knew where he could find a brick type area. But, no, he could at least see if this alarm tactic would get him anywhere. The girls stopped to look down at a stack of complimentary newspapers.

He was able to decipher that they liked this newspaper.

He said something along the lines of 'oh there it is' then took one of them up as he continued on his way. He resisted the temptation to look back and check if this had made him seem attractive.

While he walked down the street, he clicked the button several times per second. He stopped doing this, fearing that he would wear out the battery before he found his car.

How far off track could he have gotten?

He turned the corner at a gray stone building that was, most likely, a bank or something. Some politic radicals were passing out surveys. He responded to this by walking around them in a way that conveyed that he would not even hear them out.

He definitely had walked down that street there, as it was downhill, and he remembered seeing that little bit of clothing in the window.

This investigation is paying off.

He crossed the street and went up the hill, consciously lingering by the window of the clothing store to see if it gave him any more information.

He clicked the button?

Not yet.

He remembered the distinct sensation of sunlight on his neck, which was not present on this street. He went up a little more then turned to the right when his intuition wanted him to do so.

He turned back, as his intuition was wrong.

He avoided eye contact with someone that wanted to ask him for change.

Up ahead, a restaurant with an outside dining area, not currently in use. He definitely had seen one of these before, in his lifetime. A guy inside was trying his best to look pretty. The waitress had, in his professional opinion, excellent breasts.

He felt that he needed to turn right here, not by intuition, but because something else. He saw a car that looked like his, but wouldn't respond to the alarm thing.

He gathered up the garbage in the car, debating whether or not it would be better to organize it in one place or just get rid of it altogether. He filled the white sandwich bag with cups, an empty package of cigarettes, some receipts and coins of no real value.

He did not see a garbage can on this block, and decided to drive the car slowly down the road until he found one.

He turned on the headlights.

What a talented driver.

He found, at the end of the block that someone had left their trash can by the curb.

He placed the car in park, and rolled down the opposite window. The only chance he had was to throw the garbage at just the right angle that it would land inside.

He threw the bag.

It fell off the opposite side of the can.

He frowned, wondered what exactly he should do about this. Was it really the right subject to have a moral crisis over, if so, was it the right time and place? Such questions.

Would never be answered.

Waha, he drove off.

At least he had tried to get it in the can.

And he had come close, no less.

He looked over to the signs, checking to see if one indicated the shortest route back to the highway. No.

Let's leave it to fate then. He turned left.

He saw that this was not the best choice, as the highway was to the right.

He executed a skilled I might have looked as though I was turning left, but it was just my way of turning right thing. No one in the opposing lanes seemed to mind that much. They understood that he was an important guy, with stuff to do on the highway.

Yes, yes, my daughter is in the pageant this evening, opening night, you understand.

And the uncle is a veteran of a few wars, you understand, I need to drop by and give him some medals.

He shot down the street, examining the signs ahead to see which turn would take him to the North.

Success once again, he succeeds at many things.

He stopped at the stoplight, success, and allowed the dirty looking fellow to cross in front of him. The guy was holding a box of miscellaneous junk. He got bored a little, so he tried to wonder what the junk could possibly be for, but came up with no soluble answer.

I can go now.

He drove up the ramp, watching the barrier above him get lower as he got toward it. He could see the lights coming off the traffic in both directions. He thought about how incredibly personal this moment was in his life, about how this will be what he tells a fiancé on their wedding night.

What's wrong, dear?

I drove once, up a ramp.

In another country.

He began to fear that this might actually become true.

Oof.

He would have to make up some stuff.

* * * * * * *

He relaxed onto the bed, then reached his hand over to the control for the television. It was mounted onto the dresser. They did not want him stealing it.

The television itself was resting on the shelf, unfastened to anything.

He did not know what he thought about that. He leaned over to examine the control, finding the power button was a convenient red. He pressed it down.

Some leaves and stuff, a voice speaking quickly. Perhaps an educational program.

What?

The guy on television looked almost exactly like his dad!

He marveled for some time, then corrected that this guy was much shorter. He looked through the remaining channels, one advertising satisfied women or something, intriguing, but that turned out to be caused by the use of a particular type of product.

Boo.

The next channel, news.

The next channel, gray blips and noise.

He had seen that before. He turned off the television, then looked out to the balcony that he had. It was a bit cold for sitting outside, but it was a nice gesture.

He pulled off his pants, decided to keep his undershirt on while he slept. The feel of the pillow against his neck was soothing. The comforter was pretty hard, and he decided to go without that. He was a real spartan now, he did not even need an extra sheet.

The lamp on top of the dresser gave everything a nice lighting. He turned over on the bed so that he could pretend to procreate with the mattress for some time. It felt nice, he guessed, but it was not very responsive.

He had seen a nearby liquor store, if he liked.

He saw that there was an ashtray on the dresser, which was nice. He would take it with him, so that he could always remember these lovely people at this hotel.

His hair was stiff against the pillow, he needed to take a shower. Could this be delayed, somehow, until the morning? He took his head from out of the sheets, and rubbed his hair until it was softer. It no longer hurt when he pressed it against the pillow.

So relaxing.

Is this when I go to sleep?

He heard a horn outside the window, honking several times. Just when he was getting some sleep done. He should go out and beat that person to death.

Anyhow, it stopped after a time, and he did not have to kill anyone.

He found that, though he liked the idea of sleeping with the lamp on, as electricity was included in the price of the room, it was not going to happen. Not tonight at least. He turned off the lamp, becoming aware of how bright the lights outside the building were.

He rolled over onto his side, trying to fix his eyes on something as they adjusted to the new lighting. He tried rolling them into the back of his skull as though something were wrong with him.

Part 6

(a chance encounter)

One

He took his coffee out to the balcony, to have some coffee on the balcony. He set the coffee on the ground, stepping back inside to grab one of his famous chairs.

It was heavy enough that he decided to drag it.

He slid the door a little more open.

He turned the chair to face the more interesting things than the inside of his room.

Let's get started with this.

He sipped the coffee, concluding by reason of taste that it probably did not have any caffeine. They had fooled him then. As there was only one coffee thing in the lobby. Maybe he was being a little fast about it. Maybe he would drink it down and find that it just tasted strange, and was, in its heart, a good natured ordinary sort of drink.

He did not even know what it should feel like. How would he tell the difference? Maybe he would get all twitchy or such.

He watched the pavement for a time. Then he found that that guy over there was carrying some groceries. He liked the guy's coat, and debated whether to make this admiration known to the world. Nice coat, he called out, but the guy didn't pay him any mind.

He heard some sandal sounds, coming very very rapidly, and kept his eye out for a woman. She came into his view from the left, running. Her bosoms were flopping around in the cotton shirt she was wearing. She was pretty tall, and a little fat. Her hair bounced against her back.

This is the greatest thing ever.

She did not even turn up the street. He continued watching this until it was no longer a viable option. He even stretched up in his chair, taking a long last parting glance at the bosoms, and then they left forever, unless she ever needed to get something from her car or whatever.

He tried, with his imagination, to recapture the greatness of that time in his life now gone forever. He found that his mental picture was not so attractive. In his mind, the breasts flopped around without any integrity, as though they were just two bags taped to the front of her shirt.

 He went back inside, unzipping his bag to reveal his favorite magazine. He took it out onto the balcony with him.

He flipped to one of the better photographs inside. He sipped some coffee.

He tried to make the breasts move by shaking the magazine.

Not an accurate a reproduction.

If only he could see these ones in a state of urgency. That would be even better than today. He tossed the magazine to the side, it flew aerodynamic etcetera to the far end of the deck.

He felt guilty about this while he drank his coffee. Eventually, he stood up, taking the magazine into his arms, and trying to straighten it out. He had damaged the hold of the staple along the magazine's spine. He pressed it in, but the damage was lasting.

* * * * * * * *

He took himself outdoors through the lobby, making some eye contact with the clerk girl that almost cried 'Hey I'm just going outside, we enjoy each-other as human beings.' He found that the light outside the doors was much brighter, as they were tinted brown for some reason.

He decided to go up the street that way, because it seemed a classy walk along the main road. He looked both ways before crossing the street, because it was just the thing to do. He stepped up onto the curb, trying to look at the driver stopped at the sign, to see what he thought of him.

He saw a restaurant across the street that was set up in an elegant way.

That was good to know.

A place that he could get his photographs developed.

Not so much.

He'd noticed before that people were allowed, along this main street at least, to carry open beer bottles, which was, to say the least, an excellent idea. No one was making use of it at this hour. It was still a bit cold outside to have a beer, but he decided that it would be a good time.

He would do it!

As soon as he found a place that sold beer for cheap!

After some time, he saw a ratty looking store to the side of the street corner there. That's the one, without a doubt. He walked over to it, examining the shelves that were blocking his view. The store sold cans, bags of bread, telephones, aha, liquor. He studied this for some time as he was in no rush, he noticed above him, in the crack between the cigarette displays, a tan looking round thing with a mustache.

Ah!

The store guy was watching him through the window.

oh.

how disturbing.

He stepped out of view, and caught his breath, though he wasn't panting or anything. He shook his head, recovering or so and such. He opened the door, seeing the store guy in an elevated area by the window. He immediately set to avoiding any contact with that guy, until he needed his purchases rung up.

He found a small refrigerator in the back corner, full of many different types of beer. They even had one with a recognizable label, which had been translated unrecognizable. He wasn't going to buy it, of course, because it had always tasted poorly in his own language. He took a miniature wine bottle with a bottle cap instead of a cork. This is the one, it was cold in his hand.

He accidentally looked at the guy's eyes while they were interacting. The guy had droopy, nasty kind of eyes. He fished through his pockets, coming up with roughly enough. He left without his change, indicating that he had important things to do.

Outside.

He had to find a means to remove the bottle cap. The eye man probably had an opener at the counter, but well, that, no, not happening. He would find a bench or window. That should work just as well.

* * * * * * * *

He steadied himself against the wall, concentrating his vision on his laundry bag. He jogged up to it and gave it a nice kick. It flew into the corner of the room, scattering some of his laundry onto the floor.

Well, at least that's done now.

What had he been thinking when he entered the room? It had seemed important, invested with etcetera. A good thing to do, but what was it? The dresser.

Ah, he was going to eat.

He went over to the dresser, and picked up the napkins full of complimentary breakfast food. He had made several creamed cheese sandwiches with peanut spread as well. He was a little nervous, because he did not know if it was a winning combination. Particularly after sitting around for a few hours.

He prepared himself for the worst.

He stuck his finger underneath the napkin, allowing it to drop to the floor to reveal the naked sandwich. He took a small bite from one of the corners. He paused, chewing thoroughly, swallowing, and looking out the window.

Mixed reviews, but edible.

He picked up the napkin and placed it in the sock drawer or whatever that he was not using and not going to use. He walked over to the balcony, taking a few bites of the sandwich. He wondered how long this was going to take.

Maybe not too long.

He leaned to the side, so that his face almost touched the glass. From the outside, it would seem that he was watching something with some particular something, desire or such. How fantastic.

And the sandwich, he forced the last bit into his mouth, chewed, and had to swallow twice, is complete.

To make things more interesting for himself, he lurched toward the bed instead of walking like so many do. He stuck out his tongue, and then said a few things with a thin, raspy voice.

He stopped at the bed corner, and wondered if he would be able to fall against it and ricochet back into a standing position. He realized that this would take extreme concentration of the muscle fibers. It did not work out, he slid off the corner of the bed, but retained enough of his own weight on his legs that he did not fall onto the floor, but ended up in a crouching position.

He got onto the bed.

Such energy today.

He etcetera came up with something. He pressed his teeth really hard, and held his breath. He did not have any errands to run. He was not really in the position to enjoy himself, fiscally speaking.

He got off the bed, and went over to his bag. He pondered it or something.

He walked over to the door, opening it. It was cold, the air swept past him. He saw a few plants down in the foyer that were not looking so great. He looked at the concrete walkway leading to the stairs. He turned the thermostat to eight as he went back to the bed. Now passersby would see him on his bed.

Hey, let's buy you a drink and dinner.

* * * * * * * *

He checked the time on the clock, which could be correct or incorrect. The telephone was not ringing yet.

He crossed his legs in front of him.

He put his index finger in front of his lip.

Neither of these had any effect.

Though he could not move the phone from its position, he could easily pick up the clock, and take it with him out onto the balcony, leaving the door open so that he could hear the phone ring when it did. This was not a bad plan. This was a good plan.

He threw the clock between his hands. Then he looked down at the insignia on the back of it. He pressed a button that made the display light up.

Then he made it fly like an airplane, with his hand, over to the balcony.

The chair outside would be wet, still, from the rain or something. And every time he pressed it down, it would do something, and if he sat on it, it would get him wet.

He threw the clock over to the bed, where it landed. He decided that his room could use a good cleaning. This would kill time.

It will kill time.

And I will have a clean room.

He bent over, picked up a few receipts, some packaging.

He placed these items into his pant pocket, he would put

them into the wastebasket the next time he passed by it. He looked for some other thing that required his attention.

He organized his laundry into one particular corner of the room, where he would later stuff it into his laundry bag. He found some more paper underneath his hooded shirt, and some change, which went into his pocket.

Money money.

His pocket was now full enough that it would need to be emptied into the wastebasket. He filled his fist with the stuff in his pocket, and then threw it away.

He heard a sound, not the phone ringing though. Ah, it was the coins hitting the bottom of the thing.

So now he was throwing away money? Is that how he had been brought up?

He dug through the garbage, and then was a genius. He imagined that, by physics, the coins, being tiny and heavy, would gather in the corner, if he titled the basket sideways. He had to shake the basket a few times to allow the coins to get to his hand.

And then there they were.

He pulled his hand out of the garbage, and decided that the next step in the cleaning process would be to wash his hand, because it was now dirty, even though the wastebasket was only filled with paper and stuff like that.

Washing hand is good habit anyway. You can start it at any time in your life, even now. try it out.

He looked at the time on the clock as he passed the bed, then to the phone. He got onto the bed and looked around his room for mess, but he had a hard time recognizing what was out of order.

Two

At the corner of two streets that he couldn't read, he decided to make a strange expression on his face, and hold it for the duration of his walk back to the hotel. He found that the most uncomfortable position was to lock his jaw in place, extend his eyes, bare his teeth, so that he looked like the automated man.

He would like to see what people would think of this.

No one was on the street here.

He kicked his shoes out as he walked. This was getting even better. He let his vision go slack, and his mouth was about to die from prolonged mild discomfort.

He passed an ugly looking lady, he stuck his hand out. What did she think of that? She did not look at him. He started pushing air out of his mouth and made a few frothing sounds. What did she think of that? She had already passed him.

He gave up hope.

Next time he would just something and be done with it.

He paused to examine the fetid blah blah blah of a newspaper soaked in rainwater blah blah blah like a dead blah. He stepped over it, being very careful not to step in the little pieces of it that were all around.

He exhaled a smooth and elegant breath, that he could sense was cold. Almost as good as the air, but not quite.

Hello hello hello, you signpost, I cannot read you.

He saw two young guys driving towards him in a car, they were talking, they were all dressed up. They were going to find some girls. No probably just one girl that they would split. Because that just suited them better, they were not comfortable alone.

He made a big thing of it, so that everyone could see, he pounded his fist lightly on the brickwork as he walked by the building. He stopped this, because the brickwork turned into the glass window of a store, which he could not afford to break.

He stopped at the sign that welcomed him, wondering if he had any need or means to buy anything.

It was a movie place, so, he could not find a reason to go inside. Sorry.

This place ahead of him was closed, but the mannequins looked attractive. He allowed himself to stop, and to stare at the different areas of the mannequin with such scrutiny that any ordinary woman would just slap him then and there if he were looking at her in this way.

Sorry, you are too pale, wooden, and you lack genitals. I truly am sorry Miss.

He heard the great fun, just having a good time, music coming from the restaurant ahead. He could hear it faintly between slurred conversations. He waited for someone to burst out of the front doors, and fantasized using his walking speed to throw a swift sucker punch at this person, for comedic effect.

It would be hilarious, but there might be consequences.

He wanted to pass by slowly, but could not think of a reason to explain himself. He watched the bartender, who was wearing a vest.

He scratched his collar bone, which was dry.

He stopped at the menu, posted in a fancy glass case.

* * * * * * * *

He walked down the staircase, letting his finger drag off some chips of paint on the opposite side of the rail. The last two steps. He jumped, and landed on his feet, like a graceful woodland creature.

He looked at some of the vegetation, not doing so wonderfully. He could see that someone had tied a few of the plants to tiny support beams. He could see through the door, into the lobby, through the lobby, to the street. He pulled on the door.

Such a nice temperature in the lobby. He checked out the mailboxes.

Did he receive any mail?

haha.

Two people were exchanging sad words about how someone famous had died a few days ago or so. The clerk guy rubbed his temple and looked away, the guest was nodding slowly. The clerk blinked, then slid the key and directions to the room over with a respectful slowness.

The guest took the key, then picked up the handle of his suitcase, proceeded to the gardenish area.

Remember the last time at that funeral I went to? I had lost some weight, my suit would not fit properly. Before I put on the belt my pants would slip down. The front button would not hold. There was almost certainly a stain on the jacket, I'm sure there was a tear in the cloth. He went anyway though, people did not notice it as much as he did, if at all. He was not there to hit on women, or look good. He sniffed.

She grinds her teeth and says

something like 'oh, the details that we remember.'

That will shut him up.

He was tearing up a little.

Is he going to cry and be legitimate? Pound his hands and scream out My Feelings or whatever.

Famous guy!

He waits and sees.

He continued down the street, concentrating his attention on a newspaper machine. He could stop and look at the headlines. Would that help?

Of course, he had the reading prowess of a toddler.

He remembered places where he could pick up the paper, skim through it, and only then decline to read.

He muttered something about doing it to the weather, tapped his knuckle against the vending machine. He raised his head up to see if he could make out what awaited him further down the block.

Pretzel stand!

He went through his pockets for change. He looked to the side, committing to memory all the great things about the telephone service store he passed, the restaurant with the classy décor, that sort of thing, before he reached the pretzel stand, studied the prices, sad that he can only afford a small one.

To be sure, he asked the vendor if he could get a regular sized one.

The guy informed him that the prices were posted right there.

He passed over his change. He kept his hand on the counter, looked over to the side. He felt the vendor glance back at him. The vendor came back with a large pretzel anyway, took his change.

He smiled, his eyes sentimental, filled with love for the human grace.

* * * * * * * *

The proposal; if the water is hot enough, does he need to bathe tomorrow?

He ran his hand under the faucet, confirmed that the stuff was nigh scalding. He stuck the rubber stopper into the drain, tossed the towel over to the sink, where it fell onto the floor. He stepped into the growing pool, then bent down, then sat on the rubber mat that was supposed to hold his footing.

He waited for the water to fill the tub, using the time to splash some water onto the upper area of his body.

His hands wandered down onto a gross thing that was growing below his waist. He had noticed it yesterday too, and several times since then. If he pressed his fingers against it, he could feel that it was inflamed, a serious medical matter.

Did he have the courage to resolve it?

He pressed once.

and gave up.

He pressed twice.

Only a champion would be able to withstand this.

He used his fingernail to try and dig up some of the skin covering the gross stuff. Then he tried to pull out a hair that was growing in the center of it. That was even worse.

The water was now up to his back.

Into the fire gentlemen, into the fire.

He pressed with both fingers quite hard, he looked down to see if this was working at all. That is so painful, he even weakened his grip unconsciously. The water was raising, the situation was looking bleak. He pressed once more.

Fire!

Some humor stuff shot all the way up to his forehead.

He was about to wipe it off with his hand. He had the desire to look at himself in the mirror to confirm the fact.

He stood up from the tub, leaning over.

He had to brace himself against the shower rod so that he could lean the distance necessary to see himself in the mirror.

Success.

uh, yes, so I've got some vile stuff on my face.

He felt proud, and giving his reflection a military salute, pulled himself back into a standing position, sat down in the tub. He dipped his hand into the water, sterilizing it, then wiping off his entire face, then sterilizing it once again.

The water was now up to his shoulder bones.

The first thing he used the soap for was to clean off the area where the thing had been. It was still sensitive, but he had done all he can, the rest was up to time.

He was about to start soaping up other parts.

He stopped.

He submerged the soap into the hot water, counting to fifteen or so to kill the diseases.

It was safer now.

That was a close one.

He turned over onto his side, so that the hair on the side of his head would get wet. The water was now up to his upper eye. When he turned back, he breathed through his nose exclusively, feeling how pleasant the steam felt tickling behind his face.

He took the car out of the parking space looked at the shadow of the garage entrance and that sort of thing.

Was he about to collide with the car behind him?

Not really.

He changed the gear, pulling the car forward to the exit. Then he exited, turning toward the right. He consulted the napkin map. He would need to turn onto the road with the corner store, then he would need to continue to a road that he did not know the location of, turn to the right, dadadada, turn left, then he would be on his way to the address.

In this way, he would memorize the directions, know exactly how long it would take to get there for future reference.

No one was letting him onto the road, so he pulled his car out into the middle of the street. This was enough to frighten the black sedan, it slowed down, not knowing what he was up to. He sped into the street, hahaha etcetera, he let his hand out the window so that he could wave and let his fellow motorist know that he appreciated the gesture.

Going the first two stoplights or so was easy, but then he became uncomfortable because he did not know how long he would have to travel on this road, and the street signs were not entirely legible. He took the napkin and held it in the center of his vision.

This way, he could compare the writing on the napkin with the characters on each sign.

Needless to say, this hurt his travel time significantly. Many people pulled around him, one even honked the horn two times or so, until he used his free hand to insult the person. This worked effectively, the car pulled around him, the driver taking great pains to stare as he passed. He tried his best to hide the napkin, so that the guy would not know that he was having a hard time with this direction thing, instead thinking that he drove slowly because it was a thing to do today.

What he wanted most at that time was to catch up with the guy that had just passed him, get in front, slow down once again, repeating this process all day if necessary.

If it came to violence, that would not be all that bad.

Why are you all beat up dear?

Because it is what I deserved. The foreign guy, the dashing, unbeatable in a fight, foreigner, taught me that I should be more considerate.

We are good friends now, I am going to write him a check for our life's savings. Don't try to stop me.

He saw a sign that looked like what he needed, he consulted the napkin. This is probably the correct one, he pulled the car over, turned immediately afterward.

So now he had one finished, two if he counted the first turn that he made. Two turns is a good percentage of the way there.

Three

Just to be safe, he had worn his snappy little suit. No one would suspect him.

He walked down the street, consulting the promotional card that had been dropped in the lobby. He felt that he had seen this address once before, while walking in the vicinity of his hotel. The card indicated that he would receive special treatment once he got to the door.

Who are you?

Promotional guest card?

Ah, right this way, sir.

He checked the bottom of the card. The register girl had read it for him that morning. He tried to pick out which of the words meant Wine, which the register girl had explicitly mentioned, he had asked her several times to make sure that this wine would be served free of charge.

The people at the gallery would probably want to give him expensive wine, because this would set the tone for him to purchase expensive paintings. Tit for tat, as they say.

Hahaha, but I am secretly poor.

He saw what must be it.

A line.

Young people, well dressed.

He clenched his teeth, then examined the lady at the door, she was inspecting a similar card to his own, while two fashionable etceteras waited nervously.

He said;

hello!

Made a little wave to everyone.

He walked by the line, a few people looked up at him. He continued a block or so before turning back. He decided to cross the street, making his second pass from a safer distance.

From this far away, he could see into the window of the gallery. A girl was holding a glass of wine, looking at a painting or whatever.

That's exactly as I hoped.

He continued only a half-block before pausing, hopping once, then crossing the street. He approached the line once again, from his initial direction.

To be safe, he did not say hello to anyone, so that they would not recognize him by voice or his affable mannerisms. He went up to the lady, showing her the guest card. He was just checking to see er if this was the um same number as it says right there above you.

She pointed to the line, telling him that he would have to wait. He put on a big smile, saying that he was checking to see, he would have no problem waiting, he walked to the back of the line, leaving some distance between him and the last person.

He buttoned his suit coat. That worked out nicely.

I'm a big shot, traveling, art collector, guy.

The line moved ahead two steps. Eventually someone came to stand behind him. It was a girl, she stood very close to his back, intimating that she wanted him to close the distance between him and the guy in front.

Not happening.

But, if she wanted, she could grind against his back for a few minutes. We are both free creatures, you can do that.

In that case, it isn't in anyone's interest for him to poke the guy in front.

Laughter et al.

* * * * * * * *

He took an extended sip of the coffee, then crossed his legs like the women do. Knee over knee.

Ouch.

He withdrew his legs, then crossed them in a more cautious way. He looked down through the railing on his balcony to see what was going on today. Not much.

Angry guy with cigarette, newspaper on steps, sunlight.

He set the coffee on the ground, then took the ends of his hooded shirt into his hands. He fiddled with the zipper until it was good, then pulled it halfway up his chest. Now he would not get pneumonia and such unwanted things.

He took the cup, examined some coffee grinds in the bottom. He would need to be inventive with his drinking tactics to avoid ingesting them. The best way to do this is to tilt the cup horizontally, close your lips on the rim, then to slurp out the remaining liquid, blocking out unnecessary solids.

It works well, if that's what you want to do.

He saw a woman walking two dogs simultaneously. How efficient. She carried a bag of feces, which meant that she was half finished.

Approaching the woman was another younger type of woman with a little kid. They exchanged greetings, the dogs pulled toward the kid, wanting to eat him, he supposed, but reached the end of their leash.

This promised an interesting drama.

It came out eventually, though the kid was a bit reticent to tell his mother, that the darling little boy wanted to pet the critter. The dog lady asked the mother which of the dogs would prove the most pettable solution to the boy. The mother reinterpreted this question into childish language.

The answer came in the form of a pointed finger. The black one, please.

The woman gripped the leash tighter, letting the kid draw up to the dog with his hand outstretched.

The dog, retaining only a fraction of its free movement, jumped up to get at the hand. He did not think any actual biting took place, but the kid fell backward in fright, onto the ground, then started wailing a little.

He clasped his hands over his heart.

How adorable, adorable.

Negotiations set in immediately. In order to compensate the emotional trauma of falling down, the dog would have its mouth held shut, and be subject to several seconds of petting. The mother assured the child that this would work out well. The kid reached out.

Pat.

Thank god that we can put this all behind us.

The two women talked for a second or two, while the dog was still being muzzled. He could not overhear exactly what was being arranged. Dinner, conversation, slanders on their respective partners, such an evening.

Some other time.

The dogs looked back at the kid.

He just kept replaying it to himself, smiling, talking about how cute it had been, but he could not really express the reasons. The naked truth;

He loved seeing kids get hurt in petty ways, he guessed.

* * * * * * *

He had noticed before that the door to room one seven could not lock properly. He figured that no one was staying there. He had known this information for several days, but, just now, invented a use for it, as it could be applied to thieving opportunities.

Down the stairs.

He looked around.

Anonymity.

He walked over to the door. The knob felt as though it were locked, remained stiff.

However.

He looked into the room to the opposing window, the curtains were not drawn. He closed the door behind him. Should he close the curtains? Would someone notice that?

Was this going to work?

He decided that it would be best to take the receiver from the phone, dial, then lay flat on the floor out of view. This was executed. He waited for a dial tone. Success. He dialed the international number. Waited. Keep very still.

Ringing.

Success?

He could hear his brother's voice on the other side.

He whispered at first that it was him, then whispered, how are you doing?

His brother asked him what time it was. He was not entirely sure. His brother was doing well, then went into a few things about how exactly he was doing well.

He clarified that he wanted to ask a favor.

He needed some money, he wanted to know if he could borrow some money. He never specified how much money he would need, feeling so ashamed of how much money he wanted. He kept referring to this sum as 'however much you can spare'.

He kept insisting that it would not be so long for him to pay it back.

His brother thought it over.

He also suggested that his brother ask Michael as well, as he had loaned Michael money back in the day. Whatever they could scratch up, he explained. He apologized he apologized he apologized.

His brother explained that he would have to see, but assured him that he should not be sorry about anything.

He felt, who knows, terrible probably.

His brother said that they should go, as the call was costing. He cut him off, assuring that the price of the call would not be a concern. He explained the current situation with the untenanted room.

His brother found that wonderful.

He smiled, agreeing that it was a clever thing he had come up with.

He felt someone passing the window. He tried to become more flat, but it was impossible.

They were free to talk, now that that horrible thing was out of the way.

How are you doing?

His brother said some things about his apartment, doing well then, except that the drains were clogged etcetera. He stared at the pattern on the carpet, a gray cross-hatching with a red border. He pulled his hood over his head, keeping the phone inside it too.

It got around to how he was doing.

He said that he had switched hotels, not bothering to suggest the distance between the two. His brother asked if he was getting by with the locals, in particular those girls pictured in whatever.

* * * * * * * *

He took the coin out of his pocket, settled it onto his fist, then flipped it up into the air. He swatted his hand out to grab it. What a sharp type of man he was. He repeated this twice, but the third time he failed to catch the coin, actually batting it into the traffic to his side.

Money well spent.

He watched the coin settle in the middle of the road. Who would be the brave soul to go fetch it? Or was it just going to be knocked around until it fell into a storm drain?

To be honest, he asked himself neither of these questions.

Instead he looked at the dividing line in the road, said some words a few times, fell quiet, slapped his temple a bit and plodded on his weary way.

Then he went up to the hotel door, made eye contact with the clerk girl.

He did not like the way that the clerk was looking at him. She had something to say. He tried to walk past, just distracted. It could not be good news, obviously, as it involved himself.

She dug around for something. Move quickly.

She called out.

He sighed.

Turn around.

She handed him his message, saying that the guy had called earlier that morning. He thanked her and walked away.

The message was folded up into a triangle. Maybe she had gotten a little bored then. It was actually a very confusing thing, the paper expanded, then expanded again. Lastly he realized that he was holding it upside down.

He turned it over.

Girly handwriting.

He cannot make it tomorrow, will call to reschedule.

This upset him.

He held the note up to his nose, seeing if there were any pheromones on it or whatever.

He thought and thought.

He became upset. He crumpled up the note, throwing it into the garden. What was he going to do now? He was going to have to stay in this hotel longer than he wanted. Why couldn't the guy just cancel his plans? This was a very important thing etcetera. Rude blahblahblahblah.

He gave the banister a good kick. Hard enough that it hurt his toe.

He decided that he needed to keep the note for some reason, legal records or something. He went over to the bushes, started to pick around for it. He pricked the side of his finger on one of the little wooden polls.

He tore the pole out of the ground, scolded it for being a little idiot. He threw it over to the stairwell.

Nothing was going right for him.

He gave up looking for the message.

As he walked back to the stairs, he kicked the poll once

more.

He looked down at his finger, trying to spot the splinter of wood imbedded in his skin. He saw a little gray line sticking up there. He stopped on the stairs.

His nails were not long enough to pinch the wood. He tried to use his mouth power to suck it out, but that did not work out so well either.

Four

Anyhow, yes, what was it that he was doing? He stuck his hands down to the ground, then mashed them between his knees. Then he pulled on his nose for awhile. He took a sip of liquor, he turned the television on, he put that pillow into his lap, then he kicked the mattress with his heel.

He was not in the right state to watch the television. A bunch of friends, talking, problems etcetera.

He tried to pull the remote control off the dresser, so that he could stomp on it, then urinate on it.

He rubbed his face, tried to steady his brains.

What was it that he had said to Natalie? Arr, cruel, how like a gun of him.

If only he could take that back.

He could call her!

Yeah, he could do that.

He took another sip. Life is so difficult. He wished that the bottle were cold or cool.

He needed something to do.

He propped open the door, turning the heater back up.

He was now officially open to suggestions.

He went over to the pile of mail, ruffling it around with his hand. He saw that among the debris was a thin postcard with a half naked woman on it. Ah, thank heaven! He picked up the card, took it to the bed.

He looked down. He recognized the word 'perfume'.

He smelled the card. There was some perfume on it. Imagine that. He put the card to his lips, kissed it. The perfume did not taste so great. But he had kissed right along the woman's back, so that was good. Contrary to its enticing smell, the perfume's taste made him feel pretty nauseous, lying siren, an emetic or whatnot. He took another sip of the liquor.

He drooled on himself a little.

He then clenched his teeth, sucked through them for

much longer than was strictly necessary. He needed to be around some people! He walked over to the door, looking at the surrounding rooms. No one was home.

He could wait.

He took his chair off the balcony, dragging it over to the door, so that he would be ready when someone came up and offered to take him to a social thing.

He brought the postcard too. And the bottle.

He set the chair in the doorway. Before sitting down, he had something he needed to do.

He walked into the outside, held out his arms.

I too can play guitar!

He backed this up with some virtuosic syllables.

Then he sat in the chair. What was that all about? He began to wonder. Who was he trying to deceive? What fascinating material. He was the most interesting person. Following this, he began to berate himself violently. He was not the most interesting person. He decided that, in fact, he was the least interesting person.

I can't even play the guitar.

He saw that someone was entering the garden area. Unable to make out if it was a man or woman, he held his fist out to them. They did not look up.

Hey, up here.

Then they did look up for a moment, but he hadn't a thing to say.

* * * * * * * *

The headache was not something that he noticed entirely at first. He felt a strange weight resting on him so that he could not fully move his neck without exerting himself. His eyes would not fully open, his mouth was dry, he was aware of each of these things, but remained somewhat confused about what was happening.

He realized that he needed to get some water.

If he got water, he would be up.

He scratched at his stubble, but that only irritated him. He closed his eyes. With his eyes closed he could not even concentrate on anything visually to distract him.

He figured that if he got the water quickly, he could get back to sleep.

He jumped out of the bed, then jogged into the bathroom.

Faucet. He put his mouth beneath the faucet, drinking water that was cold at first, then hot.

Go! He turned off the faucet, then jogged back, dove onto to the bed.

He got under the sheets.

His heart was pumping, he had to catch his breath.

He cursed, then threw the pillow at the dark, knocking something glass off something onto the floor. Now he might as well figure out what it was. He threw the covers off the bed in an overdramatic way. He walked up to the television, somewhat able to see his face in it from the light coming through the balcony.

Ashtray.

He picked it up, then examined as best he could if he had caused any cracks in it. It did not seem that he had.

He did not even smoke.

Oh, on occasion, but please.

He tried to crack the ashtray in half with his strength. That did not work.

He tried to crack the ashtray against the corner of the television. That did not work either.

He studied it for a moment, before setting it back onto the top of the television. So, what was next on his itinerary? Did he have a meeting to get to? A doctor's appointment? Several minutes of pushups?

He got down on the floor, to see if a few pushups would do the trick. His socks were still on, they would not give him very good traction against the carpet. He removed them, then resumed his push up position.

Because he was strong, he did several pushups before he felt that he was going to die. He did not even keep count after eight because he moved so quickly that it was impossible to count.

He choked, he felt his face turning red. That's enough.

How pathetic.

He knew that he would have to do several pushups each day if he was going to perfect his physique.

which he was not going to do.

He pulled the sheets off the floor, then got back into bed. His chest was tired, he became sensitive to the stuff resting on it when he pulled the sheet overtop of him. He'd have to wait for his chemicals to settle before he would tire.

* * * * * * * *

He prepared himself ahead of time. He held the receipt in his hand, even though he was still a block or so away from the cleaners. He looked down at it. He recognized that half of the writing on the slip was in one language, half in another language, which were the instructions to the person personally in charge of the cleaning process.

Then there was his signature at the bottom, which was a third language.

What a little gem this paper is, people will find it in a thousand years, absolutely astounded at how everyone pulled together to get his suit washed.

Yes yes, the signature obviously belongs to the king and these markings having been prepared by his trans-national war conquests.

His heels were sticking to his socks.

Could he purchase socks at the cleaners?

He stuck his hand into his shirt, so that he could scratch the area of his armpit, which was dry. A lady inside of a copy shop was looking at him.

He was an attractive guy.

He caught sight of himself in the glass, over top of her, with his hand up his shirt.

Ah.

Well, what was he supposed to do then?

She looked down at the form she was filling out. The sweater she was wearing was what the layman refers to as purple, but he would call purple and red combined. He slowed down to examine just how far into her breasts he could see from the neckline.

Which is fair, considering that she had taken the liberty to deride him.

He liked her hair, her mouth was painted nicely. He could not tell, however, whether she was wearing a skirt or pants, until he got some distance away. He lowered his head to see through the light coming off the glass. Those are pants, but they hang loosely.

Clap clap. Elegant. The fat content of your leg is left up to the observer's imagination.

He saw the cleaner's up ahead. He held up the receipt so

that he could get this over quickly.

He opened the door!

Then he walked over to the gentleman at the desk, who was tying repair orders onto expensive shoes, for some reason. He did not say anything, but slid the receipt across the way, then looked out the door to the passing cars.

No need to placate one another, we're past that now.

The cleaner guy picked up the receipt, then walked over to a large rack, he pressed a button. The entire rack rotated for many seconds, clicking loudly.

He was impressed.

The guy reached in to a certain point of the rack.

He wanted to ask if he could come behind the counter and press the button while the guy was busy.

That's my suit that he's carrying. The guy put the suit down on the counter, it was wrapped, with a little hanger so that he could hang it in a variety of places. He gave the guy a large gratuity, even though people don't do that, generally.

* * * * * * * *

He was all ready to go, but still had some time to wait.

He arranged it so that his schedule book sat on top of the notebook. He buttoned the first button of the suit jacket, then went into the bathroom to see if this looked better than leaving it open.

He ran the faucet, leaned over so that his tie would not get any water on it. He splashed some water onto his face.

He rubbed water into his hair.

He did not like the way he looked when facing forward. He found that he preferred it if he stood to the side, with his one shoulder down.

No thank you, I have an allergy to inexpensive foods.

Could he stand this way during the length of the meeting? What would be his excuse?

No chair thank you, I prefer to stand, in this one particular pose, please remain in my line of vision while we speak.

He walked over to the bed, pressed his hand into it in order to test the firmness quotient of the mattress.

Not very firm.

He then returned to the dresser, arranging it so that the notebook and schedule were in concordance with the corner of the wood. He needed a pen. Lucky thing that he had taken so much time to prepare. He went over to his bag, unzipped it, then poked around for a pen.

He found one inside a pair of boxer shorts. He read the side while he twisted the pen so that the point receded into the workings.

He remembered staying at that hotel, so long ago.

He checked the time, he was running a little late. Good.

He sat down on the edge of the bed within reach of the remote control machine. He turned on the television. Without looking at the screen he pressed the channel button for a long period of time. He pressed a button that caused the volume to drop out of the programs. He imagined that he had cycled through all of the channels.

He looked up at the screen.

A program about training police dogs.

I have always been interested in that topic, but until now have had no means to pursue this knowledge.

Evidently it involved much violence. The large dog is trained to bite the man while he wears a protective suit. He wondered if the man was screaming in terror, even though it probably did not hurt at all. He tapped the channel button several times lightly, to investigate the minimum pressure required for channel changing phenomena.

He was now learning how to prepare culinary something.

He was now hearing the man's life story.

He was now being informed of the merits of a particular chain of grocers. Ugh, turned off the thing.

And then he was seeing the balcony reflected in the screen, though he could not make out any details of his room.

Not much time had passed at all, which made him somewhat depressed, other people made being rude seem so natural. He cleared his throat, he walked to the balcony and back.

Five

Though he did not write it down, as his memory was impeccable, he made a list of things to do that evening.

Twitch, sniffle, maybe urinate, if you have time.

He had finished ahead of schedule, spent an hour or so wondering if he would add —intoxicate— to this list. How much money did he have? How much money does it cost? Might mathematics help him find a congruent answer?

Hmm, hmm.

It is too bad he had never refined his science aptitude. Scientists make a decent income, their lives, aside from this, might look similar to his.

He stretched his palm out in a scientific way. He chewed on it a little, thoughtful.

He looked out the balcony window to the world obscured from his eyeballs. A hemisphere of his brain was feeling odd, but not painful, he wondered if he had ever felt such a sensation before, figuring that he must have because he has done nothing new since

Since a long time.

What ho, retching sound?

He was going to open the door to the room, but decided, as he had never done so before, to make use of a small spy hole that lets people inspect their guests, or the empty corridor. There was not sufficient light passing through to tell if the girl hanging over the rail was at all attractive.

Open the door, comfort her.

These are good things.

He approached the girl, asked if she was alright. She was letting streams of water fall from her lip onto the rail, dripping into the bushes down there. How much had she drank that night? Was it more than he could drink?

Is she alright?

He reached his hand out, and drew her hair back over to the other side, so that she could be clean. He took a look at her face, guessing her age. She rolled her head over to the side, thanking him in fragments.

I always do that for them, such things.

Does he get her water or something? Pat her shoulder?

Another voice told him to get his hands off of her. He turned around. A short girl was approaching him angrily. She swatted at him, approaching the rail.

He did not say anything. He walked away, but not back to his room as he did not want them to see his room number.

After a few steps, he staggered to indicate that he was drunk as well, but they were not looking.

The shorter girl asked the drunk such questions as, are you alright, just be honest with me, can you still go to the blah, I'm fine either way. He walked down the stairs slow enough that he would not be far from his room once it was safe to go back.

Milling underneath the stairwell, he questioned himself about his intentions. He decided that he was not intending anything all that awful. Just a civic man, maybe seeing if she, of her own gratitude, would give him one tiny kiss for helping her in a time of need. Hehehe.

* * * * * * * *

Waking up, feeling pleasant. He did not know what time it was that this had happened, so he would have to estimate ten or so when he told the story to the other people.

He had been fading in and out of fully awake for a long time. He grazed over a few memories of the previous night, a few dreams, some things he had thought this morning.

He remembered licking his gum, causing one of his back teeth to fall out into his bottom cheek. He had decided to take care of this the next day.

He was frightened. His tooth had fallen out.

He used his tongue to search his mouth cavity for it. Perhaps he had swallowed it. Perhaps the tooth was still there. He could feel a sensitive spot in his gums, were a tooth might have been before.

I am far too old to grow another tooth!

He got out of bed in an urgent way. He used his finger to pull his lip up.

All teeth accounted for.

Well, I'm just delusional then.

lucky.

He felt his mind growing sharper, sharper, as time passed. At this rate, he will be very clever by mid-evening, tomorrow. He sat back on the bed, pulling the comforter up around him. He felt too distressed to return to sleep. He decided to check the television for important events that he might have missed.

He pulled his hand out of the comforter to touch the control. He left it out in the event that he would want to change the channel.

He used his other hand to prevent himself from becoming flaccid, periodically.

The woman was on the scene, explaining how bad the weather was in comparison with all recorded history in one location.

Maintaining the comforter around himself, he stood up

from the bed to look out the window, then to grind his feet into the carpet, then to recline on the floor, while watching the television upside down. He decided that he would prefer to take a pillow onto the floor with him, did this, then just listened for a time.

He felt like sobbing for a little while, then tried to lift himself up with his legs so that his body formed a parabola, and he could see the television once again. He felt that, from this position, he legally should be able to see the underside of the desk where the anchorwoman sat, perhaps up her skirt, if she were wearing one, but his television was not large enough to have that portion of the image.

His muscles felt tired, he allowed himself to sink back to the floor. He passed some remaining time by humming a resonant frequency with his throat that shook all the junk off of it.

He could take a shower.

He could brush his teeth, maybe floss.

He could get himself in peak condition for the next day or so.

He threw his hands open and burst out of the comforter. He braced himself against the side of the bed, and stood up.

* * * * * * * *

Before choosing from the available seating, he walked over to the door, opening it to see if it was dirtier than the living room. The door led to a bathroom, which was not what he wanted.

At least the toiletries are in disarray.

At least the toothpaste is crusted up grotesquely.

He looked back at the living room. The magazines stacked on a clear glass table, a blanket folded neatly on the couch. Someone had cleaned up a bit. To impress him, no doubt, maybe.

He chose the small chair, because normally guests sit on the couch. He looked through the glass door, to the patio, where an ashtray sat next to a few chairs.

Richard came back into the room with two glasses of orange juice, stopped, looked disturbed that he had stolen the smaller chair, then set one glass onto the table, and handed him the other.

He was so pleased that he didn't feel like talking.

Richard used the opportunity to interview him as to

when he had cut his hair so short, then called the haircut quite military, not entirely suited to a high hairline, or his personality, but nice looking.

Sorry, Richard is just so honest sometimes.

He could stand up, lean over with his fist up.

I saw your bathroom, you practiced man!

He had done it a week or two ago, he said.

Richard began to ask why his assistant, what was her name, had not come along. He said that she would not be entirely necessary, without saying the name 'Hannah', making it seem that he had forgotten her name as well, as if she were a peon.

He just needed a note or two, a more thorough synopsis than the one that Richard had provided.

He cut Richard off to ask if he would prefer to be called Gordon.

Only if he wanted to, it was just an idea, he did not seem to like the idea before.

True.

He sat the notebook in his lap, taking the pen out from the inside, not taking off the cap. He asked how the story was coming along. Richard said it was finished for the most part.

Many changes?

A few, but not so much.

He took the glass from where he had placed it down, took a long sip. He looked for something to say that would not really amount to anything. He stared out at the patio for some time until Richard turned to look at it as well.

That is a nice garden, he said. He could not think of the word for patio.

Thank you. The garden is the thing that had initially and so on Richard.

He tried to say something perceptive.

He pulled the ends of his suit jacket from underneath him, giving him increased agility. He held up his hand in the air, in front of the image of the patio, twiddled his fingers. He turned back to ask if they could start the interview process.

Part 7

(continued travelling adventures)

One

He examined the remaining items in the room, which he considered unworthy of being packed into the car. However such things as this newspaper could prove useful, and who knows, a good bottle cap could prove pivotal in some situation or such.

Matchbook, have you suspected, in our brief acquaintance, that I am the master?

He remembered seeing those toenail clippers sitting in the sink. Those clippers were worth keeping, he imagined. He went to the bathroom.

Had he taken them already?

He found them in his pocket.

Fantastic.

He was always doing the right thing, even when he was not paying attention.

He kept the clippers in his hand, returned to the room. He had left out something of a change of clothes; clean underwear, two socks, shirt. He had thoroughly thought this out.

All he could do was wait until whatever, when he left.

He looked over at the newspaper, then became inspired. He decided to cut the newspaper into something more pleasant, perhaps a string of paper dolls.

Or.

He had left his good cutting knife in the car with his suit jacket. On the toenail clippers he found a small file with a sharpish point at the end, which would suffice. He folded the newspaper twice. This way he would have many copies of whatever he decided to cut.

The point of the file did not cut well, ripped the paper up. He was able to go down the stairs, go to the car, plug around until he found his knife, come back up, and finish correctly. For some reason though, this ordeal did not appeal to him. He finished ripping the paper with his fingers, which worked better.

A circle, somewhat.

He removed the thing from the surrounding newspaper bits. He pulled the circle guys apart from one another.

Now I have many circles!

How can he use this to his benefit? He tried to think of some other cause in which to enlist their aid. He suspected that he could do many things with tape. Perhaps he could make them into a stupid crown that he could wear, but not in public, or perhaps a ball of garbage. Alas, he had no tape.

He killed two of the circles with his toenail clippers. This got him worked up, slightly. He pushed the remaining circles onto the floor. Not caring what happened to them.

He looked down at the two circles speared on the file.

What if the tables were turned?

He squinted his eyes, looking to picture himself like these things, file through his chest, a little tiny man. He was overcome with pity, these poor gentlemen. He pulled the circles off the file, understanding in the back of his mind that he would have done this anyway, if he were going to bring the clippers with him.

Not even humane, this practical gesture.

He left the thing on the table.

He pushed the clippers back into his pocket. He stared and tried to reconstruct the bottom half of the photograph, with his mind's eye.

* * * * * * * *

He splashed the water over his abdomen, got rid of the soap residue. The water was getting cold though. He would have to make it fast.

He could not remember if he had cleaned off his armpits or face, so he did these two things, perhaps for the second time. He then cupped water in his fist, used it to wipe the soap from his forehead, carefully, as he was not of a lifestyle wherein he could risk soap getting into his eyes.

Because he had such nimble grace with his toes, something which other people might not have, he was able to remove the plug from the drain, then hang it from the faucet, without sitting up at all.

Then he sat up, and got out of the bathtub.

He dried off and got dressed.

He dried off and got dressed.

He waited until these things were done.

He walked out of the bathroom, rubbing his hair a few times with his hand. His hairs bending, springing back up, flicking water all over the place, which pleased him immensely. He dropped the towel at an unimportant blah blah, en route to the bed.

He looked out the balcony window, to a few lights that might be interesting. He took his sunglasses out of the pocket of his shirt, then pushed them onto his face, even though it was dark.

He stuck his hands into the pockets of his hooded shirt. He went out the door to the garden area. He could feel the water on his skin, soaking his shirt at certain places. He felt as though he were naked, this made him quite confident or bold or something like that.

He saw the young guy with the cigarettes sitting on the bottom stair. He called out that he would like to borrow one of these cigarettes for himself.

He had no intention of repaying this debt, ever.

He went down the stairs very fast.

His momentum was such that he passed the young guy then twisted on his heel until he was faced forward. The young guy held out a cigarette for him, a book of matches, smiling, there you go.

He pulled a match from the book. He debated between staying, which was polite, and going, which would make him seem stylish to the young guy.

He lit the cigarette, and sped away.

Ding ding, man on the move.

He had not planned out his destination. He figured that a good first step was to go through the lobby. He did not have his keys. He could blah blah take care of it anyhow. He even walked through smoking a cigarette. He was sure that the clerk noticed this, because he drew the cigarette away from his lips after each puff.

He even smoked it while he opened the door, with his hands in his pockets and all that!

He stepped outside, and immediately set to admiring several things.

* * * * * * * *

He checked the aisles for anything that he would like. He saw several flags that could be placed on the windows of his car. He saw some batteries, some technical looking things, as well as a few miscellaneous items.

He stopped to consider purchasing some road flares.

Hmm.

He suspected that these would be of some use. Once he saw the price on the packaging, he imagined that he could do without them. He walked off.

He went back and grabbed the flares, so that he could think it over while he looked for food.

The refrigerators were filled with delicious items. He could examine them without opening the doors.

He read the nutritional content of a chicken sandwich, but did not know what type of nutrition he practiced. Several other options included cultural foods, beef sandwich, a package of raw eggs, butter, milk.

He breathed through his nose, he looked like quite the connoisseur, he imagined. Other people would probably have decided what they wanted by this point.

He set off to see what else he could eat. Perhaps some snack food.

He looked down at the flares, considered putting them back, walk all that distance, then laid them in a box of candy.

Haha! For some reason this made him chuckle in his insides, and feel good with himself overall.

He stopped.

He went back to the refrigerator, thought about it, and decided that this chicken sandwich would not waste his time. He picked it out of the refrigerator, and then decided that he also enjoyed the flavor of chocolate milk, every once in a while. He took these two items over to the counter.

The woman that would be ringing him up had really let herself go. He had seen a more pleasant looking woman in the uniform when he entered the store initially. He waited to see if this other woman was going to return to the counter any time soon, so that he would not have to risk this woman falling in love with him.

Nowhere in sight.

He sighed, smiled, set his purchases on the counter.

Made a point not to be all that charming in his mannerisms.

She made a comment that he did not understand. He made an expression with his mouth that could be considered an appropriate response to just about anything. So that, at least, went smoothly.

He paid the full price of the items, denied that he needed a bag at all, saying that he preferred not waste them.

He examined little bracelets in a box on the counter while the woman counted out the change.

What are these for?

She said that the proceeds would go to etcetera charity.

He nodded, then explained that he would need two of them in that case, squinting his eyes and nodding even after he had finished speaking. He placed two of the bracelets in his pocket, while she deducted the price from his change. He decided to give her a wink, but waited until she was not looking him in the eye.

* * * * * * * *

He had been driving for some time now, not stopping at all. He looked down at the gauge, which told him that he had used up half of the fuel. He had not gotten out of the car since he refueled.

How bold of him.

He looked at the gauge again, to see if it had gone down since, but it had not. He set his eyes on the road, where he could see all the brake lights for many miles. He pulled into one of the slower lanes so that he could relax for some time.

He started traveling down a slight incline. He could not feel gravity or whatever pulling him diagonally into the windshield. He tried to examine his neighboring driver, but this proved difficult. He needed to stare, tensing his upper lip, and make his face all owlish before he could see that thing. Unfortunately, it was just some old guy with a beard.

A crack noise. He felt his car jerk downward, then settle flat, but he did not know what he had just done wrong.

He resolved to keep his eyes on the road.

He slapped the steering wheel a bit until that was over.

He decided that, if he listened to the radio, something

would, well, etcetera. He turned the knob on, finding that the frequency that it was tuned to was not anything all that special. Faint humming. He rotated the dial completely around, so that he would get a general picture of what was available.

Someone singing dadada, instruments.

He rotated the dial a few more times before giving up on the radio.

He had found that the time indicated on the clock was late, which he already knew by the general appearance of things, but it was good to have specifics backing him up.

He had suspected that the guy to his side was planning to get in front of him. The guy drew closer, without signaling, started to pull in front of him.

That's the game then?

He honked his horn twice in quick succession.

The guy swerved back into the proper lane.

He laughed, drew forward, said something along the lines of– don't tickle me, you blahblah.

The car guy was persistent. The guy turned on his signal to indicate that he wanted to get in.

He pulled forward to make such a thing impossible. This was his position. The guy sped up, then got in front of someone in front of him.

His heart sank.

He said something about the guy having 'the filthy disease', though he could not verify this without his medical supplies.

He sat in his seat for some time, his mind blank. He remembered something unpleasant that happened to him a few years back, something that Jake had accused him of doing the night before, but did not remember doing. He sputtered out a few words randomly until he calmed down.

He looked down at the time. He was making excellent progress, in his way. He would stop soon.

* * * * * * * *

He acknowledged the two standing at the register, to show them that he was an all-right guy. He went over to the refrigerators to browse the different wines. He saw several labels of various years. These were all quite expensive.

That is not what I meant.

He looked over to the shelves of room temperature wines, some of which were much cheaper in price.

The two gentlemen were conversing;

The thing you have to do is to make certain declarations, he turned to face them, in your taxes that blah blah not entirely, he got a little closer, dishonest, but a stretch, he held his finger, hence etcetera, to his lip, you have more money.

He broke into the silence, saying that this was what he did as well, when he did his taxes.

They looked over at him, worried expressions.

For social reasons, he asked these two gentlemen which of the wines they would recommend for his entertainment this evening. They did not answer, so he added that he was not looking for anything too expensive, adding that he would, almost positively, be drinking by himself.

The tougher looking one of the two of them piped up, saying that it was his choice which one he wanted, implying that he could bring it up to the counter once he had decided.

The two turned back to the positions that they had occupied while they were talking, but did not say anything.

The smaller gentlemen added that rabbit something was a good label, for the price.

That, my friend, is exactly what I needed to know!

He hustled over to the wines, finding one that looked to be the appropriate label, as it had a rabbit printed on it.

By the time he looked back up though, the conversation had carried on without him.

Oh.

He held up the bottle, but before he could ask, they said that he had chosen correctly.

To demonstrate how charismatic he was, he joked around with them about a guarantee. Maybe he could bring back the empty bottle if it did not get him drunk?

He would have to contact the vineyard, the information was printed on the back of the label.

i was only joking!

He paid the price, adding two pens, from the coffee mug, to his purchase in order to rid himself of the change.

Then he left, out the door, just like that.

He turned out of view, standing just outside the door to see if the two were going to start talking about how stupid he was to want a guarantee or something like that, but he couldn't hear them.

He took one of the pens out of the bag. He tried to snap it in half, but it was actually pretty well constructed.

He respected those two far too much. He walked back to his car where he would sit in the back seat, drink this rabbit whatever. He almost hoped that it had an unsophisticated flavor that he could sense and they had not.

But what were the chances of that? They worked in a wineshop.

* * * * * * * *

He drove up the hill in his automobile, wearing spectacles designed to prevent harmful radiation from striking at his eyeholes, thus preventing damage of some kind. The ordinary person does not have to worry about their eyes, because the things that they do don't require eyesight for the most part. The things that ordinary people do being; act unkind, jump around, have sex for procreative and beneficent reasons, make life harder for him by etcetera.

They don't make life harder for him at all.

They are very nice from time to time.

Who doesn't jump around?

He saw, at the top of the hill, a black building that looked quite capital.

And there's the sky as well, what good fortune.

He hit the brakes, stopped the car, searched for change that he could put in the meter. He found none, but since he was going to stand in the immediate vicinity of the car it was not so important. If he saw the police he could just speed away.

He got out of the car, zipped up his jacket. He walked up the wheelchair ramp, examining the black, polished rock of the building. He could see his reflection in it! He found a nice slab of it in front of the door that he could lie down on, but he would have to sit, first, in order to lie down gradually, without attracting suspicion.

For the first minute or so, he paid particular attention to his car. He kept his eye out for the authorities.

Then he became focused on his skinny legs.

He tried to flex the muscles, then tried the push against the muscle with his hand to test how firm it was when flexed.

I am pure stone, sweetheart.

Feel my thigh!

For a time after that he scratched the beardish thing that

was growing on his face. The hairs were getting longer on his throat than on his face, which was terrible. He was able to forget about it only with the help and aid of a growing curiosity about the set of pay phones on the corner of the building.

He stood up, walked over. While he walked he looked at his reflection, keeping it in his peripheral vision so that he would not look vain.

He picked up the receiver, but could not think of anything to say or do that would be entertaining.

He said that he would be home in a minute, dear. Then hung up.

He began placing a call to a random phone number. In the end this did not work.

He looked back at the slab, the sun was illuminating a triangle of it.

He debated some options.

He went back over to the slab, sat, reclined then so that his chest, neck, shoulder, face, were all in the warmer temperature, resolving to continue with the driving thing in another fifteen minutes or so.

He might have looked at the clouds, or something along such lines.

One looked like a vegetable.

When he looked back at the car, he was filled with dread. He said—

no no no.

Though he would have to do it, and he would not mind.

Two

He saw the dog stick its paws against the back window of the car in front of him. Obviously the dog would prefer to be traveling with him, but the transition would be too dangerous at such high speeds.

He looked at some trees growing on the side of the road. Blah!

Maintaining his speed required that he put constant pressure against the pedal. This made his large toe press into the corner of his shoe, which made him constantly aware that his toenail was too long. He fantasized that he could release his foot from the pedal, remove his shoe, tear off the bit with his fingers while still driving.

He did not do this, though.

Without looking, he put his hand down into the cup holder and felt around to see if there was anything worthwhile there. Maybe some coins, maybe something strange that he had acquired in some interesting way. The only thing in the cup holder was syrup stuff from a drink or such.

He snatched his hand out of the stuff, but it was too late, his fingertips were coated with goo.

He thought about it.

He put his fingers into his mouth, licked them clean, more or less. For good measure, he pretended to dry-heave and clear his throat, though the substance actually tasted sweet and pleasant. He spread his eyes wide, then convulsed his shoulders, neck, and hair.

He saw that one of the cars in front of him had colorful stickers on its bumper, implying that the passengers would be young women. He decided to speed the car up until he was parallel with them, so that they could see him, perhaps discuss which of them found him more handsome.

He pulled up beside this car. There were at least three women inside.

For maximum effect, he did not look at them at all, kept his eyes on the road in a rebellious way.

If they wanted, they could probably get his attention by shouting at him to pull over at the next rest area, if they wanted.

They did not do it, but no one does anything they want these days.

He was slowing down, more comfortable that they should be in front of him. He could not see them well though, he could only see the backs of their heads, from the necks up, if that.

He tapped his wrist against the steering wheel a few times.

He saw the large turn coming up ahead, so he turned the steering wheel. He looked to see a bunch of cars in front of him, which was great.

He noticed that the top of his windshield was tinted brown, which was interesting.

He turned off the thermostat, so that the air would cool down gradually. It was lucky that he noticed, he was starting to doze off. He then began suspecting that there was not enough oxygen in the cabin, so he opened his window for a few minutes.

* * * * * * * *

He stopped to tie his shoe, which he had prolonged for some time now. He stood on one foot. He put his foot back down. He braced his head against a newspaper machine, lifted his foot up, tied the shoe quickly. He could feel the pressure of the metal against his scalp, that's starting to get rather painful.

Done, he shook his foot, and done.

He stood straight, shook his foot to test the knot, and rubbed his head back to normal. He decided to go across the dirt, toward the quaint thatch type ordeal with the promotional banner in front. He tried to guess, for several steps or so, what exactly they were selling.

Would it be groceries, or shoes?

He looked back at his car, which he had left parked at the pump, even though he had already filled it with gasoline. He thought about moving it to a more polite parking spot, decided to leave it in its place because he would only be a minute, and he was just that type of man.

And what could they do? He had locked it up, had the keys right here in his pant pocket.

He arrived at the porch of the building sometime around mid-afternoon.

He put his hand against the rails, thinking that he would just climb up, instead of walking all the way to the stairs. It did not work out that way though, he walked around, then up the steps. He stopped to examine several pieces of porch furniture stuff, as well as a pleasant table, with a dirty cigarette stuffed between the wooden planks. He tried to pick it out with his fingers, they were not thin enough to reach it.

He extended his arms so that each of his hands rested on an opposite side of the doorway, while he looked through the door. He was now blocking potential customers from passing through.

Inside the shop; backpacks, rock décor.

Not his type of thing.

There were several female shirts on a rack, cut with low necklines, because a woman in the wild can't be bothered with modesty. He looked around for a changing room or mirror, to see if there were any women in the shop trying on one of these beauties.

The only person was a guy arranging boots on the back wall.

His entrance caused a sound effect. He looked up, a warning bell positioned above the doorway.

He remembered prophesying, just a moment before, that the shop would sell shoes. He had wished that he had said this aloud to someone before entering the shop, so that they may testify to his mystical doings.

The guy finished arranging one of the boots, then looked over at him. He held his hand out, explaining, so generously, that he was not there to buy anything, so there was no point in the guy standing up. Because his hand was out now, he brushed it against the breast area of one of the shirts he had admired for some time now, realizing afterwards that, because it was the first on the rack, at least one woman had worn it before. He worried for a moment, hoping that said woman had been attractive.

* * * * * * * *

He tried his best not to move.

He understood that his neck was out of shape.

The position that he had slept in did not give him much of a view, except for the underside of the driver's seat. He wondered what time it was, it was late enough that the sun had been out for awhile.

He decided to move.

He turned onto his back. His neck stung. The liquids in his head felt uneven, he felt a little dizzy. He looked past his feet to the window, examined the paint on the houses, thought about getting out of the car, as he had slept much later than was safe.

He used his shoe to pull the door handle, push the thing open. He felt the cold flood into the car, but did not move. He lay there for a time with the door open, it had turned on the light in his car, which was not so fascinating.

Since his door was open, he decided to get out of the car.

He pulled himself out of the car with his legs. Entertaining. His shirt slid up his back and all. A towel fell onto the street from his legs.

He stood up, began to stretch, blinked his eyes. Ah morning, new life.

His neck.

Does not feel good.

He closed the door. Stretched. He felt disorientated, he said a few things of no importance, dadada, stretched out his legs, both of his knees cracked.

He saw a man step out onto the front step.

He noticed this man look at him.

He strolled around the car, casually, until he was out of view. He took the key out of his pocket, ready to go in an emergency.

He peeked through the windows.

The man approached the car, leaned in to look for him.

Eye contact.

Agra! He prepared to flee, then remembered his towel had fallen out of the car.

The man said something or other. He licked his lips pretending that he had not noticed. He did notice, however, the man take some money out of his pocket.

The man asked him if he had slept well.

He could not think of a response. The man just had some clever gestures, a few things to say, no violence. The man said that he had noticed that he had slept in his car.

What was wrong?

Nothing was wrong, lalala.

The man picked out his accent, got around to telling him disrespectful etcetera respect etcetera a hotel just up the road.

Here, though the man speculated that it might be fine where he was from, that, here, they had hotels lalala.

Suspecting that the man had brought the money for a reason, he explained that he did not have enough money.

The man put the money on the hood of his car, imagine that.

Not nearly enough for a hotel room, he noted.

They reached an understanding or something, paused, the man made him say 'yes'.

yes.

Then the guy left him alone.

He allowed the wind to blow the bills into the road, then gathered them up one at a time, intending to use them to pay for the majority of breakfast, then he went around to get his towel.

He fished through the junk in his car, being careful with the manuscript, and trying not to damage the brown packaging over the frame, but being very liberal with his mistreatment of his own items, such as his suit, his jacket, a bag of toiletries. Finding at last his pornography, which was underneath some type of metal rod that he could not recall obtaining.

Magazine, he said.

He held the magazine in front of him, closed the trunk, jumped onto the top of it so that he was now sitting.

He was careful, as there was some damage on the spine. He looked through a few of the pictures. He could distinctly remember finding the pictures arousing, tried to remember what exactly his thoughts were when they had been effective.

He started hoping that someone was staring at him, amazed about him or so and such, that he could be so free as to look at his own magazine in public.

Most of the people around him were not close enough by to make out the cover of the magazine, so they did not think that he was doing anything special.

He thought that he should go into the grocery store, or perhaps the office supply store beside it with the magazine. He thought that he should read it there, then people might get upset or something.

He would just say that this was a strange compulsion.

Or that he did not know he was doing anything wrong.

Neither felt very true.

Look, see I have this card from the government that says I'm crazy, so let me do my thing.

At the entrance of the office supply store, he felt his courage fade. He redrafted his plan. He began to think that it would be enough to hold the magazine out, that would do it, whatever he was trying to accomplish here, he did not have to pretend to be engrossed in reading it.

He could just hold it at his side.

He suspected that the boy at the counter had noticed the magazine. The boy was smiling, looking away quite forcedly, said something to another office supply guy, who looked over at him.

He had to act quickly.

He raised the magazine, and put on his crazy face. He

asked the second guy, from a good distance away, if he liked naked women.

The second guy thought about this, albeit for a short moment.

Yes.

He went up, placed the magazine on the counter, saying that he did not need it any longer, and that he wanted to do his part for the youth whatever. Neither of them touched the magazine for a while, until he insisted that the first person to touch the magazine would be its new owner.

He felt good about this, he felt good.

The younger guy moved quickly after that to get it first, because the younger guy was not of legal age, he imagined.

As he left the store, he looked back, regretted, considered getting it back, saying that he was not serious.

What am I going to do without Magazine?

* * * * * * * *

He admired the woman at the counter, who was not doing anything. She had a decent smile. Then he began to wonder if this was not a smile at all, since she kept it up, but her regular face.

In which case;

disturbing.

He stepped inside, the entire pet shop smelt awful. How can a person smile in this torrid stink? He looked over at the woman. She had stopped smiling the moment that he entered.

Of course.

So he was not going to talk to her anymore.

He walked over to a row of aquariums. Some tropical things were swimming around in there. There was a light over the aquarium highlighting the fact that these little fellows could glow under the right circumstances.

Then there were the more boring fish, which had no special attributes.

Ah! A snake.

He drew back. The snake was moving around. Deciding to make a big point of it, he stepped up to the glass, then stepped up to the glass again! He was now in harm's way.

He put his hand against the glass for several seconds, did not look down. He became even bolder, tapped the glass once or twice, being careful that he did not tap it very hard. He wanted the snake to bite at him, and smack its little brain against the wall, but it did not feel like it.

He then came to a bird area, which was the place where the stink was coming from.

He covered his nose and cursed them, not loud enough for the woman to overhear.

Some of the more colorful birds kept an eye on him. What did this woman feed them? Would they eat the glowing fish if the opportunity came up?

He did not like the birds, so he went back to the aquariums, deciding to check out the opposite side of the aisle. There were a few lizards across from the snake.

They were cheap, the sign indicated emphatically.

He thought about buying one of these, for his own personal use. He looked at the lizards scurrying around. He clenched his upper lip in order to deal with the smell. One of these guys was sitting on a log. Were these the ones that changed their colors? If so, he would certainly have to buy one. He looked at the guy on the log to see if he was changing at all.

It licked its own eyeball.

That's enough of that, he decided. He certainly did not want one of these.

Next to them was a few more of the less magnificent fish. Then one that had teeth. He repeated his experiment with the snake on this fish, but it did not bite at him either.

This made him angry.

He walked back to the door. The woman asked him to have a nice day, which was a good idea. He told her that he would try his best, so long as she did the same, he looked up.

She was smiling once again.

* * * * * * * *

Headlights.

The road became brighter, a little bit. He turned the headlights off, then back on again. Yes, he now had his headlights on, a noticeable difference. He cocked his head to the side, so it somewhat rested on his shoulder, in a way.

How long has it been since dadadadadadada when will dadada hang out sometime? What about Dorothy, for awhile?

Are they still friends?

Hmm.

This driving bit is strange, I don't even have to do anything.

He let go of the steering wheel for a few seconds, the car started to turn off the road, he grabbed the steering wheel. He repeated this for a longer stretch, then wondered why the manufacturer would make a car that tries to kill you when you release the steering wheel.

Or, something else.

Well, he practically did not have to do anything, at least.

He stuck his tongue into his lower lip, entertained the idea of starting the habit of chewing tobacco, but made no definitive plans.

He looked out the side window to the jungle and the sky or whatever. He saw that the moon this evening was a pleasant crescent shape. He vaguely recollected an image of a kid sitting in the crescent of the moon, reading a book or something.

What a lie!

He would definitely tell them so, the next time he saw whoever it was. That's what he would do, if they did not like it, then they would have to stop filling valuable space in his mind with such stupid things.

Ah, such blood in me.

He opened his mouth, left it open for a good time, but nothing happened.

He queried whether or not he needed to urinate. If he did, at all, he would pull the car off the road immediately.

He guessed that he might possibly be able to urinate.

He put on his turn signal for a good period of time, so that people behind him would understand what he was about to do. The car shook as soon as it got off the road, he put pressure on the breaks, until it stopped. He could hear a strange mechanic grinding type noise. Had he just broken the car?

He climbed over the barrier, so that he could exit through the passenger side, which was less dangerous.

He looked at the tires, which seemed fine.

He unzipped his pants.

Alas, but a few drops, how pathetic.

He maintained his position for a good period of time. He listened to the cars moving passing by him, out of view. He then realized that getting back onto the road would be difficult, dangerous, irritating. He got back inside the cabin, climbed over the stuff, got back into his seat. He pressed his face against the window to see if he had popped any of the tires on this side, but they looked fine.

A car passed at an incredible speed, his car shook a little, he drew back, and cursed at them for endangering his life.

* * * * * * * *

He had passed several hotels, none of them looked dirty enough to suit his needs. He saw another coming up that was painted blue.

Hmm.

He turned into this one, even though it was not what he had planned. There were not many cars in the lot. He drew his car up to the entrance, left his lights on, got out, locked the car, walked inside.

The interior of this thing was a little classy.

Marble type tiling, spacious high ceilings.

This was not going to work.

He approached the overweight person at the counter. She asked him how things were. He decided to answer this question.

Things are fine.

He would like to rent a room.

She asked him where he was from, he told her, briefly, keeping his eyes serious so that they could get to it. She asked him what type of room he wanted. He looked over at the kitchen area, which had a waffle iron.

He could have a waffle in the morning, couldn't he, if things went smoothly?

He said that he would like the cheapest room possible.

Or, perhaps, the best value.

He imagined getting a large room with a swimming pool, perhaps a ballroom, though he did not have time to dance that evening.

She threw out a few initial prices, which were not too high.

He asked how much it would cost to sleep in his car. He leaned into the desk as he said this, looked off.

She said that the fine for vagrancy was etcetera. Her tone was no longer friendly.

Hmm. That is more affordable, he said.

He asked if he could get the suite for the price of a regular room.

No.

You didn't even think about it.

He slowly realized that she had all the power in this situation. He did not want to sleep in his car, he was becoming attached to the idea of a fancy suite. Imagine there might be a basket of candy that he could eat.

Maybe a bottle of champagne.

He asked what discount he could get.

She asked if he blah blah belonged to something club.

He did not.

She repeated her initial prices.

He considered threatening her.

He considered offering her a gratuity, just between the two of us thing.

He said that he actually did belong to the club, but that he had forgot his card or whatever. He looked down at the desk, rubbed the back of his head, while she told him that there was nothing she could do then.

Suddenly suddenly suddenly;

he no longer felt up to this.

He said that he would take the suite, tried to insist on receiving a discount. He breathed through his nose, he took his passport out of his pocket, explained that he would like to have the bill deducted from his bank account, the information was written on a card inside, he would show her how to do this if she did not know already, hoping that she would not throw him out because she did not care for the extra work.

* * * * * * * *

He flung the towel off, into a corner of the room, most likely, then spread his arms out.

Tada!

His skin wet.

He paced around the room for a few etceteras, trying to avoid getting dressed, wondering what he could do unclothed, figuring that these would be the same things he could do if he dressed, but so desiring them that he could not discern them. What were they, these things that would be done?

He sat on the chair by the eating table, stretching his arms out to grab the stack of papers.

He studied the menu of the restaurant downstairs,

imagined that they would, if he only asked, bring something up to his room, gladly.

For a price.

He looked at several brochures, caverns underground, how lovely, family entertainment, how insulting that they'd left that out for him.

He balled these papers up into his fist and said 'That's right' a few times with various alterations in tone and emphasis. The papers were matted with a firm photographic gloss, reluctant to bend, pressing into the skin of his palm.

Then he tossed the ball aside, to the floor. Someone else would have to pick it up, because, that's right.

He opened the binder, advising photographs of all the amenities he would be provided as a guest. The pool, closed, the spacious beds, which went without saying, the view, the blah, the bathrooms.

Nothing so controversial. Nothing he didn't know already.

This binder.

He examined the cover; the hotel's insignia on the front. Nice metal rings, so and such, a good looking binder.

He pulled the rings open, removed the pages, placing them in stacks on the table. He closed the rings, then waved the binder twice in the air.

New binder.

For me.

After his initial celebration, he began to fear that someone would see the papers stacked on the table, exclaim, try to take this little fellow from him. He looked around the room.

The space behind the entertainment center was large enough to stuff the papers behind it. He picked them up from the table.

I was in a tight situation, he tensed his mouth, I needed a binder, how dare you, I am blah blah, an important man of business. He pushed the papers into the space, had to divide them up into two separate stacks, one on top of the other, to get them to fit in the aperture.

He took several steps back, looked away, then looked at the space to see if these papers were hidden. Anyone could see them there, if they looked.

He decided to put on some pants. He took the binder over

to the bed, hiding it underneath one of the pillows on the side of the bed that he did not need. He took his pants up from the floor.

No underwear, not tonight!

Haha.

He stepped into the pants, pulling them up his body, being very careful that he did not get caught in the zipper as he pulled it up. Then he kicked the bed, went off to find his shirt.

Three

He rotated the plate so that he could eat the potato stuff on the far side of it. He looked over to the bar area, some distance away, where the bartender was reading a newspaper or something of that sort.

The potato thing did not receive his stamp of approval. He started smearing it across the entire plate, into the sandwich's space.

He looked up again.

No response.

He began drumming his fingers on the table. He scooped the potato thing back the way it had been before, pretty much.

If not better!

He concentrated on this task. He made sure that the pile was as hemispherical as humanly possible, given his present tools. He then set the fork at the corner of the plate, stood up. He requested an alcoholic cider. He did not think that the bartender had heard him, at first.

Then the bartender finished reading the article, walked off to the far side of the bar, opened a fridge.

He stood there, then went up to the bar. He took the cider, said thank you.

The bartender assured him that it was no problem.

He already knew that, though.

Instead of returning to his plate, as others might do, he decided to explore the entirety of the restaurant while drinking the whatnot. He raised the bottle, the top clicked against his front teeth, accidentally.

Painful, slightly.

He drew some spit across his front teeth until they recovered. He then took another sip of the cider.

He examined several pictures.

Men on horses, very nice, how true.

A photograph of people standing outside a building.

A newspaper clipping. A picture frame designed with royalish decorative trim.

He then tapped his bottle against a public telephone. The receiver did not fall off the hook, which was disappointing, for some reason.

He found a strange machine in the upper left corner of the restaurant. He could not tell what it did exactly, guessing that it was a game for kids. He placed the bottle on top of it, fished through his pockets for a few coins, not knowing which one it would take.

The machine refused to take the cheaper coins, but finally accepted a different one. Then a red button lit up, which he pressed. He watched a ball drop from the top of the machine, falling into one chassis or whatever, very interesting stuff.

The machine lit up.

What a terrible game.

Some coins dropped into a thing at the bottom.

Hello. He reached over to see how much money it was.

Big winner.

He decided not to risk his earnings by playing again, as he still had no idea why he had won, or what he needed to do to win again. He took the cider off the top of the machine, took a sip, slid the coins into his pocket, going off to tell the bartender that he had won, to give him a generous tip, which was the classy thing to do.

* * * * * * * *

He felt a genuine sense of wellbeing, or something of that sort, for a time.

He cracked his neck. Rubbed the crotch area of his pants with his free hand. He did all these things, and spoke;

Yes, at least that's finished, at least we have that done.

Then he smacked the steering wheel.

He tried to see if he could see any particular type of vegetation to the side of the road. He did manage to see, tucked away at the bottom of the hill, a small cabin. It had a pond in front of it.

He tried to study many details of this, but only got so far.

Many people would not see that sort of thing, he felt,

because it was hard to catch. You have to keep your eyes out for it. Here, he's gone and seen himself a little cabin, a nice little paradise type thing. He felt so good about this, observant so on so on.

He looked at the sparse traffic around him, to see what else his cunning senses would find. A few postings of various distances perhaps, a dead animal, rubbish, that type of thing. It was lucky that he had seen that cabin.

He wondered if it might be for sale, after all it was not all that nice of a location. Perhaps he could get it at quite a bargain or something like that blah blah blah fishing in the pond, blah blah blah interviewed by the magazine blah a preternatural business sense.

He made a move of turning the radio all the way up, then all the way down, then off, rapidly.

Then he got bored, and, maybe, did something else for a good period of time.

De de de, with his sharp tooth sticking out, quite vicious.

He wondered when he would see the next sign that would indicate how much distance he had traveled in the last few bits. He began to estimate this amount, starting small, but then, with no sign in sight, he began to expand it irrationally.

He now was confused.

He tried not to focus on this, as it probably was not true. He wasn't driving all that fast.

He saw a sign coming up.

ah.

He felt his face stiffen, he felt nervous about this. He tried to calm himself. He assured himself that he would get there, eventually. It was no good, all this etcetera. If only he'd had the good sense to buy an airline ticket.

Next time.

Why had he not bought that airline ticket? He even had the number written down on a receipt that he might still have. He berated himself, and over again, added that he was an idiot.

He held his breath longer than he would naturally do! Maybe he would pass out, wake up much further then he was. It was too dangerous, though, he kept gasping for air.

And he seemed to be moving so fast.

Lies.

* * * * * * * * *

He figured that this was a post office. It had all the right signs, a few trucks; three separate mailboxes. He was certainly correct about that.

He pulled into a parking spot, turned the car off.

He looked around the car for a piece of paper that he could write on.

A few receipts.

Well, he did not need to say so much.

Haha, no no, he caught himself. The receipts were a bad idea. Far too suspicious.

He got out of the car, figuring that he would have something in his trunk. He looked over at the door to the post office.

He could ask for a piece of paper there, right?

He opened the trunk, digging through various items. He unzipped his bag, removed his checkbook. He opened it, examined the available space on each check.

He could write on that.

No.

He took the binder out, opened that. Maybe Richard had put in an extra page or so, for note writing purposes.

He looked at the manuscript, each page had little typewritten letters, all of that. He made a few initial remarks about the quality of the ink, some capital letters in strange places. He turned to the front page where the title was written, some other things.

He did not need this page, he figured, just tear it out.

So, he tore it out

To make up for this, he smoothed out the pages with his wrist, set the binder inside his clothing bag so that it would not be damaged. He closed the trunk, then opened it again to find a pen with which to write the letter.

He saw that he had left his checkbook inside, so he took that too. Found a pen in a corner of the trunk.

He needed to be very cautious with his wording, subtle, effective.

He started the letter

Dear doctor.

Then he wrote that he was just checking in.

Over the next few minutes, he devised an excellent plan.

He would write –birthday!!!– in the purpose line on the bottom of the check. Then he would say something along the lines of 'happy birthday, I apologize for missing it'.

To all outside appearances, it would seem a decent thing to do.

When he wrote it down, he made it better. He told the doctor to tell a made up woman that he referred to as 'little Julie' that he was sorry that he had missed her birthday party. He said that the doctor should take little Julie to the amusement park, at his expense.

Little would the postman know, this innocent character was made up.

By me!

He hoped things were well.

He wrote his name legibly, adding at the bottom, that, if the doctor wanted to recommend some books to read, he could be reached at so and such an address.

He admired this letter for a few moments.

It was perfect.

He folded the paper, wrote the check, walked over to the post office to buy stamps and an envelope.

* * * * * * * *

He scanned the area for any witnesses.

Dark tree trunks, late evening, lantern light.

He removed the soda from the bag, used his fingers to pull the metal ring until it worked or whatever. Then he looked around, stepped to the side of the walk, poured the soda out onto the grass.

He watched the stream.

How wasteful, he could take one sip, at least.

The metal of the can, quite cold. He felt the soda strike against the back of his throat, stinging, he heard cracking noises. The stuff tasted awful.

Satisfied, he turned the can over, felt its weight become lighter in his hand, felt the warmth of his hand overpower the cold metal on and on conductivity of sorts, how interesting.

Haha, it is done. He picked the bag up, hustled over to the bench.

He reached into the bag, unscrewed the cap of the wine. Looked around once again.

Getting the wine into the soda can, quite difficult a task.

Some of the wine sat on the lid of the can, he swirled it around, hoping that it would fall inside, used his lips to slurp it off away, gone forever. He looked down at the can.

Success.

I am drinking a soda in this park, late at night, feeling relaxed. I am a citizen like yourself. I am enjoying this soda immensely thank you. What we must do now, is, perhaps, attend the, your choice of things, sometime in the future, you and I, not now, a compulsion to finish this soda, but later. It will be excellent, I heard the best of reviews about such matters. Shall we retreat to my small abode, talk or something? On a later date?

Maybe we could share a bottle of wine in the park. We don't do this regularly, it is not our behavior. That is why the authorities will understand, laughing, good-natured gag.

How funny.

He swallowed a swallow. There was a grape pulp in the fluid, which disgusted him.

He banged his fist against the bench. Then again and again, his last attempt hard enough to sting. He looked up.

Ah! He rapidly comported himself.

Said hello to the passing couple.

The woman wearing a big coat. The man struck him as a sensitive type. They nodded at him. He suspected that they knew what he was doing. He examined the woman after they passed. Though he did not think he was intoxicated, his visions bubbled or something, side to side.

He looked down at the can.

He shook his head, drew his breath audibly.

Could he cry on command? It is rumored to be a difficult thing.

He unfocused his eyes, calmed. His eyes felt that they were watering a little, but when he noticed this they stopped.

Perhaps a single tear on his cheek?

He rubbed his thumb against his face.

No.

But he clapped his hands to his face, huffed his back, said regrettable, regrettable, and hid his smile. He smelt the wine on his lips, wondered if his mouth were purple, which would ruin the entire thing. That can of soda, he looked down, purchased for no reason. A waste.

He looked into the pharmacy. A dim light coming from the back. He wondered if someone was inside, staying late. Or if it was a thief, a robber. Should he call the police?

Or.

He stepped up the steps, to the little area that he found pleasing.

He admired some of the tiny plants. He also avoided stepping in dog feces that someone had left just to get him, how inconsiderate. He sat on one of the planters, under the withery tree.

He reached his hand out, pulled off a few leaves.

They were almost as large as his hand, quite nice looking. He thought that he might be able to do something with them. He considered writing his name on them with a pen, but he had not brought one.

He put one of the leaves over the zipper of his pants, entertained by this. Then he imagined that he would do well if he was stranded in the wilderness.

In such a case, he now knew how to make underpants.

He would make some for the ladies too, if they asked him.

Haha, perhaps not!

He looked over at the sidewalk, then at the nice night or whatever. He stuck his hand up through his hooded shirt, scratched his arm, his skin was irritated. This did not help. He pulled the sleeve up, to see if his skin was flaking off.

He wondered if he was infected, he had not been to a doctor for some time.

There was a small red patch on his arm, where his fingernails had scratched it. He resisted the urge to repeat this, believing, in his heart, that this would only make it worse, even though his instincts wanted him to do so.

He needed to shave, duly noted.

He studied the topography of the street. There were a few passersby on the other side of the area. He scratched his arm. A few kids were walking down the street. He wondered if they would see him, he flexed his muscles in his hooded shirt, as he was a tough type of man.

He pulled his sleeve down, then looked at the side nearer to him. A man was approaching him, with his eyes quite fixated.

On me.

Smiling.

But why?

He looked down, wondering what the problem was. What was he doing wrong? He had something on his face. Or did this man think he was handsome or something along those lines.

How are you doing?

The man still walked nearer to him. He said, under his breath, that he was fine. The man passed by, but kept looking at him, happy or something. He did not look.

As soon as the man was out of view, he felt that this guy was just a nice fellow. He regretted acting the way he had.

He turned his head, shouted loudly 'have a nice night', waited for a reply or something, but figured that the guy had heard him.

He pulled his shoulders up. He shuddered, then stepped down, then down into the street, intending to repeat his compliment.

* * * * * * * *

He ran his index finger down the wall of the hallway, held it up to his hand, inspected for dirt or something. He shook his head, sadly, sadly.

This would not do.

He licked his fingertip, then tapped it against his thumb a few times.

Then he rubbed his tongue against the roof of his mouth, made a face.

Following this, he snapped his fingers, while waving his hands around gracefully, made two swift punches, all while walking perfectly.

He saw Angelo, looking through the hotel door. He pursed his lips, whistled some great song or something of that sort, quite pleased with himself about how loud he was able to make it.

Angelo sat up, said a greeting.

He asked if Angelo had a hammer and nail behind the desk.

Why?

He wanted to hang a painting in his room.

Angelo said that this would depend.

Depend on what, exactly?

Angelo asked what type of painting it was, whether or not it was a good quality painting, so on and such things, this hotel had standards to uphold.

He began to assure Angelo that it was a fine painting, expensive. He looked up, Angelo had a grin.

His eyes dropped, he was confused.

Angelo laughed at him. Then told him that he would have to pay for the holes in the wall, it would be deducted from his security deposit, not a good idea.

He stared, blinked, looked away.

Angelo then invited him to take whatever he needed out of the closet, if he was that set on the idea.

He bowed his head, thank you.

He thought of something.

He told Angelina to have a nice day.

take that!

Angelo told him to put the hammer back in the closet when he was done with it. He looked over at the hall.

He figured that he knew where this supposed closet was, he had seen it a few times. He could picture the door to it, he thought, smaller door, no handle, he could imagine moving past it. He walked down the hall.

He thought that he would not return the hammer to the closet, that would show them. He would keep it in case he ever wanted to move his painting.

He saw a door.

That is the maintenance closet. That is definitely it.

There was no handle.

Only a lock.

He held his hand to his chin.

scientific.

He pulled against the lock to see if he could open the door, twice or so, before giving up.

He would have to go back, get the key. Angelo must have known that he would have to do this.

He walked a few steps back, then stopped.

He decided that it could wait. He could wait several hours until he went back, say that Angelo had forgotten to give him the key, a rude thing, how dare you. He placed his hand against the rail, hopped up the first few steps until he reached the second flight.

Part 8

(the triumphant return)

One

He set the chair underneath the light thing.
Hmm.

How to go about this?

He took the package of light bulbs from the desk, removed one. He took the marker out of his pocket, removed the cap. The thing was dry or something. It would not write on the glass. He rubbed the tip against the bulb several times.

Aha.

A line of black.

He drew a little man on one side of the bulb. He felt that this man should be doing something entertaining. He considered several options that he could not think of.

Fine, this little man will have a wine.

The marker was too thick. The bottle did not come out clearly. He drew several curved lines, as well as an exclamation point over the fellow's head.

It is done.

Standing on the chair, he reached toward the ceiling. He used his fingers to take out the screws that were holding up the glass elegant light cover thing with no function. Its weight fell into his hand.

Underneath, a light bulb.

without a drawing on it, interestingly enough.

That's something to think about.

He then went to work or something unscrewing this inferior bulb. He hoped that he was not putting too much pressure on the glass. Maybe it would shatter in his hand? Maybe he will die? My hand, my hand. He looked at his hand, disturbed that he could see some skeletonish bones in it.

He resolved to eat more.

He put the other light bulb into place. He decided that it was possible to replace the glass covering at a later date.

Haha, he jogged over to the light switch.

He could see the room illuminate.

He squinted at the bulb.

Yes, a drawing on it.

If his calculations were correct, there would be a large reproduction of his masterpiece on one of the walls. He looked around the room but he could not find it. He did this again. Where was it?

He did this again.

ah.

sad.

He walked to the other side of the room. He looked at the walls, then up at the drawing. He held his wrist against the window. He had a fantasy that he could ooze through the window as might the phantom-ghost. Then he wondered if he was about to enact this fantasy.

Nope.

He picked up a few articles of clothing from the floor, figuring that cleanliness is good. He could not think of a place to put them, so he dropped them into a pile next to the dresser, realizing that he could, if he so desired, put them in there, but then he would have to take them out again someday; blahdadadada, pathos! He looked at the room, at all the things around him.

And where was his gigantic drunk man?

He stretched his fist toward the wall, shook it a few times.

He gave up on this, put both of his hands inside his shirt, wrapping them around his rib cage. His hands were very cold. Bones bones, he needed to eat more, he had just eaten.

* * * * * * * *

He saw both of them sitting on the couches in the lobby, chatting. They did not see him immediately, so he looked around the lobby to check if Angelo was at the counter. He imagined that knowing Angelo's name, shaking his hand and such would impress them, because he, himself, was a man of the people.

Angelo, not at the desk.

He waited to see if Angelo would pop up from underneath

the counter, as he was set on the idea of saying hello to
Angelo.

He told them that it would be a short walk to the
restaurant. They stood up, the woman said that she could not
wait or something. He held the door for the two of them, even
though it took them several seconds to reach him.

Outside, he walked in front of them, very careful to
stay on the sidewalk. He could hear them talking quickly,
he imagined that they were holding hands. He was positive
that the woman's name was Betsy. The man's name was maybe
Robert, Judith, Jacko.

Fergll?

What was the woman's name? It could not be Betsy. He
closed his eyes. His suit swished around beneath his arms. He'd
messed this up. What was her name? He started to generate
random female names such as, but not limited to, Betsy.

Perhaps she was the elusive Fergan?

He clapped his hands, stopped. He turned to the man,
expressed, more or less, that, though this was embarrassing, he
had forgotten his name.

The two laughed, ho ho, quite social.

The man's name was Jude. They shook hands.

He pointed a finger at the woman, and said,

cautiously.

Betsy.

Correct.

Clap clap, debonaire, we're all friends now.

They all began to walk together. He thought about telling
Judith that he had considered Judith in his list of names.
Judith began complimenting him on his suit, which was nice.
Betsy asked him, afraid, if they were under dressed for the
restaurant.

She had thought of this for some time, he imagined. He
assured them that it was a, he did not know the right word,
normal dress place.

He assured them that they would enjoy it. They agreed
that they would.

Betsy went on about an anecdote that involved his being
in a sweatshirt earlier in the day, then she saw him in a suit
just now. She had thought something shocking about the way
she was dressed. Her hair was tied behind her. She kept falling

onto Judith's arm as she told the story.

He indicated the restaurant with his finger. He would walk them all the way to the door though, as that was the classy thing to do. No one talked for a little bit. Betsy told Judith that she was starving, then she said that this looked an excellent restaurant, from the outside.

He tried to walk away from them once they reached the door. He instructed them to have a nice meal.

Where was he going?

Isn't he going to join them?

* * * * * * * *

He opened his eyes. He estimated what time it was. Early. He slept for a little more, he needed to drink water. He got out of the bed. He needed to drink water from the bathroom sink.

Headache.

He clenched his teeth. His eyes went out of focus. He stalked over toward the bathroom. It was dark blah blah, he put his hands beneath the faucet, drinking several waters in rapid succession. He shook his head.

It was not until he saw the phone, hanging from the dresser.

Oh no.

He got back into the bed, he pressed his hands against his face. He could not remember who he had called, at first. He pulled the comforter over his head. Sleep sleep. Who had he called? That phone thing was nothing but trouble.

Perhaps he could press redial, and apologize for embarrassing himself.

Then he began to think about the international rates. Oh. Such robbery. Maybe he hadn't called anyone, maybe he had knocked the receiver off the hook with a wild kick, as he was inclined to such things. He assured himself that he liked to kick things. It would make perfect sense. He had even kicked a telephone or two in his days.

He started scratching himself sporadically.

His back, his chin, his hair.

He sat up in the bed. He held the receiver to his ear.

Hello? Hello?

No one was there.

He moved to place the receiver back. He held it in front of his mouth.

Wouldn't it be funny if he said something else into the phone? Wouldn't that be grand?

He paused while he thought of something else to say.

Not now, I'm busy, I have to go.

Thus, the conversation ends.

He got out of bed, pulled on his pants, he wanted to get breakfast from downstairs. He stuck his tongue out, picked up a shirt, then leaned his head into the wall for many seconds. Then he knocked his head against the wall several times with a smooth rhythm.

At the door, he looked back into his room.

He looked at his shoes. He let his eyes fall half closed, so that he looked disconcerted. He slapped himself gently, clapped his hands.

He set off, destination; probably breakfast!

And if the wind gets to him, then he'll come back for his jacket.

In his hallway he walked sideways for a while.

He tried to remember whom he had called.

He tried to pat down his hair.

The stairwell was cold. The architect never had intended this terrain for the pedestrian without shoes. He held his hand against the handrail, that's it. He jumped down the last two steps, landed.

The bottom of his foot stabbed his mind with little impulses. He lifted it up. He had landed on a sensitive nerve. He stopped to nurse this wound.

There was nothing he could do.

He ran his thumb over his foot to locate this weak point in his biology. He did not find it.

* * * * * * * *

He studied the line at the counter, then set his hand against several boxes of medicine. He would have to wait a few minutes until the line was clear.

He picked up one of the boxes.

Hmm, yes, green.

He looked over at the counter. Unfortunately, it was a man, an old man.

Someone else passed by the aisle, got in line.

Patience.

He looked around the pharmacy, there was no one else

inside. If he was going to do this right, he would have to purchase something. He would have to purchase something ordinary, as though he did this all the time.

oh, by the way, nonchalant.

Heheheh, he rubbed his hands in his imagination.

He decided to buy himself a toothbrush, it would make him seem hygienic. He initially selected a green toothbrush.

Bell.

An old couple had entered the store. He would have to wait.

He wished there were a girl at the counter, so he could use this to his advantage. Smile and such stuff as that.

Honestly my darling, this is my strange way of getting close to you.

I'm actually a lawyer or something.

Actually, I am a professional money incinerator.

Not professional actually, it's just a how I pass my time. I pass my time wasting money.

Well, let's just have sex or something, then you can talk to your boss.

The old couple was lingering at a rack of pills. The counter had cleared. It was time for him to make his move. He took two toothbrushes instead of one, just to do it right. He also needed some toothpaste, while he was at it.

The old man looked down at these items.

Hello.

The old man rung up the purchases, told him something, money out of his fancy little wallet, gentleman, hand to hand.

Oh, by the way, are you hiring?

He had his head turned to the side. He could hear the eyes move over him. He tried his best not to twitch at all. No one was saying anything.

i've always wanted to work in a pharmacy.

We are not hiring.

He took his change, looked at the floor. He took the bag, said that this would be no problem.

Oh no, ah, it had happened like that had it? He felt ashamed. He passed the old people, who had heard him ask for a job, get rejected outright.

He stuck his wrist through the bag, then started down the street towards his car. His wife would not be at the house, she needed to pick up the kids first. Then on to an athletic competition. He had wanted to go, but, as the saying goes, you've got to pay for things by means of money. What was that guy's problem? Didn't he know that he was asking only as a lark? Who would want to work in a pharmacy?

Hmm. He should stop and see his mistress, he had told her he would stop by.

His face tensed, he ducked behind a wall. Out of view. He reconsidered the scene.

What had given him away?

* * * * * * * *

He found the address book filed in the space underneath his laundry bag. He ran his fingers over the carpet, which was looking a bit disgusting. He sat down on the floor, his knees cracked as he stretched them out, opened the book.

A grotesque sketch of a beautiful woman disturbed him.

Yet, if viewed from the right angle.

With closed eyes.

He found the number, then placed his index finger on the page, closed the book around it, stood up. He used his eyesight to scan the local area for any coins, that he could make the call from the telephone downstairs.

No change.

He guessed that he must have done laundry recently, which made him pleased with himself.

He would have to make the call from here, no real shame in that. He walked over to the desk, gathered the binder into the corner of his armpit. He took these things over to the side of the bed.

maybe he should make the bed.

He set the binder and address book on the pillow, set to work. He picked up some pants, a few socks, etcetera, until his hands were full. He took these items over to the laundry bag, dumped them on top of it.

Back at the bed, he drew back the comforter so that he could find the first layer of linen, which was bunched up at the foot of the frame. Dede, he felt nervous, rotated his shoulders, an unusual amount of light and such, pulled the linen taught, walked around. It was simple enough to get the comforter, stop, tap against his heart with his fist, say a few words that he didn't catch, forget what he was doing, oh yes, make the bed.

Ah, he sat on the fancy and clean bed.

He fluffed the pillows, placed the binder on the center of the sheets.

He had lost his place in the address book. Oh, what else could go wrong, he would have to find it again. He found the phone number. He scratched his chin.

maybe he should shave first.

He picked up the phone, dialed the number. The phone rung a few times.

Outside the sky was getting dark, because it was night.

She was not home, he decided. He could let the phone ring as long as he wanted.

Hello?

He whistled quietly.

He asked Hannah if she was sleeping, she said no. She was not so happy to hear from him, he could tell, so he decided to mention the money as quickly as possible. He said that so and such, he needed her again, translate the manuscript that Richard had given him. He could not write the article etcetera very urgent crisis.

She said that she was not a translator. He needed to act quickly.

The sum that he threw out was roughly twice what he had planned.

She did not say anything, which means– yes.

He apologized for the hour, he would talk to her soon.

He hung up the receiver, made his hands into claws, and raked at the air with worried eyebrows, cursing quietly that things were not so good.

Two

He stood in the elevator next to a fellow with a suit on. He leaned back against the wall so that he could get a good look. The hood of his shirt bunched against the back of his neck. He sniffed. The guy was balding on the back of his head, with a good amount of hair growing out of the collar of his shirt. He sniffed.

Did this man stink?

He sniffed.

This man did stink!

He stuck his hands into the pocket of his shirt, pushing it down so that he could scratch at his lower abdomen with his fingers. Haha, this man was a real stinker. He decided to say something clever. The elevator doors began to close. The elevator moved up.

Do you think we'll make it?

The man did not respond to him, except by stinking for a while longer. This was great. He wished an additional someone were standing next to him so that he could make some eyes about it.

Eyes that said;

This man does not bathe, and I am charming.

The elevator opened at the second floor. He waited to see if the man was going to exit here, in which case he would wait. The man pressed the close button on the apparatus.

The doors began to close. He jogged out at the last second.

The doors shut behind him.

Peril.

He held out his hand so that he could grab the corner of the wall, pulling his trajectory towards his door. The corner thing pinched his hand. He walked down the hall, pulled his legs apart so that his testicles were not sticking to his thigh.

Hmm hmm.

There is the door.

There was a white bag set against the front of the door. He leaned forward, could not remember leaving it there.

Paper bag with a dainty handle. He could see some tissue paper inside.

His name was written on it.

He held the bag in his hand. He looked down the hall, he turned his head.

He pulled up the tissue paper. Underneath was a metal canister with black trim. He pulled it out.

A flask.

Class act!

He took out his keys, went into the room, leaving the door open.

Who had given him this flask?

He figured that Angelo, Angelo's cousin.

Or.

or, some secret admirer.

He found a note in the bottom of the bag. He took this

into the bathroom with the flask. He turned on the faucet,
removed the cap. He tried to look over at the note, but it folded
closed.

He took a sip of water from the flask. The opening did not
allow much liquid to come out. The water tasted a bit dirty.

Refreshing.

He opened the note.

Thank you note?

Interesting.

He took the note out into the master bedroom, taking sips
of water from this little fellow. He deciphered that it was from
those two, probably thanking him for dinner etcetera. Good
luck with newspaper.

* * * * * * * *

He placed his foot against the side of the desk so that he
could get some leverage to tilt his chair onto its back legs. He
succeeded at this. He took a sip from the glass, shuddered, his
eyes wet.

He experimented with making the chair tilt back further.
He felt the weight come off his foot, so that the chair began
to tilt back, oh no, doom, shifted his torso forward, the chair
returned to the floor.

A sound.

He moved his head towards this, then stood up, taking
the glass with him. He pulled the curtain to the side, looked
out the window. What was that? An animal? He leaned in to
the glass.

streetlight, car, vegetation.

Blah blah, yet another mystery.

He leaned back, drinking the last of the glass. He walked
over to the bottle, put his index finger on it, waltzed around at
a radius until he ran into the corner of the desk. He suspected
that he could have another, but could not set himself to the
task, immediately.

He performed a drinking dance, snapping his fingers,
dragging his socks against the carpet.

The dance was, by all accounts, a wild success.

He decided that his problem was that he did not enjoy the
taste of the gin when it was mixed with bathroom water.

Ah, this problem could be solved, somehow.

He could purchase a soda in the break room.

He found some coins in his jacket pocket, returning to the desk for good measure, refilling his glass so that he could have a cocktail for the road. He walked over to the door.

In the hallway, he began to act like an entrepreneur. He toasted several doors with his glass, nodded, continued walking.

Yes, yes, good luck with that.

He spilled some of the gin onto the carpet. Someone would see him with his glass, report him to some authority, get out, take your little glass with you.

Even though the stuff looked the same as water.

What, I can't drink water now?

All the same, he lowered the glass, keeping it by his waist so that no one could see it. He pressed the button for the elevator, looked around, looked around again.

He sipped.

heheh.

Alas, he could have made an excellent spy.

The doors opened up. No one was in the thing, he stepped inside, pressing the button that would take him down to the lobby.

He sipped his glass, felt sick. The elevator doors opened. He rubbed the top of his head against the side of the elevator. He shook, then pumped his free hand and shoulder in small concentric circles. The elevator doors had closed by this point.

Was he trapped?

The elevator began moving upwards.

Ah.

He pressed the button for the lobby, but it did not work. Someone had called the elevator. He would look like a stinky idiot, just standing there, wrong way confused and all.

Oh you dog. Tap water and gin?

Stuck in the elevator? How entertaining.

for us.

He pressed two. The elevator stopped. The doors opened.

He escaped! Sipped the last of his glass, walking over to the stairwell.

* * * * * * * *

Angelo was taking a break evidently. He saw him walking outside the main doors of the lobby, turning right dada. He hurried up so that he could see where Angelo was going. He pushed open the doors. He looked to the right.

Angelo was nowhere to be seen.

He decided to walk a little that way. He turned the corner. Angelo was descending the hill, sticking his fingers into a packet of cigarettes.

What upset him about this was that there would be no way that he could walk down the hill without being obvious that he was following Angelo. He thought about giving up on the matter, returning to his room, planning it out better. He might even etcetera, do something else.

Angelo pulled out a slip of paper from his pocket, blue looking.

He walked down the hill, etcetera, just passing by. He stood behind Angelo, saw that the paper was a record of Angelo's working hours that had, at some point in time, been attached to a paycheck.

Perfect.

He stood behind Angelo, not really wanting to say hello or anything like that. Eventually Angelo noticed that someone was standing behind him, but did not turn around. He did nothing either.

Angelo turned his head, took back. Then said hello in a suspecting way. Angelo folded the paper, and pretended to burn it with a cigarette. Angelo pulled the package of cigarettes from his pocket, then asked if he smoked at all, mentioning that he did not believe so.

He put his fingers into the package, taking one of the cigarettes. Instead of a match, Angelo offered him the other cigarette, which he used to light it.

He said that he needed to talk to Angelo.

Angelo walked closer to him, asked what he needed.

Hey, hello, hey, remember that time when I lent you that money?

What?

He told Angelo about how he had written a check when Angelo had asked to borrow some money, asked if he had gotten back the money yet.

Angelo said that he had not gotten back the money.

Angelo looked away.

He puffed on his old cigarette.

He did not want to continue. He felt that he had explained

himself already.

He said that he needed the money back. Angelo flicked the cigarette, said that he didn't have any money.

He decided to cut this short. He said that he did not need it all right away. It was just that obviously something. He stopped, he punched Angelo in the arm, said that he needed to run a few errands, so long.

He walked down to the retaining wall, put his cigarette in his lips. He jumped down, landing dadada.

He looked for the most reasonable direction to go and perform these supposed errands. He walked towards the intersection that way.

He looked back at Angelo, who had turned his back, scratching his scalp.

He waved.

Angelo did not react to that.

He turned, rubbed his hand against his forehead. He flicked the cigarette, the ashes falling on his pants.

* * * * * * * *

He could not feel any heat touching his fingertip through the bottom of the coffee cup. He raised the cup to his mouth.

The coffee was slow to come, viscous, pretty nasty.

He choked on it for a while, made a face, tried to set the cup down on the windowsill outside the photo thing. It was not wide enough, the base of the cup would just not rest on it, no matter how hard he tried. He had some misgivings about setting it on the sidewalk, which might etcetera infect it, maybe.

Since he was not going to drink the coffee, he set it on the ground.

Hello, Miss.

She did not look up at him as he had, somehow, said this in a menacing way. He turned back to his coffee cup, picked it up, looked at the bottom, tossed his head back. It was not so bad before he swallowed it. He pushed his tongue back to force it down.

He let his eyes roll into the back of his head, wavered his forearms as if about to faint or something, cracked his neck, opened his eyes, looked down the street to see if anyone had seen him do his little bad coffee routine.

Some people were on the sidewalk, but no one was

applauding.

He looked over at a mailbox that was some distance ahead of him. He thought about disposing of the empty cup by placing stamps on it, send it to a nemesis of some sort. He did not have his address book on him, nor stamps, or any real desire to do this.

He saw a trash can the other way.

Since he had some freedom in his schedule, he walked back to the trash, until he was a short distance from it, he tossed the cup to the can. The cup landed on the garbage, success, it fell off the other side though.

He paused.

He looked around for some evidence. Had someone seen him?

He walked over to the cup, picked it up, rested it on top of the garbage.

Conscientious man that I am, I don't balk a minute at giving myself the shorter end of things.

He used both of his hands to brush his scalp. He steered himself out of a passing person's way, so that he almost scraped against the side of the partition of a bus stop.

This being done, he examined his memory for the varieties of shops that this way would lead him to. If he turned right, he could go to a park. If he went straight, he could get a sandwich, perhaps.

He stopped at a corner to see what amount of money he had brought with him. He pushed his thumb against various pockets, checking for the shape of his wallet. He found it, pulled it out, counted out a few bills.

Haha, so he was a rich man today.

He figured that he might go get something to eat, then, if he felt up to it, he might stop in some place for a drink.

* * * * * * * *

He selected a few books, one of them hardcover, that he would sit on the table. They looked respectable enough, judging by the covers.

He hoped that they were respectable enough, at least.

Oh so now you read 'how to be pregnant', do you?

Ah.

She already knew that he could not read, didn't she?

True. How true.

He could not remember where he had gotten the books, exactly, so he set the stack of them on a clearance table, figuring that some employee would take care of it someday.

He walked back over to the coffee stand, where his binder was. He felt relieved that no one had stolen it, which had been weighing on his conscience or something.

He took the package of cigarettes out of his jacket pocket, opened them, removing several cigarettes so that the thing did not look new. He considered removing the envelope, keeping it on the table, but that seemed pretty much what he wanted to do.

He set the cigarettes on the table, looked for an ashtray, saw one.

It was difficult to reach the ashtray from his seat, he nearly fell out of the chair.

He bent off one of his matches, lit the cigarette, placed it in the ashtray.

He aligned the cigarette pack to the room's geometry.

He held his lips up for awhile so that anyone interested could see his teeth, if they were so inclined.

Hmm.

He imagined that this was Hannah, he could not be sure. She looked about the same. He made a nod at her, took the cigarette up from the ashtray, tried to puff on it.

It had gone out.

Hannah walked into the coffee area, said hello to him. She was happy to see him now, which threw him off. She pulled the chair out, he realized that he needed to light his cigarette once again. He pulled out another match, looked away from her, pushing the cigarette pack towards her.

No thank you.

He held the flame in front of the cigarette longer than he needed to, figuring that he looked pretty good.

Blahaha, little do you expect.

He pushed the manuscript over to Hannah. She made a comment about how it should not take so much time to translate, as it wasn't very long. He said that this was good, as blah blah tight schedule.

She did not believe him about this, he could tell. He wished something would happen that would prove it to her. A phone call for him, an urgent call from a famous person.

He took the envelope out of his pocket, slid it over, said that he would give her the rest upon completion.

She did not count the money, which was disappointing, as it was all there.

Did she want a coffee?

Actually she has a few things to do now.

He said that she should go in that case, he would talk to her soon enough.

She did not go immediately, she sat still, looked at him then out the window.

Three

He rubbed his fingers into the carpet in front of him, making several crumbs pop out of the threads of whatever.

Not feeling so grand.

He put these hands of his over the back of his neck. He stood up, walked over to the desk where he suspected he had some alcohol or something like that left over because he never finished it. It's so hard to complete a bottle of gin.

He found that the bottle was empty, groaned, suspected that he might have poured it into his flask. He found the flask in the bathroom, swished it around.

That might be water.

He sipped the thing. He could not tell what it was, figured that it was his gin, probably. He took another sip, tried using his senses to discern what it was. He went back over to the floor. Sat down, reclined onto his back. He pulled his abdomen up, so that he could sip from the flask. He set his head back, slowly, rolled it to the side.

Broad daylight.

Lunatic!

blasé.

He heard door sounds, wondered for a moment if his neighbors were up to something. Enter the maid. He looked under the bed. Without knocking blah blah.

He shifted his back and legs, again. He slowly worked himself under the bed, reached over, took his flask so that she would not see it, though he did not feel like drinking it now. He could not see well in this position.

The underside of the box spring is covered with black felt.

Good to know.

He heard the maid walk around the room. He began to

suspect that she would find him. He choked a little bit.

strange strange man.

What was the appropriate thing to do? Stand up, hello hello. He moved his head to the side, he saw her hand reach down, picking up a shirt of his. He hoped that she would proceed to do something odd with his things, so that he could roll out from under the bed.

Aha, sniffing my underpants are you?

I was only underneath the bed for reconnaissance purposes.

He heard her tear the sheets off the bed. The danger increases. His breath kept hitting the felt, felt a bit stifled, he could feel the moisture in his breath. His cheeks were red.

Bah, bah, change my sheets.

He heard the air sweep underneath the fresh linen as she draped it out to unfold it. He could not see up her skirt, but could not help thinking about it, that he should be able to and such, considering.

He suspected that she had seen him by this point, he could hear her snickering a little under her breath. She let the mattress drop back onto the box spring. She laughed, gathered the dirty linen.

What's so funny?

She walked over to the door, closed it.

The encounter is over.

Getting out from under the bed, he scraped his back against the carpet.

* * * * * * * *

He walked down the hall, tada. He used his hand to rub the interior of his pockets against an irritated splotch on his thigh. Several threads were bunching up into lint, rubbing against his leg, maybe falling off, who knows. He stopped at the break room.

The night auditor had put two chairs together, sleeping.

He thought about banging the door, wake the guy up. But, to what point?

There's a fire in the bit over there. The poor woman burnt up. You should not be sleeping.

You killed her, I'm going to sue you for these emotions.

In the lobby he stepped up onto the back of one of the couches. Made a survey of the things to see. The lobby desk, the lobby windows, the lobby in general. His shoes slid off the back of the couch. He stamped his feet into the material, wondered if there was any dust on his shoes.

He got off the couch, walked behind the desk.

He wanted to take something.

He took one of the pens, rubbed the tip against his hand to check if it had run dry.

It had.

He placed his hand against the shelf full of mail. He inserted his index finger into his mouth and sucked on it.

He had some mail then.

He took his mail out of the hole on the shelf. He checked through it. He balked.

Hello.

Doctor.

He opened the envelope to see what exactly was inside.

It was empty?

The bottom of the envelope was filled with confetti. He poured a bit of this into his hand, interested to see what this meant. He turned one of the slips of paper over. Some numbers on a green background.

Interesting.

It was one of his checks.

He closed the envelope, folded it over. He moved to throw it away into the wastebasket behind the desk, but it occurred to him that someone, most likely Angelo, would find it, figure him out.

He walked over to the door, checking to see that he had his key card with him. He stepped outside. It was cold. He walked over to the trash can, etcetera, threw away the envelope.

He walked back to the entrance, braced himself against one of the columns, rubbed his temple, grit his teeth.

He looked out at the night or such things.

The sky lifted around.

He rammed his shoulder into the column a few times. Alas, alas. He thought about calling the doctor somehow, explaining that he had not meant any offence, apologize. Even if he did not get anything out of it.

He decided that it was not too late for a walk.

The grass was wet from natural processes. He could feel it soaking the tip of his shoes. He continued down into the gulch, where he could not see anything. He stopped at the creek bed or thereabouts.

He looked for stones that he could cross.

It was too dark.

He stood in place for a few seconds before turning back up the hill. He could feel his muscles tensing in the back of his legs.

* * * * * * * *

He stopped by the bathroom, with a suspicion that he did not have everything that he would need. He felt his wallet in his pocket. He felt his keys.

What else was necessary?

He might need his passport. He walked over to the desk where he remembered seeing it underneath some junk. He moved several papers around.

His second attempt was to check the pockets of his laundry. He went over to his bag.

He saved himself some time by folding the pants instead of doing all that hand in the pocket stuff. Each of his pants bent easily at the pocket, so his passport was not inside there.

Had he lost his passport?

Hadn't he felt a weight fall out of his jacket as he stepped up from the street that time?

He did not need his passport at the moment, he was only traveling domestically. Hm.

He was fairly certain that he had left it on his desk. He walked over to the desk, figuring that it might be underneath some etcetera paper, or shirt, or this or this. He lifted the shirt up from the desk.

He checked by the bed, where he kept several things.

His face got red. He said 'why' a few times softly and in quick succession. He had lost his passport before. He turned over the pillow. This type of thing always happened to him. He knew how to get it replaced though. Underneath the bed, a few socks, a shoe or so. He pushed his thumb into his eye. So, lost your passport once again have you? You are such a wellspring of entertainment to us folks at the embassy.

He tilted the dresser away from the wall. Many people, perhaps him as well, fling their arms around while they sleep. He had knocked it off the dresser, that much was certain

He gave up, walked over to the door. There was nothing he

could do about it. He ran his hand over the desk. The passport was certainly on the desk, that rascal. He was making such a to do about it. He stared at the desk for a while, hoping that it would pop out at him.

He coughed.

He had lost his passport then.

No big loss.

He decided to check underneath the pillow one more time. He had been lying in bed, looking at his painting before he'd gone to sleep. He turned over the pillow, reached his hand inside of it. Oh, hadn't he been derided enough? He said 'please' again and again.

He smacked the bed frame, then threw the sheets off. He huffed.

His passport was wrapped up in the sheets, with a pack of cigarettes. He grabbed it, knelt. He held out his hands, and prayed for several minutes.

Thank you.

He pressed his face into the linen.

He kept his eyes closed, kept praying, but reached over for the cigarettes, found them blindly, took the package to his ear, shook it to see if there were any left.

Yes, there was a couple left.

* * * * * * * *

He saw that some unsuspecting soul had left their drink on the top of the wall. He walked over to it, pointed his eyebrows down.

He roared.

He smacked the drink off the wall, it hit the sidewalk, fell into the street. The soda poured out of it, running back to the gutter, and he felt generally pleased with himself. He fled the scene casually. He took his little flask out of his jacket pocket, unscrewed the cap.

He tensed his face up, swallowed.

He opened his eyelids halfway, let his vision go out of focus and made the most disquieting smile he was capable of. He looked across the street thinking that someone might want to see this.

deserted, late afternoon.

A car approached him, passed him by.

He made a rough estimate at how much alcohol he had

left in his flask. He could always refill it at a liquor store, if he deemed it necessary. He pushed it into his pant pocket. He shook his leg so that it would settle on the bottom of his pocket, where it would not fall out.

Following this he reached out for a signpost, touched it gingerly. He swung around it once, not as fast as he would have liked, the metal dug into his palm. He lost his footing for a second, but his grip on the post prevented him from falling down.

Restaurant.

He spread his arms out, trotted across the road to the doorway. All of the windows were blocked by shutters, he could not see inside.

He decided to investigate this matter further.

He adjusted his shirt, rubbed his face, made sure that he looked harmless.

He opened the door. The interior was rather festive, orange lighting, red booths, some blue colors by the bar area. He blinked a few times, then saw a couple coming toward him. He decided to hold the door open, they walked past.

He considered whether or not to tell them to have a nice evening.

He walked over to a little wooden ordeal where they kept the menus, took one for himself, walked over to the bar.

He asked the bartender if she had a list of drink prices that he could use to make his decision. She walked away from him, allowing him a good look at her from behind.

Haha. She was a little overweight for his tastes. Her hair was done up nicely.

He decided to take out his flask.

He took a sip, closed his eyes. He looked up, the bartender had noticed that he was holding his flask. She walked back over to him. Going to say something. She held out her hand.

oh no. quick.

Before she spoke, he explained that he was wondering what price it would cost for her to refill this flask with a mid level alcohol.

She paused. She looked at the flask, saying that it would depend what type of alcohol.

He did not have much money in his pocket.

He said that this would be up to her. She thought about it.

* * * * * * * * *

He looked down at the coins in his hand, extended his fingers. He placed his other hand on top of this one, and rattled them up and down. The coins flew around in his hand. He considered throwing these on the ground, as though he were throwing dice.

He did not do it however, because he would have to pick them up off the carpet.

At the elevator area, he opened his palm up, counted off the coins in a row, added up the value a few times. He pressed the button to call the elevator.

He licked his lips, cracked his neck.

He stood with his back against the elevator door, so that, when it opened, he would fall inside. He heard the bell, he felt the metal pull out from under his shoulders. He put his weight back onto his feet, walked backwards into the elevator. Pressed the right button and such things as good men are inclined to do when traveling by elevator.

The elevator shifting downwards made him aware of his urinary tract. He felt as though it might evacuate automatically, ruin his pants, and such things that gentlemen do but that would not happen, actually.

He practiced his phone manner. Hello, how are you, how is it coming along? My son back home is a little sick, but my harem will take care of that.

I was working on some experiments, thinking of you.

He walked down the hall to the pay phone, withdrew the door. He debated whether to stand or sit during the ordeal. He sat down on the stool, reached his hand up to place the coins in. He consulted the number that he had written on his thumb. He needed to bend it at the knuckle, making the number a bit more readable.

He inhaled through his nose, lifted his head in an elegant motion.

A man picked up the phone.

Questionable.

He moved to hang up the receiver. He decided to be polite, ask if he had the right number. He asked for Hannah.

She was not there at the moment.

He did not know what to say.

Would he like to leave a message?

He explained quickly that he was a friend of hers, she was translating a story that he was working on, calling for no reason really. The man took this all in.

He said goodbye, then said wait, he said that he needed to know if the story was any good, so ask her that. He said goodbye quickly, then hung up the phone.

He blew his breath, felt lucky, placed his elbow against the counter, rubbed his hair. He thought of calling back to ask what, exactly, was the relationship between the two of them. Then he felt embarrassed that he had said the word friend. He rubbed his nose. He pictured that they would get a good laugh over that.

He smacked the receiver hard, enough so that he thought it might fall off the cradle. He mashed his fingers on the numerals.

Four

He took off his shirt, went to the bathroom to see if he had any towels left. His lower eyelids were swollen up from trying to sleep. He stretched them out, lowered his jaw, moaned.

He put his hand into the bathroom, which was dark, pressed it against the wall, found the light-switch.

Toilet, above the toilet, towel shelf. He saw that he had one towel sitting on the shelf, folded up. He went over to the shelf, reached up, took it down, draped it out.

The towel was small. Not big enough to wrap around his waist. He decided that it would do, for the moment, adding that he could go get one of the other towels from the floor if it proved insufficient. Who would require a towel of this size? Why had she put it on his shelf, knowing full well that he was a regularly proportioned man?

He bunched the towel up and set it on the toilet. He turned on the faucet over the bathtub, put the drain in.

The water on his hand got onto his pants as he undid them. This annoyed him. His foot got stuck in one of the legs, and he had to sit on the side of the bathtub to remove it properly.

He wobbled on the edge, tried to maintain balance.

At long last, after weeks of labor, he removed his pants, kicked them under the sink. Removing his boxer shorts was fairly easy. He threw these over toward the sink. They landed on the counter. He stepped into the tub. The hot stung the top of his foot in particular. He debated whether or not to add more cold water to the thing, entertained the idea of taking his bath at an unheard of scaldingesque temperature, felt quite tough about his willingness to do this.

He sat down in the water, which was too hot, stood up, added a little cold water and got out of the tub to wait for things to calm down.

Passing some time, he grabbed his testicular sac in his fist, squeezed it until he could see veins and such biological things. He studied some marks in the skin, wondered what those were until he gave up.

Some steam went this way and that up the tile.

He placed his hand underneath his back.

The water had cooled enough by this point that he felt comfortable getting back in, standing for a moment. He sat down, splashed some water onto the top of his legs. The hair on his legs flattened out, turned a darker brown. He complimented himself on the density of his leg hair.

Leaning back, into the water, he felt as though his shoulder bones might crack from the temperature, and he would be generally rejuvenated. His hair got wet, his neck got wet, the back of his ears got wet, he scratched them, then put his foot under the faucet.

He closed his eyes, and wondered if he was tired now. If he would be tired when he was done.

* * * * * * * *

He picked up one of the bags of corn chips, staring at the price tag, then up at the matching sign above the display, a yellow board with black figures.

Did he want these?

He looked at the bag to see if the price on the display was different from the suggested price on the bag. He could not find one. He placed the chips back on the shelf, deciding that it would be best to think it over.

He could eat them, he guessed.

He stopped at some milk cartons, put his hand on his head. He tried to think of several menus that he could invent and keep in his room. It would save some money to have them. He did not have anything to cook with, though. He wanted something delicious, with a particular flavor that he liked.

He could get some bread, make sandwiches.

Hm.

He walked down the line, looking for the correct aisle.

He touched a pack of batteries, thinking that he could use some. He remembered that he no longer had his electric razor, and, in general, did not have many things of his own. So he did not want these at all.

An older gentleman, with a grocery cart and all.

He stood against some cleaning stuff, in order to let the guy get past him. His nose almost touched an orange box with blue writing on it. His jaw tensed, and he thought that he should leave. He could just wander to the front of the store, make his getaway.

He calmed himself down, making a sidelong glance at the older fellow, who was holding a pack of nails with a picture on the packaging. He shot off down the aisle, put his hands into his pockets. He looked back, realized that he had not gotten a cart for himself. He wondered where they were keeping them, as no one had told him about those.

Nearer to the front of the store, he saw some movie things for sale at the checkout. He wanted to go a little closer so that he could make out the covers, but did not as there was that clerk girl at the checkout, and he did not yet have any purchases.

He walked a few more steps, saw some bags of bread. He took one of the loaves, a brown one, then decided that he would need some excellent meats to go with it. Cheese as well, if everything went correctly.

Then I'm done.

It was noticeably colder in the aisle of frozen foods.

His nose was stuffed up, but he hadn't brought any tissues.

A teenaged boy was shopping with his mother. She probably knew how to cook, he figured, and he wished that he could ask her for some advice. I'm having some trouble, laughter. He began to feel mildly angry that someone might see him and have a condescending opinion of him.

He looked down the back of the store, where there were many things. He saw some orange coloration at the far corner, then walked toward it, figuring it was the right way to go.

* * * * * * * *

He nodded, then put his hand down against the dog's nose. Cold, the dog pushed its nose into his hand. He then patted the little tuft of hair on its head, smiled, then told her that this was a terrific animal.

He looked back down at the dog, wondering if the comment he had just made was at all plausible. It stuck its tongue out of its mouth, licked its hair, then walked several steps away.

She bent down, then picked up the dog, laboriously, as it was fat. She pressed it against her face, asking it if it had heard his compliment.

Alright.

He tried to plan a maneuver of some sort, something that would lead to him walking around with her for an hour or so, getting invited back to her place. He said that he had a terrier back home, which was true in a way. She bent over, putting the dog on the ground. He surveyed the surrounding area for other people.

The dog walked over to his shoe, put its nose onto it, then remained still for some time. While she looked down at it, he shot his head up to examine some of her key facial features. Her skin was tan, she had some freckles, her nose was thin.

I have a terrier back home, he said.

She told him to have a nice day, clapped her hands together for the dog to follow, not making much sound because the leash prevented her palms from slapping together. The dog coughed, its neck garroted by the collar, it trotted after her.

sortof denim jacket, he said.

She looked not so attractive now.

He thought about following her under some pretense. He would explain that he was interested in her, that he was a writer, and a foreigner. He put his foot onto some mulch, kicked it over. He looked at the girl, who was pulling the leash tighter to get the dog to follow.

I need to follow you because I am doing research for an article that I'm writing. You will be symposium, museum, limousine– sleep with me! He gave a swift punch to a tree in front of him, withdrawing his muscle early enough that his knuckle received no injury from it. The girl was walking up the paved portion of the hill by now.

He dragged his feet across the mulch, noting, and feeling glad, that he was knocking things out of order.

He asked himself what he wanted with a girl that age, deciding nothing.

Then he thought about the poor dog.

He stuck his hands into his pockets, checked to see if he had brought any cigarettes with him. He pulled out a napkin from his pocket, which he had drawn on earlier. He unfolded it, wondering why he had kept it instead of throwing it out.

A stick figure with large breasts, two helicopters overhead. His name and the date written in the margin.

Ah, life.

He pushed the napkin back down into his pocket, looked up the hill.

* * * * * * * *

He looked down at the pavement, keeping the man that was about to pass him in his peripheral vision. When they were about to pass, he looked up, nodded, smiled. The man was dirty, poorly dressed, presented no real threat.

He put his hand into his pocket, rubbing his finger against one of the coins. He withdrew it, slipping it into his mouth, using his tongue to push it into his right cheek. Metallic taste. He raised his head up, so that he could see the hotel.

He turned the corner, decided to take the sidewalk up to the door. He put another coin into his mouth, positioning it in the other side. He sucked his cheeks in underneath his molars, as much as he could, at least.

A few trees.

He thought about what he was going to do when he got back to his room, he felt there was something he'd intended to do that he could not recall. A blue truck pulled down from the hotel, turned toward him. He shook one of his tennis shoes.

Angelo's cousin.

Driving a truck.

He raised his hand toward her, letting her know that things were good. She flashed her lights, slowed the car down. He opened his mouth, worried about her seeing coins in there. He discharged them into his hand, some saliva trailed out from his mouth.

He did not want to put them in his pocket. He kept them in his fist, and felt uncomfortable about touching the saliva stuff. Angelo's cousin waited for him to approach the car, which he did. She was wearing her uniform, with a tough-looking jacket overtop of it.

She asked how he was, she had not seen him much.

He looked around at some nature, the hotel, then back at

her.

I'm fine.

She said that this was good, many people were worried about him. She looked over at the light at the end of the street, then back at him. He put his hand into his pocket and casually released the coins and wiped his palm at the same time. He did not know what she meant, or how to respond.

He kindof smiled, said that he was doing well.

She had to go, but they would talk soon. He stepped back onto the pavement, paused, then waved at her. The truck pulled away, he saw her move her head over to look down the road. He turned back to the hotel, started walking.

He thought things over, wondered who was worried about him.

Angelo, he figured, although she had said many people, which worried him.

He began to console himself, things had not been so well lately, he discerned. He felt sympathy for himself, regretted some general aspects of his life. Money was tight, his emotions were not good.

He felt irritated that Angelo had been talking about him, particularly to her. He thought that he would tell Angelo not to do this again. He had enough troubles in his life. He turned up through the lot, walked on some grass.

* * * * * * * *

He flipped through his checkbook, noted that there were not many left, as he walked down to the elevator. He figured that he could order an additional checkbook, worried that the bank would not want to ship it to him. He shook his head, then pushed the checkbook against his neck.

The elevator door was open, though there was no one in the waiting area. He ran over toward it, catching it just in time. He pressed the lobby button.

He realized that he had not brought a pen with him.

He moved to press the button that would return him to the second floor. He realized that he would first have to go to the lobby, as the elevator was already headed down.

He could take one from the front desk.

The doors opened. He walked out, then looked at the stairwell. He could go up the stairs, grab a pen, and return relatively soon. He saw the back of Hannah's head, she was looking out the lobby window. He walked softly so that she would not hear him.

He got over toward the desk.

Hannah looked over.

He stopped.

He said that he would write the check immediately.

He took one of the pens from the mug on the desk, then walked over to the couch. He sat down as far away from Hannah as the couch would allow. She tried not to look at him while he wrote the check, though he noticed that she glanced over at him a few times.

He looked at the binder on her lap, he signed his name.

He put the pen into his shirt pocket, hoping that she had not noticed that he had taken it from the front desk. He held the book in one hand, then carefully tore the check out of the binding. He handed it over, thanked her.

He moved nearer to her, pointed his finger down at the papers sitting on top of the binder. He asked if the story was any good, she finished placing the check into her purse, then lifted up the binder and papers, handed them to him.

She said that he would like it.

It was good.

He did not know if she was saying these things to appease him. He thought of insisting on her honest opinion of the story, but could not find a good reason to do this. He put the papers onto his lap, then held out his hand for her to shake.

She did this.

He said that he would send her a copy of the article once it was printed.

He said that he would place her in the thank you portion of the article, at the top of the list.

She raised her hand to her ear, pulling her hair behind it. She stood up from the couch, pulled her skirt down. He withdrew the top sheet of paper, stared at it without reading.

He figured that she wanted to go, but was waiting for his permission or such.

He rubbed his throat.

Did she want a hug or something?

He said that he would keep in touch, stood up, pulled the stack into his arm.

Part 9

*(a disturbing quiet
followed)*

One

He stopped by the gum ball machine, took out a coin, and placed it in the apparatus. He turned the dial, looked through the glass. He hoped that the candy would be one of these gentlemen with light blue dots on them. He put his hand underneath the machine, in case the candy fell toward the floor.

He lifted the metal door.

Pink.

He lifted up his sunglasses so that he could confirm this.

pink.

He checked over his shoulder, for some reason. He felt relieved that there were no witnesses.

He wedged the candy into his mouth. It had gotten stale, a bit hard to break. He thought that he might have to remove it. He clenched his jaw down tightly. The candy slowly split in half.

He held open the door for an old woman, stared at her face, hoping that she would look up at him appreciatively. She refused to make any eye contact. She almost brushed past him.

Going out of his way to be polite.

He walked down the street, chewing on his gum ball. He put his hands into his pockets, leaned back until he felt pressure on his lower spine.

The candy was hard, his jaw exhausted, the flavor, not to be found in nature.

He decided to spit the thing out of his mouth. He arranged his lips into a circle thing, situated the gum in front of his teeth with his tongue. The gum ball shot out of his mouth, quite far. A tiny cannonball! He was amused by this, impressed with himself. He wished, for a moment, that he had bought several of them, as to have an arsenal for emergencies.

He crooked his mandible back into place, thought about romance, classy furniture, politics.

He had lost track of his location, looked around for a crossroad or advertisement that he might recognize. Outside the shoe place, he saw a yellow banner that seemed a bit familiar. He figured that he could, if he wanted, be back in his room within a half hour.

Out of the corner of his eye, he looked at the reflection of his shirt in a store window.

It is a nice shirt.

Quite a nice shirt, after all.

He saw someone inside, a small woman with dark hair. He hoped that she had not seen him admiring himself. He looked down at his shoes. His sunglasses slid down his nose, he held out his hands to catch them, but the temples caught behind his ear, which was their job.

Someone's car horn.

He felt irritated by this, looked up to find the disturbance. Someone was making an illegal turn, the black car beeped once more to indicate that its driver was dissatisfied. He sniffed, hardened his facial features.

Across the street a man was standing in front of a closed gate, looking at his watch, pulling on the handle once again. He smiled to himself about this. The young man looked around, confused, then sat on the steps.

He entertained the idea of going over and explaining the particulars of the situation.

They are not inside.

* * * * * * * *

He sat on top of his hands, scratching his fingernails into the leather of the booth. After some time of this, he felt confident that the blood flow was sufficiently cut off from his wrists, and that he could remove them. His hands twitched and did not respond to his commands.

He slathered his hand on the menu, wondering if he was numb enough not to feel it.

He could.

How disappointing.

His waiter was leaning over the bar, so that it stuck into

his abdomen. He felt neglected, thought about calling him over to the table, but he had not yet decided what he would order, probably a sandwich of some kind.

He stuck his finger into the space between the backrest of the booth and the cushion he was sitting on. He felt a few suspicious crumbs. He then ran his finger further down the line until it ran into a small object. This he decided to pull out for further examination. He pinched it between his finger and thumb. It popped out onto the cushion, rolled, fell onto the floor.

He bent down, ran his hand over the carpet until he found the thing in question.

Aha.

A small glass vial.

He withdrew the cork from the top of the vial. He thought that this might be some type of poison that he could put to use. He held it underneath his nose.

Perfume, elegant fragrance.

He fantasized that he was running his nose along a woman's neck.

He held the vial against his wrist, dabbing some of it onto his skin. When he moved the vial, the remainder of the perfume spilled onto his forearm and pants. He looked at his waiter, then around the bar. He paused, sniffed to see if the odor was detectable. He drew his forearm to his nose.

Scent of young girl.

The waiter neared his table, and he felt afraid. He could not stand up to go to the bathroom sink.

He smelled his forearm once again.

The waiter took a pen out from behind his ear, smiled at him, asking if he had gotten enough time yet. He felt pretty, small, coy, and happy, petrified that the waiter would look at him.

Let me get you some candies from the podium.

He picked up the menu, placing his finger onto one of the items in the entrée list. He said that he would also have a glass of water.

And a shot of raw alcohol, hc said.

The waiter sniffed, asked what type of alcohol he would like. He said bourbon, the first thing that came to mind. The waiter took this all in, wrote it down, sniffed.

Looked up from the paper.

He stared at the waiter's collar, forcing his eyebrows down, clenching his jaw.

The waiter said that he would be right back with the order.

He placed his palm on the underside of the table, rubbed it vigorously until he could feel it heating up from the friction. He glanced over at the waiter, placing his order at the bar, and felt that circumstances so and such.

His lips pursed into a grin, smelled the elegant fragrance again, and waited around to go to the bathroom.

* * * * * * * *

The man nodded, licked his lips, removed a blue handkerchief from his coat pocket, looked for a place to set it so that he could get a good look at the necklace. He noticed a small hole in the man's overcoat, the area around it was singed.

The man set the handkerchief on top of a newspaper machine.

He looked down at himself, and, while the man was not looking, zipped up his jacket.

He put his finger on the edge of the cloth, made note of the coloration of the necklace. Two braided bands of gold. He could feel the man standing behind him, looking at him. He turned back.

He nodded.

The man began nodding, drew closer to him.

He then picked up the necklace, pressed the metal between his fingers. He felt guilty about what he was going to say, and did not want to give this information too quickly. He held the necklace up to the sun, pointed his finger at it, and nodded intently.

He explained that the gold in the necklace was alloyed with copper, which was the reason for the pink coloration. The man did not know how to interpret this, kept saying 'alright' for some reason, then made some eye contact with him. He looked down at the sidewalk, then over at a woman standing across the street at the bus stop.

He placed the necklace back onto the handkerchief, handed both of these over to the man. Was this man going to sell the necklace? Had he just bought it?

He instructed the man to touch the necklace. He explained

that he was sorry to say that the stiffness of the material, as well as its lack of shininess, indicates that the necklace is not strictly golden. He felt that this would explain that the necklace was not worth much.

The man.

Lalala.

He looked down.

The necklace isn't worth much.

He added that it was a fine looking piece of jewelry, it would make an excellent gift.

He moved his wrist up, as though he were looking at a watch, then said he was on a pressing schedule, he had an urgent meeting with a medical contact. He needed to get back to this schedule that he had.

The man tried once more to get an exact estimate of the necklace's value, saying that his terms had been vague, and that he didn't expect the necklace to be worth a fortune. He said that he could not give a good assessment of this, as he did not know the exchange rate or something.

He walked a few steps away. Some pressure in the back of his nose felt as though it would pop out one of his eyes. He smiled, waved back to the fellow, then turned back and concentrated on the far corner of the stationary store ahead of him. He planned to take this turn, though he hadn't planned on it.

He looked over his shoulder, and saw that the man was walking after him. He arrived at the turn, then jogged a few steps ahead.

* * * * * * * *

He sat along the side of the bed, touched his hand to his ribs, wondered about the exact state of his health. He wondered if his organs were holding up well with all of this. He closed his eyes, and felt his head lift up, down with his sighs.

He arched his eyebrows, felt a little confused for some reason or another that he could not hear what was going on in the hallway. Then he felt flustered and stupid. He stuck his tongue out, then placed both of his hands against the side of his temple, and performed ancient soothing massages. He pushed his feet against the carpet.

A callous along the side of his toe.

Curious.

The skin had yellowed there, and his tried to see if he could rip it off with his fingernail.

He stood from the bed, walked over to the window, and without looking outside of it, returned to the bathroom door, knocked on it twice with his knuckle, then, without waiting for a response, returned to the bed, where he resumed his massage treatments.

He made guns with his hands, then searched the room.

He looked at the breast on the painting, which was revealed in the lower corner. He held his hand up towards it, so that it, to his eyeballs, it seemed that he was touching it.

He turned the lights on, without looking.

He studied some red marks inside the painting, and made note that the bathroom presented in the painting looked to be a public facility. He had not thought of this before.

He felt happy that he had thought this out.

He could not picture what was happening any further than that. The woman was drawing on her eyebrows with some sort of pencil. He could not remember the title of the painting, which he thought might be of use.

His attention turned to the chair.

He pulled the chair out from the desk with his foot.

He sang a note that stimulated the congestion in his nose.

He sat down in the desk, and looked at the manuscripts in the corner of it. He made a mental note to read them when he felt up to it. His vision and thoughts and skin were too out of sorts at the moment for him to undertake the task. He stuck his fingers in between the pages of it.

He placed his head down on the desk, on top of his arms. Rest.

He moved his head so that his nose sat on his wrist, he inhaled some of his pheromones, and brushed his nose with the hairs of his forearm. He pushed his weight back, intending to move the legs of the chair. Traction, carpet, the chair tilted back into a perilous position, and he was forced to stand up, move it over to the side.

He walked a few steps.

He lunged forward, waved his index fingers, said some things placing a curse on the dresser.

ja ja ja, take that.

He laughed at this, and repeated the scene to himself. He felt for his keys in his pocket, thinking that he might go on a walk if he had them handy.

Two

Some emotions got at him for a bit of time, he rubbed his ribs underneath his shirt, studied some air between his face and the window. Eventually, he decided that the thing to do was to get up, go to the bathroom, shave.

This did not happen immediately. He rolled his face over into his pillow and tried to recall the exact thing about the dream that he'd had last night. He tried to recognize the exact sensation of his upper back striking against the metal, which he'd remembered that morning.

A sort of feeling of sorts.

He kicked his leg up, then let it drop to the floor.

There.

He repeated this for the other leg, got up from the bed in an entertaining way, walked to the bathroom, keeping his movements exaggerated, as they would be if he were a marionette. He let his arms drop to the side. He flailed his hand at the bathroom door, pulled it open.

He stood up straight, looked into the mirror, then at his razor, which he had laid along the edge of the sink so that the blade hung freely over the basin, and would not get infected by local bacterium.

Evidently, he had closed the faucet tightly when he had last used it. He admired his strength.

The water began running, he splashed some of this onto his face. He applied some shaving cream on his fingers, ran it along his neck, his cheeks. He yawned, some shaving cream got into his mouth. He fished this out with his small finger, cleaned off his lips, tasted this water.

He drew the razor over his neck. The trail left behind felt warm and such things.

He shaved for awhile.

He clenched his chin so that he could get a smooth cut on it.

He looked at his upper lip, still covered in shaving cream.

He paused.

mustache.

He ran the razor over his right cheek, rinsed it in water.

He then splashed some water onto his face, wiped the cream off his neck.

He could not see the mustache yet, the white residue on his face distracted his vision, he feared that it might not work out. He reached over to the toilet, taking one of the hand towels, wiping his face. He put the towel into the basin.

He took several steps back.

He had a mustache now, which is good.

It was just the beginnings of one. He would have to try at it for awhile, it would not be easy. He had given himself a good start, and things were going to work out, if he kept at it.

A faint dark line across his lip.

Hello, madam.

He licked his fingertip, ran it through his eyebrow. He bobbed his head, laughed, turned the lights of in the bathroom.

He decided to wear a nicer shirt, in concordance with his new style.

His suit shirt was bundled in the corner of the room with the rest of his laundry. He moved a towel from the pile, then found it hidden among some miscellaneous things. He unbuttoned the shirt, then pulled his right arm into it.

* * * * * * * *

He tossed the knife between his hands, then pointed it at the lobby area, in an action pose. He snapped his fingers, shifted his weight onto his left foot, and thought about which restaurant he would go to, once he got outside. He stepped into the lobby area, saw some people.

He stepped over behind the wall, slid the knife into his pocket.

Two men in suits were speaking with Angelo.

There were a few boxes on the floor, Angelo came out from behind the desk, scratched his head. One of the men pointed at one of the boxes, then over towards some point on the wall. Angelo picked up the box.

Hahaha, Angelo is weak.

He came out from the corner, said hello to everyone. Angelo was the only person to respond. He asked if these people needed any assistance. The first man, with his beard and everything, said that they would be fine. Angelo asked him if he could help, if he wanted, to get these boxes over to the elevator.

He stopped at one of the boxes, pulled the sleeve of his shirt up. He bent over, made an initial calculation about the force that would be needed. He pulled the box up, it was much heavier than he expected. He needed to brace it against the desk.

The men behind him picked up the remaining two boxes.

Thank you.

He said that this was nothing.

Angelo was having some trouble with the elevator button. He hoped that he would be able to get to the elevator before Angelo was able to press the button, so that he could be the tough one of the group. He lowered his brow, walked toward the elevator. His lower back stung, stressed.

He walked into the back of the elevator, braced his box against the back rail. Angelo held the elevator for the other two fellows. He faced the back wall of the elevator, and he felt that everyone had come in.

The doors closed, the elevator lifted.

He wondered if they would be staying on his floor.

One said heavy.

He agreed.

He tried to look into his box, to see what exactly he was carrying. He imagined that it was debris of some sort. He felt a little strange that everyone else was facing the front of the elevator, but he could not release the box.

The elevator stopped on the fourth floor.

Angelo moved a box so that the door would stay open. The two men left ahead of him, walked over to the hallway, uncertain which way to go.

He caught up with them, he was at the point of asking for their room number. Angelo turned down the hall.

He wondered if these men were going to insist on paying him for his hard work.

Perhaps a drink or so at a secret river, where you will meet the beautiful women.

Angelo stopped at one of the doors, said that this would be it.

He held his box against the wall.

* * * * * * * *

He set the container on the side of the wall, punched the lid in, pulled it up. His head swayed, he reached in and took out the piece of bread, figuring that it would level things out. He closed the container, walked up the hill. He held the bread in his fist, smelled the butter that had melted on it.

He stuffed the bead into his mouth. He had some difficulty getting it down.

He swallowed, clenched his teeth. The bread sank to his stomach.

He stuffed some more of the bread into his mouth.

arr.

He smacked his lips, looked over to the gulch. He looked over at the noonday sun, coming in through the nature over that way. He felt confused, the bread had passed through his esophagus, causing some pain that forced him to pause. He beat the last bit of bread against his heart a few times. He took several breaths of air.

He stuffed the last of the bread into his mouth, continued walking.

He chewed thoroughly, until it was no longer pleasant. Some of the bread caught in his outer cheeks, refused to move. He scooped this out with his tongue, and got it down his throat. He approached the door to the lobby.

He placed the container against his nose, and sniffed it. He could smell the tomato portion of the meal, and a pungent rich flavor. His stomach tensed up. He took his key card out of his pocket, slid it into the door.

Hello.

He made staccato steps across the floor of the lobby. He just needed to get to his room, as quickly as possible. He felt a sense of danger in this so-called lobby area. He slowed his pace, and looked back to the couch area, felt quite bold.

He blew cold air down his shirt as he walked down the hallway. He saw a tub of towels outside the vending area. He snuck up towards it, bumped his waist against the tub, stood up, looked through the portal.

Angelo's cousin was looking at the vending machine.

He kicked open the door.

Kra!

She jumped back.

Hello.

She caught her breath. He walked into the room, and set

the container on the table. She laughed a little, and studied him. He said that he was just getting in. He asked if she wanted this, he opened the container, showcased the food with a sweep of his palm.

He said that he wasn't hungry.

She eyed the food, and assured him that she was fine. He insisted that he was about to throw it away, and that he had not taken any bites. She judged whether or not she wanted what he had gotten.

He pulled a fork out from his pocket.

He dropped it on the floor.

He bent over to pick it up, apologized several times. He felt rotten that she would not be able to use it now. How would she eat now? He apologized, stuck the fork back into his pocket. She closed the box, and said that there were forks in the dining room.

* * * * * * * *

He cackled, putting the corner of his shoe against the curb, lifting himself up. He heard the car pass by him, felt some air move against his back.

He examined some of the finer points of the park. The benches, trees, the general people. He put his hands onto the iron fence, squeezed it. The fence was topped with tiny spears, which made him loose courage. He walked over to the entrance, then down the path.

He settled down, went over his itinerary.

He decided to walk straight through the park.

Some kids.

He saw a young woman with a young man, sitting on the bench. He looked down at the book in her lap, then away and back again. He feared that the young man might stand up to him.

She agreed. She said what she liked about the book, then pulled closer to the young man. He slowed down his pace, walked over onto the grass. He looked back at the young man's hair, which seemed a bit too fashionable.

He considered several possibilities.

I overheard that you were talking of books, and such classy things as I am aware of. He brushed his knuckle against his back.

I recently completed my short story.

Oh, you are too young to kiss.

He blinked. He pictured the young man looking away from him, while the girl stared. Yes yes, it is a good story that I finished. It involves comas. It is about a man coming out of a coma. A commentary on things, satirical, nuance.

He stopped on the path.

He thought, sighed, then set his eyes on the space underneath the bench. Book satchel, leather, clasp.

Aren't we all in a coma, or something? Little girl, have you thought of that?

He bent his shoe into the trunk of a tree, then stood on it. He looked over to the edge of the park, where the kids were screaming. He studied the light coming off the face of the brick.

He stood.

He tensed up his shoulders, sighed, walked back over to the path.

Wine glass, he insisted.

He held his fingers up, twitched them around, walked out of the park. His thigh brushed against the side of the fence, injuring it. He rubbed it with his palm, and cursed, continued down the street.

He saw a sign in the window of the office and smiled, and thought about his mother. His knee bone shifted out of place. He raised his leg, shook it, satisfied that the kneecap had set back into its proper location.

He saw that the cigarettes were being offered at discounted prices, an illustrated woman on the packaging with seductive eyes. As he studied this he realized that the smile on her lips made her look like a rabbit. He titled his head back from the poster, blinked, and looked down at the pavement.

ah, alas.

He looked at a black car, with no top on it. Someone had left their sweater on the passenger seat, to be stolen. He looked around him, stepped closer to it, and examined the nearby shops.

Three

He tensed his legs to see whether or not his need to urinate could be postponed until he got back to his room. His lower stomach tickled, he trembled, stepping off the sidewalk, down the hill toward the gulch.

Eyes wide.

He began to trot down the hill, the bottoms of his feet slid into the front of his shoes, throwing him off a bit. Once he had gotten down a good portion of the hill he looked for some inconspicuous places. He could urinate on the stone there.

He could go behind the tree.

He unzipped his pants, taking aim at the side of the creek bed.

He put his hands on his side, making it look as though he were just standing there quite innocently. His urine sprayed onto the stone. Hmm hmm, I am just admiring this view. He turned a bit to the side so that he was not making as much noise.

As his bladder emptied, he found that the pressure was no longer sufficient, he needed to use his hands to prevent any of it from falling on his pants.

He looked over at the hotel.

so close.

He felt a bit ridiculous, finished up, so and such.

He decided to make use of the fact that he was now in the gulch. He walked along the side of the creek, making note of several things of note. He saw a beer can stuck into the dirt, and recollected drinking such a thing. He, however, had deposited his garbage into a trash receptacle.

That's right.

He saw a toy sitting along the stones, it was green. He neared it, huddled over.

Fascinating.

He stepped over the stones in the creek, walking up the hill. He thought about his earlobes, looked at the evening sun, felt the exercise in his calves, and figured that he was becoming physically fit.

I go on walks all the time!

The thing about canoeing through the rapids is to keep your head up. Keep brisk gentlemen. I jump up to the treetops in my fancy suit, and read books of philosophy. Stalwart, and dressed in ironed shirts, haha.

He rubbed his nose, then looked up the sidewalk. An old woman dragging a cart, moving quite slowly. He stared at this, and placed much significance in this.

She was walking slowly.

the wheels of the cart squeaked.

He lost interest, and walked over toward the parking lot. He touched the various pockets on his clothes, trying to find his key card ahead of time, and so be well prepared when he got to the door. He could not feel it, feared that he might have left it on the desk.

He balled up the cloth along his pant pocket. He felt the edge of the card against his thumb. He inserted his finger into his pocket, touched the key card, under the impression that this gesture felt slightly erotic, and smiled in his mind. He scratched the interior of the pocket, chuckled, and withdrew his finger subtly, clearing his throat.

* * * * * * * *

He yawned, then placed his fingers over his mouth. His eyeballs became wet, and such biology. He needed to brace himself against the panel on the inside of the elevator. He finished up, stuck his tongue out of his mouth, then folded it back up.

He walked out of the elevator onto the carpet. His breathing was a bit heavy. He looked down the hallway, impressed by the length of the carpet. He wondered how many segments of carpet were involved, what lengths they had been originally. How one would go about getting one's hands upon such a length of carpet, if it were available to the general public.

He looked over at the clerk, meaning to say hello in some way.

He coughed, groaned.

The clerk began digging through some papers on the desk. He tried his best to pretend that he had not noticed this, continued down the hall, figuring that he would go to the dining room, where he would do something or other.

Wait.

He put his head down, his hand against the wall.

He looked over at the clerk.

The clerk was coming from the desk with an envelope in hand. His hair was standing on end, as though he had been pulling on it.

He stepped closer, holding out his hand. The clerk made eye contact with him, looked back toward the entrance, moving towards him. They made eye contact twice more before they were within reach of one another.

The clerk is tall.

He corrected his posture, so that he also would be tall.

The clerk held the envelope out, saying that this had been delivered for him. He took the envelope, looked at his name.

He clenched his teeth, and looked up. He thought that the clerk might know some information about this.

It is a subpoena.

Someone had brought it a half an hour ago, the clerk had thought he was not there.

He nodded as though this were interesting.

He thanked the clerk, he said that he needed to go. The clerk stood still as though he expected an explanation of some sort. He walked over to the break room, waved goodbye.

Err.

His head felt light, he pushed the envelope up his sleeve. Once he was out of view, he opened it.

He whistled.

He could not make out any of these words. They were quite long.

He looked behind him. He coughed to cover the sound of the paper tearing in half, then again. He stepped into the break room, figuring that he could hide some of the paper beneath the vending machine. He closed the door gently, bent over. He looked again at a bit of the paper, thinking that it might be a mistake.

He slid the paper under the machine, then stood up.

He walked over to that wall over there and checked if he could see the bits.

He could put the rest in his trash, he figured, or he could tear it up more and leave some of it in the ashtray. He moved out of the break room, quickly. Some sweat gathered on his lip.

* * * * * * * *

He turned the chair, so that it faced the bathroom mirror, sat down, then looked over to the side, judging the hour of the evening from the hue of the window.

He pressed his hand against his shirt, where he could feel some irritated skin.

mirror.

He looked at the size of his head.

He breathed.

He felt some air build up in his chest, he spread his

mouth, yawning until his mandible hurt, the air pushing out from his mouth, he braced his hand against his knee, let his eyelids drop. Relieved. He coughed, wondered if his yawning indicated that he could go back to bed.

Touching his hand once more to his chest, he decided it would be best to remove his shirt and get a good look at the skin there. He stood up from the chair. His shirt caught against his neck as he pulled it up. He snapped the shirt off, then tossed it into a corner of the bathroom.

Light switch.

His eye adjusted to the light.

He saw pink trails across his chest, crossing over his pectoral region, as though someone had been scratching at him while he slept, begging, begging, mercy, please, on an old battlefield of some sort. He flexed his entire body, stood, ardent.

He turned the faucet on, then ran his hand beneath it. He smeared this water over the wound on his chest. It stung a bit, then the skin grew darker.

fingernails.

He looked at the counter, wondering if he had nail clippers.

He remembered having one of those.

He stuck his finger into his mouth, pushing the skin against his lower teeth so that he could get a bite on the nail. He pressed his teeth together shearing the nail at the corner. He dragged his head to the side, growled a little. He began to tear at his cuticle.

He stopped, then bent the nail to the side. He turned his finger over then bit down on the nail, it falling into his lower lip. He tried to spit this out, it stuck to his lip, and he used his finger to pull it off. Some saliva trailed off of it, a snailish plasm.

He examined his remaining nails.

He put his hands over his face. A lack of blood in his fingers causing them to seem much colder than himself. He used this coldness to cool his eyes. Then he molded his face in his hands, looking at himself in the mirror, quite satisfied at how disturbing that expression looked.

He walked over to the doorway.

He did several graceful bends, as dancers do.

He looked at his shirt, thinking to put it back on. It had fallen in a pool of water by the toilet. It would stick to him, until it dried off. That would be uncomfortable and he did not want it to go that way. He turned off the lights in the bathroom, then walked out, knocked his knee into the chair, and consoled it as he walked over to the bed.

* * * * * * * *

His hips swayed as he walked down the hallway, and he raised the cup of coffee into the air. Some heat drifted off the top of it. He held the coffee so that rim of the cup sat level with his eye, the steam seeming to drift off the horizon as it would in a foreign country.

He turned into the lobby.

He looked over at Angelo behind the desk, who had not noticed him. He said, loudly, that his mission for the day was to drink twenty cups of complimentary coffee. Angelo raised his head.

That's not good for you.

He turned his head back, adding that he planned to spend the remainder of the afternoon in a seizure of some sort. He would lie on the stairwell, and laugh, clutching at the ankles of the guests, asking them if they could spare money for a twitchy wretch.

He opened the door with his foot.

The outside air!

Have a nice morning.

Angelo gave him a salute, and he walked out onto the sidewalk, looking back twice or so. He felt a little pity for poor Angelo, who had no free coffee to speak of.

He felt some sunlight streaked against his brow, jutting into the corner of his vision. This caused him to make an erroneous step to the side of the pavement. Some coffee slapped out of the cup, falling onto his wrist, burned it, cooling off in a matter of seconds.

To prevent further accidents of the sort, he raised the cup to his lips, intending to drink the coffee down. He found this action aggravated by his walking, the coffee waved up to his lips, then back. He stopped walking.

He sucked some of the coffee into his mouth. He took several quick breaths to facilitate the cooling process.

Some gas crept up from his stomach, and he took a

moment to try and figure whether or not he enjoyed the taste. The coffee was a little strong, this is true, but he could not recall if he preferred it this way.

Ahead of him, he saw that famous bit of cement around the base of the lamppost. This, he decided, would be the optimal location for coffee placing. He stepped onto the asphalt, keeping his eyes focused on the texture of the cement. He began to feel a sense of urgency, excitement, at getting to this destination. He moved slowly though, as he did not want to spill any more coffee on his hands.

He looked at the cement once again, then at some light.

He clenched his teeth.

He thought about bark, he set the coffee on the cement, and, once this was done, snapped his fingers, walking several steps away from the coffee onto the grass.

He looked back at the coffee, then looked down the hill at the grass.

lovely!

He returned to his coffee drink.

He lifted the coffee, tasted it once more, set it down, and retreated back to the grass.

* * * * * * * *

He drank the wine, choking a little on it. Some pulp stuck to the top of the glass, and his throat lurched when he thought that he had swallowed some of those things.

He set the wine against the wall.

He looked down the hallway, then at the glass in his hand.

He sipped, then set it down with the wine.

He walked away from the things. His mind went off, he began to feel nervous. He wondered how long it would be. He sank down to his knees, then crawled along the floor. For a period of moments he felt that no one would ever understand him. He huddled into a ball, putting his hands over the back of his neck.

His nose began running.

And how would he explain himself?

He rocked back and forward. The thought occurred to him that someone might walk out of their room, see him, and call the police on him. He rolled his neck, soothed by the motion of rocking himself, and so, thinking that he still had a few minutes, continued to rock, little baby boy that he was.

He must stand up.

in a few seconds.

He raised his face to the lights in the ceiling. He felt exhausted. Ah, and oh, what would he do, such things. He wanted to stay in his position for just a few more seconds, he heard no one opening any doors, he did not have to stand up just yet.

He stopped, then braced his hand against the wall.

He pulled himself up, then walked back over to the wine, feeling a weight in his head that indicated he would not need to stay awake much longer at all.

He heard some conversation.

He poured another glass of wine, quickly, then hid the wine bottle at the doorway.

He walked down the hall to the corner, peeked out. Two gentlemen were coming from the elevator area, dressed well. They looked over at him and nodded, he stood up, walked over to them.

He approached them, asking if they had had a nice evening, and, to be frank, he was wondering if either of them had a cigarette that he could borrow for a few minutes.

The more exotic man stopped, then padded down the pockets of his coat. The other tried to walk away.

Eventually, the man pulled out a package of cigarettes and a book of matches.

Let's get you set for the whole evening.

The man slipped three cigarettes out of the package, and asked if he would need the matches. He looked down at the ground, yes. He thought of shaking the man's hand. The man handed him the cigarettes, which he put behind his ears, except for one, which he took to his lips.

He ripped one of the matches out of the book, then admired the pink lettering on the back. He struck the match, puffed, and lit his cigarette, handing the matchbook back.

thank you.

Smalls tufts of smoke drifted up into the hallway, and his eyes, as he looked at the man so thankfully.

* * * * * * * *

He estimated the distance from here to the pavement behind the hotel, pushed his hand against the window, then tried to lift it up, ventilate the room. He turned his head to the side, stared at some laundry that he had left on the floor.

dirty, dirty.

He felt some pain in his back as he bent over to pick up the pants. He shaped his mouth, pressed his knuckle to his spine. He jiggled the pants, wondering if they had any loose change in them, and heard the sound of metal clapping.

He figured that this might be the belt.

He stuck his fingers into the pocket, removed his wallet, and several receipts.

He felt some loose change in the bottom of the pocket. He walked over to the corner of the room, setting the pants onto the laundry bag. Then he turned, spread his arms out.

He looked at the room.

He used two hands to scratch his hair, and walked toward the desk. He touched the cover of the binder, then picked it up, throwing it onto the bed. It landed on the pillow.

Getting a good ground under his feet, he started toward the bed, wherein he made a sudden leap toward the headboard. His chest impacted against the springs, his face touched the linen covering the pillow, and he rubbed his hands around him.

He felt some shame that he'd kept his shoes on.

He pulled the sheet over his body, twisting his ankles so that they laid flat. He concentrated on some disturbance in his stomach, so and such, he slid the sheet up underneath his shirt, and stuffed it up to his belly.

Lo, I am the fat man.

amused.

He found it difficult to move.

A glance at the window revealed nothing, and so he asked and thought and thought of what the time was. He pondered whether he could reliably click his tongue to count off the seconds exactly.

Click, and, after a time, click.

click clock click.

Come closer, dear daughter.

Oh, kick the maid out of the room, lock the door on her, I have much to tell you. Don't quibble over the will, etcetera, let Henry take the golden boat. Let it be a simple death, build a statue of me at the age of thirty in the living room, grasping a lightning bolt in each fist. He pressed his ear into the pillow. He has learned much about the state of things in recent weeks, etcetera, oh, blah blah, so weak, his throat is dry!

If only he had more time, he would explain the secrets of poetry.

He turned his head over to the other wall, then stared at the manuscript, sticking his small finger in his earlobe, trying to relieve a sensation on the right side of his face. He moaned several times, pleasurably. He rubbed his knees together, in order to create a little warmth.

He pulled the sheet out of his shirt, then, setting it over his shoulders. He pulled it up to his neck, sniffed at it, trying to see if he had a scent.

* * * * * * * *

He supposed he would have to take the room by force.

He brushed his wrist against his side, turning his head away from the vagrant standing by the greeting cards. He looked down at the cards, pretending that he needed to find one for a special occasion, hoping that this would soothe the vagrant, that he wasn't scared of him or so on, he just needed to get that card.

The bear holding the balloon struck him as a poignant bit.

Some flowers, thank you dear.

He reached the end of the aisle, feeling a momentary confusion that he would not find what he was looking for, and wondering, if that would be the case, if he could leave the store immediately. He tapped his lip with his index finger.

Several bottles of wine.

obscene.

He jogged over to these.

He studied the prices, then bent over, his hands clasped behind his back, bringing his face right up to the label, sniffing it once. He did not feel like carrying this bottle, which was unfortunate. He stood upright, and, giving a glance over at the middle aged woman dressed fashionably, fantasized for a moment that she might give him a little kiss on his eyes, tear off his necktie.

Ah, he had no necktie.

problematic.

He looked over at the refrigerators.

A man at the end was setting down a box of sodas, he

thought about asking this fellow for some help.

He walked by, pausing for a moment at the refrigerator, behind the man's shoulder. He did not say anything.

He stood for a moment.

The man opened the refrigerator, then began stocking the sodas.

He apologized twice, and walked off toward the front of the store. He saw the lady once again, then, putting on a smile, said hello to her. He saluted as he passed her, and she nodded to him, and he saw a display case ahead.

He pointed at it, then looked behind him.

He got over to the display case, and looked at the items. Red leather wallet, things of that sort. He saw some refillable lighters, then saw a particular one that came with a bottle of fluid. He tapped the glass, then snapped and looked away.

He looked for someone that could get this for him, pulled at the hem of his shirt and bunched it up in his hand.

He entertained the idea of haggling on the price, and spotted a girl towards the front of the room. He titled his head back as he walked toward her, hoping that she would notice this, and come over to him. He tilted his head further back, until he was looking out the top of the window, at the telephone pole outside.

That's just what I need, he said.

The girl looked up at him, and, with a disconcerted face, asked him what she could do to help him. He stuck his thumb over his shoulder, and, turning back, and turning back to her, said that he needed to buy something out of that thing.

* * * * * * * *

He tore off the sheets, thinking that he had seen it there, some nights ago. He stared at the linen for a moment, then saw that the pen was sitting underneath the pillow. He swept his hand down, scooped it up.

And now I have my pen.

He took the pen over to the note pad.

He wrote his name down in block letters, then crossed it out. He stuck the pen into his mouth, sucking on its end. He thought, for some time, that the bitter taste in his mouth might be ink, which he had siphoned out of the well. He took the pen out of his mouth, stuck his tongue out, rubbing it along his front teeth.

He touched his finger to his tongue.

His finger was not black, not inky by any stretch of the imagination.

He tasted his tongue, inquisitive.

The telephone began ringing, and he imagined that this might be in a different room. He looked over at the telephone, then rubbed his head. He stood up from the desk, the phone rang once again. He walked over to it, holding his hand out.

He stopped.

He saw the phone ring.

He looked over to the window, then moved over to the side of the bed, where he glanced back over at the phone. He imagined that this might be his brother, checking in on him, and nothing really to worry about.

The phone rang again.

He rubbed his hands in his lap, clenched his teeth. The phone continued once or twice more, before cutting out. He blew some cold air out of his mouth, then waited to see if it would continue.

Satisfied that this was over, he stood up from the bed, walking over toward the bathroom. He struck a pose, then lighted up the bathroom. He glanced at the hair at the collar of his shirt, then tilted his head down.

He turned on the faucet.

He waited for the water to cool.

He stuck his hands beneath the faucet, and, shaping them into a bowl, got himself a few gulps of water. He swallowed the first of these, deciding afterwards that he needed to swirl some in his cheeks, spit it out, and remove the taste on his tongue. He heard something dropping in the living room, turned the faucet off, his mouth full of water.

The phone was ringing once again.

He kept the water in his mouth for a moment, then opened his lips, quietly, allowing the liquid to dribble into the basin of the sink. He looked at the coloration of the wall.

He sat down on the toilet seat, tried to close the door with his foot softly as the phone rang once again.

No no no.

He pushed his palm against his right ear, pressing excess air into the canal, then considered that this might be an emergency. The ringing cut out once more, and he waited

another moment. He wiped his fist against his mouth, to clear
the water from it. He squinted, trying to make out what his face
looked like in the mirror, and how he seemed emotionally.

* * * * * * * *

He felt the wind press against his cheek. He shivered, then
looked over at the trees at the end of the road, which bent
slightly, their colors still muted by the hour of the dawn and
whatnot. He looked down the street.

Behold, the lone hipster.

He stared at this young man, wondering if he were going
to his car, or something of that sort. He hoped that the young
man was drunk, or had not seen him. He pulled the cord of
his laundry sack out in front of him, as the bag was dropping a
little far into his back.

He approached the barrier at the end of the road.

He placed one leg over it, then the other.

He looked down into the woods, thinking that there
might be a path of some sort. He saw some garbage that way,
which relieved him a little. This was an excellent place, and he
thought of himself as quite nearly finished, as he had walked
all this way. He stepped down onto a dirt trail, which tilted
him down a bit.

The binder slapped into his shoulder.

He bared his teeth, letting his lower lip drop to his chin.

He felt the breeze dry out as he passed through the tree
line. He looked for the some light coming out of the horizon,
for some homes or something of that sort. He decided it would
be best to walk halfway into the woods.

He crouched, then looked up.

He could see some roofs in the distance. He felt happy
that he would not have to walk much more.

He looked at the area around him, for a fire pit or something
that he could use, a campsite perhaps.

You never know, people do love nature.

He saw a log tipped over, with its face having been chipped
away, exposing yellow insides that worried him for a moment.
He saw that the hill dropped off a little, and he could probably
find some suitable spot nearby.

He made a note to himself that he should not do it near
any dry trees.

He saw a small hole, which an animal might live in. He

thought he could use this, then decided against it, as he did not want a snake to come out of it and snag him or some tragedy of that sort.

He decided to kick away some of the nature at the bottom of the hill, some twigs and things, as this really was a good spot. He looked back, then forward, and saw neither buildings, nor people.

He set the sack down, then drew the mouth open. His arm was shaking.

He slapped his coat.

He took the binder out of the thing, then set it down on the ground. He lifted up the bag, taking it some distance away where it would be safe from fire. He took out the lighter fluid, and touched the lighter in his pocket.

He decided to keep the binder, which would only inhibit the burning process. He could toss it into a garbage can on his way back, if he liked.

* * * * * * * *

Thinking that it would be about time, he walked over to the door at the end of the hallway. He jogged a bit, at first, slowing down once he heard that the dryer was still active. He listened as a button clapped against some metal, and then once again.

He thought that perhaps the dryer might be in the later phases of the cycle. This he would have to check on with his eyes. He opened the door to the room, then looked at the machine.

The indicator light remained on.

He looked around the room, to see if someone might have removed his laundry, so that they could use the machine. He had it in his mind that they might have folded it for him, to make up for touching his possessions. Nothing.

He pulled the door against his chest.

Help! I'm being sawed in half!

The edge of the door felt pleasant against his abdomen, but no smile came to his face. He decided to drop the matter altogether, and go out into the hall. He let his mouth drop into a rather fashionable expression, and he stood with his back against the wall.

He did not have to return to his room, and it would be a waste of energy to do so.

He let his arms drop to his side, then thought about

nothing special, then thought about the sound of a television coming from one of the rooms to his left, then felt generally disconcerted, and hoped that he looked sexually attractive in this position.

Some people, in the far off hallway.

They came out of their room, two men.

They began laughing after a few steps, and one of them closed the door. One of them held up his hands, he imagined, telling the other to wait. The man padded his pockets, then stuck his hand into his pocket, and, finding things satisfactory, continued to their jobs or whatever.

So that's all good then.

He began to snap his fingers rhythmically with the washing machine's music.

This was not so easy to do, and he made some mistakes.

He bent his fingers, then got the timing of it correctly. He kept this practice up for longer than it entertained him, and he made notes to himself that he should check to see if the machine were in the later phases of the cycle.

He opened the door.

The light was on, but he kept the door open, thinking that it might change, perhaps, at that very moment.

Yes.

He walked into the laundry room, then over toward the vending machine that was full of delicious looking soaps. He thought for a moment, then walked over to his machine, and placed his hand against the door. The metal was slightly warm.

That's my laundry getting done.

He heard someone open the door to the laundry room. It was a woman. She said hello and looked away from him, and he stepped back, feeling inappropriate for a moment. She examined the vending machine, wore a shirt with violet flowers printed on it, overweight.

Laundry day?

He clapped his hands together.

* * * * * * * *

He stopped at the edge of the lobby, then stamped his foot into the ground there. Angelo looked over at him, up from the desk, and somewhat laughed and said his name. He pumped his hands up into the air, as though he had won the championship.

He held this position.

He dropped his arms and walked over to the desk, Angelo looked down at the papers there, then asked him what he was doing.

He pointed both of his index fingers at Angelo.

Pretty drunk.

He stepped back from the desk, closed his eyes, and nodded for a moment. He was not very intoxicated, but his throat and vision were a little out of sorts.

Angelo laughed, and said something about wishing to be drunk.

He told Angelo not to say this, as it was a very vile state that he was in. He should be proud of doing his little job, and the afternoon was not the best time for such business.

he's slurring his words.

Angelo said that he had not been drunk in the afternoon for some time, then pushed the papers, and looked down.

He felt ashamed for a moment, then asked if he was bothering Angelo.

Good, good.

He thought of nothing to say, then looked out the window of the hotel lobby. He said that, in fact, it was a rough position to be in. He caught Angelo looking down at the papers.

I'm bothering you, he said.

not at all.

All the same, he needed to go get some snack foods presently.

He walked over toward the door to the lobby, he looked back. Angelo called out to him, saying that they would have a cigarette together.

He made a hand gesture at this, then watched Angelo gather some stuff, dig around. He wondered if he should wait at the door, or go outside and stand against the wall. He decided to step outside.

He looked around.

He waved some air up into his face, and sniffed it. He planned on saying some things to Angelo about the breeze. He wanted to calculate out some conversation that would be minimally embarrassing. He stepped away from the door, over to the side of the wall. He tapped his head against the wall a few times. He put his hands between his back and the brickwork.

He took several breaths of air, then looked out of the top of his eyes.

Angelo came out of the hotel, wearing a jacket now. Angelo tapped the package of cigarettes against his wrist, then looked over at him, asking if he had any of his own.

No, he said, and felt quite bad about it.

Angelo undid the wrapping of the package. He looked down at the floor, thinking to say that he did not need one of the cigarettes. Angelo took one out, and, handed it to him, fished for a lighter in the jacket. He held the cigarette up near his mouth, and pretended to smoke it for a moment with a stupid face on his face, thinking that Angelo would find such foolishness amusing and worthwhile.

* * * * * * * *

He slid his hand down the sheet, underneath his shirt, then scratched his stomach. His mouth was full of dry air, and his throat hurt, but he suspected that his head felt fine, and he would be alright. He turned to the side, pressing his cheek against the pillow in a lazy way.

He looked out the window.

dark blue.

He shivered, and smacked his lips together. He tried to drift off to sleep.

He thought about the water from the sink, which was the only drink he had available.

He tossed the cover off, then sat up in the bed. The taste of the tap water contained a slightly brown metallic flavor, which was not a good thing. Still, he blinked, then looked dazed. He slid off of the bed, feeling his boxer shorts slide up, pleasantly enough. His knees cracked.

He walked over to the bathroom, the arches of his feet brushed against the carpet.

A wet spot.

He looked down at the carpet, then over at the bathroom, where he'd left the light on. A trail of water lead from the bathtub, gathered in a pool at the doorway.

He scratched his chin, then looked at the desk. He saw some coins there, and thought of going down to the vending room, where he could grab a soda of some sort.

He took the coins, and, as it was a weekday dawn, thought he could make it down to the lobby sans pants, as they say.

Sine qua non, in fact.

He stepped towards his laundry, in search of his keys. He had the thought to grab one of his shoes and prop the door open that way. And he did so, briefly fearing that burglars might come and take his things.

He walked down to the stairwell. He jiggled the coins in his hands, and thought about casting them onto the carpet. Come on, give me a soda!

He heard a creaking sound from one of the rooms, he picked up his pace into a casual run.

Everyone, there's a spirit in one of the rooms, run, forget the pants. There's a time and place for modesty.

He got to the stairwell, and, quickly, padded his feet down the stairs, thinking that he needed to get there quickly, and back, if he was going to go back to sleep. He could already feel himself becoming awake.

His momentum carried him to the wall of the stairwell, he pushed his hand against the wall to increase his speed as he turned to the second flight.

At the bottom door, he stopped. He pushed the door open a crack, and looked to see if any witnesses were around.

A quiet laughter in his eyelids.

He took his time with it, pumping his elbows as he strutted over to the vending machines. He thought of walking over to the lobby. Yes, no pants, that's just how I do things now.

He looked into the vending room at the soda machines, then calculated what drink he could purchase that would not hurt his throat.

Part 10

(defeat!)

He saw that the people had organized themselves and were heading down the street to a local sound. He crossed the road, checking to make sure that he would not be hit by a car, fairly important.

He bumped his elbow into a meter on the edge of the street, and, waiting for a break in the flow of people, saw some younger women touching each other, and consenting to something.

He decided to stay off the sidewalk, so that he could move more swiftly. He heard some sounds coming from down the street. He looked out into the road, no danger, ran up the street, passing many people who had not thought of this. He saw a street vendor up ahead of him, selling meats.

He gave this man a pump of his fist.

Coming to the corner, he turned. He saw some arts and crafts, and heard the faint blare of horns and many conversations. He picked up his head, with an odd sense of urgency, jogged up the next street toward the park. He pictured that they might be giving out prizes of some kind, or that he might be able to snag himself a glass of lemonade.

A kid crying, not so audible in the crowd. The mother looked down, then buttoned the kid's little coat, the kid trying to slap his mother's hand away, to no effect. She reached into her purse, looking for something, he guessed, to wipe some goop off the kid's face.

He put his hand on the side mirror of a car, then looked at the entrance to the park. There were many people filing in, he became a little nervous about this, for a time thinking that he would have to abandon the dream altogether.

He moved sideways, pushing his shoulder into the crowd. An old man turned to let him go by. He was pleased with his tactical ability to move through the gauntlet, without touching many people. He slid to the side, allowing the girls to pass by him, then into the space that they had created.

Once he had gotten through the gate, he moved over onto the grass, where there were not as many bodies. Drums were playing, and by this point the music had become somewhat unnerving. On top of it all, the parade of conversations raised in volume over the music.

He stepped over behind a tree, chewed on his lower lip.

He needed some surveillance.

He stood on his toes, checking over the crowd. He could see some tables at the far end of the park, out of his reach. The music kept up.

He turned, then looked at the fence. He mussed his expression on his face, and kicked a paper cup over towards the trash receptacle. He stood on his toes again, then looked over at the tables.

A small group of men were looking over at him, suspiciously. He waved, and smiled, then walked toward the fence. He figured that he could buy something from one of the street vendors. He looked behind him.

Whistling, no ill intentions.

He climbed over the fence. His feet struck the pavement, and he stood up. A woman across the street grinned, mildly amused at his antics.

* * * * * * * *

He stood at the window of the room, looking out. He became enamored with the idea that someone might be looking at him, cutting such a ponderous figure in the window as he did. He pledged his hand onto his breast, arched his eyebrows.

He turned his head to the side, thinking that someone was about to knock on the door. He stared few a few moments at the block of light coming from the hallway.

He looked down at his collared shirt, quite sophisticated in his manner of dress. He rocked his shoulders and felt his skin, dry, sliding against the cloth hanging loose enough that it was still cool. He walked a few steps over toward the desk. He saw the light beneath the door darken.

He waited for her to knock.

Knock.

He rushed over to the door, hoping that he would be able to open it before she could. He heard her getting out her keys, he reached for the handle. He pulled the door harder than was strictly necessary, the handle struck against the wall.

He stood in the doorway.

Tada again.

Angelo's cousin was taken back again.

Do come in again.

He stepped to the side, she smiled at him and came into the room. He began to close the door, then saw the cart of towels and realized that it would not be in the best interests of efficiency.

Angelo's cousin was pulling his laundry off the bed, which was where he had planned to sit. He walked over to the corner of the wall, and, thinking quickly, stared up at his painting on that wall there. He waited for her to notice this.

Ahem?

Sorry, I'm just distracted by some beauty.

He glanced out of the corner of his eye, thinking that she must have noticed, by this point, that he was being a very tasteful man. He folded his arms in front of him, and began humming at regular intervals, staring at the pale color in the upper corner of the canvas.

Now that's a painting.

She looked from the bed, at the painting first, and then at him.

She agreed, and paused, looking at the bed.

She threw the pillows onto the floor, saying that she liked it because the woman looked very tired, that she had been out all night.

He agreed, she began pulling off the sheets. He pointed a finger at her, examining the skin on her chest, her hair. It occurred to him that she had looked at it before, perhaps stopping altogether to look at it while he had been out on business.

You just won yourself a painting!

She looked up.

He ran over to the wall, and lifted the painting off the nail. He took it out into the hallway, then looked for somewhere to set it down. He placed the painting in the cart of towels, and thought to run in and write her name on a paper with a little heart on it.

She had stepped away from the bed, and was looking to see what he was up to. He gave her a little clap, and she shook her head, trying to stop him.

But she couldn't, his mind was set on the idea, though he hoped she might compensate him a bit if she knew how much it was worth.

* * * * * * * *

He yawned, setting his hand against the desk. The coffee continued to percolate, popping every few seconds, and he looked at the amount of black in the bottom of the coffeepot.

Where was his dignity?

He thought of other people's lives, and felt that other people look down at him in general. He bent his shoe so that his ankle rubbed against it, and he sat down on the bed. The coffee was on its way. He decided that he could fill his glass with it, when he had the motivation to do so.

He was the poorest wretch. He lived in his hovel, making barely enough to pay the rent. These other people thought of him as pitiful, walking their dogs and kissing their spouses.

He chewed on his lip, walking over to the desk. He picked up the glass, and waited for the final drops of coffee to fall into the pot.

His arm stretched behind his back, pulling the muscle tighter until it stretched out enough.

He was so exhausted, his life was so exhausting.

Meanwhile, others sing and dance.

He took the first sip of coffee. He was pleased that he had made it so weak, as there was no unpleasant aftertaste to it. If only he were someone else, he would have a loved one massage all the cricks in his upper back, sitting in an evening chair and all of that.

He took another sip from the glass, walked over to the window where the light was coming in. He touched the curtain, and looked at the weather.

It was nice enough outside.

He used to have a better view.

His fingertips began to sting from the heat of the coffee. He moved the glass into his other hand, and kissed his fingers. He then took another sip of the coffee, hoping that it would wake him up a little. He pushed his face against the glass, looked down at the trunks of a few serene trees.

He moved away from the window, drinking some more of the coffee. He took several sips in quick succession, but could not muster the courage to drink the entire glass in one go. His throat lurched a little, his mouth filled with gas from his stomach. He rushed over to the desk, putting the glass down.

He set his hand over his heart, and blinked slowly.

He had better watch out for his health, it was no good to drink so much coffee at once, particularly when one is getting on in years. He set his fist against his mouth and blew into it.

He looked at the glass, then scolded it several times. He would have no more of its tricks.

After a few moments, it began to depress him that he had nothing to drink now that he was not going to finish the coffee. He wandered over to the bedside, then made an evaluation of his bodily state. He felt a bit healthier now. The gas had receded. He figured that he could finish the coffee, if that's what he wanted, but decided not to, as an act of will.

*   *   *   *   *   *   *   *

He pushed the form underneath the window, then looked at the number that he had written in the corner, the legal disclaimer part of it, which he had not read, and his name. He had signed in all the correct places. The clerk stared up at him, through the glass.

Passport.

Oh yes.

He tapped his pockets, then stuck his fingers into his coat. He whipped the passport out of his pocket, holding it up for one moment. Without making any eye contact, he slid it underneath the glass, watched the clerk's hands as she opened it.

He glanced out of the top of his eyes, trying to see if she was still attractive as he had thought a moment ago while he stood in line. She looked up at him.

She was somewhat attractive.

He made the smile that he often made.

She indicated that he could sit in the couched area while they contacted the bank. He strutted over to the couches, money, money, money. He twisted on the balls of his feet, spinning to face the register, falling down onto the couch.

He padded his knees, and looked back at the clerk, who stood from the chair to go and get him his money. He sucked on his tongue, and made a detailed analysis of the potted plant sitting on the end table. Both his face and an area along his upper thigh felt cold, for some reason.

He leaned back into the couch, allowing his hair to touch the window.

After a time, he saw a dirty, crazyesque fellow passing the window.

He moved his gaze so that he would not see this person, without making any sudden movements that would give away his presence.

He looked up.

The crazy thing had drawn in to the window and was now staring at him. He tried not to look disconcerted, and pursed his lips, pretending to whistle idly. It's from the musical 'Crazy Face with a Red Face and a Beard', do you like it?

Please, please, go away.

The fellow left, and he felt relieved at first.

He sat up, to prevent further such incidences. He looked over at the clerk who was working with a machine of some sort. He hoped she would get him his money quickly. The thought got into his mind that the crazy would try to follow him, take his money. Trick him into a dark dead end

And then rape him!

Ah!

He tried to dismiss this scene. His muscles tensed, and his eyes watered. He tried to think of something he could use as a weapon. He scratched his hair, then tried to dismiss the whole thing altogether. He imagined that he could out run this person, that he was not so attractive anyway. His imagination was leaking. He winced, tried to chuckle. Ha, paranoiac, ha.

He soothed himself by imagining that he would ask the clerk if she would like to go dancing or something, his treat. He would slap the money against his hand, and look like he had just thought it up.

* * * * * * * *

He picked up the empty bottle, admired the field that was pictured on the label. He set it back down on the desk, then ran his hands across the wood, trying to find a pen and paper. He stood up, then went over to the dresser.

He removed a slip of paper from a note pad that he had, then took the pen out. He smiled and made his new label.

He spent some time refining the lettering, and made a mistake in the spatial etcetera so that the last two letters ended up much thinner than the rest.

Poison.

That'll do it.

He took the label over to the wine, debated whether or not he wanted to tear it so that it was the exact size of the current, inferior, label. He held the label in place with his fingers, lifted the bottle from the desk.

Can I interest you in a glass of poison?

He thought that he could set this on his windowsill, as a decorative bit. All he needed was some tape to hold the label. He did not think that he had any tape. He looked around the room.

He set the label on the table and sat down, placing the bottle between his thighs. He looked into the bottom of it, faintly making out some pulp at the dark bottom, then pondered the reasons why it hadn't evaporated.

He blew out some air, then pushed his shoulders into the back of the chair. He looked at his hotel room.

He saw a bug in flight, then another. They went at each other.

Doing battle.

Then they pulled away, and he wondered if this were some bizarre mating ritual, and, if so, which of the bugs was female. He rubbed his knee through his pants.

Yes, but which is the female?

He repeated this question to himself several times, without trying to think of any evidence to resolve it, then fantasizing that the female bug was desperate to procreate.

Tired, he turned his face over to the light. He let his cheeks go slack, his mouth hang open. Casually, he grabbed the bottle from his legs, and lifted it to his mouth. He took several imaginary mouthfuls, then set it down. He waved his hands at the side of his head, claimed that he was drunk, and set his head on the desk. He felt the temperature of the desk against his nose, keeping his eyes closed shut.

Enough of that.

He sat up in the chair, then stood. He walked straight to

the toilet, where he urinated, set his hand against the wall, flushing the toilet prematurely, as brusque men like to do. He tried to urinate as fast as possible, so that he would not have to wait for the toilet to refill with water.

The water began flowing down into the pipes.

He made it in time, then zipped up his pants, clapped his hands together. He fantasized getting himself a dinner somewhere, as he ran his hand under the faucet.

* * * * * * * *

No one spoke.

He looked at the carpet, then glanced over at his glass of wine, wondered if they would let him drink it, they could all have some, relax a bit. He looked over at the lawyer fellow, who was tapping the cigarette on the tip of the cigarette package, so that he would not get ash onto the floor.

Richard touched the pages of the translation, shaking his head, then looking up at him every so often. He stepped backwards, keeping his front towards them so that he could rest himself on the window. The back of his foot hit against the wall, and he let his weight drop onto the windowsill.

So the security light has turned on for the evening.

At least we're safe.

He noticed that they had not closed the door to the hallway. He muttered something to the lawyer fellow politely asking him if he could close it, but, for some reason, neither of them responded to this. Richard looked up at him.

You stole it to burn it.

Richard stared at him until he made eye contact. He thought to say that this was not his original intention, but kept quiet. He let his hand rest on the windowsill. The lawyer fellow looked at him once again, then at Richard, placing both the cigarette and the package into one hand so he could touch Richard's back, his face having a serious face to it, and the smoke rising into the corner of the room.

Richard blew air out of his mouth, slapped his palm against the manuscript several times.

He looked down at the laundry bag. It occurred to him that he should have hidden the manuscript in one of the washing machines down the hall. And he thought that he might apologize or something.

Richard looked as though he were trying to read the first

page, then stopped, then started to form a question.

Why did you do this?

Is this what you do?

Such things as people say.

He felt insulted.

No, he said.

I suppose I panicked.

He parted his hands in front of him, trying to think of a good argument, smart insults, a criticism or two. He wondered if this was going to result in physical violence. He watched the lawyer fellow's suit, trying to think of the official color of the suit, or the type of suit it was, or a sophisticated compliment of some sort that he could say.

Richard smeared the translation off the desk, a good part of it falling onto the chair, the other onto the floor.

Richard pulled himself away from the lawyer fellow, then walked to the door, kicking it open.

He was happy that Richard had left.

Richard needed to calm down.

The lawyer fellow put the cigarette back into his other hand, ashing it into the package once more, then looking down at something he could not see, perhaps some underpants of his that he had left out by the bed, then looking up at him once again, curious with white hair.

He noticed that the lawyer looked like a turtle of some sort in the facial area.

He looked down, unsettled.

Did you mean to publish it?

He looked up at the lawyer, responding that no, he did not think so.

* * * * * * * *

He thought about it for some time as he walked into the corner of the park. He wanted to put his hands on the fence and look at things. He turned sideways so that he could pass through the bushes without touching any of the twigs.

He put his hands on the fence.

Some traffic.

A few shops.

He turned and looked back at the park. He saw a nice little spot between the trees where there was no grass. He wanted to sit down there with a wine and a friend or so. He imagined that this was illegal.

Some breeze came up the street, brushed against his face. He closed his eyes, sniffed through his nostrils, one of which was congested, and would not work too well.

He realized that his jaw was clenching, his molars fit together nicely. He looked over at the park, thinking romance, romance. He imagined he cut quite a figure. Contemplative man at the gates of the park.

In a cotton undershirt.

He scratched his hair, then walked through the bushes. One of the twigs scraped against his leg, and he felt that his socks were dirty, as his feet were secreting an oil of some sort and he could feel the balls of each of his feet each sticking its respective sock.

As he walked he balled up his shirt at his back, so that the cloth was taut against his chest, abdomen etcetera. He looked down at himself, then posited what adjective a woman would use to describe his physique. Would they say that he was too thin now? That they could not sleep with such a thin man?

He mashed up the fat in his pectoral muscles, assuring himself that he had not gotten to that point yet.

He stopped walking, realizing that he did not want to return to the hotel for some time. He felt tired and dreamed that he might recline on the grass, take a little nap, as it were.

He looked around, seeing a few key pedestrians.

He imagined that he would be accosted by a vagabond of some sort if he lay on the grass. He imagined someone shaking him, going through his pockets.

He had not brought much money with him.

He rubbed his eyeball, then walked over to the path that would lead him out of the park. He thought that he might browse somewhere, at a shop most likely. This sounded like a good idea. He thought that he would find a knickknack shop, or something of that nature.

At the entrance to the park, he stepped off the walk so that he would be out of the way of the thug ahead of him. He felt somewhat intimidated, kept his eyes averted from the man's cigarette.

He hopped back onto the walk at the first opportunity. He looked at the store with the red awning, which looked to be a bakery. He then saw a postal type business, as well as a few restaurants, but none of these struck his fancy.

* * * * * * * *

The weight of the bag pulled at the skin on his palm, but he refused to switch hands in front of her.

I can carry a bag up to the third floor, sweetie.

He insisted that they take the staircase, then tired to think of a reason for this. He said that her room was much closer to that side of the hotel.

She took off her glasses, then slid them into the purse hanging from her shoulder. He kept looking down at her neck, her breasts, pleasantish enough. He began to feel nervous though, and moved ahead so that he could walk in front of her.

He looked down at the carpet, searching his mind for some charming conversation topic. He felt tired.

She caught up with him, he glanced over his shoulder. She held the pamphlet up that Angelo had given her.

He told her that she should read the history section of the pamphlet, there were some interesting bits in there.

The entire hotel is haunted, he said.

He went up the first flight of stairs.

There are many ghosts on the third floor that go after the women. If they bother you, just run down to the second floor and sleep with me. The ghosts are repelled by the diminutive size of my phallus.

He blinked then let the weight of the bag pull his shoulder down. He wished that they had taken the elevator.

How long have you been in town?

He said that he had not been here very long.

Is there anything to do?

There are a few things to do.

He switched the bag into his other hand, then looked back at her. He asked her to repeat her room number. She did. He then calculated whether it would be to the right or the left of the stairs, figuring that it would be to the left. He breathed through his nose, then rubbed his fingers against his palm where the bag had injured it.

He arrived at the top of the stairs, then turned to the left.

Your room should be right here, he said.

Just up ahead.

He considered how he would go about asking her if she was seeing anyone. He set the bag at the door, then turned around.

All set.

Handshake.

Elicia.

She thanked him for carrying the bag up to her room. She was so tired from her trip, etcetera, going straight to sleep. He waved her off, assuring her that this was not a problem.

Anything for a lady.

He said his room number, if she would like a tour of the town.

She repeated it correctly, then took the key out of the pamphlet. He nodded, then walked toward the elevator, which he could use to get back to his room. He looked over his shoulder, but returned his head to the proper position before he saw her.

He repeated a few things, then felt somewhat overwhelmed. He wondered if she would hear anything about him.

* * * * * * * *

The music playing in the shop was loud enough that he could not hear the questions that the clerk was asking that woman. He looked at the bag sitting on the counter. There was a picture of a young woman there, an attractive girl looking to the side of the bag. The clerk stuck the things into the bag, shirts a set of pants, then handed the woman her receipt.

He stuck his hand into the rack of neckties.

He admired one that had some racing dogs on it.

He felt that he could use one of these, to go with his suit.

He pulled the tag up, trying to locate the price of the necktie, then dropped it. He tried to imagine the reasons why a necktie would be so expensive as he then walked over towards the female section of the store, saw several females, and could think of no reason to justify his presence in this section. He had no wedding band on his finger, obviously there just for kicks.

Hardwood floors, elegance.

At one of the columns, there were a few belts of various lengths and styles. He found one that would fit him, then looked at the price.

He took the belt.

He held the belt in his hand, and continued over to the collared shirt area.

The collared shirts were individually packaged, with stickers on the front of them. Above him, two paddles were mounted to the wall?

He looked over his shoulder, then back up at these.

He disregarded this, and located a pale blue shirt that looked to be his size. He picked it up, then imagined how he would look in it, imagining, in particular, that he would be smoking a thin cigarette, walking fashionably down the sidewalk. He set the shirt down, figuring that he could come back and get it, if he wanted.

He took the belt over to the counter, then looked at a stack of greeting cards, a few advertisements.

He looked up at the clerk, wondering what he had said to him.

yes, that's everything.

He took his wallet out of his pocket, then asked if he could have a bag for it. He pulled out the correct amount of money while the clerk leaned down behind the counter for some time. He slid the money over towards the register.

The clerk pulled out a small bag that had a different picture on it.

A picture of a suave guy.

That's me.

He and I often go to the dance place and brush off teenagers.

He looked at the clerk's face while taking his change. It was a more handsome face, he admitted, sullenly. He said a thank you then took his change and pushed it down into his pocket. He took the bag from the counter, then thanked the clerk, and walked toward the front of the store where the outside light was coming in. He used his shoulder to push the door open, then stepped back out to the sidewalk.

* * * * * * * *

The water of the bath was cooling before he was finished. He amused himself by submerging his arm into the water, and then allowing it to rise to the surface. He wondered whether there was an amount of air in his bones that was causing this phenomenon.

His wrist broke the water, floated there.

He rolled over to his side, then stuck his face down into the water, letting his mouth open. He found that, in this position the air was trapped inside of his mouth. He pushed his tongue out.

Denizen of the bathtub.

He rolled over, pushing his shoulder against the edge of the tub so that his torso came out of the water. His hair was still dry on the one side. He picked up some water in his hand and ran it through his hair. He decided that he did not need any further cleaning.

He drained the tub, then stood up. He slapped his temple a few times, then grabbed the towel and ran it between his legs. He decided not to put on the same boxer shorts that he had been wearing thus far today, walked out of the room, back to his bed.

He sat down on the chair, then rubbed himself with the towel. He rubbed the towel over his hair for a bit. He felt water drip down his back, onto the chair, thinking about what he would wear for the rest of the evening.

Suit jacket.

He figured that he could put on his suit, that he would walk around respectably, though he did not have anything in particular to do that evening that required that he seem like a gentleman. He allowed the towel to fall to the floor of the hotel room. Some water had leaked down his legs, forming a wet spot on the floor that would dry in time.

He did not see the suit in the corner where he normally kept his laundry. He imagined that it might be under the bed or in the closet.

He jogged past the bed, then opened the closet door. He had hung his suit in there, on a hanger no less. He took the hanger out of the closet, then draped the suit onto the bed. He brushed his hand against it, smoothing out the wrinkles, moving quickly so that he would not get it wet.

He looked around the room for some boxer shorts.

He stopped at the bed corner, then executed several stretches. He stuck his hands at his side, swiftly twisting his chest to the left. His spine pressed, then cracked.

He felt relieved.

He took a pair of boxers from the area in front of the dresser. These seemed relatively clean, though he thought he would have to do his laundry soon enough. He stepped into them, then went over to the suit. He removed the jacket from the hanger, then set the pants on the floor and stepped into them, pulled them up.

* * * * * * * *

Outside of the hotel doors, he stood, looking around to see if someone was looking at him. He tried to figure out where he would go for the course of his walk, coming to the point that he decided to purchase a bottle of wine, or, if the mood struck him, some cigarettes.

His stomach was a bit heavy, he could feel some liquid inside of it.

His nerves were out of sorts.

He walked down the sidewalk, looking over the grass into the gully to this side. He sniffed air into his nose, hoping to clear out his nostrils, the skin along the bridge of his nose pulled inward.

His mind went about and he let his eyes fall open, watery.

He rubbed his hands together then noting that he would have to turn to the left at the corner ahead of him, as he often did. He would get a whole bunch of cigarettes, he decided, for himself. That would do it, he figured. He would have several cigarettes on the walk back.

A woman in a car was stopped across the street, she looked at him, he nodded to her. He imagined that she might have wondered what exactly he was doing, such a well dressed man, at such an hour. He shot off a few vain thoughts as he walked, imagined that he was good looking.

He touched his pant packets to see how much money he had brought with him, thinking that he might have brought enough money to purchase both a package of cigarettes and a bottle of wine, which would be good. He felt his keys, then touched the interior pocket of his jacket, touching some shape that had the thickness of his wallet.

He stuck his finger into the pocket.

He felt some money there.

He stopped, realizing that he had placed all of his money in this pocket sometime earlier. He did not feel comfortable carrying it all while walking around like this, he thought of taking it back to his room.

He wanted to count the money, but disregarded this, continuing on to the store where he would buy both cigarettes and wine, whatever he liked, as might a successful politician.

He took the roll of bills out of his pocket, keeping it tucked closely to his chest, he looked down at the bills, then made a rough estimate of his wealth.

He felt excited about this.

He turned his neck to the side, figuring that someone would have seen him counting off the money. He drew off two bills, then stuck them into his pant pocket as though this were the only money he had, the rest of it he put back into his jacket.

He used both hands to rub his hair, he thought he might go somewhere nice for a meal. His calves felt light against the pavement, though a string of the muscle felt worn. He would not have much further to walk, and then he would have quite an evening.

* * * * * * * *

He walked out from the elevator area. His head went up, down, and an amount of light entered into his eyes. He pulled at the fabric at his thigh, then looking to the right, towards his room, where he would go. His mouth open.

Someone called after him, he turned to see that it was that woman he had met before.

Elicia.

Dressed in a dress of sorts.

He stopped then smiled a little, she walked over to him, asking if he had change so that she could use the machine. He licked his lips, then looked over her stomach, thinking that he did not have any change. It occurred to him that he needed to sleep with her.

He turned, turning back, taking the money out of his jacket.

She took back at this, some bills dropped on the floor, and she bent over to pick them up for him. He waited until she could see his eyes, then instructed her to take the money and sleep with him. That she could have all the money if she did this, near crying with stress.

He felt sweat on his palms going into the money. She looked curiously at him.

He said that he was very serious about this.

I need you.

She thought it over for some time, he reached out then took her hand, which she pulled back. He put the money into her hand, then closed her fingers. He pointed over to his room. He cracked his neck, then walked toward it. He did not want to look back at her. He pulled the key out of his pocket, he unlocked the door, then opened the door, then looked back to see if she had come.

She looked much more serious.

He was not a killer or something of that sort.

He looked into the room, seeing a towel in the hall, thinking that she might give him a moment to clean up. He walked inside, hoping that she would not throw something at him from behind.

He heard the door closing behind him. She was closing it with her back, he walked over, then took the money out of her hand and placed it on the desk. She walked into the room, she would not stop looking at him.

He pointed to the money on the table, then approached her. He slid his hand underneath her coat, intending to take it off, then rubbed his thumb against a bone in her shoulder, sliding his hand then onto her back, looking at her neck.

He touched a clasp on the dress.

He felt a wet sensation on his ear, nearly pulling back. He could smell some alcohol in her scent.

She touched her tongue against his earlobe. He slid his hand down to the small of her back, then pulled her closer to him, that she nearly fell. He felt her breasts compress against his chest, hoped that she did not find it uncomfortable. He groped her then caught some of her hair in his mouth, then kissed her forehead, tasting saltish along his tongue.

He grit his teeth, then slid his hand into the neck of her dress, under the cup of her brassiere, feeling as much the wire scrape against his thumb as the flesh drop into his palm.

* * * * * * * *

He looked at the gate. He would have a good bit of time to spend here. The benches were padded with leather, and many people were sitting, reading papers, books, etcetera.

He thought of setting one of his bags onto the bench so that he could save himself a place to sit if it got crowded. He imagined that his bag might be stolen though.

A small kiosk at the corner was selling many juices, muffins, things to eat, and candies for him.

He walked over to this, then looked at the candies. A woman in front of him turned to look at him, accusingly glaring at him, as though he intended to go in front of her. He waved his hand, calmed her down, then pointed down at the candy bars, which he had come up to the counter to inspect.

He stuck his fingers into the space between the fingers of his other hand, then rubbed them vigorously. He decided to get himself a length of taffy, which would give him some energy, clear out his throat. The woman approached the counter then leaned onto it, yelling to the clerk that she wanted some tea.

He set his bag down next to a stack of newspapers in a wire display.

He picked out several bits of taffy for himself. He imagined that the blue ones would taste the best, so he got two of those, then one each of several other colors.

The clerk set down a cup of hot water with a bag floating in it, then looked down at the numbers on the register, ready to punch in the information. The woman asked how much it cost.

He waited for the woman to hand over her money.

She remarked that this was too expensive, pulled the money out of her purse.

In order to make the transaction more efficient, he calculated the approximate cost of his purchase, then put his hand into his pocket to withdraw several bills more than he needed. He touched his ear, rubbed his eye, waiting for the woman to get out of the way so that he could go sit down and eat his candy.

He handed the money over to the clerk, took his change.

He stuck his arm through the handle of his bag. This way, he would not have to put his candy down. The bag dragged onto his elbow as he picked it up.

He tried to peel the packaging off with his teeth.

He eventually got to a seat, then dropped his bag onto the ground. It bent the sticks of taffy as it dropped. He fell onto the bench, then used his fingers to open the packaging. He stuck the stick into his mouth, cutting it in half with his front teeth.

He smiled, then chewed the stuff, looking at the airplanes

out the window of the terminal.

He was quite impressed by one with silver décor.

The candy stuck against his back teeth, like the thick saliva in the open mouth of a creature.

* * * * * * * *

He looked at the empty glass on the dining table. His brother was drinking somewhat slowly, and had a particular grin on his face. He asked his brother if he would like another drink. His brother invited him to go and get himself one from the kitchen, as he was not quite done.

He pushed his chair back from the table, walked over to the kitchen.

He found the liquor on the counter top, poured himself a nice bit of it. He added a little more to it, which would make the drink much stronger than necessary. He placed the cap back onto the liquor but did not screw it very tightly. He opened the door to the refrigerator, thinking that he would add something to the drink.

He pulled out a carton of apple juice from the top row, then looked at the color of it, then thought about adding milk to the stuff instead, declining to do so in the end, for health reasons.

The window looked down into the alley, he could see some cans of garbage, some orange colors spreading onto the concrete, it was quite serene.

He spilled some of the juice onto the counter. He solved the problem, wiped it up with the sponge sitting in the kitchen sink.

There we are.

He threw the sponge back in there.

He looked at the clean clean counter.

He lifted one hand up, the other grasping the glass.

He tasted the drink.

'Tis drinkable.

When he walked back out into the living room, he saw that his brother was going into his coat pocket, most likely for his cigarettes, without asking. This annoyed him mildly. His brother pulled out one of the cigarettes, then went back to his own chair.

He decided to sit down on the couch, so that he could keep his legs up. His brother lit the cigarette with the matches from the table, pushed his back into the chair.

He complimented his brother on the apartment.

His brother began singing a little song. For lack of a better reaction, he assumed a bemused expression, then stared at the door. His brother asked him if he had ever seen that movie.

He asked him which movie.

His brother turned the chair, then continued the song, lifting his glass up into the air, drinking from it at the point where he no longer knew the rest of the lyrics, then slapping the table.

He decided that he liked his brother very much.

He tried his best to read the poster sitting over the television set in the corner of the room. He could not make it out well, then cursed, rubbed his temples, and joked that he was going to have a hangover. His brother set the glass down on the table then asked him something that he did not catch.

He took another sip from the glass, his brother stood from the chair then walked over toward the kitchen.

He set the glass down on the floor, then heard a bottle breaking over there outside. He asked his brother if he had heard this.

* * * * * * * *

He decided that he would go downstairs to the restaurant so that he could take his pill with a cup of coffee instead of the drinks available in his brother's apartment. He took some of the change off of the dining room table, then searched the apartment for the key to the door, so that he would not get locked out.

He found the key on the coffee table.

He picked it up, then slid it into the breast pocket of his shirt, along with the pill.

Out the door.

He moved down the stairs as quickly as possible, his hair stood on end. He jumped down the last three steps, then landed on his feet, shocking his right knee. He looked at the mailboxes, some things on the bottom floor of the apartment building, then went outside.

He looked at the grocery store across the street, then jogged over to the door of the coffee shop. His innards bobbed up and down, but he made it to the door without slowing his pace.

The bell rung.

The clerk said hello to him, in her cute demeanor. You little darling, get my coffee. There was a chalkboard over her head, the menu was written in cursive, and a little picture of a sandwich was drawn in the corner. He decided that he had enough money that he could get himself a slice of buttered toast with his coffee, if he got the smallest cup.

He snapped his finger, then walked over to the counter. He read the items off the menu that he would like, then made some nice eye contact with the girl. He pulled the coins out of his pocket, then placed them on the counter.

He looked at the tip jar while she filled up his cup.

He felt awful that he had no more money.

He put his hand into his pocket, and found only a bottle cap. He felt the ridges of it with his finger, then waited until she was not looking at him, dropped the thing into the jar.

Go fantasize yourself some nice perfume.

ding!

The clerk heard this, smiled at him.

She placed the coffee onto the counter then invited him to take his toast from the wicker basket on the counter. He picked out a slice that was not cold at all, thanked her, then walked over to one of the little tables. He took one of the paper napkins there, folded it out for his toast to sit on.

He blew into the coffee, got out his pill, slid it between his lips, covertly, took a sip of coffee and swallowed it down. He then turned his chair to the side so the clerk could look at him while he ate his breakfast.

The butter had soaked into the toast.

He enjoyed this.

He leaned back then held the cup to his mouth and took a sip of coffee while he admired the décor. He began to feel a little guilty, deciding that he would go back up to the apartment and find some additional money to place into the tip jar at a later hour. For the meantime he felt content, cracked his neck and rested his ear against his palm.

* * * * * * * *

The circle ahead of him, the fountain in its center, how nice. The sky etcetera, and what a lovely fountain. The folder rested nicely in the joints of his fingers.

He turned his head to look at the girls, carrying their bags, perhaps heading over to the train station, going home, getting a bite to eat, generally doing well for themselves. His throat felt rather dry, his neck could not move in many directions because it was stiff.

The little dog stood on its back legs for its master, doing a little carnival type maneuver. He found this impressive, then turned onto a side street of the circle so that he could pass a few of the bars.

He imagined that he could get someone to take him to one of these bars, have them buy him a few drinks, a nice to see you again type thing.

He saw the restaurant with the blue and white awning. Oh such great times he'd had there, he imagined. He used to go there on occasion.

Steam rose out of the ground, coming from the train station no less. There was a sign with an arrow indicating that stairwell that descended from the street. It was lined with bathroom tiles, which seemed urinesque in the yellow light at the bottom stair, where the path turned left.

He thought about some things, blinking intermittently.

He pulled the folder up into his armpit, he imagined that he could find a printing shop nearby, but could not picture one that he had seen. He needed to draw up some copies of his little resume, perhaps get someone he knew to write him a letter of reference of some sort.

Oh him, why he's an amazing worker.

A very skilled man, talented in the dark magics, if I recall him.

He looked at the restaurant over that way, which served expensive foods on the upstairs patio. He would not mind eating at this restaurant, which served reasonably priced beer. This was a good thing. He turned his head down, looked at the reflections in the pools of water in the cracked cement, showing little more than the air above the buildings and the general weather.

He figured that he might return to his apartment and watch some television programming.

Fortunately, he was walking in the correct direction for this.

Put his feet up on the couch, dirty socks and such.

Tried my best today, as you can see.

He could feel that the gel in his hair was melting onto his scalp, that it would drip down his forehead, perhaps into his eyes. He figured that he would take a shower or two when he got back to the apartment, that he might as well put on a pajama suit and make himself a fancy drink.

Ah you're home, I toast you.

I'm home, a toast is in order.

I've eaten all your condiments.

He looked at streetlight at the end of the sidewalk, where he could make a turn that would bring him home quickly.

* * * * * * * *

His brother took the phone into the bedroom, which made him curious as to who might be calling. He turned his head to the hallway, unable to hear from the movie that was playing on the television. He stood up from the couch, then turned the volume down so that he could listen in, in case it was someone that he knew.

There's a reasonable volume.

The cord from the telephone stretched into the bedroom, where his brother stood. He imagined that his brother might have left the room so as to be polite, and not talk over the movie.

He looked at the bathroom suspiciously, held his breath, then went back to the couch. He took the can of soda up, took a sip of it.

He's looking well, doing well, got in so long ago.

He imagined that his brother was talking about him there.

He imagined that it might be a woman, this drove him mad, he thought of asking his brother who it was exactly. Then he relaxed, leaning his back into the back cushion of the couch. He watched the man on the television screen explain something with the aid of the toy figurine, while the others looked on, confused.

He then looked out then window, clenching the muscles that controlled his eyebrows. He imagined that the person on the telephone might want to speak to him, as they were interested in the topic of him, how he seemed, when he'd come into town, and his state of being.

He could hear his brother laughing now.

He rubbed his nose then looked at the bottom of the

radiator, dust, paper, and a metal cog of some kind lying underneath it. He thought for a moment that there might be a mouse hole in the wall, then found none.

He got off the couch so that he could resume the volume of the movie, as he needed to know what the scientist was saying to the pretty girl. He turned the dial up, their voices coming out of the speaker so that he could not tell if they were whispering or speaking in an ordinary way until he heard static beneath them.

His brother walked back into the room with a handcuff draped over one of his wrists, fiddling with it. He was organizing some dates, suggesting that they meet on the weekend perhaps. His brother looked over at him, then held his fists together as though the cuffs were locked and he were unable to escape, making an amusing facial bit.

His brother set the phone down. He held out his hand, hoping that his brother would give him the handcuffs to play with, but, no.

He asked who had been on the phone.

His brother said that they would go and see Dorothy and Matt that weekend, if he liked. He nodded, then said that this would be a good time, they had not seen each other and it would be a good time, certainly. His brother then looked at the soda on the table and asked if he wanted a drink from the refrigerator.

* * * * * * * *

He found the boxes in the corner of the warehouse, near the basins where the cardboard was to be disposed of. He did not see a knife in the vicinity, then touched his pockets, and went over to the shelf to look for one.

He found a tin full of washers, a few batteries.

On the lower shelf, perhaps.

He found a hammer, but nothing that he could use to cut the boxes.

He walked back over to the trash area. It was fortunate that he was such a problem solver. He tried to use his fingers to take apart the tape on the boxes, but this did not work.

He pulled his apartment key out from his pocket. He stuck this into the tape, then dragged it down to the bottom of the box. He was then able to pull the side apart, and tear apart the first of the boxes. He put his apartment key in between his bottom fingers, then lifted the box and threw it into the basin.

He counted the remaining boxes, feeling disappointed that there were so many of them.

He decided that he would save himself some time by breaking down several boxes, then collecting them and throwing them into the trash. He got down on one knee, feeling the temperature of the cement, painted green. There were no windows in this room, some sunlight came down through ventilation holes of some sort.

He broke down two more of the boxes then threw them into the basin. His key touched his finger, he felt that it was covered with residue from the adhesive on the tape. He began to fear that he was going to break the key if he kept misusing it in this way. He tried to rub the reside off with his thumb.

He stuck the key into his mouth, scraping off some residue with his teeth. He rubbed the length of the key between his index finger and thumb until he had gotten the majority of it off. He felt better, then crossed the warehouse to the shelf where they kept many binders.

He looked for a knife of some sort.

He found several rolls of tape, which was the opposite of what he was looking for and he found this smile worthy.

He eventually saw a large screwdriver sitting on the floor. He looked over at the foreigner whose name he did not know, rolling a wooden crate with a dolly. They nodded at each other, and he waited until the man passed from view before he stole the screwdriver.

He jogged back over to the boxes, he waved the screw driver out in front of him, then stabbed it into the box, missing the tape by several inches. He got back down on the floor, sitting cross-legged. He began to smack the box with the blunt end of the tool, figuring that he might as well take his time as they would only have something else for him to do afterward.

He used the tip of the screwdriver to break up the tape of the next box, then pulled the two sides apart from one another and flattened it out.

* * * * * * * *

He used his tongue to gather the available saliva in his mouth. He sucked his cheeks in, pulling the blanket further up his chest until it left his feet exposed to the air inside the apartment. He swallowed then turned onto his side, attempting to draw his legs in so they did not hang off the side of the couch.

He noted some music coming from outside the window. Some people were still up, being inconvenient to him, though he would have to be up soon, he imagined.

He heard the clock ticking in the kitchen at a set interval, then imagined that he could get a few hours more rest before his brother woke him.

He breathed from his nose, then slid his hand onto the underside of the cushion, where the couch had not been heated by his body.

He could not sleep with the night coming through the window.

He rolled onto his other side, so that he faced the backrest. He slid his hand up, clasping them in a praying fashion so that he could pinch the bridge of his nose from both sides. Soon enough he felt that he could feel the humidity in his breath trapped in the air between his face and the couch.

He wished that they would stop that music, his eyes watered, and he imagined going over to their door, pleading that he needed to wake early, and make them feel ashamed of themselves that they did not have to think of such things. His cheeks felt nervous, stiff, and he thought that he might be awake for the remainder of the night.

He imagined that he could sleep, if he got into the right position. One of his knees was extremely uncomfortable, bent as it was, and he let it slide from the couch, hanging to the side.

He turned over, then used one hand to pull the coffee table next to the couch. The feet squealed as they moved along the floor, he worried of waking his brother, but it must be done, and his brother had a bed and could not feel angry with him because he bought a couch that no sane man would fit on.

He found that he was more comfortable if his heels hung off the end of the table. He then twisted himself to the side, resting his anklebones off of the table because they were sensitive. He pushed his head into the cushion, until his ear heated up from the lack of air.

He sniffled a little.

He wondered if he needed to blow his nose.

He cursed at his brother for owning such a loud clock.

He began to drift off, thinking of dreamy things until he heard the sound of an unmuffled engine passing by the alley's end, blaring an additional music, without regard any for his life, the lives of others. He clenched his eyelids, desperate, and covered his ear with his palm.

* * * * * * * *

He set his bag of snack food down on the table, then looked over at the clock. He had some time until he needed to go back down to the floor and do work.

He felt apprehensive about this.

He read a list of items that employees could keep in the refrigerator. The idea occurring that he could eat better if he made his meals before work, then brought them here. He could keep some sandwiches in the refrigerator, he could maybe have a glass of wine with his lunch.

He looked down at the papers that he was supposed to fill out, read, initial. He had not brought a pen with him, and figured that he could sign them while he was crossing through one of the offices. He looked at an illustration of how he was supposed to lift things to avoid injury.

The stick fellow lifting incorrectly had painful lines coming out of his back.

He scratched his hair, then ate another handful of the chips from the bag, the taste becoming more distinct as he forced additional chips into his mouth, breaking them up with his teeth, turning them into a thick past on the top of his tongue with a pleasant salt flavor.

He let his eyes drop, he stood and walked over to the refrigerator to see what items were inside. Some water was leaking from the door, a pool on the top of the green tile that he stepped in, displacing some of it to the side.

Signed photographs lined the room.

He opened the refrigerator.

Mostly sandwiches, some drinks lined along the shelf on the door.

He thought it would be funny if he put his snack chips into the refrigerator.

Yes, I was meaning to save those.

A woman opened the door to the break room, then looked at the ground, walking over toward the refrigerator. He imagined that she must answer the phones, as she wore a loose fitting blouse. She said hello to him, then mentioned something about not wanting to go back out, while she took out one of the drinks, opening it.

She walked back over to the door to the room.

His mouth was full, so he nodded several times, then waved at her back as she went back out.

He threw the bag into the trash, then turned the faucet on so that he could put water on his face. He did this, felt the water drip down the collar of his shirt, then opened his eyes, turning off the faucet, and drying his face with the sleeve of his shirt.

He leaned against the counter and dreamed that he would be going back home soon, that the rest of the day would pass quickly. He breathed heavily, putting his hand into his pocket, staring over at the clock moving slowly, waiting for the time to pass until he would leave the room, and the time to pass until he would leave the building for the night.